RED AFFAIRS,
WHITE AFFAIRS

FELICIA NAY

Published by Cinnamon Press, Meirion House, Tanygrisiau, Blaenau Ffestiniog, Gwynedd, LL41 3SU

www.cinnamonpress.com

ISBN 978-1-78864-069-5

Designed and typeset in Garamond by Cinnamon Press. Cover design by Adam Craig.

Cinnamon Press is represented by Inpress and by the Welsh Books Council in Wales.

The publisher acknowledges the support of the Welsh Books Council.

RED AFFAIRS,
WHITE AFFAIRS

The Beginning of Winter
Tuesday 8 November

Cruising and circling, they spiral downwards in a near-death experience, only to rise again on undeclared powers of hot air and faith. Black eared kites. It is an illusion, of course, the idea of their death, a human tribute to frailty and invisible energies. *Hope is the thing with feathers*, above the South China Sea as much as anywhere. I watch them, admire their perfect balance, my mind drowsy with jet lag and leftover November heat, dipping and diving like the kites.

Suspended over the tired turquoise of the sea, the kites write question marks into the sky, searching curves that thrive on their own fullness, turn in on themselves, invert their fates, make endings into beginnings, to finally come to a full stop with hunger: *Now*.

Fragrant Harbour, Incense Port, Pearl of the South China Sea. I roll the words around, shift them playfully back and forth like the melon seeds in my mouth. They have become an addiction lately, my afternoon snack on the ferry to Wanchai, their aromatic sting so much stronger than the mild salt of the air, their brittle shells accumulating in the saffron hammock of my lap. Amid dark-clad businessmen and Filipinas escorting their white charges home, the seeds have become my hungry ritual, a secret almost, like the black eared kites. In this mass of dozing people, I fasten my eyes onto the haze, take a flight of my own. There are moments when keeping still and blending in almost feel the same.

Heung Gong, the locals call it, a name that resonates with music and fragrance; the opium-laden, bible-wielding colonisers didn't know any better than to render this with harsh diction: Hong Kong.

A phone rings. It's barely audible amid the thumping of the ferry and I am slow to understand that it is mine, buried deep inside my olive backpack. *Virginia Ngai*. I let the call die under my fingertips. They burn with guilt, afterwards.

She must be a few years younger than me, in her late twenties perhaps, and a whole decade younger than Virginia. A 'girl', I have learned to call her, just as I am a girl for those around me, *neuihjai*. Like me, she must be travelling home, back to a flat filled with plastic boxes and chopsticks and a battered Hello Kitty on her bed. So often, I am grateful to Virginia for being different. Less polyester, more rosewood.

Moments ago, boarding the ferry, the girl and I collided. I thwacked the back of a folding bench into her, not seeing that she was already sitting down, ready to ride backwards. 'Sorri', I said in my German English, and 'So-rih', she said in her English Cantonese. '*Neih mouh yeh a ma?*' I apologised further, enunciating carefully as if speaking to Virginia in class. I walked around, sat down alongside the girl. Still, the incident has left an aftertaste and the force of my blow to her, still singing in my elbow, is battling with a feeling of unease. Wasn't I right, trying to reorient us?

I am still rubbing my elbow when my phone starts again. An Internally Displaced Person I am, dumb with sleep. I lift my skirt, vent my legs that the humid air has welded to the wooden bench. And still I ignore my mobile, heavy with something that I declare jet lag although it could be many things. The wish to belong. The urge to understand. The desire to come to a full stop once in a while.

My phone continues to ring. I heave my rucksack, bulky with books, into my lap. *The World of Suzie Wong*. Borrowed from the library at Spielberg's urging—'A classic. Part of your education as a Hong Kong expat, my dear.' *The North China Lover*, Marguerite Duras. My own choice. *Cantonese for Intermediate Learners*. My copy, filled with Virginia's teacherly scribblings. *Lives in Limbo: New Paradigms in Migration Studies*. Irina's magnum opus, which I have yet to read for work. Once more, I let my hand dive into the hot plastic darkness, finger the humidity for my phone.

'Reini.' My aborted call from Virginia, glaring at me from the screen. And now, Auntie Hilde. Deft mistress of time zones, unlike so many other friends and relatives who never manage to call. Her husky voice sounds as if she is only metres away on the upper deck, washed out jeans clinging to her petite frame, her white short hair shining in the quickly goldening evening. 'Did you have a good trip back? Everything alright back home?' It aches, how she understands me. I think of my daily walk across the wet market, the blue crabs, the fish still flipping with life, the fist-sized cauliflowers and the metre-long beans. The translucent gecko that has made my living-room its home.

'*Ja,*' I say, 'Everything just as it should be.'

A short exchange only before we hang up. The smell of hot motor oil is pungent, almost obliterating the salty spiciness of the melon seeds in my mouth. On the opposite shore, the Wanchai skyline glitters, the Arts Centre like a cheap echo of the Sydney Opera House, the International Finance Centre drilling itself into the sky in pursuit of foreign records. Only the library building in Central seems to be itself, its coin-like windows truest Hong Kong.

My chin starts to pucker on my chest. With a jerk of the head, I open my eyes. I slip another melon seed into my mouth, as if that small act of hunger could combat sleep.

My fingers touch paper. It crackles as if startled by my touch and, for a moment, I am confused. Then I remember. *Gwaapei.* I am not good at cracking their hearts blindly, like the Chinese. I need my fingers. The sachet under my hand reminds me of the other type of paper pockets that I have seen, funeral giveaways. Jim, the amateur ethnologist, showed one to me, a small white bag with the name and address of the supplier on the back. Printed in artful blue characters but nonetheless a reminder that somebody's death is somebody else's daily bread. *Your death is my business.* The envelopes contain money, like the laisee pockets given out for Chinese New Year, auspicious red siblings to the sober white ones handed out at wakes. Like my unmarried

Chinese sisters, I receive laisee, but resent it less. Sometimes, exoticism makes things more palatable.

Motor whining, the ferry butts against the tyre-lined bay. I gather the husks from my lap and, pretending not to know myself, scatter them into the water. The sea is quick to disperse my secret, forgives my small trespass. My eyes cast one last searching look at the sky but the kites have disappeared into the haze. Where will they be now, hurtling towards death?

At the pier, the *Shining Star* is waiting, a twin of our own white and Muslim green vessel. There is something comforting in their friendly uniformity. The passengers are filing down the ferry, a swarm of dark heads and lithe bodies. My steps thunder down the gangplank and a familiar jealousy surges in me—to be able to not keep still and yet blend in, instead of towering over the crowd with my white skin and down-to-earth sandals.

The display on my phone pulsates with another caller. *Spielberg Lam*. '*Waai?*'

'Kim. Welcome back,' he says. 'So, *lengneuih*. You haven't forgotten your Cantonese, then.' Another envy builds in me. Awake, that is what he is, not only today but always. Fresh, alert, curious. A man obsessed with invented worlds. A mint-striped personality where I see the shades between the shades.

'Oh, stop your Chinese nonsense. Only yesterday I messed up the tone for "nine" again.' If you pronounce it in the wrong tone, you end up with a word related to the male anatomy. A word so rude that Virginia refuses to speak it aloud, even for teaching purposes. I am following the masses streaming in direction of the MTR station, a multitude of black trousers and bright shirts, silk tofu legs and plum black manes.

'*Gau*,' he pronounces it for me. 'Have you been back for long?'

'The jet lag isn't quite gone yet but the effects of the holiday already seem to have worn off.'

He laughs. 'Welcome to the modern world.'

'It also feels as if the population of domestic workers had doubled while I was away and they all have problems which I need to solve. Anyway— Has Spielberg called?' This is our running joke. If a name can invoke success, Spielberg is up and coming, waiting for that magic offer from his namesake for a leading role in his latest star-studded enterprise. His chances are small, though, too small at five foot five, even though he looks like a soulful Bruce Lee.

'No-o. But I have a casting next Saturday. For a weirdo kind of movie, really. An ironic take on the kung fu genre, kung fu with a gay twist. So, how was Germany?'

'Oh well, Germany in October,' I say, almost bumping into a woman with two expensive-looking carrier bags. '*So-rib*— Visiting family and friends, that's what it was about.'

'Getting stuffed on your mom's food, right? Ah, mothers around the world.'

'More or less,' I say. The Angelic Apothecary and the Philosopher King. My parents.

'Although I always wonder where you put all that food you consume,' he says. 'You're slim like a chopstick.' In this city of dieting ads, it feels undeserved, to own this body shape without going hungry.

'Hey, guess what?' I say. 'My brother and I were best man and bridesmaid back home. Well, the German equivalent. For my *parents*.'

He gives a fake howl. It sounds a bit tinny from his Chinese-register voice. 'And I thought you were from a decent family.'

'I am,' I say. 'It was just the church wedding they postponed. It must be some kind of mellowness that comes with age. My father is an agnostic. Or used to be.'

He laughs. 'Aren't we all, on some days? Listen, are you meeting Virginia anytime soon?'

What an odd pair we must make, she short even for a Southern Chinese, hair glossy like a polished helmet, and me in my crinkly, blonde lankiness. And yet, people have come to take us for granted ever since Virginia started Hong Kong Heritage Hikes and I became her unofficial English language assistant. In return, she teaches me Cantonese. I cannot read, though, not really, and so I remain a child in this culture.

Spielberg's voice continues, the phone's heat now insistent against my ear. 'Yesterday she seemed… deflated. Maybe another quarrel with her father. She said something about spending the weekend at Zoë's place.'

'Zoë? Zoë Mok?' Our most colourful hiker lives with three hundred pink garden gnomes and a husky on Lamma. With her purple fringe and tattooed shoulder, she is everything Virginia is not. But she is one of the regulars at the hikes.

'There's talk about an anniversary party for Heritage Hikes. At Zoë's place. Anyway, I just thought I'd let you know. You know how she is, never letting on how she really feels.'

'Virginia, you mean.' A shift on my skin, an exchange of hot humid warmth against cool dry air so familiar that I hardly notice it. 'I'm getting on my train in a moment— Spielberg, I'm a foreigner. I can't… meddle in her family affairs.' Family affairs which I, the *gweilo*, don't understand. A foreign ghost. And who am I to understand families, me, the recent bridesmaid?

'Just cheer her up, cheer her up. You're a model for her, whether you like it or not. Kind of… running your own show.'

Something in his description makes me squirm. 'But she does the same. Even more so with the Hikes. Being self-employed and all that. Me, I'm just a small potato, getting lost in third world capitals with MediMission.' I run my Octopus card across the turnstile and enter.

'Are you calling Hong Kong a third world capital? You inspire her. Nobody thought that this sort of specialised tour would work. For a full-time living, I mean.'

'And what should I do? Tell her father to be proud that she is a struggling self-employed rather than a history teacher?'

'Don't be unfair. He gave her the money to start the business.'

'And all that nagging about her not getting married,' I continue. Mr. Ngai, trying to create his daughter in his image. No, that is not true. In his wife's image, probably. Her mother. The *sin keih leung mouh*, the good Confucian wife and mother. 'No, thank you.'

'Ah, Chinese families. Darling,' he croons, 'I'm sure you'll manage.'

10

Like Jesus bugs, our conversations are—skating across the water, never quite touching, never quite breaking the surface, zigging and zagging. But there is a sense of lightness in them I crave.

Moon Ten Day Ten
Friday 11 November

It is almost dark when I emerge from the MTR. Night falls quickly in Hong Kong, darkness latching onto darkness. The air acquires new density, sandalwood scent and sea spray mixing with diesel fumes and the remaining warmth of the day. At this hour of indecision between day and night, the burning of incense is a gift to the Earth God. It still stings, that second commandment, although I am learning to ignore it. *You shall not make for yourself an image in the form of anything in heaven above...* Instead, I seek them in temples and doorways, my painted and gilded friends: Tin Hau, patron saint of fisher-folk, and Kwun Yam, Goddess of Mercy, the Earth God and even the God of Wealth. I with my Catholic upbringing and bleached out convictions. Mostly.

I love this stretch between Causeway Bay and Wanchai, love it for its mysterious household appliances, for its cheap clothing overflowing onto sidewalks and for its wet market busy with office workers on their way home. But love it most of all for its gods.

I slow down and call Virginia. 'Sorry again about the other day, I was just too tired,' I say, pushing the memory of my daydreaming and the black eared kites away, as if they had anything to do with us. 'And now I'm running late.' I give a dripping air-conditioner a wide berth, swerve to let a delivery boy pass and almost walk into an Earth God tucked into the entrance of a Maxim's bakery. He is magnificent. Only his eyes with their unclear messages are unsettling, either dangerous or distant.

'You're still out running?' In my mind, I see my friend narrowing her eyes, either in doubt or simply to hear better.

I raise my voice against the traffic noise. 'No, I do my running in the morning. I was saying that I'm going to be a bit late. *Mh hou yihsi.*' Out of the corner of my eye, I see a head turn at the sound of a foreigner shouting in Cantonese into her phone.

That's how we talk, going back and forth between English and Cantonese. Code-switching, linguists call it, as if we were trading secrets. The truth is, it can be a lonely business, trying to learn Cantonese in Hong Kong, where nobody is used to slowing down for a foreigner. Only Virginia is different, correcting my tones with endless equanimity, making soup into sugar, ears into clothes, linen into a mother. 'Not *mah*, *ma*,' she will say and only allow her mouth to twitch. I need her friendship for all kinds of reasons, most of which are selfish.

Like a mother, Virginia explains the world to me, makes sense of the thousand secret signs everywhere. In this city of shiny surfaces, she has something unlikely about her with her hiking trousers, her no-nonsense haircut and her historian's fussiness about details. She waits in front of Kosmos, oblivious to the crowds around her, legs slightly apart, white trousers gleaming, her face already indiscernible in the dusk. I push past another batch of glossy girls and gangly boys and wave.

She smiles and moves towards me. '*Ah* Kim!' Her hand flutters a greeting on my elbow and my heart expands at her use of the intimate *Ah*.

A waitress approaches, a petite, agile Neil Armstrong, her helmet antenna bobbing. She assigns us a table and I look around, take in the black and silver décor with a smile. 'That's cool. You want a helmet with an antenna as well?'

Virginia's smile looks diluted. It must be the black light, making each highlight appear even whiter. 'You're the one who could be an astronaut. Don't they choose them for height, like pilots? Or maybe a model.'

'With this kind of hair?' I rub the bristle on my head, finger the creole that nestles underneath. 'In sixth grade they used to call me the Toilet Brush.' I blush. 'Don't look at me like that. That's the way children are.'

'But it's cute, the golden curls.'

'Dishwater coloured, you mean.' I pull a face. I learned it early on, that the right compliments for the wrong things are no good at all. It also annoys me how shame and anger wrangle in my face, all wrongly directed—shame at my schoolmates and anger at her.

'What happens when you let it grow? That would be a bit more feminine.'

'Then it looks like some sort of llama fleece. It's practical, short like this. And when you can't communicate, a men's haircut is something any hairdresser can do.'

'*Aiya*, it's not easy, being a woman.'

'It has its moments.'

She hears something in my voice, looks up to quickly look away. 'And children. Children are important.'

'And a lot of work,' I say, peering into the black and silver darkness. 'The service certainly doesn't work at lightning speed.'

She giggles. 'She probably has to fly in from another galaxy.' Her eyes scan the room. 'But you cannot *not* have children only because they're hard work. You could get a maid. For the children. You and your husband.'

'The imaginary one,' I laugh. 'Domestic worker, you mean.'

'But don't you want to get married? Somebody who—' she catches sight of the waitress and waves— 'takes care of you and you—'

The waitress scurries over. Behind her visor, the bean-shaped eyes move expectantly.

'I'll have the Kosmic Surprise,' I say. 'Extra hot, please.'

When the waitress has disappeared, Virginia leans back. 'My Chinese doctor doesn't allow me to eat hot food. It's bad for my skin.'

It's not just the lighting, she really looks tired.

She continues, 'It's a pity you were away. We missed the

German Beer Festival again.'

I toy with my water. 'The beer isn't good for my running. It's not even German, it's Bavarian. It's called *Oktoberfest*.' As if that was the point. Virginia has been badgering me to join her for the past two years. For the Beer Festival, held on the roof of the Marco Polo Hotel, which normally functions as a parking lot, and for the spa she frequents to offset the tanning effect of her walks. 'Anything new here? Did you finally walk that missing loop on the MacLehose Trail?'

'We did, right after the Grave Sweeping Festival. There's a new member at the Hikes. From New Zealand. He seems to like it. An engineer.' She fingers the place mat under her glass. 'How was it back home? Did you meet anybody nice?'

'*Ok-la*,' I say. 'It was good to get away from work.'

'And your parents, are they well?'

'As well as can be,' I say. She has never met them, of course, but she still asks. It takes some getting used to, the way your parents become public property in a Confucian culture. I think of the wedding but drop the thought. I don't talk much about my parents with Virginia, as if this could make her understand them better. My mother, running her pharmacy like a well-maintained machine and my father, who doesn't believe in paid philosophers but, instead, in my mother's ability to feed us all.

After the main course, Virginia starts to rummage in her handbag. Her lipstick ritual always makes me cringe. She goes for voluptuous reds, shades that sit askew on her mustard coloured skin.

A line of slim shadows assembles next to us, rustling in cheerleader-like outfits. 'Special promotion! San Miguel,' the girls chant, hardly looking of age themselves.

'Oh no,' I roll my eyes. 'Visitors from outer space. Beer girls.'

Virginia shoos them away and picks up her lipstick. I feel annoyed. There's not enough secret about her, applying make-up in public. Although, am I not the same, even without lipstick? 'Oh, I have to tell you something,' I say while the girls start their spiel at the neighbouring table.

She looks up.

'My parents—I attended my parents' wedding while I was in Germany. Crazy, isn't it? The church wedding.'

Her pocket mirror sways. 'Your parents were not married before?'

'No, I mean—they only had a civil wedding, years ago. Because of my father. So, for their thirty-sixth anniversary, my father gave my mother a church wedding.'

'That's so... romantic.' She returns to her mirror. When she has finished, her hand teases me, the golden lipstick container poised over my fingers. 'Few people get to attend their parents' wedding. So, when will you find Mr Right?'

'Oh gosh, wrong topic.' I knead my earlobe as if to erase Joel, that birdlike man who used to gorge himself on Shakespeare and then feed him to me, *I would I were thy bird, my nyas*. Until he boarded a plane and flew away.

Virginia smiles; well-meaning, her gaze wanders over my face. Even so, my skin flares.

'Tell me, why do I need to find somebody?'

'Girls should marry, shouldn't they?' With this pronouncement she disappears in direction of the toilets, a fresh coat of cinnabar shining in her pale face.

Our desserts arrive as Virginia returns, something called 'Gagarin's Dream' for her and 'Yang Liwei's Delight' for me. She shoves the mango dish towards me. Her face has blanched even more. 'That must be yours.'

'Are you alright? You look awfully white.' I close my eyes, follow the electric taste of mango across on my tongue. 'Mmmh. De-li-cious.'

She takes a stab at her dessert but ignores it. Churning her silk tofu into a puree like a child, she says, 'My parents introduced me to another man.'

My head jerks. Her family sends marriage candidates on her outings who view her unpunished only to disappear forever. 'And?'

'A nephew of one of Mother's mah-jong aunties. They sent us all to have dinner together, with his cousin and one of mine. *OK-la.*'

I take another mouthful. 'I tried to make coconut dessert at home, but it only tasted very plain.'

'Perhaps it's the salt. This dish needs salt.'

Now that I know the salt is there, I can plainly taste it. 'Yes, but did you like him? Do you think you'll see him again?'

She looks up. Her eyes have a wet shine. She lowers her spoon. 'Kim. It's not just a matter of me liking them. They also have to like me.'

I return to my dessert and finish it in silence. I'm not a good girlfriend, not the kind to giggle with over magazines or to make tearful boy confessions to. 'This is so good.' I take my last bite. 'You have to teach me to cook.'

'This really is Thai but I could show you some Chinese things.' She smiles at her spoon, a thin smile. She will be seeing herself upside down now.

'You're not eating,' I say. 'You haven't even tried it.'

'You can have it.' She pushes her dessert away.

There is something wrong with her. What did Spielberg say? Deflated. Without looking at her, I ask, 'Is it still that blind date? Did you like him a lot?'

She shakes her head, opens her mouth but no sound comes out.

'Is it... Are things with your father difficult again? After that blind date?'

Another shaking of her head. 'My mother... My mother is sick.' Her voice is almost soundless. She folds her lips in and turns away, wipes her eyes with the back of her hand. She trembles, the shoulder blades like trapped wings under her T-shirt, the burgundy fabric contracting and expanding as if of its own volition. Her next word barely reaches me through the din of the restaurant. 'Cancer.'

Unbidden, my parents rise in me as they emerged from church only weeks ago, beaming and clasping unseasonal flowers for an unseasonal wedding. I lay my hand on hers, feel it cold and clammy under my fingers. Still not looking at me, she pulls away.

'Is it... Is it bad?'

She quivers as she swallows, and swallows again. She nods, still turned away. There are more nods, or maybe gulps for air. After a while, something in her quietens. She breathes in sharply, fishes for a napkin and blows her nose. 'You don't understand.'

How can I understand? The Angelic Apothecary, the recent bride, with her short hair, slim build and lab coat, never even catches cold and overall is as immortal as mothers are meant to be. So immortal, and so different from her mother, semi-literate like most women of her generation, and married to somebody who probably was half a stranger on her wedding day.

'Sorry. Never mind.' She blows her nose again, takes a few measured breaths. 'We have to take it a day at a time.'

The waitress appears, bill in hand, but when she sees us turns so abruptly her antenna whisks the air.

'I'm so sorry,' I whisper. My fingers stroke the table, smooth and cool like a hesitant beast under my skin. I focus on the still life it frames, something precious to be remembered: soy sauce, chilli paste, toothpicks, sachets of sugar. *Nature morte*, isn't that what the French call it?

'Maybe it only looks very bad now.' My eyes hunt hers, will them to life, but they don't even flicker and remain fastened onto her handkerchief. 'People do recover from, from these things. Sometimes quite unexpectedly.' I sound alien even to myself and somehow from the angle of her shoulders I can tell that this is not what she has been hoping to hear. I start to move the things on the table around.

'You don't understand,' she repeats, in English, to make sure there is no mistaking her words.

Like chess figures, I arrange and rearrange the chilli paste, soy sauce, sugar and toothpicks, until I finally let go.

After the black and white world of Kosmos, Victoria Park is a relief, the humidity of the greenery as palpable as the steady hum of the city around me. An unusual row of tents stops me in my tracks. It looks like fair booths strung along one of the main walks, with bright lights dangling from awnings and a sign saying *Hong Kong Daoist Association Annual Festival*.

'*Mi-si*. Face reading, fortune telling.' A woman looks hungrily at me, a look I recognise from hairdressers and other professions aimed at straightening out my life. 'Your face, easy. Good face for reading, today is free.'

'No thank you,' I say and flee. I slip into one of the bigger marquees. The tent is stuffy, pretending a heat that this day, so late in the year, never had. Lights assault me from the darkness, blue and purple and green they pick out figurines clad in traditional Chinese clothing, arranged in life-like sequences, almost like nativity scenes. Another still life. I can hardly make more sense of this one than of the arrangement on our dinner table an hour ago. Jim would enjoy this diorama as a running commentary on the vicissitudes of modern consumer culture, black light and disco balls coming to the aid of folk religion, which more often than not is about making money. Although in here I cannot see any of the usual symbols associated with wealth and good fortune, no gold coins or oranges, no paper blessings or charms. Only humanoid forms, twisted and distorted as if in agony. Suffering.

Moon Ten Day Eleven
Saturday 12 November

Same bed, different dreams, the Cantonese say, meaning the togetherness of two persons ends where their dreams begin. This is a new bed for me but already it seems destined to be filled with my same old dreams. *Wild Nights! Wild Nights! / Were I with Thee*…With a conscious effort, I banish Emily Dickinson to let the IKEA delivery men in.

'Here. Right underneath the window, please.' I step and turn awkwardly in the confines of my bedroom.

'No, that is the place. Much better. The right place.' The older one passes an elbow over his glistening forehead and runs his fingers through maroon-dyed hair.

My gaze wanders over the whitewashed walls to my right, the inbuilt cabinet to my left, the pile of entangled bras, T-shirts and bed sheets behind the door. He is right. 'But I want to see the stars at night.' I can already feel the night air caressing my skin, stars blazing from a tropical sky.

The junior, a spotty guy with a gold chain around his neck, shoots his superior a glance.

'It should be here, *Mi-si*,' the boss says.

Even so, I cannot bear the idea of thirty beds being invisibly stacked one onto another in this building, bedrooms running like a vein through the whole block. Life as it was pressed into form by an architect twenty years ago. The dictatorship of the proletariat, the Philosopher King would probably say. 'No,' I say. 'Under the window, please.'

When they are finished, I smile. 'Thank you.'

But they don't smile back. 'The feng shui. You shouldn't sleep under a window,' the younger man blurts out. Concern widens his eyes, gives him a doggish look that invites you to pat him.

'Never mind,' I laugh. I envision it years from now, the IKEA range for the Chinese market, complete with an Annika incense cabinet and a do-it-yourself Lars altar. I have always loved the God of Wealth at the IKEA entrance, snugly put up in his rosewood home next to jelly beans and overly thin towels. In this moment, I love him even more, despite his commercial intentions. Irina would probably call this inculturation.

When I hand them their tip, the maroon-tinted man pockets it impassively. The junior recoils as if from danger. 'Not necessary, no money,' he says, evading my eyes.

As I watch them trudge out, I catch the junior sending one last disapproving glance over my arrangement. Just before the door closes behind them with its usual metallic sigh, their voices echo through the empty corridor. 'Only... *gweilo*... no need... feng shui.'

Moon Ten Day Eighteen
Saturday 19 November

Her eyes seem to follow me as I press the doorbell, a benevolent yet distant gaze from sky blue tempera eyes. For once, her cloak looks right in this climate and a handful of crumpled leaves add to the European feel of the arrangement. The Virgin in Zoë's Lourdes grotto, overlooking the comings and goings of the house. In summer, the path from the ferry pier to Zoë Mok's is steep enough to make my skin tingle with sweat, but tonight a cool breeze is coming over from the sea and there is a hint of winter in the air. I search the Virgin for signs of grace but only find tiny holes. Termites perhaps, or woodworm. The leaves at her feet stem from the mango tree towering over her grotto. I brush them away, blow on the hem of her gown to clean it from dust.

A sound makes me jump. 'Walk all the way up,' Zoë's voice is roughened, by the intercom or too many cigarettes, 'we've taken over the roof for the party.'

I never know what to make of Zoë on the walks—listening to Virginia's explanations without comment, blowing her fringe every now and then, her green-tinted sunglasses pushed on top of her head to keep her hair back. I give Mary a last smile and wipe my hands on my trousers. Then I brace myself for the ascent, ninety steep steps past overgrown greenery and the three hundred pink garden gnomes.

On the roof, I almost bump into a statue of Kwun Yam, awkwardly placed between the outer wall and the door. I give her an apologetic pat and move away from the doorway.

'Two hosts rather than one. That's what I call double happiness.' Panting from the stairs, I kiss Zoë on the cheeks, brush Virginia's elbow and lift a bottle of wine from my backpack. '*Grauburgunder*, flown in by my very own self.'

'Thank you.' Virginia's eyes search mine. Her composure

strikes me more than if she had swollen eyes. *Now and at the hour of our death.* Deep inside, something in me grinds to a halt, something I had not even noticed was there, all the way up the stairs. I hand her the bottle. 'Happy birthday to Hong Kong Heritage Hikes. The first year is the hardest in a private business, they say.'

'This is also your success. You help a lot.' She takes the wine and walks me over to the drinks, where she inserts the bottle into a Chinese flower pot that serves as an ice cooler. An improvised dance floor has been cleared but still sits empty in the middle. Tables, chairs and even a sofa are lined up against the low wall that frames the roof. 'I think you haven't met all of the guests yet.' She turns to the group next to the buffet. 'This is Kim, with wine from Germany.'

'Welcome to Hong Kong. And welcome to Virginia's party. We celebrate everything from the Communist takeover to Buddha's birthday.' A man with coppery golden hair extends a bottle of Qingdao. He has eyes like a fox, of a green-brown so fluorescent they seem to give off light on the dim roof, lit only by candles and a bulb above the door.

'Thank you,' I say. 'Actually, I've been here for three years already. Four, almost.'

'Reini.' Jim steps closer. 'Welcome back.'

I kiss him on the cheeks with that vague unease I can never entirely shed. Kissing a Catholic priest and a young and handsome one at that. But Jim spent time in Cuba—'doing my socialist bit,' as he puts it—and insists on being treated like a friend in every way. And he is a colleague, ministering to the Filipinas I work with. Father James Antonio Donnelly.

'We used to celebrate Queen's Birthday as well,' Jim remarks. 'Not that she would have been my queen or anything.'

'Listen to you, old republican. Those were the days.' The blond man drains his beer.

'Talking about holidays,' I say. 'Have you ever wondered why Chinese New Year moves around all the time but Qingming always falls on April fifth?'

'No, I haven't,' Jim says. 'I know the answer.'

'Good for you,' I say. Sometimes, his know-it-all qualities get to be a bit much. Recently, he has been trying to enlighten me about migration issues. He has already digested Irina's pièce de resistance. It was Jim who first brought me along on one of Virginia's outings, when she was still doing them on the side. He attends them for professional reasons, he claims. After all, he is only a part-time pastor to the Filipinas. The other half of his time is dedicated to studying local culture and religion.

'It's because the Chinese use two calendars,' Jim begins. 'A solar calendar and a lunar calendar. Some festivals follow the sun—agricultural holidays, for example—and some follow the moon—'

'Like Chinese New Year,' the red-haired man interrupts him.

'It's called a lunisolar calendar. When the Jesuit astronomers introduced the Gregorian calendar at the Ming court…' Jim is in full flow and, although I was the one to ask, my attention strays and the murmur of conversation fuses with the hum of jungle night and human habitation. In the distance, the lights of Hong Kong Island burn like a thousand early Christmas lights. On the other side of Lamma Island, the chimneys of the power station pierce the silhouette of hills like exclamation marks, their industrial illumination making them stand out even at night.

Now I have time to examine it, I see how exquisite the Kwun Yam statue is, her face finely crafted, the robe flowing across her alabaster body falling in graceful folds. Kwun Yam, Bodhisattva of Mercy.

'Kim, this is Frank.' Virginia is crouched on Zoë's love seat, a purple affair with zebra pattern and lime green stripes. A strong, old-fashioned aftershave hangs in the air.

'Hello.' The man standing next to her lifts his glass in greeting. 'Named for Frank Sinatra, they say, which I mostly try to ignore.'

We laugh. I attempt to piece them together, Frank Sinatra and this white-haired man with bottle blue eyes and a shirt that tries too hard, frangipani and passionflowers wrangling on his chest.

He has followed my look. 'Believe me, I sing better than I dress.'

We laugh again. I rub my nose, twist a non-existing wisp of hair behind my left ear. 'You must be the newcomer,' I say. 'From New Zealand? Virginia mentioned you.'

'Did she?' He smiles and smooths his hair with one hand. After depositing his beer on the wall, he adjusts his trousers on his stodgy frame, pulling on the belt. 'Not quite sure if I still count as a Kiwi after, er, twenty-eight years in this city. Came here for a two month job and never left. Same old story everywhere.'

'New to the hikes, I meant.'

'Ah, the hikes,' he says. 'Great idea, that. Forget about Shanghai or Beijing. You can't beat life here. Great people and with that famous can do spirit. Like Ginnie here, with her own business.' He gives a slight bow in direction of the love seat. 'You missed her vote of thanks at the beginning.'

'Virginia,' I say. 'Oh.'

'Frank's daughter is studying in Vancouver,' Virginia says into the breeze. In the dim light, I sense her blush more than see it, something twinned to an eager strain in her voice. 'And his son is working in California.'

'Congratulations,' I say. 'And welcome to Hong Kong Heritage Hikes. You're in good hands here with Virginia.' I tilt my glass towards her. She wriggles as if to brush off my compliment but smiles.

'Ginny was just telling me why she studied history,' he says.

She runs a hand over her hair, straight like an accountant's. 'I suppose I—I learned a lot from my father,' she says. 'Most parents want their children to study business or economics, something of that kind. My parents never were like that.'

'I have to say, I can't see you wheeling and dealing in a tight suit,' he says. 'Although it would suit you.' He lifts his glass again.

'You know, history is…' She frowns. 'You know how things look different when you see them through a microscope? I think that's what historians do—look at the details to, to understand the whole. And the most ordinary things and people look… amazing when you see them from that perspective.' She half turns away, moving out of the lamplight.

I search the darkness for her face, virtually feel my pupils enlarge, but only see the shine of her teeth, an animated brightness in the shadows.

'Well put,' he says. 'Well put. Ah yes, the families. Look around,' he gestures towards the clusters of people, the men with rolled up shirtsleeves, the women with smooth legs normally hidden in hiking gear. 'My late wife was a lawyer. Her mother could just about write her own name. And her mother's mother—' he takes another gulp of beer— 'her mother's mother still had bound feet.' He nods appreciatively. 'Strong families, pooling their money and pushing their children to burn the midnight oil.' He frowns at the drink in his hand. 'After my wife passed away—' His upper body stills, becomes fluent again. 'It's the families that make things happen.'

He loosens his shoulders and emits a soft burp behind a hand that is a denial of his Hawaiian shirt, a signet-ring glinting on mature skin, the nails too well buffed. 'Excuse me. Strong families. All for one and one for all, like the Boy Scouts. And great food.'

'Hi.' He has slipped over, stealthy as a fox. Under the gaze of Kwun Yam, he looks unlikely, a suave pretension that life is easy. Or maybe it is Kwun Yam who suddenly lacks credibility, an alien intruder watching over us gweilos.

'Hi,' I say. 'I'm Kim.'

His eyes glide along my legs in what is probably supposed to be a surreptitious look. 'Like Kim Basinger?'

'No. Like kimchi.'

His eyebrows shoot up.

'Kim like kimchi,' I say and dip my satay stick into the chilli sauce.

A smile curves the corners of his mouth. 'I thought Jim called you—Ray…? Something like that.'

'Rye-nee,' I pronounce it for him. 'Spelled R-e-i-n-i.'

'Is that Chinese? Your Chinese alter ego?'

'No, that's me. Short for Reinhild.'

'You say no a lot. Is that your default mode?'

'No,' I say and we laugh. But he is right, I seem to be saying no a lot these days, something I am not used to. It may be good, who knows. I am a helper, or used to be. I can't say no. It tends to land me in trouble.

'So, how come you have two names?'

'I work with domestic workers. The Filipinos love nicknames, nobody just goes by a single name. And Reinhild is... very Germanic.' I pull a face. With care, I dab at a crimson spot on the table. 'I was named after my godmother,' I add and immediately regret it. As if Auntie Hilde could help my name. Or hers.

'I see. I'm Bertie, by the way.' After a big gulp of beer, he leans over and whispers, 'It's really Cuthbert.'

I grin, take another snack and push the plate back to him. Lathering my satay stick with more sauce, I say, 'I once was the most famous patron of the only Korean restaurant in a thousand square miles.'

'You got stuck somewhere on the mainland?'

'I work for MediMission,' I say. 'We're an NGO specialising in migration issues. I used to work in Sudan, with IDPs.'

'With what?'

'Internally Displaced Persons. Sorry for the jargon—people who are refugees in their own countries.'

'But the maids here aren't refugees.'

Our eyes travel to Zoë's domestic worker, passing around drinks on a tray. People who are at home and not at home, Joel used to call the refugees with his nomadic insight. Bertie's gaze lingers on the girl's bottom, tightly packed into a pair of black trousers under a pink T-shirt softly bulging just where it should.

'They're not,' I concede and pull the snacks back to me.

'But?' He makes a conscious effort not to look at the girl.

'But. There's always a but.' I glance over the guests, women who own made to measure silk outfits and men who still use cufflinks. In a corner, Jim and Spielberg are bent over a mobile phone.

'Physical abuse, molestation.' My eyes meet his, ever so lightly. 'Wages that are never paid, extortion from the employment agencies…'

'And what do you do? Why hire a *Germanic* staff member and not a local?'

After another bite of chicken, I say, 'Why not hire a Filipino is more like it. I studied migration studies. We run a shelter, give legal advice. Lobby with the government, that kind of thing. I started out as a support worker for individual cases. I guess it also helped that I'm a woman, and Catholic.' I grin. 'That's discrimination because of gender and religion, I know.' I nibble down the rest of the meat from my stick. My mouth half full, I add, 'Recently, I've been doing strategic work. Devising campaigns and so on.' I set down the bared stick, the neatness pleasing me, tidy and clean like the knowledge of my new work, the promotion barely hidden in my last words.

His eyes roam my body again, scurry along the loose linen trousers right down to the shoes which Auntie Hilde would call *Jesuslatschen*, Jesus sandals. They get stuck on my feet. Feet that would look good next to a water buffalo.

'So, are you some sort of nun? The Medical Missionary?'

'Heavens, no.' I say. 'The poverty, I could probably live with. But the rest?' I fight a vision of Irina in a nun's habit, demanding absolute obedience. 'MediMission isn't even very medical any more. So, what do you do here?' I have to bite my tongue not to add, *Cuthbert*. What promise does this name make which it doesn't keep? But who am I to deplore names and their claims.

'I'm here to make money. No dreams, no good deeds unless you count selling things a good deed.' He lifts his satay stick, notices it is all eaten and drops it on the table. 'But it's a damn good life here. Cheap maids, cheap taxis, great food.'

I watch him leave, crumpling a napkin onto the table, watch it drift to the floor. Expatriates. As if I wasn't one myself. The breeze caresses my skin with not so much as a whisper and for a moment all is well. I close my eyes, allow myself darkness and quiet and concentrate on the flavours in the air, an unnamed tropical sweetness, barbecued meat and sea salt. When I open them again, I look right into the face of Kwun Yam. Tireless, the Merciful is watching over us, waiting to bestow her blessings on the suffering world.

Jim has followed my gaze. 'Zoë, what is this, on your roof? This Kwun Yam statue is a real piece of art. Magnificent.'

'Here, try some sweets.' Spielberg appears before me, holding out a plate with rice balls. He leans over, voice lowered. 'I overheard your talk with the glib guy. The womaniser. Hey, since when are you so direct?' He grins. Louder, he says, 'It's good to see you again.'

'You have no business being jealous of other men.' I give him a pretend pout.

'Women, darling, you mean women. I'm with you when it comes to being upset about men.'

'Checking out Zoë's orthodoxy, are you, Father?' Frank's voice booms out, flushed with beer and the pleasure of being onto something untoward. 'Zoë, we've all seen your Lourdes grotto downstairs. Come on, spill the beans.'

'Jim,' Jim says. 'I'm in civvies here. This is not the Congregation for the Doctrine of the Faith.'

'The grotto is my mother's. My mother went through a Catholic phase years ago.' Zoë glances at Jim. 'The Kwun Yam statue also was her idea. She felt that the chimneys of the power plant produced bad feng shui. They look like incense sticks in an offering. I put up the statue to stop her nagging.' Everyone laughs good-naturedly.

'Two Virgins under one roof, that's the spirit.' Jim raises his glass. 'To Kwun Yam and Mary.' But the conversation has already moved into a thousand different directions and nobody follows suit.

When the air has grown so fresh as to be almost cold, Virginia ambles over, a piece of leathery pizza in her hand, chewing.

I raise my arm in greeting.

Her mouth still full, she asks, 'What's that?'

'Sangria.' I peer into my drink, let it circle until a few orange and yellow pieces float to the surface. 'Frank's extra special version with star fruit and pomegranate.' I get up to fetch her a glass. My blood hums with the drink and I allow my hands to follow the wall, let its rough, cold surface tickle my palms. When I come back, she is sitting on the floor. Her glass still in my hand, I slide down next to her. '*Ah* Virginia.' I hand her the drink. 'Cheers.'

'Call me *gaje*.' She takes a sip, frowns. 'Like an honorary older sister.'

'Blood sister,' I say. 'Like Robin Hood and his men.'

She turns towards me. 'You've done so much for me. Like a younger sister, you are for me. And you don't have any sisters.'

'Right you are.' I rub my eyes.

'We used to have sworn sisterhoods.' She resettles herself against the wall, extends her legs. 'Sworn spinsters, they really were, in the Pearl River Delta. Women who refused to marry and lived with their sworn sisters in old age. In Buddhist communities.' She takes another sip. 'What is that? It tastes weird.'

'I think he put in some five spice powder as well.' I take several swigs, will the alcohol on as it grapples with my sleepiness and the growing chill in the air. 'Uggh, it really tastes like cold mulled wine.'

She laughs. 'He's too crazy.' She sets down her glass. 'Can you believe it, I met one such sworn spinster last time I accompanied my mother back to Foshan. She was tiny and fragile and looked about a hundred years old.'

'But you want to marry,' I say. I pull up my legs, hug my knees, rest my cheek on them. Travelling with her mother, only recently.

'Of course I do. But you can still be sworn sisters or brothers with somebody. Men do it more than women. There is a proper ritual for it, to become sworn brothers.'

I lift my head. 'For blood brothers or sisters, you would need to exchange blood.' I shift my legs, pick up the blunt table knife on my paper plate and pretend to cut my index.

She leans over. 'Really, I mean it. I can be your sister.'

I lift my hand with the knife as if for an oath. 'Not sworn spinsters,' I say. 'Sisters.'

Gently, she pulls down my hand, extracts the knife from it. 'Knives are bad luck.' Her hand is warm against mine as she lifts it. 'Sisters,' she says.

Two different palenesses, our hands are against the Southern Chinese sky, and the cool breeze brings our fingers closer together.

When I feel the wine leave me like a forgotten promise, I get up and stretch. 'Let's call it a day.'

'See you, *gamui*.' Her voice brings me to a halt. I thought we had faked it, our sisterhood, and here she is, calling me little sister. My one and only.

Now and at the hour of our death. On my way out, I say it consciously, a Hail Mary for my blood sister's mother, directed at the still blue lady in her grotto, where more dead mango leaves have accumulated in the course of just a few hours.

Moon Eleven Day Fourteen
Wednesday 14 December

After a day of hammering out project reports, I am itching to leave. My finger is already on the button that releases our office door when Irina's voice pulls me back. 'Kim. Have you done your Word for the Day yet?' She leans away from the photocopier, rubs the small of her back. Like an afterthought, she adds a smile, as if to soften the impact of her voice.

Although it is not really part of our job, we are all expected to support Word for the Day. Lynn Cameron, a Methodist minister, coordinates it for Voice of Faith and last winter roped my boss in. 'MediMission is like Noah's Ark,' she had said to Irina and me at the Save the Children Christmas reception.

'Yes,' I replied, 'we only get to help one or two for all those that drown.'

Irina had shot me a punishing look, then smiled back at Lynn. Probably seeing herself in the role of Noah.

'So colourful. The right mix of ethnic backgrounds and

denominations,' Lynn continued with a look onto Irina's face. 'You know what I mean.'

With its tiny compartments and countless piles of the *Manual for Migrants* and *Seafarer's Quarterly*, our office certainly feels crammed like the Ark. A vision of our boat people surges in me, each of us staring out of a personal porthole. Irina the giraffe towering over hers, only revealing golden and brown patches through the window. Ed the chimpanzee smiling through the glass, his dark face as round as the porthole. Maybe he would even be waving a banana. Eva would be a Chinese mongoose, and Jim—

'You know Lynn is always desperate for new voices.' Irina hauls me back into the present. With a half glance, she sets the photocopier into whirring motion. 'And the recording?'

'Done,' I say, 'The story of Mary and Elizabeth. A typical Advent reading, with a bit of feminism thrown in.' I grin at her and she grins back.

'The broadcast is next Wednesday,' I add. 'Lynn liked it.' When you grow up with this kind of thing, it is not difficult to formulate a few well-rehearsed ideas that you can live with, even if you feel numb saying them.

Downstairs, I habitually look at the door god who guards the entrance to our building as if he could revive my religious zeal. But he looks weary, his tea cups half empty. When I was a child, Advent lived from the happy ending that I knew to be guaranteed. These days, I fear the stories whose endings we can predict and find it difficult to derive hope from them. 'A spiritually dry phase,' Jim would diagnose and surely know a remedy. As it is, I don't even mind the dryness and that is where the real sin lies.

A blast of moist air washes over me as I step outside. The air in Hong Kong is a presence of its own. Whether you acknowledge it or not, it is always there.

Moon Eleven Day Sixteen
Friday 16 December

Rising and falling with the softest of sighs, the snow sways in the breeze of the air conditioning. The airstream lifts the hairs on the reindeers' nose, makes them tremble. Rudolph the Red-nosed Reindeer, decked with snow like the hut he is watching over, appears to be shivering with cold. The unintended effect makes me smile. Hong Kong people have a fondness for Christmas displays and the Country Club is no exception.

I sneak a look at myself in one of the gilded mirrors of the lobby, smooth down the suit jacket that Virginia mended for me. Somewhere out there, between dark green hills and the sluggish sea, far away from the invented worlds of Christmas installations, she is carrying around the knowledge of her mother's illness. My blood sister. Sometimes, I envy her the solitary moments of her work, exploring a walk in the New Territories, sitting down in the cool haven of Central Library to read up on colonial Hong Kong. I sigh, pull at my T-shirt and give myself a tentative smile. Fundraising talks still make me nervous.

In the depth of the lobby, the dark wood panelling opens and April Lindsay strides over, her steps ringing on the marble floor. A girl struggles to follow her, a perfect, miniature echo of her mother's English Rose blondeness. April is Secretary of the Ladies League and in charge of Social Affairs. The girl, four perhaps, peeks at me from behind her mother's sleeve.

'Laura, say hello to Auntie Kim.' Gently, she pushes the child forward. 'Sorry. I know we always tell our members no children but I had to bring her. She'll be very good—right, darling?' She brushes a few stray hairs out of the girl's face. 'Our helper is down with the flu and Matt is away on business. I didn't want her to catch Anita's flu. We want to go to Boracay over Christmas.' She stops her breathless flow of information, smiles at me. 'Right. There'll be brunch first, then the floor will be all yours.'

I nod, my mouth feeling shrivelled.

'Mummy, look!' The girl breaks free from her mother's hand and darts to the manger scene. 'Real straw.' She fingers the grassy mattress under the baby Jesus. Another envy: that things acquire beauty simply by being small.

I step closer to the arrangement. A gaggle of ducks, a handful of goats and a water buffalo. A hut that looks suspiciously Chinese, complete with red paper blessings framing the double door. A dark-haired Mary in traditional peasant trousers and a group of farmers with Cantonese straw hats. Jim would love it.

'Such an unusual nativity scene,' I say. 'I love the water buffalo. And Rudolph and the snow add their own special note to it.'

April laughs. 'It raised quite a few eyebrows last year. Apparently, it was a gift from a local artist which they couldn't refuse. The Caucasian members didn't want a Chinese Holy Family and the Chinese didn't want to be depicted as peasants.'

I smile. 'Yes, a Cantonese manger scene would have more electronic gadgets in it.' It is easy enough to imagine, the new Chinese version—a Mercedes breathing soft diesel fumes down Mary's neck and Joseph busy posting the birth on Facebook.

'This year, the general manager just set it up. Mr. Singh probably doesn't care either way.' She turns to the girl. 'Let's get you to the bathroom.'

They set off, the girl's voice chirping through the lobby. 'But why didn't they go to a hotel? Mummy? The helper with the baby and the father?'

'I told you, darling, the hotels were all full. And they were strangers. And, sweetie, the girl in the manger scene isn't a Filipina. Mary and Joseph were Jews.'

'Say what you want, the colonials had an eye for views.' My neighbour has caught me gazing out at the sea. Behind the panorama windows of the dining room, Deep Water Bay lies hidden in the haze. To our right, the South China Sea stretches into the horizon, shimmering and grey like the inside of an abalone.

I will myself back, to this room with its humming crowd, the fleet of Chinese waiters, their steps muted by the plush carpet. 'Sorry. Yes.' I smile and focus on the woman to my left. Her hair is cut in a Lady Diana, 1990s-like style, betraying her nomadic status better than her raw silk jacket. In my nervous frame of mind, I cling to an insight borrowed from somewhere, long ago—that expat communities, like Jewish refugees in the 1930s, tend to lag behind fashion but that your status grows with your time on the road.

'Yep,' a plump woman with a rasping voice agrees, licking her spoon with devotion. 'Think of the Peak. Can't beat the view. You have to try the chocolate cake.'

'The fried noodles are also excellent.' I lift another unwieldy skein of curry-flavoured rice noodles to my mouth, careful not to stain my suit before the talk. Across the table, a pale woman looks up but says nothing, struggling to pick up a spring roll with her chopsticks.

My neighbour turns her attention back to me. 'So what does your husband do?'

'My husband? I—I live alone.'

'But then, why are you here?'

I stare at her. Into the sudden quiet, the spring roll breaks with an explosive noise as the pale woman finally bites into it. Her mouthful rumbles like distant firecrackers, provoking her to blush. *Because of the blue crabs. Because of the abalone coloured sea. Because of the pineapple buns without pineapple and all the other mysteries.*

'I work for MediMission,' I say. 'I'm today's speaker.' But their image replays in my mind, April and her daughter, their perfect symmetry as they walk, Laura reaching for her mother's hand, April's back in its tailored outfit swaying like an uncertain flower. The memory of that back, safeguarded and beautiful, aches in my chest. I lie to myself most of all.

A spoon rings out against a glass and stills the room almost at once. April smiles at the assembled guests. 'Ladies, while you swallow your last delicious bites, allow me to bring your minds back to business. In a moment, Kim Kranich will talk to us about the latest, er, developments at MediMission.' Applause. 'A big thank you again to all who supported the Autumn Bazaar in aid of migrant workers. Altogether, two-hundred and thirty-seven persons attended, that's without maids and children.' Applause.

Mirth is the mail of anguish. I chew my lips and concentrate on their faces, so fresh and innocent above their manicured hands folded into their laps. 'Thank you,' I say, 'for allowing me to introduce our work.'

A woman in a suede two piece has raised her hand for question time. 'I know that you help these women, but what do you actually do?'

'You mean, apart from the legal advice and the shelter? We lobby with the government for better policies that we believe protect employers and employees.'

'No, you personally,' another listener interjects from the side, her hair dyed midlife-crisis red.

'That's my job, what I was just trying to explain. To work on policy recommendations. To come up with ideas for fundraising campaigns.' I smile at them, the skin on my face tight from the effort. 'I also act as a support worker for individual cases.' I pull my skirt down a few inches.

'So, do you have a maid?' somebody wants to know. A giggle follows the question and a teasing hiss from somewhere else.

'I—I don't have a maid,' I say, tugging at my jacket. 'Domestic worker.'

'Does this mean you don't want a helper?' A pale, dark-haired woman near the window gets up to make herself better heard. I strain to see her against the brightness of the silver sea outside. My lunchtime companion with the spring roll.

'I really don't think that my private… living arrangements are of interest here.'

'We give them honest employment,' the Lady Diana look-alike interjects.

'Why don't you want one?' the pale woman asks. 'My helper feeds seven persons in the Philippines with her salary. She puts her children through school with my money.'

'Yes, why?'

34

The quiet in the room condenses. The Lady Diana look-alike clutches the silk scarf around her neck. Laura is huddled into her mother, her small fingers spread onto April's arm. A low whine leaks through the door. One of the Chinese amahs is vacuuming the lobby. The noise stops—it must be the nativity scene she is working around—and resumes.

'Because... I just cannot see myself as part of this,' I say. Crossing the line is not painful, but that could be numbness, or a death. I move back to the projector where I showed pictures of the shelter moments ago. 'You think you're good employers? Maybe you are.

'Maybe you are, maybe you're not. According to our surveys, seventy-five percent of domestic workers work fourteen hours a day. And all of them have to play by the rules of the system.' I pause, search through my files. 'A system where losing your job means losing your visa and losing your home. And these are the good moments. The post-colonial, no, the proto-colonial moments,' I say and savour the word. 'The moments when the air conditioning is turned on for the master's dog but never the "maid".' There is an intake of breath in the room, a stifled something. 'In the bad moments—and I get to work with the bad moments, remember—it's modern slavery.

'It starts with withheld wages and confiscated passports, wrongful promises by employment agencies and employers. Curfews are also popular. Curfews that prescribe adult women when to return on their day off.' I consciously look away from them, from their cheeks that bloom in the semi-darkness. 'But this is only the, the warm-up. And when I say warm-up I mean it.' I open a file. A scorched, heavily burned body appears, the face set into a grim expression.

'This woman suffered third-degree burns because her employers routinely locked her into the flat. By the time the firemen were able to break in she was already damaged for life. She had to return to the Philippines.'

I click on. 'Jewel Longakit was repeatedly sexually harassed by her employer. Her friend Milma was beaten and hurt with an iron. See the burn marks?' The pictures rush onto the silver screen, more than I'd ever need to make my point. 'To answer your question: No, I cannot see myself as part of this system.'

The audience is motionless. The pale woman focuses on the spotless table linen, her thumb taking in its texture. Outside, the leaden sea pulses, laps against the shore.

The pale woman stands up again. She is very young, I see now, and there is a ladder in her tights. 'Bravo!' She claps her hands. The sound falls into the quiet as if unheard.

Icy sweat trickles down my armpits, along my knees. I have broken every possible rule of professionalism, confidentiality, prudence. And fundraising.

'I have to go,' I say. 'Thank you for the invitation.'

The silence of the room hammers in my ears. Somewhere, a chair creaks. Deep inside the folds of a handbag, a mobile phone starts to vibrate. I give a half-cough and turn away.

'Thank you,' April says, more to the group than to me, and finally they are free to talk among themselves. The room erupts in conversation. My fingers are so clammy I struggle with the computer cables. April comes over to help and, with a shock, I feel our skins touch.

'Thank you,' April says, her eyes travelling around my shoulders, only her green tea perfume reaching out to me as if heated. 'I'll get back to you after Boracay.' She winds up a cable. 'Did I tell you that we're leaving next summer? Going to Singapore.' She still can't look at me, but there is a new edge to her voice. Pleading. 'The children are so tired of moving, poor things.' Her hand reaches out for her daughter, lingers on her head. She sighs. 'So, the Philippines will be our last holiday for a while. We'll be in touch.'

As I pass the wood-panelled lobby again, my homespun business look casts dishwater-grey shadows on the gilded mirrors. Rudolph still looms over the manger scene, dwarfing the water buffalo and the Chinese Holy Family. Soon enough, Mary and Joseph will have to migrate again, this time not for a census but in response to a threat to their family, their young son, internally displaced persons like so many of us.

*

What do you want to be burnt at your funeral?

Like a hungry, unhappy ghost, I wander Ma Tau Wai Road. I have given myself the afternoon off, to postpone the confrontation with Irina, but my suit cuts into my stomach and my shoes injure my feet. Going home would be the sensible thing to do, to curl up on the sofa and plump up my ruffled self.

Instead, I roam this area where red and white affairs converge, matters of the living and the dead sit side by side, incense burners and ashtrays, cross buns and Buddhist pastry. I love the double happiness coconuts with their red, lacquered characters. Sitting in chaste, crumpled pairs, the shoots barely showing, they are ready to burst their skins and propel new life in green, forceful fronds.

I almost pass the shop—sports shoes and polo shirts, blouses and caps—without a further look. They won't have my size anyway. Then I see what is on offer and my heart stops. Gifts for the departed, lovingly created from paper, to be committed to the world of the dead by burning. Jewellery and handbags, laptops and perfumes, bras and underpants, dental hygiene sets and mobile phones. And food—dim sum and sandwich and pizza, complete with a western set of cutlery giving off its faux metal shine. All to nourish and redeem the dead, so they in turn may bless the living.

Inside, the shop is like a fairyland stationer's, crammed with shimmering paper goods in all colours of the rainbow. Buddhist chanting seeps out of one corner. A tape, set at a volume so discreet it is hardly noticeable against the sound of vehicles outside. I try to find myself in this array of goods, look for earrings and wonder what I would get for the Angelic Apothecary and the Philosopher King. Books and medicine but what else? They are strangers to me in this place and the realisation hurts.

A call from Virginia interrupts my browsing. 'Sorry, I need to cancel tonight.' Her family has arranged another blind date. There is new urgency in her voice.

'Just be yourself,' I say, my eyes lingering over a pair of fetching paper Prada shoes. Taking the art of plagiarism to new heights. The copy of the copy. Where does our invention of invented worlds end? Where is that kernel of truth, like that innermost part of a Russian doll?

I finger a golf cap for a dead person with an unknown handicap. How we long to be recognised in life and in death. 'Just be yourself,' I repeat, 'isn't that what everybody says? You'll be fine.' I wonder who could love her and why, and feel like a traitor. 'Anybody who doesn't want you is an idiot,' I say and strangely enough that feels closer to the truth. She is hard to define but has no defects either. She is easy-going, accommodating, always striving to be cheerful.

I go on, 'You're running your own business. Don't you always say Hong Kong people look for mates that are financially secure?'

'*Ah* Kim. People look for different things in women.'

'You have a great body,' I say. 'Not as stick thin as most Hong Kong women.'

'Do you think so?'

I know what she means. After Sudan, it was a shock to move to a place where people pay money to look starved.

'What do you look for in a man?' Her voice startles me, its matter-of-fact quality.

I look at the papier-mâché figures around me, well-dressed specimens in traditional Chinese pyjamas, servants that will never ask for legal advice or a flight ticket back to the Philippines. I move to the shop entrance as if to see clearer. Outside, cars and double-decker buses rush by in clouds of heat and smoke. I struggle for a simple Cantonese truth that I can formulate. Finally, I say, 'He has to be a good person.'

Her answer, genuine curiosity in her voice, floors me. 'Why?'

I look around, at the endless forms that love can take, and try again in English. 'He... has to recognise me.'

Somehow, we decide this is no way to talk and she promises to get back to me. I stare into the traffic, louder and greyer with the sun's passing.

'*Mi-si.*' The owner has followed me. 'We can also make tailor made, anything you want. Pets, musical instruments, servants.'

'I don't need this kind of thing,' I say. Although for once it doesn't matter they may not have my size.

I step out. *You don't understand.* And then I do understand. It is her mother's desire to find a companion for Virginia. A loved one, trying to provide her daughter with a loved one.

Again, I marvel at the way night falls in this city, darkness generating itself in the briefest of times: a phone call, an errand, a distraction. You exit and the outlook on life has changed.

Winter Solstice
Thursday 22 December

Winter solstice. A day which seems to mend things or at least to turn them around imperceptibly, like the sun which changes direction ever so subtly. What a distant memory Germany is, where the forces of darkness are so palpable at this time of the year. Here my colleagues are more concerned with the big family dinner winter solstice gives rise to.

'Another one,' Eva sighed before she hurried off around lunchtime. 'And Chinese New Year still ahead of us.' Eva likes to be different. Sometimes, I suspect this is what attracted her to Christianity. *Another one*—Virginia will be thinking the same, albeit with a different tinge.

'But it's a beautiful tradition. I wished I could attend a family dinner tonight.' I stopped. It must sound as if I was angling for an invitation, even if from Eva.

'It's difficult for me, with my mother and uncles not—come to Christ yet. All the gambling and drinking. It's good I'm not a son. At least we can skip the discussions about ancestor worship.' She let the glass door go, handbag shivering on her shoulder.

Irina comes to my cubicle. Only occasional beeps and whines of electronic equipment break the silence. We are still reeling with the effects of my performance at the Ladies League, which has left the League deeply divided. One half is adamant not to support MediMission anymore—'this hotbed of aggressive leftism'—while the other half congratulates us on championing women's rights. And the money pledged by the League for this year will not be forthcoming.

Irina was less disappointed about the money than my 'extremely unprofessional behaviour.' 'Passion is good, yes,' she declared when she heard the news. 'We hire you for passion, but we pay you for prudence. Passion and prudence.'

The Formica creaks softly as she sits down on the empty desk next to mine. She crosses her legs at the ankles, tucking one cream coloured pump behind the other. 'A Mrs Partridge called.' Trimmed with beige, her pumps are. They have wooden heels, showing rings in the material like tiny trees. She glances at her note. 'She said… she now realises her behaviour was post-colonial, no, excuse me: proto-colonial.' Irina's heels swing slightly. Is it real wood? Do they fell trees for shoes? 'She has dismissed her maid.'

She folds her glasses, deposits them on the table and sits up. 'This is the fourth such call.' With a soft slap, the note comes down in her left palm. 'This has to stop.' Another slap, even softer. 'You'll call her and explain why she will not fire her domestic worker.'

'Yes, Irina.' *Her legs don't even come down to the floor*, a little voice in me whispers. They are hanging freely now. She could dangle them if she wanted.

She crosses her legs, slowly wrings the paper into a ball. 'I was thinking of letting you help Ed with the Ronda Pajarillo case.'

I look up, into her face which is so well put together. 'The one who had her nose broken during a beating?'

'No, that's somebody else, leave the criminal cases to Ed. This one is termination without prior warning and no compensation.'

'So, it's back to case work,' I say. I don't want it to be taken from me, the crazy campaigns, the strategy papers and roundtable meetings.

'I wouldn't put it that way. But you have to stay in touch with our grassroots work, get to know our constituency. Alright?' Irina talks as if she was paid for her lingo as well.

'Irina, I'm not a social worker or anything. It feels too… old, grown-up somehow.'

'Now, isn't it a bit late for that? If the Filipinas are old enough to come here, you're old enough to help them. It'll do you good to work with Ronda. Jim will do all the regular pastoral counselling if she needs it. But you'll remember that not all of them are half burnt to death. Get some perspective on things.'

In one single move, she slides from the desk, straightens her skirt and eases her upper body. Well-oiled, she seems. She picks up her glasses and flips the crumpled note into my bin. 'Any plans for tonight?'

All my Chinese friends will spend the evening with their families, and the Westerners are busy preparing for Christmas. I hesitate. 'Not really.'

She looks down at her hands, smiles. 'My parents never got over winter solstice, not even after forty years in California. "Look!" My father would show his hands to everybody—"No frostbite, not like Novosibirsk."' Her hands share her blondeness. 'And he was proud of it.'

She turns to leave. 'I never got over the sight of my father's hands blistered from hauling fruit crates. So. Go out and do a bit of emotional pampering for the girl. Ronda.'

I nod, shift in my seat, feel my thighs relax.

Halfway to her desk, she swivels around. Against the yellowing afternoon light, it is difficult to read the expression on her face. 'You do realise that you've got a… kind of history with this organisation, right? I'd hate to see you repeat that sort of experience while you're here in Hong Kong.' With these words she disappears, her voice too bright in the empty office. Next to Eva's desk, the photocopier still gives off its mechanical sighs.

Moon Twelve Day Two
Sunday 1 January

'Happy New Year!' As usual, Auntie Hilde sounds as if she were just around the corner, not nine thousand kilometres away. Outside, the tree under my window flashes its blinding green while the street breathes its usual Sunday morning quiet. A fishmonger hurries by on a bicycle, his black rubber boots reflecting the sunlight. (A thought, to be pursued later: That those dealing in dead lives—butchers, fishmongers—wear white.)

'Oh,' I say, 'Happy New Year.' I glance at my wrist but under my pyjamas my arm is still bare. Nine a.m., the display on my phone says. Two a.m. in Germany. I will have to call the Angelic Apothecary and the Philosopher King. They claim not to adhere to conventionalities but they expect me to call, my mother because underneath her love dispensed in the form of vitamins and health tonics she misses me, and my father to complain about the inevitable party at the Schmidt's, with '*Fondue* and *Fischli* and people who talk all the time but have nothing to say.'

'Sorry about not calling earlier,' I say. 'Calendars are such a relative thing. We follow a different truth here.'

'Ah, don't you sound just like your father. So, no New Year's resolutions for you, then?' She could be Asian in her way of approaching difficult revelations, turning them around for effectiveness.

To help Virginia through a painful time. To be more prudent at work. I blow onto the surface of my phone, watch the dust motes rise and fall. To be a better housewife. 'To give up smoking,' I say and we both laugh. 'Hong Kong has got one of the lowest smoking rates in the world, did you know?'

'So, still faithful, still there. No hope of luring you back any time soon?' she asks in that perky, unbelieving tone that relatives reserve for my life here. It is difficult to talk about the taste of jasmine toothpaste, the dubious, unvegetarian qualities of sea cucumber and the shaded tonality of the language.

'No hope,' I say. 'But you're always welcome to see for yourself.'

'*Ach ja*, I really should.'

Of course she never comes. It is like a game you play, these invitations, because in the end they expect you to come home. They think they know where it is. Even Auntie Hilde. Especially her.

Moon Twelve Day Three
Monday 2 January

Belatedly, I call my parents. 'Any plans for the New Year?' I ask.

'We were thinking of going on a honeymoon,' my mother says. '*Wer A sagt, muß auch B sagen.*' Her voice sounds happy, happier than the duty she implies with her expression, while I picture the Angelic Apothecary and the Philosopher King in a hotel full of retired newlyweds. Sometimes, I wonder how she will ever retire but the mere question seems heretical.

'Hong Kong is so far away,' she continues. 'You know how Papi hates to be jet lagged.'

And humid heat. And strange crowds. I know. 'So, next will be a birth announcement and the purchase of a terraced house in the suburbs?'

'We've done that already, my darling, you forget. I guess you're next in line for that.'

Suddenly, it makes me squirm, all of it, makes me seasick in its topsy-turviness.

Moon Twelve Day Five
Wednesday 4 January

The ballroom of the Mandarin Oriental Hotel is almost full, humming with waiters, brimming with conversation. My eyes skim over dark suits and pencil skirts, are hooked by islands of colour: a group of Muslim women in matching lilac headscarves, an assembly of monks in rust coloured gowns. Across the room, next to a towering arrangement of orchids, I spot a familiar wiry figure in black jeans and dark shirt. I help myself to a drink from a passing waiter and cross the room.

'Jim! Happy New Year.'

'Reini.' He kisses me hello. 'Join me for some rare capitalist grandeur.' With a sweeping gesture, he takes it all in, the tinkling glasses and the polished silverware, the buffet and the stage. To our right, a Sikh is deep in conversation with a Daoist monk. 'This reception gets nicer from year to year. Even if it's all rather meaningless.'

The New Year's reception of Hong Kong's official religions. 'So, how's life on the hill?' I ask. Jim lives in the Catholic community above Stanley.

'Uphill.' He grins and shrugs. '*Salud.* I hear Irina wants you to go back to case work?'

I blush. I look at him, then pull at an imaginary length of hair and say in an affected voice, '"To stay in touch with our constituency."' We laugh. After gulping down some more orange juice, I say, 'She wants me to start with Ronda.'

'Pajarillo. Medium height and from Leyte?'

'I haven't met her yet.' My stomach rumbles, as if to voice my discomfort with my own lassitude. Avoiding Ronda as if this could make her less true. Or my problem with Irina.

A voice booms out from the stage. 'Good evening.'

'I'll see you later.' After a look at the podium, Jim dashes off in direction of the washrooms. I shift my weight from one foot to the other, almost teetering on the plush carpet.

Well-bred applause ripples through the room while the first speaker descends from the stage. My stomach seems to be rattling with hunger. I position myself closer to the buffet. Silver cupolas, shining like Orthodox church towers, hide rows of dishes but do not manage to disguise the smells: butter and fish, lemon and tomato. An ant is crossing the tablecloth. I attempt to blow it away but it doesn't budge. With a quick flick of my wrist, I brush it from the starched expanse. Under my fingers, humidity bleeds into a suspicion. I lift my hand from the black streak that was, moments ago, a living ant.

'That act of killing looked very much unlike you.'

'Me?' I give a start. The voice is so serious it rings like a gong through me. Scolding me for my ugly secret. I brush some invisible crumbs from the table and try to calm my heart.

'You don't look like a serial killer,' the voice continues. The accent is hard to place, a bit of Hong Kong, a bit of Canada maybe. Finally, I look up. A body to match that voice, a body for an opera singer. A Cantonese opera singer.

'No, I don't see myself as a serial killer,' I say with the same levity.

'You?' He hesitates, opens his mouth, closes it again. Looks at me from the side, probing. 'No. You… You've got hair like a pedigree ram. And eyes like an El Greco nun.' He lets his gaze fall between the dishes, wedges it between mustard and napkins, brings it to settle on the white fabric.

My cheeks burn. I weigh the possibilities of these words, smallness against maleness against darkness. Push the words around in my mouth like melon seeds. Sift them for shells and find nothing to discard. I turn away, feel the linen under my stroking fingers, dry, noncommittal, the unintentional murder still burning on my fingertips.

I look up, smile, wish to infuse the situation with the light-heartedness it deserves. 'I hate it if the day starts with a killing. There are these bugs that make my shower their home.'

'Ah well, how do we judge the right to live. Who is allowed to live and how.' He is almost speaking to himself now. All treacle and caramel, his voice is, rich and dark hued.

'I lived in Sudan for a while,' I say. 'It's a place where you learn to fear pests, especially near food.' Locusts, for example. What a place of biblical proportions it was, Sudan, and, as usual, something in me aches for not being able to love it back on its own terms.

'Mice probably, they're everywhere. And locusts, I would expect in an arid climate.' He raises his voice as if in question, this voice whose forgiveness I already crave.

'Yes, how did you know? We used to get the Locust Watch by email in the office. Although the country isn't dry everywhere. The south can be pretty.'

'I should know. I'm a biologist.' He digs in his pocket for a card. 'I work for Green Lotus. We're a green Buddhist organisation.'

A dark green lotus flower on cream coloured background. *Ben Chan, Fundraiser.* 'Did you choose Ben yourself? Hong Kong is so full of self-professed Rambos and Swallows. Ben is nice.'

He laughs, runs a hand over his thinning crew cut. 'I hit six foot in grade nine. I guess I wanted to stop growing, be a Benjamin. And I have an Uncle Benedict in Macao.'

I take an appraising look at him, breathe in the lighter air we now share. He must be in his mid-thirties. 'Well, it worked.'

'Six foot one,' he grins. 'Almost. The rest,' he pats his stomach, 'went into girth.'

As we stand there, listening to another address, the stillness between us slows and condenses, becomes less rough-hewn. I sneak glimpses at him. Shoes that look like dugouts next to mine, and trousers that seem equally secular. On stage, a speaker in a long Chinese gown drones on, his English hardened by his Cantonese inflection. 'New technology threatens our cultural achievements, in particular Chinese writing, the mother of our beautiful classics. As guardians of our cultural heritage, we call on all leaders in society to preserve Chinese calligraphy…'

Mirth is the mail of anguish.

'Emily Dickinson. That was Emily Dickinson you were quoting.' Ben Chan seems pleased. What a gift it is, this voice.

It takes a few seconds, then the force of our connection hits me. 'I didn't even realise I had said it aloud,' I say and see he is the one who looks startled.

'So how's your calligraphy?' I ask. 'I really thought Hong Kong had other problems.'

He smiles, searches my eyes, and something in me stretches, oozes. 'Such as?'

'I don't know,' I say. 'The environment. Social justice. Property prices that don't allow people to get married.'

We stand there, take each other in.

'So,' he says, 'you know your Emily Dickinson well.'

'Yes, I love Emily Dickinson.'

'That sounds dangerous.' He smiles with his eyes first, just the opposite of other people who curve their lips but sometimes forget to let their eyes laugh along, or only crease them in afterthought. 'So, are you going to spend the rest of your life locked into a room, wearing only white?'

We both glance at my clothes—my one good suit, again—and laugh. 'No, not white,' I say.

He looks at me and breaks into another easy smile. 'Yes, you would probably be considered pretty eccentric. Dangerous even. Unlucky.'

'So what about you?' I ask. A Daoist monk is climbing the steps to the stage, robe rustling. I lower my voice. 'What's your story with Emily?'

'Shh. Later.' Behind the polo-necked sweater, his body is aligned differently now, more at home. 'Yes. I love poetry.'

'...As the communion of faithful, we contribute to Hong Kong society spiritually, politically and economically, to build a prosperous society with a thriving business world...' More speeches follow but in spite of my hunger I mind them less, the smell of food more anticipation than delay. Next to me, Ben Chan's presence pulsates, changed as if in colour or notation. Like humid air, the space between us is dense with information, with the smell of gingko shampoo and aniseed and a lot I cannot name.

After the last speech, we join the quickly forming food line. 'Is this all?' I say. 'A hardly veiled endorsement of Hong Kong's

47

cut-throat capitalism? At an interreligious meeting?'

'Were you here last year?'

'No,' I say. 'I'm standing in for my boss.'

'Last year,' he says, a mini quiche between silver tongs suspended near his face, 'the official declaration was about the dangers of information technology. "Avoid the corruption of our youth" and so on.' He rolls his eyes.

I lift a prawn roll, wave it. 'Would you like some?'

'Prawn? No, thank you, I'm a vegetarian. Most of the time, anyway.' He laughs, his plate wobbling with the movement of his belly. Tiny wontons, crispy tofu sticks, mini quiches and filled cherry tomatoes fill it to the seams. He looks at me, doesn't seem to know where to place his eyes. 'Well. It's six official religions, after all. Maybe capitalism is an easier topic.'

'It's difficult to get all this straight,' I say. 'Buddhism. Daoism. Confucianism. Folk religion. For example: what is the difference between Buddhism and folk religion?'

'For example: folk religion is very much concerned with making money. Think of Chinese New Year.'

'Laisee,' I say. 'The red envelopes.'

He nods. 'Whereas Buddhism, pure Buddhism you could call it, would probably share your opinion of—cut-throat capitalism.'

Oh Emily, if you could hear his voice. My harbinger of mirth and anguish. Cut-throat capitalism. My gaze wanders as if the word alone could conjure Jim. He is talking to one of the women in lilac headscarves. Even with a plate in one hand, he is gesturing like a Sicilian. Discussing the situation of Muslims in the Philippines. Or perhaps having a theological heart-to-heart about one of the finer points of the Koran. Or maybe they share a passion for Murano glass or fruit bats. With Jim, you never know. Somehow, I hope that he won't be finished with the Muslim woman too soon.

Ben Chan has followed my gaze, chewing.

'A colleague,' I say.

'So, will you let your boss come back next year?' His eyes again. They have the colour of his voice, molasses.

I smile, trying to picture Irina in here. 'Her favourite hymn is

"Onwards, Christian Soldiers." She's second generation Russian American and first generation born again.'

He laughs.

'She's not all that born again,' I say, 'but still.'

'Not like you, then.' His eyebrows rise. 'So, what are you?'

'We're a mixed bunch in our office. I'm a Catholic. German Catholic.'

His smile broadens. 'You make it sound like a denomination of its own.'

'Oh, it's mostly about anti-nuclear involvement and fair trade coffee.'

He laughs so hard now that he has to set down his plate.

'Well. I think I could stand another one of these receptions.' I smile. A shimmering translucent brown, his eyes are in this light, the colour of *peihdaan*, preserved Chinese eggs.

After focusing the tablecloth for an inordinate amount of time, I ask, 'So are you, are you some sort of monk, working for a Buddhist organisation?' My eyes barely brush him.

When I look up, his smile is even wider than before. 'No, I'm a layperson.'

'...and don't forget to get in touch if you have any questions about fundraising.' Ben Chan's voice still echoing in me, I bump into Jim, outside, where he is smoking while practising his Cantonese with the bell boy.

'I'm leaving,' I say. 'Tell me, how do you reconcile your landlord cigars with the Revolution?'

'The tobacco farmers have to make a living.' Jim takes a slow puff. He delicately balances the cigar between his fingers, contemplating. 'Mind you, it's harder to reconcile Latin America with Hong Kong. Liberation theology and working with domestic workers under post-colonial circumstances is difficult.'

The mention of post-colonialism makes me blush but he seems oblivious to the ring the word has for me now. 'They should be a match made in heaven,' I say.

'In heaven, maybe.' Jim's face grows serious. 'You would be surprised. For many of them, the Filipinas, religion is just some sort of...' He exhales a cloud of blue smoke and rolls his head, relaxes his shoulders. 'Escapism. You forget the establishment, my dear. Their bosses and mine.'

Moon Twelve Day Six
Thursday 5 January

'Do you like it?'

Blushing, I drop the skirt and Ben Chan from my mind. As if by secret agreement, we have gone out, Virginia and I, pretending to be girlfriends on a shopping spree. Pretending that my blood sister never sobbed, shoulder blades quivering under her T-shirt, in a restaurant that was a playground for adults. Pretending she is buying something for herself, not for her next blind date.

'What do you think of this?'

Shopping is an act of imagination. We dress up a new self, make up a life in which we will need that flimsy dream in shades of pink, that hell-and-leather-black underwear. It is an intensely private affair, to see your summer coloured hopes and silken aspirations spread out under your hands, which is why I never go shopping with other women. Shopping is an act of revelation. I steal a look at the Earth God at the shop entrance, try to make an ally of him. Cotton and wool are my disguise, my everyday habit under which I hide.

'*Ki-im.*' Her voice attains an ethereal quality, like a fairy, and she waves her fingers as if she was holding a wand. 'Come back to me, Kim oh Kim— Do you like it?' Holding up a soft black dress, she furrows her eyebrows. Sometimes, doubts seem to hold her personality together. We have already gone through a number of loam and silt coloured pieces that remind me of refugees. They could be mine.

'The black looks good with your hair,' I say.

She holds the dress out in front of her and clamps her chin on the hanger, extending her arms. She is more substantial than most Cantonese, more angles and more curves. The dress's jersey undulates across her body. 'What about the length? This is for petite women—'

'You know,' I say, 'you can really carry this off, with your cleavage.' If only the city wasn't littered with placard people whose bodies resemble ironing boards. Virginia is Cubist, all alien perspectives imposed on her. Sometimes it is hard to find her between the shards of self packed into an unconvincing surface.

'The price is not bad,' she says. 'Do you think— Do you think the others will like it?'

'Sure. Simple but elegant.' I pull the dress into shape. 'Perfect from head to toe.'

She narrows her eyes at her image in the mirror, stretches out her left foot in its health sandal and inspects it. 'I need another pedicure.' Her voice sounds distorted, her chin still pressed to keep the dress in place. 'All that walking.' She drops the piece onto the clothes rack next to her.

'You know,' she says, picking at the price tag, 'my mother had this ingrown toenail. I should have nagged her, told her to go and see a doctor.'

'You can't prevent this kind of thing, Virginia.'

'Such an embarrassment it was, the ugly toenail, when they put her into the machine for the scan. What shall people think of me, not taking care of my mother in her old age?'

'Old people and doctors,' I say. 'Really, you shouldn't— What about your sister?'

'Rebecca.' She lets the price tag go and for a moment it flutters in the current of the ventilation. 'Rebecca never worries about anything. Until now. She can't do much from Vancouver. *Yihga*—now she is *freaking out*.' Her face distorts with the foreignness of it.

'Really, our siblings should form a club. The Club of the Absentee Siblings.'

She hesitates over another dress. 'You know, that's Hong Kong. People pass through for a generation or two and then move on. Like a water heater.'

I laugh. 'Hot it certainly is. And humid.' I hold up a white halter-neck dress that would set off her tan nicely. I don't mention it, though, because like all Hong Kong women, she wants snow white skin. 'What about this?'

'No, nothing white,' she snaps, although I have seen her wearing the colour before. My arm falls back and I remember. Ben Chan and Emily Dickinson. White is the colour of death. Red, on the other hand, is auspicious, the glaze of happiness, the hue of protection. Red affairs are weddings, that lucky joining of two individuals, two families. And so bright red underwear sells well in Hong Kong. Last year, the Year of the Monkey, collided with Virginia's sign. She is a monkey and to live through the year of your zodiac animal is dangerous. All horoscopes advised her to wear something red at all times, or to stick to her particular lucky colours. I keep to my nunnish Schiesser Rippenstrick pieces. You can boil them at one hundred degrees and they come out white as before, unchanged.

'*Hou chan neih.*' The shopkeeper, her rice box growing cold next to her on the counter, nods to Virginia.

'What is she saying?' I ask, my fingers finding their way back to the printed linen skirt, brown with light green butterflies so tiny that they could be dots.

'"That suits you, it's just right for you."' Virginia turns from the shop assistant to me. 'Do you like it?' The print has a faded, low-key quality to it, like the friendship that comes with a pair of washed-out jeans. Because that is the other side of shopping, the possibility to reinforce ourselves.

'No trying on! No extra large sizes!' The shop assistant glares at me, her eyes roughing my body.

My cheeks glowing, I let the skirt fall back, the linen running drily between my fingers. 'Never mind.' On most working days, I wear a self-devised office uniform of dark trousers and white blouses. Spielberg calls it the Friday Look, 'like somebody stranded with Robinson.' It puts me in a work mood.

Hou chan neih. Later, in bed, I toss the new words around in my mouth, memorise them. *That suits you, it's just right for you.* A while ago, Spielberg complained that he couldn't keep any secrets from me any longer. It was meant as a compliment for my Cantonese but, like most compliments, it is double-edged. For the past one hundred and fifty years, the locals have mostly guarded their secrets with success—the joke about the fat gwaipoh hanging from the bus strap, underarm hair bulging from her sleeveless dress, the provenance of the almost-antiques for the sun-baked tourists, the price of brides and jade and shark fins, the rules of temple festivals and gods' birthdays.

I also lift Virginia's pain, examine it, try to feel it as if it were mine, and put it down again. She is right. I don't understand.

Listening to the neighbourhood throbbing behind my window, I resent the blindness of my forebears. How could they resist this city, its whispered secrets and yelled atrocities? That suits you, it's just right for you. I turn around, lower my sheet. Perhaps it was fear. Fear of being disappointed once we have broken through the multi-mannered smiles, the glittery packaging of snake oil and the sugared surface of a pork bun. Even so, I compliment myself: *Hou chan ngoh*. It suits me, it's just right for me.

Moon Twelve Day Seven
Friday 6 January
Epiphany

The black eared kites again. Like a screen-saver, they appear and disappear throughout my working days. In winter, their habits change, push them deep into the ravines between buildings. Against the metallic shine of the sky scrapers, their floating, feathered selves look surprisingly sturdy. Real. I step closer to the window, see my reflection merge with the image of the kites. I watch it disappear to leave only the birds.

'Kim. Sorry to interrupt you.' Eva rustles into my cubicle, silver pen in hand, a couple of sheets brushing her chin, her navy skirt swishing against the support tights.

'Hmmh.' She wants the tights more than she needs them, on her twenty-eight year old legs. It strikes me as very Chinese, this pretending of something to make it happen, like the paper coins in Chinese New Year displays. She and her husband are hoping for a baby, have been hoping for quite a while already.

I turn towards her. 'Yes?' She always looks immaculate without being dressy. It probably comes with being born again. Irina is committed but Eva is the real thing. Spirit-baptised, as she would probably put it.

She feels my gaze on her, pushes her white blouse sleeves up. 'The AGM minutes. I need a signature from you before I can paste a copy into the company records. The green ledger over there.' She points to the shelf next to my desk. It has mutated into a space for general use, crammed with files, dictionaries and videos that look oddly out of place next to my meticulously sorted documents.

The moss coloured volume feels heavy for its size, the faux leather cover sucking softly under my fingers. MediMission's Articles of Association, a list of our founding members, addresses of Board Members. I fan out the last part. *List of Staff Members.* Águilar, Edward. Bernstein, Irina. Kranich, Reinhild. Sim, Eva Waih-sze. And, behind each name, the declaration *Occupation: Missionary.* I stare. The book suddenly feels hot under my fingers and even heavier than before.

'Anything wrong?' She leans closer. Her perfume is unobtrusive yet feminine like all the rest of her.

I point to the list. '*Missionary.*' I attempt a laugh. It sounds thin. 'I thought I was programme officer.' My face burns.

'But we're here to give witness, right?' She smiles, files a strand of hair away behind her ear. She thumbs a few pages back. 'I remember Jonathan Chan. Very nice. And so committed.' Her hand starts to finger the filigree cross around her neck. 'This is not the Sudan, you know. No problem with… standing for our Christian values.'

'Well,' I say. 'I'm not Jonathan.'

'You should consider it a title of honour.' Her mouth slopes downwards. 'Aren't we called upon to be witnesses?'

'Eva. The word "missionary", it's—it's old men thrusting Bibles into the hands of people, of—*natives*. Of delivering fire and brimstone sermons. It's so—nineteenth century. Colonial.'

An odd expression builds on her face. 'You forget the cannon boats.' Her hand drops the cross. 'Bibles on one side, opium on the other. That one will haunt us forever.'

'See?' I allow myself a weak smile. 'I do see that converting to Christianity for some people is a sort of liberation. Like you, you don't want all that family stuff.'

'No, that's not true,' she snaps. 'That's not true. But… don't you think it's… selfish not to share your faith?' Her face reddens. 'What if you are condemning people with your laxness? It's not as touchy-feely as people want to believe, you know. Our faith is not only about feeling good. God has expectations towards us.'

'And the revolution is not a dinner party. Sorry, wrong department. That's Mao Zedong.' How did we get to this point, discussing religion and revolutions? My cubicle is very hot now, two wills wrestling in a confined space. 'People should ask first,' I say. 'I can't believe in the kind of god you believe in. Where's the all-lovingness? And human free will?'

'Are you saying my god is not loving?'

'I thought we had the same one.' I shut the green volume with force, catching her slim index between the pages. 'Oops, sorry.'

A shadow cuts between us. 'Anybody knows where the leftover copies of the last Annual Report are?'

I give a start. Irina. How much has she heard of our conversation, in our egg carton-like office with its flimsy cubicles?

'Well—' Eva's eyes challenge me— 'you can always talk with Irina if you have a problem with that.' Her pupils are ablaze. Life must be easy when you own this kimchi-like heat. That is the worst part of it, the envy.

Irina's gaze wanders back and forth between us. 'Is anything the matter?'

'No,' I say, my palms suddenly moist. Not another thing after the Ladies League. I carefully measure out a smile, aim it at both of them. 'Nothing.'

Later, Irina squeezes into my cubicle. 'You do realise the word "mission" is used differently nowadays, right?'

Warily, I look up. This sets her off; incites her to tell me more than I ever needed to know about 'global churches witnessing together' and 'intercultural theology'. On and on she goes, about the 'prophetic role of the church' and 'ecumenical partnership—'

'So, it's all about interreligious learning?' I interrupt her. 'And about Christians working with other Christians?' I spin on my chair, turn a few inches away from her. 'If you ask me, I don't think it's good to continue using a word if it has acquired a new meaning. Especially if the old one is so loaded. And if others continue to use it in that loaded sense.'

As if following a secret choreography, our eyes move to the window, away from Eva's desk.

'Irina,' I say, 'I would like to suggest that we consider bequeathing as a way of fundraising. You know, getting people to include MediMission in their wills.'

Her eyebrows rise.

Quickly, I add, 'I heard it from a Chinese friend.' I hate it how my voice goes in such moments.

I am still suppressing a vision of the Chinese departed with their Hell Bank notes in denominations of millions when the office doorbell jingles, 'Oh my darling Valentine'. (That is another Hong Kong specialty, doorbells. Yet more invented worlds full of promise, castles and snow.) Our heads turn. Jim, literally darkening our office door, dark clad, dark haired. Almost Chinese, he looks from this angle. *Father bless me for I have sinned.* Although in this very moment, I could not name my sin.

'Welcome!' The waitress at the Revolutionary Café is wearing a camouflage miniskirt and a Che Guevara T-shirt. '*Sikh mh sihk yin?*' she asks, *Do you eat smoke?* As if we were ghosts ingesting incense during our lunch break, feeding on the smoke that the living offer us.

'Non-smoking,' I say, casting an apologetic look in Jim's direction, while Ed nods.

'What kind of place is this?' Ed's glance falls on the hammer-and-sickled walls, the pipes veining the black ceiling, the face of the revolutionary on the staff uniforms. 'Do I have to eat that Russian stuff in here, borschtsch? Or whale fritters?'

'Isn't it great?' Jim's grin is wide enough to take in the whole of Cuba. 'You'll love it. They also have a great selection of cigars,' he adds as if struck by an afterthought.

I raise my eyebrows at him. 'We did try socialism in Germany, you know. For forty years. It doesn't work. *And* we're sitting in the non-smoking section.'

'Socialism cannot be implemented north of the 38th latitude. Look at North Korea.' Jim has a theory on everything.

When we have ordered, he discreetly disappears. I tell Ed about the green ledger. *Missionary*.

'But we're called "Mission",' he says. Ed is a Catholic in that most straightforward of ways, Filipino Catholic.

I noisily stir my Yin and Yang. 'Oh come on, MediMission. Medical Mission for Migrants. It's like, like a health insurance slogan. *Your health is our mission.*'

'So you always read it like that?'

'Vision—Mission—Goals. That's how NGOs talk,' I say. 'Don't tell me you dream of handing out Christian pamphlets.' Ed may be a passionate lawyer but he hates all the rest. The mumbo-jumbo of NGO work, he calls it, his accent making it sound like an exotic religion. I take a sip of my drink but recoil. Too much sugar. I can never make up my mind about Yin and Yang, this local concoction with its unlikely marriage of tea and coffee, East and West, but continue to order it wherever I go.

'And what is your mission at work? You must have told them something.'

'Oh, that. That was ages ago.' I glance in direction of the toilets and hurry on. 'People aren't exactly lining up to go to Sudan. I even told them something about Islamic values. And threw in faith, hope and charity for good measure.'

I look up, into his round, brown face that even now seems

ready to smile. 'Missionary sounds so… wrong. The White Man with the Bible meeting The Heathen.' I steal another look into the back of the restaurant. 'You of all people should know. The Philippines were colonised for hundreds of years.'

'You forget the missionary boiling in the cannibals' pot.' Ed grins. 'As a child, I used to find that so romantic.' He takes a sip of his ice water, his face turning serious again. 'But see, without them we wouldn't believe.'

There is something about his faith and mine, a kind of lack that stings. 'I used to find nurses romantic. And doctors.'

'Excuse me.' The waitress reaches over and sets the appetiser down. In a swift move, she deposits a second plate on the table, laid with a red napkin and a mini hammer and sickle. I look quizzically at the arrangement.

Ed chuckles. 'Getting a bit corny, isn't it?' When the waitress has left, he asks, 'Do you want to talk with Irina?'

'No,' I say and there is another kind of sting, a lack that would hurt her if she knew. Irina is not bright, she is brilliant. Her paradigm of 'refugee agency' and 'participatory ownership' has revolutionised our field. I stir my Yin and Yang some more. 'Why is it so difficult to talk with her?'

'Yeah, it is difficult.' Ed fidgets on the bench. 'The grand old lady of migration issues.'

'Not so old, really.' I nod, submerge the ice cubes floating in my drink and watch them rise again.

'Talking about cannibals. We've got headhunting tribes in the Philippines, did you know?' With professional oversight, Ed shifts topic. Jim is back.

'Cannibalism?' Jim says, reaching for his ice water. 'You must be hungry. But I wouldn't say the cuisine here goes quite that far.'

At the sight of him, something in me flares up again. 'Have you been to the Philippines?' I scowl. 'Of course you have. Do you know why people are leaving?'

He almost cowers under my assault, unsure of what is going on.

'No jobs,' Ed throws in, his chopsticks lingering over the

peanuts. 'And a government that stinks with corruption.'

I ignore him. 'They have beautiful land in the Philippines, three harvests a year in some places. Beautiful rice-farming land.'

'Very beautiful.' Ed nods, then turns to the waitress. 'Over here.'

'Which the farmers don't own.' Jim throws a handful of peanuts into his mouth. 'They work for their landlords. Three back-breaking harvests a year.'

'People like Ronda Pajarillo leave to work abroad because their country is overpopulated.' I set down my drink, the brown liquid threatening to wash over the rim. 'And guess why, in this nation of Catholics?'

Jim, his cheeks still bulging with peanuts, doesn't respond. *Oh no, not this discussion*, his eyes seem to say, and then, *From you?* How I hate myself in this moment, the untruth of it all.

'Guys,' Ed says, looking anxiously from me to Jim, 'our food is growing cold.' He points to the table, where a monumental salt block has been deposited. 'At least I hope that's our food. What... is... this?' He picks up the hammer and taps the salt block.

'Isn't it great?' Jim grins and snatches the sickle, elbows Ed for the hammer.

'No, I can do this—'

'Let me, let me—'

Like boys, the two wrangle over the tools. In the end, they tackle the salt crust together, hack and hammer away, cheeks flushed, tongues stuck out in concentration. I rub my face. It must be my mood that I see weapons where they see toys, their faces alight with enthusiasm.

With an aching sound, the crust breaks. Underneath, a whole fish appears, glistening in its own juices, unadulterated by spices. Ed lowers his head for a short blessing, then tucks into the dish.

'Go ahead,' I say, ignoring Jim's bowed head. 'Cavemen.' I push the fish on its snow white bed towards them. 'How is it, fossilised?'

Jim eyes the dish, carefully selects a piece. He puts down his chopsticks, chews. His sky blue eyes search mine. 'Reini.' They

59

seem more liquid than moments ago. The heat of the food, probably. 'What's the matter?'

At the sound of his voice, I just want to lay my cheek on the table and be patted like a dog. Or have a good nap and forget about it all. Instead, I pick up the toothpicks, shake the little container, hear its empty rattle, set it down again, feel the soy sauce slop darkly in its bottle, and finally drown a piece of fish in chilli sauce.

The zing of the spices tickles my nostrils, massages my lungs. 'Nothing,' I cough, my chest still hollow and tight. Still, I lean into the unambiguous taste of the fish until my eyes water. 'Nothing, really.'

I take the company records with me after work. With some effort, I extricate the ledger from the overflowing bookshelf. And then, in an impulse of sick black envy, I pull Ed's files down as well, delve for a moment into their shining injustice: *Grievous bodily harm.* How anaemic Ronda Pajarillo's case looks in comparison. *Dismissal without warning nor compensation.*

I glance over at Irina, still staring at the computer screen, and nurture opaque visions of correction fluid. Perhaps I will change the name I have been given, like so many other names. The ledger doesn't fit into my backpack. Hurriedly, I shove it into a plastic bag. It crackles thunderously under my fingers. Here I am, smuggling office property out in a red and white Yue Hwa Chinese Products bag.

How red and white my affairs have become lately. More white than red really, with no news of Virginia's mother. Or Ben Chan. I shift the bag into my other hand. On my walk to the MTR station, the book seems to radiate heat on this cool January day, a particular epiphany gift of its own.

Moon Twelve Day Eight
Saturday 7 January

At home, I have buried the bag with the ledger in a corner, let it steep in the stink of my running shoes, a task waiting to be done.

I sip coffee at the window, hugging myself against the cold as music drifts up from the building platform. My old Malmö mug from university has a chip. Twelve floors below, a group of women is exercising with Chinese fans. In the mornings, there is always something happening on the podium, t'ai chi and fan dancing and everything in between. I like to watch the women flailing their arms about like insecure birds. Their dancing has become the soundtrack of my Saturday mornings, a whole weekend of Heritage Hikes, church with Jim and the Filipinas and meals with friends stretching out before me. My lips brush over the chip to assess the danger. I drink on.

Finally, I set my cup into the sink and fetch the ledger. Pond-scum coloured. Duck shit green. I try to work my way into outrage, watch the book accumulate weight until it seems an obese obscenity on my small pine table.

On Monday, I have to smuggle the company records back and the whole cringe-inducing enterprise had better be worth it. I get the correction fluid and set to work on the ledger. It smells slightly musty and reminds me of the darker corners of our office and the passionate humidity of summer, so different from the damp cold that seeps into my bones these days.

Kranich, Reinhild. Occupation: Missionary. The bottle with correction fluid rattles as I shake it, a playful noise that seems not grown-up enough for accountants and lawyers. One by one, the fluid obliterates the letters, makes *Missionary* into *Mission* and then *Miss*. I toy with this, tongue in cheek—*Occupation: Miss*—but discard the option.

A white space is left beside my name. I hover over the page, waiting for inspiration while the correction fluid congeals. Its chemical smell burns in my nostrils. I hurry to screw the lid on and wait some more. The discoloured patch on the sheet grows more disgusting by the minute, but my mind remains as blank as the page.

Slowly, the leatherette leaving my skin with reluctance, I fold the ledger shut, unable to name myself.

Moon One Day Three
Tuesday 31 January

A sharp-edged day with Virginia that burns itself into my memory. Like a diagnosis. Or a death sentence. Or a declaration of love. An ending and a beginning—the holiday crowds in Festival Walk, shopping and eating with abandon; the cinema with *War of the Worlds* and the ice rink; the cold of the air conditioning in winter, battling same with same like Chinese medicine; our hopeless mix of languages.

'I'm freezing to death,' I say to Virginia, rubbing my arms after the cold of the movie theatre, '*dong sei le*'. My eyes, still struggling with the brightness of the shopping mall, search her face in the hope of catching a small nod for my colloquialism. But her features, framed by the silk collar of a traditional jacket, remain serious. It is one of the mysteries of this city, why a culture obsessed with avoiding bad luck will emphasise remarks by invoking death, *he was deadly annoyed* and *I am hungry to death*.

'The film was deadly violent,' I go on as we amble towards the ice rink but am stopped by her hand on my arm.

'Shh,' she says, leaning into me to let a family in brocade jackets pass. 'No unlucky words for the New Year.'

'Sorry,' I say and duck a balloon trailing behind a boy in silk pyjamas. To our left, two young men in matching short-sleeved outfits are smoothing the surface of the ice, their arms and legs mirroring in twinned curves. 'Think of the energy that goes into cooling this in summer. Only to be able to say: Yes, you can ice skate in the tropics.'

She laughs. 'That's the famous Hong Kong spirit. Making everything possible.'

'That's a nice jacket, very festive,' I say and smile until my lips seem to crack. 'What a lucky golden colour.'

She smiles, flustered, and fingers the uppermost button of her padded jacket.

I continue, 'I'm sure the New Year will be very lucky for you,' but her face, creased with pleasure from my compliment only seconds ago, turns absentminded.

On our way to the café, she lets her hand shiver along the balustrade of the ice rink. 'What did you think of the ending?'

I catch myself scanning the restaurant entrance as if looking for a friend. But it would be too much to expect an Earth God in the sleek surroundings of Festival Walk and not even a God of Wealth is in sight. There is a New Year display though, a group of sages with shiny scalps enjoying the best of Chinese old age: handsome children, long life peaches, and the knobbly yellow fruit called Five Generations Together. I say, 'I liked it how the aliens d— got the stomach flu. It's the small things that make cross-cultural encounters difficult, right? The jellyfish in the fridge…'

When we have ordered, she pats my arm. '*Ah* Kim.'

I look up.

'I have to ask you a favour.' She folds her face into its habitual frown, stirs her drink with a clinking noise. Through the foggy surface of the glass, it is indiscernible what is inside.

'Sure,' I say and take another murky sip from my drink.

'We need a maid,' she says, 'a proper live-in maid. Our Chinese helper doesn't come in anymore and with my mother… in hospital, we need more help. Do you know anybody?'

'That's easy enough,' I say. 'Why did your amah go?'

In a series of small explosions, the ice cubes in her tea dissolve. She looks away and it is difficult to read her expression. 'She thinks we are… bad luck. My mother—' She rubs her finger against the glass, leaving a clear window on the foggy surface. 'It has gotten much worse.'

I swallow. 'I'm... sorry.'

'I'm so scared.' Her words are a mere whisper.

'They can do lots nowadays. Against the pain, you know.' I also lower my voice.

'You don't understand.' She pushes her drink to the side. 'I'm afraid that—that my mother will go to hell.'

It falls like an anchor, this piece of news. In slow motion, I feel it slide along the lining of my insides and sink until it hits the bottom of my stomach.

'*Nein*,' I say and pull away from the table. 'No.' I shove my Yin and Yang away. Somewhere deep inside, I feel a task grow out of this knowledge, although I do not know what it might be yet.

Her glass has sweated fat drops, tear-like, they bleed into the place mat underneath.

Across from us, on the ice, the children are oblivious to the cold. Duping the senses is elevated to an art in Hong Kong. False idols. I have always taken that expression for something referring to rock stars and cheap celebrities, nothing in the way Eva would mean it. Finally I ask, 'How can a good person go to hell?'

She balls up her handkerchief and runs it across the table. She clears her throat. 'Don't forget about the maid, right? Maybe somebody with nursing experience, nursing old people.'

I nod.

On my way out, the gaudy fuchsia and fake gold of the New Year scene strike me with sickening force. How the Hello Kitty-like pinkness of people's aspirations has fooled me. The bald skulls of the wizards look ravaged by disease and there is not a single female in sight. How could I fail to see what this is about? Making money and obedient offspring. An invented world to ward off evil. Because some evils are so powerful that you cannot beat them same-same. You cannot beat them at all. You can hope to avoid them or to beat them with different things. Alien things.

Moon One Day Six
Friday 3 February

On the last steps of Jordan's apple green MTR station, inside and outside temperature are in perfect balance. I stop for a moment and close my eyes, shut out the pedestrians hurrying past. Throughout most of the year, the inside of buildings is a cool haven against the temperatures outside; a strange reversal of my childhood spaces I keep bumping up against. For a moment, I let the traffic noise wash over me, shut out the smell of exhaust fumes and settle on the warmth of the sun on my clothes. Across the street, a fashion model broadcasts radiance from a billboard spanning several floors, her white smile unfazed by the twenty-four lanes of traffic, the siren-red taxis spilling out of every corner.

'*Mi-si.*' A monk in lentil coloured robes appears before me, smiling. He must be mistaking me for one of the tourists that roam the area. I ignore him and his beggar's bowl and direct my steps towards the women's shelter, past newspaper stands and one of the last hot snack vendors of the season. On this blazing day, the smell of coals hangs incongruously in the air. The vegetables look shrivelled in their purple skins, an alien root or tuber I cannot name. I will have to ask Virginia and that fact fills me with an odd satisfaction. Surely, I cannot be a missionary if I do not know the names of things. Weren't the missionaries explorers, name-givers?

The off-white colonial building that houses the shelter, nestled against an old brick church, probably used to house missionaries. It always puzzles me, the effortless way in which the colonials paired beauty and violence, their elegant houses inhabited by the free and the unfree. It will be good for me to work with Ronda Pajarillo. Finally. I don't know how I did it, shirk this task for so long, and it surely will not help me with Irina.

Ronda has been waiting for me. 'Ma'am, please, here.' Her

smile is many things at once, too many to grasp. She leads the way, leaving only her willowy back for me to admire. Flip-flops clacking along, my work shoes ringing on the tiled floor, we pass bunk beds, threadbare underwear dangling from their rails and metal wash basins stacked with clean dishes. The smell of chlorinated detergent almost makes me sneeze.

I wave a greeting into the kitchen, where Norma Delgado is ticking off lists. As usual, she looks very much at home, like a wife with an oversized household and plenty of children. They aren't children, of course, the women she takes in and mothers with Filipino *sinigang* and plenty of hugs. But like a mother, she is the only one in this building who is allowed to stay indefinitely.

'Norma. Hi. I'm going to sit down with Ronda for a talk.'

'Kim!' She takes off her glasses and lets them dangle on her chest, breaking into a broad grin. '*Kim-chi*. Long time no see. Go on into my room, there's nobody in there.'

In the office, Ronda lifts a stack of brochures from a plastic chair that reminds me of garden fêtes. 'Please, take a seat.'

When I am settled, she disappears. In another world, this room would be a basement den with its metal filing cabinets, boxes of publicity materials and a water fountain greying around the edges. On the largest cabinet, three rows of identical bottles are lined up, filled with an amber liquid. They remind me of Khartoum, of the recycled containers in which street vendors used to sell petrol by the litre.

'Twenty-four bottles of baby oil,' I say when Ronda returns with a cup of tea. 'Do you have any children in here at all?'

'Here, Ma'am.' Deftly, she places the cup onto the filing cabinet next to me. 'The oil, that was a donation,' she says. 'People love to give.' Her features change and I cannot decide whether she is hiding a smile or pulling a face. She takes another plastic chair and looks at me, her smile unafraid. It is her hair that gives me a jolt, that mass bound into a loose ponytail. Ronda has got hair like a wiry terrier. I yank my eyes away from that halo of spiky corkscrews. I frown at my green tea in its Styrofoam cup and ponder her, lone wearer of an afro in an archipelago of sleek black beauty. I should have visited her much earlier and, in this moment, I cannot even recall why it has taken me so long. Then I remember. I like Norma but I don't like the shelter, the sight of adult lives wasting away in the dim shadows of bunk beds.

'You don't have to serve me, you know,' I say, twisting the paper flag of the teabag between my fingers. 'We're here to work together.'

'I'm used to it, Ma'am.'

'Call me Kim.' I take a sip but recoil from the unexpected heat. I glance at the papers in my lap, clear my throat. 'Ronda.' I smile and feel the gesture run into emptiness. 'You've been in Hong Kong for quite a while.'

'Nine years,' she says. Her chest shifts as she speaks the words, seems to acquire substance.

'Wow,' I say. 'An old Hong Kong hand, then. Like the permanent resident expats.'

'Not like the permanent residents,' she says, her eyes suddenly bigger and rounder. 'We can stay here forever, for three— lifetimes and not become permanent residents. You know that.'

I wriggle in my chair. 'Let me confirm I've got the basic facts right.' Together, we run through her biographical details: a native of Baybay on Leyte, the third of five children, she started on a nursing degree after school but had to drop out for financial reasons. Her marriage and a series of irregular jobs followed, so that she finally decided to try her luck in Hong Kong. Here, her employment history was uneventful until she made a fateful change that landed her in her last family.

'We will work towards another visa extension,' I say, 'so that as long as your case is pending, you are exempt from the two-week rule. You know, that would normally force you to leave Hong Kong within two weeks unless you find a new job.'

She nods. 'Ed explained that already. And that I cannot work while I am waiting.'

'Yes, that's the big snag.' I take another tentative sip of tea, the scalding heat giving way to leafy-green fragrance.

'Ma'am—Miss. Kim. How long will it take, until my case is solved?' She resettles her feet in the flip-flops. 'My family, they expect my income. Ed said it could take some months?'

'I'm afraid he might be right. These things are unpredictable.'
I blow onto my tea. 'How many children do you have?'

Her heart-shaped face expands with pride. 'Three, two boys
and a girl. My husband also sends money, he works in Dubai.
But it is getting hard for him, the construction work.' Her smile
slopes downwards. 'My youngest, she just turned ten. My mother
looks after the children, together with an aya from the
countryside.'

The domestic worker paying a domestic worker. For
childcare. 'And do you get to go back?'

'I go every two years.' She reaches over to collect my cup,
brushes a strand of unruly hair out of her face. 'My mother is
good with the children, really. Very good.' She picks up the tray
and marches straight-backed out of the room.

I follow her. Her back swings as she walks. Three months
younger than me and packing about double the amount of life
experience and responsibilities between her finely chiselled
shoulder blades. Suddenly, I am annoyed. Annoyed with Irina for
exposing me to this kind of work. Annoyed with Ronda. She
wants me to help her so that things stay the same. I want to
change things. Annoyed with myself for being annoyed.

I call out, 'Ronda.' The sharpness of my voice makes her spin
around. 'For how long do you want to continue with this?' How
I despise myself, forcing her to lie. As if I didn't lie just like her,
keep secrets from myself.

An uneasy smile flickers across her face. She looks at her feet,
lifts her toes. 'A few years.'

A few years, so that her eldest can go to college. Like my
mother, who spent my childhood getting her pharmacy off the
ground. A few more years of night duties and emergency shifts.
I tremble with the indignity of the comparison. I had the
Philosopher King and Auntie Hilde and breakfasts and lunches
and dinners with the Angelic Apothecary. Eva appears in my
mind with her support tights and the folic acid hidden in her
handbag—what she would say to Ronda.

'A few more years,' I repeat, my voice flat and hard, and force a smile into my face. I am learning this Asian art, smiles that reach out in many different ways at once, like a thousand-armed goddess. A few more years. A few more tears. I turn to go.

'Ma'am.' Her voice is a command. Dutifully, I face her once more. Her eyes are glazed over. 'Kim. We only have one life. One world to be happy in, to make our children happy. But only some get to make the rules.' Her chin challenges me. 'If you ask me, I didn't make the rules.'

The angry beating of my heart forces the air out of my lungs. 'Good luck,' I say and leave.

In the kitchen, Norma is stacking rice bowls with more force than necessary. 'Kim. How did it go?' Her broad Filipino-American accent is as soft as her body, rolling and rounded, but her arms seem sharper than an hour ago, more agitated. *Stack stack stack*, her hands move, her elbows piercing the air.

'Isn't she bright?' I get a cup from the draining board and run it under the water cooler, but there is only a gargling sound. 'Oh, this is empty.'

'Yeah, welcome to the world of non-profit: food, mattresses, air-conditioning. Everything barely enough to get by.' She leans back, runs a hand across her forehead and hair, sighs. She takes a step and parks her hand on her hip. Her elbow unsettles the pile of enamel bowls. They clatter onto the draining board.

'Oh fuck.' She rubs her eyes and stands for a moment, lids closed, her chest heaving. 'Sorry.' She picks up a 7-Eleven mug from the top of the refrigerator and gets herself a cup of cold, boiled water before passing the jar on to me. 'We had the Buildings Department here while you were talking with Ronda. I thought it was a routine check of fire precautions, something like that. But they found out how full we are. Overflowing, really.'

'But you always are.'

'Yes but now we have to, quote, "evict twenty-five percent of our tenants within the next fortnight or face judicial consequences according to the Buildings Ordinance".' Her laugh sounds bitter. 'Twenty-five percent is six-point-five women. Tell me, which half of Ronda should I kick out?'

'But these cases take months,' I say. 'And the women have

nowhere to go.'

'Tell that the Buildings Department. Sure, I can live with not taking new people in, but how can I turn somebody out onto the street?'

Outside, the white-skinned woman still smiles languidly from the billboard, but the sun has disappeared. It is cooler than an hour ago and the delicate balance has left the air, the smell of coals, of winter barbecues and chestnut stalls dominant again. Sweet potato or taro, I decide as I pass the snack vendor on my way back.

The traffic light changes to let pedestrians cross. The noise around me builds to a roar as I try to keep the magnitude of my idea out of sight. A lorry rumbles by, its tremor growing through my feet. Virginia and Ronda may seem a natural fit but if Ronda works for her, both of them will violate her Conditions of Stay. She can be reported to Immigration. And I would be the one who instigated them. My heart starts to pound with the traffic. Under my arms, trickles of sweat build.

'*Mi-si*, please.' Out of nowhere, the monk reappears, undeterred and with a smile even more ingratiating. The traffic light changes once more, beeping, drilling its message into my brain. Ronda, who has to put her children through school and no income in the foreseeable future. I throw some coins into the monk's bowl.

'Thank you, *Mi-si*.' Ceremoniously, he sounds the bronze vessel. Its ringing echo seems much too small for the surroundings. And then, my hand reaches for my mobile phone and I call Virginia.

'I'm in a hurry, but it sounds good. Let's talk about it tonight.'

'Yes,' I say, knowing already that I will keep the most important piece of information from her, my blood sister.

Moon One Day Ten
Tuesday 7 February

Ben Chan. A name, compact as its owner. I am flicking through my name cards, searching for the details of the friendly giant from the reception. When Ben didn't get in touch, I dispatched him to my professional contacts, the card frayed from the constant probing of my fingers. *What's in a name?* How Juliet was wrong. A name can blame, like *Jaaudi*—Wish For A Brother—for yet another female child. A name can heal—like *Swallow*, for a coltish girl with an awkward gait. A name can be a promise.

I try to imbue the phone's mechanical emptiness with signs of hope. Outside, ten floors and a traffic-packed street away a boy—a young man, really—is dismantling a bamboo cage, the type of scaffolding used for smaller repairs.

'Hi, this is Kim from MediMission,' I say to a girl who gives her name as Cindy. Waiting for her prince like all of us. I suddenly feel uncomfortable, being thrown together with this stranger. If only Ben had given me his mobile phone number. If only he had called.

'*Feizai*, a girl for you on the phone,' she shouts. Fatty, she calls him and I cringe even more. Outside, the boy is wearing a double harness, one over his hips and another one over his legs. It reminds me of medieval chastity belts.

'Happy Year of the Dog,' I say.

He immediately remembers me. 'How's the born-again boss?'

The Voice. How could I almost forget? The question sounds tricky from a Buddhist. Across the street, the boy is removing the plastic binding that holds the scaffolding together. 'She's into Second Life these days,' I say and immediately wish I could take my words back. 'For professional purposes. "We need to be present in the virtual world", "address new audiences", that kind of thing.'

He laughs. 'It's full of cyber criminals out there. Give her a fair warning.'

I give a laugh, a carefully measured exchange for his own. The boy is a meticulous worker. Before handing the bamboo tubes back into the flat, he shakes them to remove stagnant water. I am starting to fear that staring at him will cause him to trip.

'How's your First Life these days?' Ben asks.

'I went hiking over Chinese New Year. A beautiful waterfall, do you know it? The Bride's Pool.' Heat creeps behind my ears and onto my neck. 'Things have been rather quiet at work. Which is good.'

'Same as here. People are only returning from the holidays.' A pronounced silence follows.

Outside, a whirl of bamboo poles and plaster. I clear my throat. 'Remember the reception? I mean, how we were talking about fundraising through bequeathing?'

'Sure,' he says and his voice gains strength. 'Sure I remember the reception.'

'I mean, how you get people to include your organisation into their wills.'

'What I told you about, yes.' More bamboo going back into the house and an impression of trainers. His voice again, with a different tinge. 'Why are you asking?'

'Well, um, my boss. I suggested that we might consider it as a form of fundraising.'

'I guess the key is to be tactful about it. Respectful. You need a long-term relationship with somebody before you can propose it. It's difficult.'

I shift the receiver from my right ear to my left. The plastic clings to my hands as if not wanting to let go. I take a deep breath. My mouth clamps shut again. I will myself not to look at the emptiness soaring underneath the boy. 'Yes.'

'Look.' He coughs. And coughs again, in a slightly higher pitch. 'Look, I could pass some of my materials on to you for your colleague. We could grab a bite to eat afterwards.'

'Sure,' I say, glad he cannot hear the hammering of my heart. 'I mean, thank you so much, that would be most helpful for our work.'

He laughs, quietly. He laughs at things, not at people. The line grows still. Across the street, a glimpse of long sports trousers and an *I love HK* sweatshirt. 'Reini.' He says it to perfection, even the German r. Where did he get that from? His voice is dark, like the tarmac underneath the boy. 'It was nice of you to call. It—it was Chinese New Year and all.'

More silence down the line. My smile is so wide, my cheeks almost hurt.

'Sunday evening?' His voice pulls me back. 'I'm working on your side. Can I call you over the weekend?'

'Sunday is—' Heritage Hikes day. Jim and the Filipinas day. 'Sunday is fine,' I say.

How the beauty of this city sometimes hurts. After our call, I keep stealing looks at the boy, like a secret lover. For ten, twelve, twenty entire minutes, I am soaked in sweat and his every move provokes a new outburst of panic. One long prayer, my contemplation of this unknown worker is, with his shock of unfashionably long hair and the love declaration on his chest. One by one, the bamboo poles go in until he climbs back, unharmed. What a beautiful sight it is, to see his lone hand appear again, like a greeting, to unbuckle his harness and remove a leftover piece of black binding. I don't know which gods his mother prays to every day but they must be powerful, perching in her soul. Hoping.

Moon One Day Fourteen
Saturday 11 February

'*Josan.*' Voice lowered, I take a few hesitant steps into the Ngai's living-room in house shoes, Ronda following me, until I remember Virginia's mother is in hospital. I am used to sneaking past her, settled among a flock of elderly girlfriends, the clattering of mah-jong tiles shrouding them in noise. The rosewood furniture sits deserted, the dining table across the family altar gaping hungrily in the corner, only illuminated by a pair of elongated red bulbs, lights for the ancestors whose black and white faces stare into the room.

'You look well,' Virginia says. I will never get used to the way Hong Kong people study you. 'Glowing.'

I blush, heady with Saturday morning happiness and perhaps more. 'For a moment I thought you'd say 'growing'. That's probably the one thing I'd try to avoid.'

She scans my face and laughs. 'You're not that tall. Just taller than the rest of us.'

'I had a good week,' I admit. With a soft shove, I push Ronda forward. 'This is Ronda, the domestic worker I was talking about.'

'Good, good.' Virginia takes an appraising look at her. 'We really need somebody, the kitchen is in a mess.' She turns back to me. 'My father should be back any moment. He's out with the birds.'

'Isn't it a bit late to bring the birds to the park?' I glance at my watch. Almost eleven.

'He's out a lot these days. The house is so empty without my mother.'

As if on cue, the doorbell rings, 'My Bonnie lies over the ocean'. Seen together in the doorframe, it is striking how Virginia and her father resemble each other with their angular faces and broad foreheads. But he looks even thinner than a few weeks ago, two birdcages straining each of his wiry arms.

'*Josan, Ah Suk*,' I greet him with my politest Cantonese.

He gives me a distracted smile, kicks off his street shoes, the birdcages still in his hands, to tiptoe into the flat.

'*Ah Ba*, your house shoes.' Virginia hurries behind him in direction of the balcony. I follow her, leaving Ronda in the doorway, her hands clasped behind her back. As usual, the birds have a power over me which I cannot ignore, with its push and pull factors: their big wills in the small cages against their shimmering plumage, their hithering and thithering, the fragility of lacquered bamboo against the sturdiness it hides. Terror and beauty twinned to such perfection it seems impossible to think

74

one without the other.

Uncovered, the birds are luminous, a black mynah, two finches and a bird which I cannot identify. It is olive green and appears to have white eyebrows pencilled onto its small skull. Ben would know its name. No wonder I glow. It isn't even a secret yet, just a hope, and yet I feel it seep through my pores like unwanted sweat.

'Your birds are beautiful,' I say and rub my nose. How a full truth can also be a half truth, following the mathematical rules of fractions and musical notations. I shift on my feet, awkward in their borrowed house shoes.

Her father smiles fully for the first time, the movement creasing the whole top of his head. 'That one, the green one which you like, is a Hwamei,' he says and points to the eyebrowed bird.

The birdcages hung back onto their hooks on the wall, we return to the living-room where Ronda is still standing with a polite smile.

Virginia turns to her father. '*Ah Ba*, this is the maid Kim is introducing to us. Ronda...'

'Ronda Pajarillo,' I say. 'She's got lots of experience, haven't you, Ronda?'

'Yes Ma'am.' She seems demure now, the barbed wire look a disguise, only her eyes bright as ever.

It all starts off well, Virginia showing Ronda around, her father throwing in a question or two, while I invoke all the advantages of this setup to myself: school for Ronda's children, assistance for Virginia—

'Why did you leave your employer?' Virginia's voice is directed at Ronda, but runs through me hot and fast.

Ronda looks at me.

'There's one thing,' I start, my heart gaining speed against my will.

Virginia turns from Ronda to me.

I clear my throat. 'You know how she comes through MediMission. The shelter we work with, I mean. She...' I tilt my head, feel the back of it against the palm of my hand. 'The thing

75

is, she's got a labour case pending.'

Virginia stiffens. 'I don't want any trouble-maker.' Her voice sounds starched. She looks back at Ronda, with her billowy mass of hair and her face which is wrong for somebody intending to clean toilet bowls. The truth thwacks me, how my blood sister would prefer a different kind of person, somebody called Rosie de la Cruz with downcast eyes and a soft voice. There are many Rosies among the domestic workers.

'No, it's not that. She's not an activist. She was wrongfully dismissed, so we filed a complaint with the Labour Department. And while her case is pending, she's not allowed to work, while her former employers are free to seek somebody else to exploit—'

'So how can I hire her?' Virginia cuts me short, her librarian's haircut shivering. 'We've got… enough going on as it is.'

'But she will help you,' I say. 'She's practically a nurse.'

'What's that, "practically a nurse"?'

'I finished two years of nursing school, Ma'am.' Ronda's voice is impassive. 'Two out of three, and I got good grades. But then, my father fell ill. We couldn't afford it any more.'

From the balcony, Virginia's father calls out, 'What do we need somebody with nursing skills for? *Ah Ma* is in hospital. Getting the best care and medical attention possible.' A brief argument follows, Virginia retorting something and her father hitting back, too fast for me to follow.

'Kim,' Virginia says, 'this is not you, I can't believe it. How can I hire somebody illegally? With no insurance, nothing. It's crazy. It's difficult enough to keep the Hikers legal.'

'Please, Virginia.' My eyes almost liquefy with intention, hot they run over hers. 'The shelter is full. Her case is really minor in comparison with all the other women, beaten and—and everything. Irina will be so pleased to hear that—that Ronda got to stay with a friend.' The enormity of the lie almost bowls me over. Another half truth.

'I will work very hard, Ma'am.' Ronda's eyes, almost black, seek Virginia's lighter brown ones, before she casts down her lids with a movement that could be Irina's, so supple is it. 'All that you want. I need the money for my family in the Philippines.'

Virginia's pupils travel uneasily between us, take in Ronda's capable young body, my pleading whiteness. 'Alright,' she says. 'You can start right away. Tomorrow. The minimum wage.' Her eyes flutter back to me.

Before I can say anything, Ronda replies, 'It is Sunday tomorrow, Ma'am. I will come with my things tomorrow after church. I will start on Monday. Thank you, Ma'am.'

Moments later, the grated entrance door falls shut behind Ronda, her figure diminishing behind the bars until it disappears in direction of the lift. How easy it was to spring her from the shelter and settle her behind this door.

'You're a good girl, always helping Virginia.' Her father's voice pulls me back in. He has settled down on the balcony, in his favourite rattan chair next to the birds.

'She is helping me,' I say. 'Without her, I wouldn't have learned any Cantonese at all.'

Virginia and I set to work, go through the website, list specialised vocabulary for her to learn. Outside in the rocking chair, only a newspaper and a pair of legs are visible, the knees in the light coloured trousers standing out like hooks, the pages moving softly up and down.

'Fallen asleep again.' Virginia says with a look at the trembling newspaper. Once in a while, the puffs end in a soft moan. 'At night, he hardly sleeps at all.'

'He's gotten so thin.'

'Yes.' She twists the pencil between her fingers, studies it, raised like a bar between her hands. She lays it down with care, her fingertips extending the moment. 'And not getting any younger. That's why it's not bad to have somebody with nursing skills.' She pushes up her glasses with her fingertips. 'In the long run.'

'*Ah Ba.*' Lifting the newspaper with care, Virginia wakes her father for lunch. He stumbles back in, squinting against the darkness inside, and turns on the TV. It fills the room with sudden noise, newscasts and jingles that rally in vain against the emptiness of the flat as we sit down to a meal without her mother. Outside, the sun is blazing but inside it is so gloomy the lights on the family altar throw the corner into pulpy, maroon shadows. For a while, we eat in silence.

Her father lifts his eyes from the screen. 'You're neglecting our guest.'

Virginia jumps. With expert moves, she debones the fish and puts another piece into my bowl. 'Have some more. Cinnamon Flower Fish.'

Her father watches me between mouthfuls of food. 'You're such a good girl. You should go out, make friends, meet people.'

'Thank you, *Ah Suk*.'

'So, where are you taking the Hikers today?' he asks Virginia.

'The Lover's Rock and the Police Museum. There's soup on the stove and a fish left for tonight.' She turns to me. 'I've also been thinking of checking out the Heritage Trail for the hikes one of these days.'

His chopsticks stop in mid-air. 'Lover's Rock? Don't forget to burn some incense, then.'

She shifts in her chair. '*Ah Ba*. We go on… educational outings.'

'*Ah* Kim.' He turns his attention back to me. 'Are there a lot of single women in your country?'

'I, we—' I shoot Virginia a glance. She's shoving rice into her mouth, her eyes averted.

'Do Western parents hope for their children to get married?'

'Usually, yes.'

'And,' he continues, chopsticks pointing at me, 'at what age do women in your country get married?'

Next to me, Virginia exudes a peculiar warmth. She is six years older than me. I keep my eyes fixed onto my rice. 'I—I don't know,' I lie.

'Your parents must be worried about you, so far away from home.'

My *Ah Ba* and *Ah Ma*. Oh well.

Virginia dissects a piece of tofu. 'Her parents got married last month.'

78

I smile into my food.

'What?' Her father drops a piece of fish into his bowl. His eyes search his daughter's to see if he has misunderstood.

'They had a church wedding,' she explains. 'Thirty-some years after the civil wedding.'

'You should get married soon, make your parents happy,' he says. His eyes rest on mine, brown orbs paled by age, thin and diluted like all the rest of him. 'Like our daughter here.'

'Thank you, *Ah Suk*,' I say, my face glowing again. I add, 'Husbands are not all that important.'

Her father looks at me. 'Have you ever been married?'

'*Ah Ba…*' Virginia pushes the tofu in his direction.

'Chinese people don't divorce,' he informs me.

'Apart from those that do,' Virginia says. 'And those that decide to stay formally married and each go their own way. And those that keep second wives.'

There is a stunned silence around the table. And then she adds, 'Kim is Catholic. Catholics also don't divorce.'

I nod, although something feels wrong about it.

Virginia's father lifts his chopsticks again. 'And do they hope to have grandchildren? She should hurry up, make her mother happy.' He returns to his food.

I push my rice bowl away. On screen, Audrey Eu is reading a new manifesto for direct democracy. *Saudoidong*, the Cantonese call women politicians, the Handbag Party, but her arm is bare, without a big black handbag dangling from her elbow.

'Hurry up, that's what she should. Give me a grandson. Who's she waiting for, a prince on a white horse?' Her father seems to be speaking to the TV, oblivious of his daughter's carefully emptied face, her body frozen into silence. *Pain has an element of blank*, indeed, and I wished I could unlearn this knowledge. He grips the remote control harder, increases the volume, and Audrey Eu's voice rises from the screen. Handbag Party. I used to find the term derogatory but maybe it is a title of honour in a city where concubinage was only abolished in 1971. Three years after Virginia was born.

Outside, the birds have quietened down, muted into headless

feather balls that could signal submission or contentment or both. In the ancestral corner, the lights burn dimly, casting their obscene blood-red shadows onto the living and dead alike.

'Too much education spoils women,' Virginia's father mutters and it is not clear whether he means Audrey Eu, Ronda, his daughter or me.

How medieval it can be, this city, with its clusters of trade that seek strength in togetherness, its seaside dwelling women who don't know how to swim, and magic forces invoked on every corner. On our walk from Wanchai MTR station to the meeting point at the Hopewell Centre, I watch Virginia climb the narrow sidewalk of Wedding Card Street, hunched into herself. She looks up just in time to bypass a group of mainland Chinese tourists filing down. They speak Cantonese but even I can tell that they are not locals. They don't look Eastern German at all but there is the same kind of *otherness* that is difficult to find a tactful word for.

We stop next to a shop window. Virginia looks around as if taking in her surroundings for the first time: wedding invitations, laisee envelopes, birthday cards. It is also doomed, this alley, to be redeveloped into something less medieval, more capitalist.

She fingers a wedding invitation dangling in a shop entrance. 'You know, my father…' She frowns over the card with its pop-up design, forces it along the folds. With a soft snap, the double happiness character in the middle jumps out, golden against the cinnabar of the card.

'I understood nothing of what he said,' I say and reach for another card. 'Nothing, really.'

She follows the group of mainland tourists descending the alley with her eyes, brings her fingertips to her glasses. Seen from the side, it is both realignment and a shield, this gesture. 'My mother is better with people.'

My cheeks suddenly burn.

At the bottom of the street, the tourists turn the corner. 'My mother is the one who stays in touch with our Foshan relatives. She usually— She used to go back at least once a year.'

'Do you discuss politics with them? Your relatives?' I ask, thinking of the forced cheerfulness and awkward silences of visits to Eastern Germany in the past.

'Not really. I guess everybody has had enough of that.' Carefully, she inserts the card back into the display. 'You know, my father was labelled a rightist when he was still on the mainland. During one of the anti-rightist campaigns. On my mother's side, we came to Hong Kong right after the civil war but my father only came in 1963. He married late for that generation. Very late.' She gives the display carousel a push, setting it into trundling motion, and we move on. We are walking next to each other now on the tiny sidewalk, very close.

'So your father really was a refugee.'

'His only crime was that he had an interest in calligraphy and dealt with antiques on the side. Petty capitalism, they would call it.' She snorts. 'It's quite ridiculous, because he made a very bad capitalist here in Hong Kong. Rags to riches, you know, that generation is full of these stories. I've got a friend whose father came with fifty Hong Kong dollars in his pocket and now owns Citibus.

'Sometimes I think that's eating at him,' she continues. 'He tried to get into antiques but with no money or goods to start with it was difficult. So, for the first few years he did all kinds of things, worked as a clerk and later a private tutor... That generation was really tough. Living on rice with soy sauce, always burning the midnight oil. In comparison with them, we're spoiled brats.' She laughs, a brief laugh that her hand erases quickly as if to make the intimacy of the moment less painful.

'Size matters!' Spielberg is almost roaring. A silly grin spreads on his face while the rest of the group assembles at the foot of the monolith. There is hardly enough space for all of us and we have to be careful not to step on the offerings scattered around, leftover candle stumps, oranges and paper slips that do not even whisper in the windless forest. Like so often, there is a certain kind of small-mindedness to the surroundings, bushes and rocks and shrines huddled and clustered together under a uniform canopy of green against grey. Jim once complained about the 'pusillanimity of Chinese landscapes' with their vegetable gardens and toy ponds, for once missing the wide vistas and deep-breathing gusts of his Canadian past. But here, small is only half of it.

'Wow.' Frank stops to catch his breath, the white chest hair lining the collar of his Hawaiian shirt trembling. 'It certainly doesn't take rocket science to figure out how the Lover's Rock was named.'

'Rock science, in this case. Geology,' Virginia says in a rare attempt at an English joke. Or perhaps she is correcting him.

Frank smiles at her, indulgently.

'Looks just like yours, doesn't it?' Bertie comes up behind us, panting from the steps, Celia Chan following him. The daughter of the Citibus mogul, a sliver of a girl, all sleek and lithe. Seeing her so close to him makes me wonder.

'Ts, ts,' I wag a finger at Bertie and Spielberg. 'In front of ladies.'

'It's hard to stay serious in front of— this.' Spielberg opens his eyes until they shine white, drums his hands on his chest like a gorilla.

'*Hard*, yeah,' Bertie says with a leer.

It is not only the graphic form of the upper part of the rock that has made it into what it is. The phallus is naturally hollow and the u-shaped, tunnel-like cavity at its bottom forms a perfect vulva.

'Okay. Please—' Virginia claps her hands. 'About the Lover's Rock.' She glances at the index card in her hand. Even she has succumbed to outdoor textiles, although she complains that they make her look like somebody who has been hiking through Patagonia. 'The Lover's Rock is popular with girls and women who want to get married, or bear children…

'Any questions?' Virginia scans the group. If Jim were here, he would ask all kinds of things, working in words like 'paradigm' and 'pre-Sinitic influence', but we all nod, ready to walk on.

In ones and twos, the group descends from the rock platform and disappears back into the forest. When the others have moved out of sight, Virginia sets down her backpack. 'Do you want to burn incense as well?'

'No thanks,' I say, fighting an image of Joel, who as a matter of principle was only interested in illegal kinds of smoke. The idea of lighting incense for him, or for any other man, would have provoked him to hysterics. Joel, who deserted me without warning, leaving half a cubic metre of English classics in his wake. Now, Ben… Another thought to banish, for all kinds of reasons.

I squat down and watch her dig for something in her bag. The incense, probably. Sometimes, I cannot read her, separate enlightenment from innocuousness. To bring us to this super-phallus, even if this is an officially recognised tourist site, must point to one or the other, but which? I chase an insect away.

She has lit her joss sticks and is bowing, careful not to step on other offerings. Somebody has used a beer can as an improvised incense holder. *San Miguel*, sun-bleached almost to illegibility. I struggle to reclaim archangel Michael from my memory, his particular field of responsibility, while another part of my brain puzzles over this combination, beer and maidens. Beer girls. And the German Beer Festival. In an instant, I see us again—sitting on the Ngai's flowered chintz sofa, leafing through a whole album of merry Chinese hoisting steins, almond-eyed waitresses in Bavarian *Dirndl*, and a stage full of men with *Lederhosen* and obscene-looking musical instruments. Extra large.

'*Alphörner*!' I leaned to take a closer look at the flushed faces. The pictures seemed to reek of beer. 'Wow. They're—having fun.'

'There was this game.' Virginia turned a page. The musicians were still on stage but were naked except for some odd looking implements in front of their beer bellies. 'Copper frying pans,' she said, smoothing down the loose corner of a photo. 'Aren't they typically German?'

'Frying pans?' I saw it clearly, brassy shine against hairy legs. 'They are wearing them like… loincloths?' I giggled. 'That must be so uncomfortable.'

'People from the audience came forward for this game. You

had to answer questions about Germany. I thought I should give it a try.' She looked at me. 'I mean, I pick up a lot from you. For each correct answer, you were allowed to sound the frying pan like a gong.' Her cheeks reddened.

I squirmed, sudden accomplice of the gong girl.

'People had three chances. And,' now her cheeks turned crimson, 'for three correct answers you would get to look behind the pan.'

'And did you get to lift the pan?'

'Yes.' Her voice harboured disappointment. 'They were wearing a kind of, of tanga underneath. Nude coloured so that the audience wouldn't notice. Wouldn't you also have wanted to take a look? To see if it's really as ugly as in the books?'

An ugliness of its own peculiar beauty. I kept my mouth shut. My hand hovered over the pictures. Surely she must know. Surely she must have—

I saw her how she saw me, the chaste single girl who never mentioned any previous boyfriend, just like her. I blushed, turned the last page of Beer Festival photos. 'We used to cook with such pans. Hundreds of years ago, I mean.' I paused. 'They don't look microwave-safe to me.' I closed the album.

In moments like this, I hate my paper cut nature in her presence, this flat version of myself created out of all I do not dare to be. And Ronda now binds us together in a different kind of dishonesty. I brush another fly away.

Virginia places incense at the foot of the rock, frowning here, adjusting there. I do not know what she hopes for but, seeing her bending her joss sticks just so, a new truth smacks me: whatever she aspires to, I cannot hope the same. I have different wishes for her. Again, I feel like a traitor.

'Husbands are not what they're cut out to be, all in all.'

What a strange repetition of my earlier pronouncement. I turn around and see Zoë, clasping a bundle of incense sticks. Her blush looks like a faint echo of her pink fringe but she seems unapologetic. 'I'll happily settle for a lover.' Her face folds into a mischievous smile. 'Don't you want to burn some as well?'

'I can't,' I say. 'I'm a Christian.'

'Gotcha!' Spielberg reappears around the corner. 'We were wondering what's taking you girls so long.'

'Burning incense,' Virginia says. '*So-rih.*'

'Miss Mok and Miss Ngai, ladies, allow me to guide you away from this... overpowering, pernicious influence.' Spielberg sends a last glance up the Lover's Rock.

'Is that envy I see?' I ask. 'Do you wish you could burn some as well?'

'Nah, I'm not big on tradition, Kim. Especially if I don't have a place in it.'

We step into the forest, Virginia and Zoë chatting in front of us, lengthening their steps to catch up with the group. Spielberg's glance follows mine, takes in Virginia in her sand coloured trousers and trainers, Zoë in her cargo pants, her Husky heeling like a devoted shadow. In a move that gives more than it takes, still absorbed in her discussion with Virginia, Zoë lets her arm fall down. Her hand, Indian bangles rattling, reaches between the dog's ears, setting the animal's tail into quicker motion.

'You know,' Spielberg says, 'sometimes I don't even know what I need. Need most, I mean. Maybe I'm happy just loving. Some people need to love and others need to be loved.'

Lantern Festival
Sunday 12 February

'Copy watch! Copy watch!' The Indian touts at the southern end of Nathan Road are indefatigable as usual, their voices husky in the sharp winter air, their accents foreign. Aliens targeting the alien and, yet, our two strangenesses don't make for sameness in these surroundings. I hurry along, step around the tourists and skirt the be-mirrored Indian slippers, batik shirts and Chinese minority headdresses that never had a homeland. 'Invented tradition,' Jim once called these items, with his keen ethnologist's eye, and flipped a finger against the *Made in China* tags. 'Polyester as well.'

I cross the street at the mosque but almost immediately switch sides again, undecided about bumping early into Ben, his fundraising drive in Kowloon Park probably not over yet. I could have taken the MTR to Jordan but decided to walk through the purple-blue evening instead, to allow my rasping throat and skipping heart distraction: the shimmer of silk in shop windows, the fishy smell of dried scallops catching dust on the pavement, the brush of carrier bags against my elbows as shoppers jostle past.

The Beijing Restaurant turns out to be on the first floor. I wait downstairs, sneak glances at myself in the glass, tug at my socks and sleeves and seams. A working day for him and a Sunday for me; I struggled with what to wear until the cool weather relieved me of choice and I slipped into my warmest sweater. The walls of the restaurant entrance are plastered with advertisements for Chinese palmistry and fortune-telling upstairs.

'Would you dare go and see him?'

I swing round. Ben is beaming at me, his face rounder than I remember. Slightly breathless, he adds, 'To find out about your fortune in the New Year?'

'Oh, er,' I pull my cuffs down. 'I don't even read my horoscope for fear it might come true.'

His laughter shakes his whole body, makes the backpack on his shoulders tremble. 'They only tell people what they want to hear. Lucky in love, successful exams…' His smile softens as he gazes at me and my arms in their sleeves quieten down, settle into the folds of the fabric.

I move closer to inspect the images, figures with oddly square faces and Chinese characters written across them. He sets down his bags and joins me, his rucksack touching my shoulder. 'What does the word on the forehead mean?' I ask. A smell of aniseed skin escapes from his collar, something warm and almost familiar in the cold. 'The guy on the wall looks like Mao Zedong.'

He laughs again, more quietly, and studies my face. El Greco and the pedigree ewe, my memory purrs. 'That's *yantohng*, The

Hall of Seal.'

I extend my hand and compare it with the diagrams. 'Is that the life line?'

He leans over, lifts my hand and holds it for one breathless moment. My skin tingles and I relax my fingers into his, ever so lightly, while my pulse thunders in my ears.

'It looks good, clean and long. Do you often have cold hands?'

My fingers twitch. Heat rushes into my face. 'N-no. I run. I do lots of sports.'

'You sure? It would go with your build. Slender people tend to have problems with their circulation.'

'It's just the cold. Damp winter cold.'

'In that case, I recommend a hot ginger water. And some nice northern Chinese food.' He smiles, places his hand on mine and, for a moment, delicious warmth sandwiches my fingers. Seconds later, our hands part. Dangling empty at my side, my palm suddenly feels dangerous, a hot thing left alone.

I inhale. Exhale. 'So. How come you know Chinese medicine?'

'Oh, I like to dabble in this and that. I used to study it on the side. Until I realised how many endangered species ended up as ingredients.' He laughs again.

I almost hesitate to follow him inside, into this room darkened by old-fashioned wood panelling where even the smallest tables are huge for two persons. Neon light glares from the ceiling and a troupe of elderly waiters rushes back and forth. Finally, I lower myself onto a seat next to Ben.

He is already preoccupied with the menu. 'Do you mind if I order?'

I lean into him to avoid raising my voice. His hair prickles against my face and his spicy smell hits me once more. 'Go ahead, I feel in good hands,' I say. 'You're the vegetarian.' I pull away.

He blushes. 'Maybe I'll join you for some meat. The winter lamb here is famous.'

A waiter approaches us. Whistling under his breath, he takes out his pad. 'Ah Ben, long time no see.' He breaks into a broad grin.

Ben's cheeks flush once more. He smiles back. '*Ah* Lei, I've brought a guest to make up for that. What do you say?'

Ah Lei takes me in and nods. 'Excellent, excellent.'

With the first slice of hot, fragrant lamb, the fluttering in my stomach starts to subside. My mind clears and taking in air seems to get easier. Only my chopsticks still tremble when I go for more. I have forgotten how exhausting this can be, with taut nerves, shaky limbs and a shivering heart. 'Mmh. Cumin and something else—'

'Five spice powder,' Ben says, his mouth full.

I tuck in but wished we had not ordered lamb. Its taste brings up lost aromas, of *bamya* sauce, of kebab… Maybe it is the situation, sitting here alone with Ben, but the immediacy of my memories upsets me. It has been slipping away from me, Sudan, and I have been allowing it to, until all that remains are the sound of the muezzin and the smell of wood fires.

'You seem far away.'

I open my eyes. 'The taste of lamb always brings back Khartoum.' I glance at him and give him a smile. 'It's funny how taste always brings back memories. You know, Proust and the madeleines…'

He smiles. 'The part of the brain that's in charge of smells is in the same area as the one in charge of memories, that's why.' He pushes the plate with the meat over. 'Come on, create a few more memories.'

A relationship soured by its ending and, like all those widowed in one way or another, I have created a new angle from which I look at the past, acknowledge the grating feeling of something that was never quite right from the beginning. Me, with a volatile man. Me, in a country where whiteness created its own dangers and blackness required an eye for distinction finer than mine. Or maybe it is the shine that comes from newfound love, the glittering of the sea under the noon sun, the flickering of neon lights at night, the trembling of the shadows at dusk, a brightness that casts things past in shadow.

Before I came to Hong Kong, I used to think of myself as a cosmopolitan. I do not have a name for it yet, the way in which I am a stranger here, so unlike my strangeness anywhere else. I sit up and poke my chopsticks into the food until my hand almost touches Ben's.

'You'll have to help me,' I say, 'with the memories. And the food.'

In spite of the lamb and the chive dumplings and the bak choy, my body seamlessly trades one sort of queasiness for another, moves from jitters to fatigue. The dessert restores me; glutinous rice balls, peanut-coated, deep fried and filled with sweet bean paste, a dish that warms my skin, my toenails, my heart. 'Mmh-mmh.' I am reduced to ecstatic chewing.

'Today is Lantern Festival. That's the specialty of the day.' Ben smiles, more to himself than to me. 'On this day, girls were traditionally allowed to go out unchaperoned. Some people call it Chinese Valentine's Day.'

I finish my rice ball, so sweet and crisp on my tongue. 'Do you really believe that? To me, it seems almost an invented tradition.'

'What's wrong with that? Think of the poor boys, getting to see the girls only once a year.' He points at me, his rice ball almost skimming my lips. 'In Canada, every second festival seemed to be an invented tradition. *Mmh.*' He finishes his dessert.

'I was starting to wonder whether you were overseas Chinese.'

'With this accent?' He laughs and runs a hand over his scalp. 'No, I came back a few years ago. I studied at the University of Victoria.'

We step outside, into the cool winter air. For once it feels like Germany, this passage from hot to cold. 'So what about the palmistry and face-reading?' I ask. 'Is it genuine or a tradition invented for the tourists?'

'That? That's genuine.'

'Do you believe in it?'

'Sure.' He pulls his collar up. 'Most of the time, anyway. Ask me on Tuesday and you'll probably get a different response from

Monday.'

My heart jumps. The way he says it, I might take him up on this and call him, just to hear his voice. I am getting used to his voice. It is true, each gain inhabits a loss.

He moves closer and for the first time I notice how even his teeth are. My ears grow warm under his gaze. 'I believe what I want to believe,' he says.

Moon One Day Sixteen
Monday 13 February

'Are you going over to the shelter today?' From across the cubicle partition, Irina waves some papers at me. 'Ed's got some documents for Ronda.'

'Er... no,' I say, my mind somersaulting. 'That's a great piece you're wearing. I like the colour on you.'

'Oh? Thank you.' Irina smooths her bisque skirt. I must have seen it a hundred times. Her hand sends the papers into a questioning flutter. She gazes at me over her halfway glasses.

I reach across the partition to take the documents. 'I'll pass them on to her. The shelter was full. She's staying with a friend of mine.'

'Really? Now that's... effective case management. Thank you.' She departs, a perfect hourglass silhouette against the azure partition walls in our office. She has almost reached her room when she gives a half turn. 'Does she know that this is going to take months? Your friend?' Her eyebrows, never lazy, seem to hover under the ceiling.

Moon One Day Seventeen
Tuesday 14 February

Virginia looks terrible. Ugly, violent bruises line her neck along the collar and probably underneath as well. Shadows frame her eyes, and her hair, bereft of its sleek shine, encases her head like matted fur. *Please mind the gap*, an automatic voice warns. The train doors beep and close. The first car is our meeting point when we take the underground to go somewhere; she boards in Tin Hau and I in Causeway Bay.

'What happened?' My voice shrills into the silence of the train carriage. I pull her onto the seat next to me. Out of the corner of my eye, I see a head come up, and another one, people raising their gaze from their mobile phones and Apple Daily.

'*Aiya*, no need to worry. Crazy girl.' She pats my arm. 'Moxibustion. I went to see a Chinese doctor. I'm not sleeping well these days.'

Moxibustion. I've seen these burn-like marks before, on waitresses' necks, on clerks' arms. I let out a relieved breath. My heart catches up with some difficulty. It takes a while until I can speak again.

'I see.' I smile in apology and watch my unpleasant thoughts scurry away like cockroaches, back into the darkness.

I cannot bring myself to ask after her mother, not in the bright, clinical light of the train, and so I ask, 'How's your father coping?'

She looks at her health sandals, gathers her feet in. 'In hospital, he pretends to be all strong. Brings food and Chinese medicine and all our relatives to see her.'

A man with a huge flower arrangement has boarded the train. It's Valentine's Day and the city is spilling over with blossoms, growths that have mushroomed over the past few days on every corner. Something about the way he holds the pink cloud of foil, or the worried look on his face, makes it look like a weapon.

Virginia lowers her head until she seems to be speaking to

her lap, her voice barely audible. 'At home he's… it's awful. Asks why he has attracted such bad fate. Yells at Ronda and barks at me to finish my rice. Tells me not to let myself go.' She has switched to English, as if this made things less true.

'But you don't let yourself go,' I say. Her blouse is freshly ironed and she's wearing lipstick. Cherry coloured, today. But of course, the blouse is Ronda's doing.

'It's not my clothes. He's developing these theories about going out, about our air and drinking water. Getting scared of everything.'

'A friend of mine works for a green organisation. They campaign for better air.' Does she notice it, how he hovers between us? How my fingers twitch, itching to check my phone for messages? How I own him already in my mind? *Do you believe in Chinese medicine? I believe what I want to believe.* Today, I believed what I wanted to believe and I was wrong. *Please mind the gap*, the warning sounds and once more the door closes next to us.

Moon One Day Twenty-one
Saturday 18 February

Because I could not stop for Death. I have never liked this poem and lately it grates even more. Today, I will have to stop for death, for a whole morning of gravestones at Happy Valley cemetery. Odd, this choice of Virginia's, now death is kindly stopping at her mother's door. I remember what she taught me; that it is a nineteenth century euphemism for cemeteries, the expression 'Happy Valley'. How very Chinese.

When I arrive at the main entrance, Virginia is waiting together with a young man whom I do not recognise, both of them half hidden by her familiar umbrella. With its UV coating, it looks like an outlandish instrument against the marble angels and granite headstones that surround us.

'This is John,' Virginia introduces him, a second cousin back from his PhD studies in Edinburgh. 'You two must have lots to talk about,' she says. 'John is a dentist. Kim works for MediMission, they used to be a medical organisation.' Her eyes dart back and forth between him and me, the rest of her pretending not to notice what she is doing.

'Hi, John,' I say. 'So nice to meet one of Virginia's cousins.'

'Oh.' He blushes like a girl and extends a soft hand. Slowly, his gaze travels up until it brushes my face. 'Virginia only mentioned that you're so clever.' His smile widens. 'Speaking Cantonese and all that.' He lowers his eyes again. 'Your Cantonese is really good,' he says to my feet.

When the group sets itself into motion, Virginia whispers, 'His wife died a year ago. Breast cancer. So sad.'

It takes me a moment to realise that she means the dentist, John. His slim figure blends effortlessly into the group and it takes me a while to locate him. He is speaking with Jim, laughing and gesturing. A widower. 'So young,' I say.

We stop at a planter filled with shrubs. Some of us sit down on the rim of the flower-shaped basin. Virginia's eyes take us in: Jim and Spielberg, Bertie and Celia, Jim and Frank and a Swedish tourist with a crewcut and a developing sunburn. 'All over the cemetery, you can see that this really is an... ensemble. Four different cemeteries, for the different religious communities, in one place. An ensemble that was developed during the nineteenth century cemetery garden movement.'

Her shoulders tilt to address the rest of the group. 'This was a, an ornamental fountain...' One hand in a trouser pocket, the other one clutching her umbrella, only the faded moxibustion marks along her skin remind me of that other life. Something in her feels my gaze. Without interrupting her speech, a hand fans out protectively against her neck, goes to her face and makes a wiping movement across her right lid. I look away. 'You can find the same form on the Parsee and Jewish cemeteries. It is a symbol of life, of the rivers flowing out of the Garden of Eden.'

'God as the Spring of Living Water.' Jim peers into the basin filled with earth and dry leaves. 'A victim of mosquito-prevention measures, if you ask me.'

The group, with its umbrellas, sunscreen and water bottles, swarms out again, taking pictures or inspecting stone tablets. '*In memory of the engineer officers R.N. who have died on the China Station. Erected by their brother officers—*' somebody reads out the lettering at the foot of an obelisk. '1858. Gosh, they died young. Twenty-eight, twenty-nine, thirty-four.'

'Tropical diseases,' John remarks, his voice timid. 'Many of them died from typhoid or cholera.'

'Served them right. Bloody colonialists,' the tourist says. 'Them and the bloody missionaries.'

Suddenly, I know it all without ever having seen it—the frugal surroundings back home, all cabbage and patched trousers, a burning desire coupled with modest means. 'I think they came out of conviction,' I say.

'They were social climbers.' He stops for a moment, panting. Around us, the gravestones seem tiny against the skyscrapers framing the cemetery from all sides. Like the inside of a mouth, it feels, surrounded by high-rise teeth.

'Don't be fooled.' Bertie is fanning himself with his cap. In the bright sunshine, he has lost his phosphorescent quality. Or perhaps it is the new girlfriend who pales his colours, turns his glowing beauty inwards. He is holding her umbrella while she applies more sunscreen. 'The missionaries were part and parcel of it, opium and extra-territoriality and all the rest. Colonial privileges.' He resettles his cap. 'Well, that's history and it's alright by me.'

'You forget the Mormons,' Jim interjects from behind.

'Oh well, they're nutcases, like Jehovah's Witnesses. Roaming the city in dark suits, in this heat. Each to his own.'

'Theodosia!'

'Oliphant!' We find ourselves yelping at the names.

'Ruth Pettigrew,' I read aloud. 'A missionary. *How beautiful are the feet of those who bring glad tidings.*'

'That's from Romans but don't ask me the exact chapter,' Jim shouts back.

Gingerly, I step over a cracked tombstone and join him. 'Hong Kong is the only place where people get to choose their own names.'

'English names, you mean.'

Of course I have my own bone to pick with my parents. Reinhild, for God's sake. 'At least, in the West, everybody knows that your name is not your fault. Here some people get stuck with their pubertarian phantasies in their passports. I once shook hands with Ivanhoe.'

'Do you really think it's such a modern phenomenon?' Jim turns to the Chinese among us. 'I always thought there was an awful lot of Chineseness to it. Naming the things you aspire to. "The Aroma of Cultivation", "Mountain of Virtue".'

'That's the Chinese names,' I say. 'Aren't there rules about how your name has to match your horoscope?'

Suddenly, we are all talking at the same time, enumerating the English names we have come across. Rainbow. Sushi. Cinderella. Napoleon. A woman named Lenin. Burberry. Samson.

'And Royce,' Jim says.

'What's wrong with Royce?' Zoë asks. 'And would you please pass me your lighter, you Mountain of Virtue.'

'Such an... automobile name,' Jim says, prodding his pockets.

'Capitalist, you mean,' I say. 'Oh come on, Jim.'

'Eulalia Culpepper!' Spielberg's voice rings out next to a very European looking pine.

For a while, I meander on my own, startle magpie robins into flight, watch a squirrel-like animal rush up a tree. Finally, I slow down at a stream lined with lichen-covered stones.

After a moment, I see it. A creature, hump-backed and archaic, sitting absolutely still. An amphibian with a very long tail. I hold my breath, freeze to a similar stillness and pray that nobody will scare the animal away. Movement builds in me like a sneeze, seeking an outlet. *No.* The creature blinks. Crude, it seems in that moment, like a potential calculating lover. I allow myself to swallow. *No.* I dismiss all other movement until my body heat wraps around me like a cloak on this mild morning.

On and on, the animal forces me to a stillness I did not know I possessed, giving me time to see its green grey tint, the delicate black band cresting the eye. Another flashing of the lids over the trapezoid eyes. It winks at me, as if we share a secret. I blink back without conviction. Not understanding.

'What's that? God, I'm hot.' Spielberg joins me, running his hand over his brow in an exaggerated manner. 'And it's only February.'

'What's going on?' Jim catches up with us just as the animal disappears into a cluster of leaves. 'Oh, a Changeable Lizard,' he says when Spielberg describes the amphibian to him. 'I used to see one in the seminary garden. They're not that rare, really. The difficult thing is to spot them.

'They have surround vision,' he continues as they move on. 'And during the breeding season, the male's neck turns bright red…'

Before I follow them, I cast another glance at the stream, the dark green foliage suggesting emptiness where moments ago it hosted a miracle, something materialising out of nothing.

'Okay. A few words about the oldest part of the graveyard.' Virginia's glance shepherds us into a group and her eyebrows twist up and down while she silently counts the participants. We have gathered in the shade of an acacia. Everything here is off balance, seems to be veering and teetering like a drunken dream. Bamboo shoots up between burial sites; banyan roots finger across graves and upset headstones until they lean at precarious angles. Bertie jumps towards a drooping stone. With grand gesture, he leans against it, pretending to keep the inclined tablet from falling.

'Hey, that's great.' Celia snaps a picture.

Bertie shakes the stone. It doesn't budge. 'Good British quality.' He jumps back, brushes off his hands on his trousers.

I step forward, bend down to decipher the inscription.

'Careful!' Frank sounds concerned. 'Not so close. These things weigh a ton.'

'R—something,' I read. '*Braid*. I can't make out the first name.

Robert?'

At that moment, the stone's shadow to my feet trembles.

'Jump!' somebody shouts, a pair of wiry hands pulling me away. John. I rub my upper arms.

With a silent heave, the gravestone crashes over. We watch, stiffened, as a cloud of dust billows. I stare hard at the tablet that almost killed me. My brush with death, and still I feel sorry for the unknown missionary family whose foundations we have shaken.

'That was dangerous.' Jim's face is ashen, laughter lines around his eyes erased.

It happened so fast I had no time to be scared but, at the sight of Jim's face, fear grabs me. Images flash, of myself lying hurt in the dappled sunlight, of John the Dentist giving me the kiss of life, of Celia fanning me with a leaflet, of frantic calls on mobile phones, of Father James delivering last rites on a grave, of simply being dead.

'I'm… alright.' I move a few steps into the shade, lower my head, rub my face. When I take off my backpack and crouch down, my cotton shirt is plastered to my skin.

'Drink water, that will be good for you,' Virginia says. She comes over and squats next to me, massages my shoulders, my neck. How she always knows where to touch me. I latch onto the bottle and close my eyes. Gulp by gulp, the plastic-scented water calms my furious heart. An ant crawls across the dry earth, carefully circling our feet. *Death kindly stopped for me.*

After the walk, Virginia wants to foist a joint meal on us, John, herself and me. 'So sorry but I have to go,' he says, avoiding my eyes, his apologetic look aimed at his cousin, and I do not know whether to be hurt or relieved. Instead, Jim and I go to Tom Lee's, where he buys guitar strings, before stopping for a quick dinner around the corner.

'How are you enjoying working with Ronda? Isn't she quite a character?'

The mere thought of her makes me smile. 'So—unmeek,' I say and Jim laughs.

I set down my cup of lukewarm tea. 'There was supposed to be a conciliation meeting yesterday, with her former employers. The Labour Department had scheduled it. But her employers never turned up.'

He nods. 'These cases drag on forever. How did she take it?'

'So far, so good,' I say. She seemed almost relieved the investigation never got under way and I know why. It was stupid, to make her work for Virginia without being able to tell anyone and never did I regret it more than yesterday, my fear transparent on my skin. My pulse quickens and the air between Jim and me suddenly thickens.

'Virginia's mother is dying,' I blurt out. My words sound operatic in these surroundings, all chrome and efficiency. Behind us, in the shop window, chickens and ducks drip their oily promises into gleaming trays. For a moment, I seek comfort in their blonde and rosewood glaze.

I turn to the chopsticks standing on the table. They look just like the sticks used for fortune telling in temples which you rattle and shake until a single wooden strip slips out of the container. With that piece of bamboo, you go to have your fortune told by the resident soothsayer. If he has anything soothing to say.

Without looking up, I say, 'Virginia believes that she is going to hell.' My eyes are drawn back to the chopsticks, eager to hear their message.

The waiter approaches us, a dish with steamed chicken aloft. 'White-cut chicken?'

'*Nidouh*.' Jim gestures for his food to be set down and shakes a pair of chopsticks from the holder. 'It's difficult, Reini.' He bows to pray and for once I give thanks with my whole heart. Ant-sized, my faith is these days, bent on survival.

I look at his plate, the chicken pieces next to the rice, blood still oozing from the bones. It keeps the dish extremely juicy, steaming the meat just so, but today I only see the blood. My fried rice with salted fish is innocuous in comparison.

He shoves rice onto his spoon. 'The Chinese believe that the dead continue to exist in some other form, right?'

'They become ancestors.'

'That is the ideal case, you become an ancestor venerated by your family.' He takes a large mouthful of rice. 'But see, what kind of being you become depends not only on your own behaviour. How you die and how your family takes care of you after your death also influences your fate. If you die through an accident, you are likely to become an unhappy ghost that haunts the location.'

'That's what the Hungry Ghost Festival is for,' I say. 'To appease the unhappy dead.'

'Yes. Suicide victims also are likely to become Hungry Ghosts. The thing is, these unhappy ghosts are somebody else's forebears. So, what is a dangerous ghost to you can be an ancestor to me.' His spinach coloured chopsticks cut through the air as he points from me to him. His mouth half full, he continues, 'To make things more complicated, it's a reciprocal relationship. The ancestors also influence the living. They can bestow blessings on the living or, if they are unhappy, exert a harmful influence.'

'I know, the Chinese believe in this netherworld, that's what all the rites and paper objects are for.' On my plate, the fried rice suddenly seems unappealing, a brownish mass that exudes a fishy smell. I should have ordered chicken. 'I thought if you do it the right way, the ancestors would certainly... go to heaven.'

He tilts his head. When he speaks again, his voice softens. 'Reini, name one religion that's not about hope. Where people can be *sure*.'

I shove the rice on my plate to the side and feel foolish.

'It's not a religion without hope, you know,' he says. 'Maybe there are different degrees of hope, for those with boys to do the rites, those who only have girls, the childless and so on.'

'What's that, a priest classifying hope? Shouldn't hope be boundless?'

'You do realise that it's not the clear-cut—' he chews, swallows— 'assortment... of religions that the travel guides present us with, right? Daoism, Confucianism and Buddhism.'

'Yes,' I say, 'I'm learning it the hard way.' Learning to ignore pretend truths. 'Like the reception.'

'Exactly.' Jim smothers another piece of chicken with ginger dip. 'That's what you could call the Great Tradition——the orthodox, pure forms. Orthodox Confucianism. Classical Buddhism as you probably find it elsewhere.'

'Among forty-ish German women.'

He grins. 'If you say so. But see, what most people here practice is Chinese folk religion. And that's syncretism, a messy combination of everything. Ancestor worship. Buddhist ideas of the Western Paradise. Daoist ideas on cosmological forces and how they interact. The whole feng shui stuff. Plus some indigenous traditions and shamanism thrown in.'

He swallows. 'Lots of liturgy, little systematic theology, so to speak. So, many people can tell you what they do but not always why.' He dips another piece of chicken into the light green sauce, carefully nibbles around the bones. 'It's difficult.'

Moon One Day Twenty-eight
Saturday 25 February

Drowning is not so pitiful/As the attempt to rise. Suspended from a bottle blue sky, our cable car trembles uphill like an oversized metallic bug. Ben and I are travelling to the Giant Buddha. Setting out on an act of faith. Rising pitifully slowly. I lay my hand against the cabin wall, draw on its cool, metal confidence to still my stuttering heart but only sense my fear condense against the hull in anticipated doom. Unobtrusively, I slide my gaze back into the centre of the rising cabin, shut out the olive green hills falling away under us.

Ben is bent over his camera, busily clicking away. A sudden swerve. I stare at the floor, as if to memorise it one last time, like the advertisement on the back of our return tickets. *Ngong Ping Cable Car is a visually spectacular 5.7 km cable car journey.* We should have taken the bus.

He looks up, beaming. 'What a day for photos! Look at that

sky.' The skin around his eyes folds with pleasure, and through my fear I cling to his scent for comfort: talcum from his collar and Chinese spices from his skin.

'Any good shots?' I force a smile, anchor my eyes in his. They are the colour of Chinese wood ear mushrooms, speckled with flecks of amber in the bright morning light.

'Yep,' he says. 'Great ones. Everything is so fresh. Spectacular, really. When do you ever get to see the Buddha from this angle?' He points to the Giant Buddha.

I risk a glance and nod. Another jerk of the cabin. One. Two. *Three times, 'tis said...* I steady my breath, focus on the sight of my knees.

From afar, I hear him, 'I'm coming to think more and more that the angle makes or breaks how we see things. And with digital photography, the angle is about the only thing that you can't change afterwards.' His voice seems to fade.

I sense warmth on my elbow, a brush of skin on skin. A whisper of a touch only, but it echoes in me like a shout. His fingertips on my arm. 'Only a few more minutes.' He smiles at me, not sure what he is seeing in my face.

'What about the lighting?' I force myself to ask, drowning.

Moments later, the cable car trundles into the bay and shakes me back into my usual self. Ben jumps out first and extends his hand. Suddenly, I feel reckless with relief. I squeeze his hand with all my might before letting go.

'I'll see you later.' He nods apologetically. The truth is, I am glad to be left alone for a while, to shed the last remnants of terror from my blood and shirk the awkward question of religious observance. Ben has to see the monks at the temple about a cleanup campaign that Green Lotus wants to do later in the year. I send him off to his appointment with a small nod in return, watch him weave his way through the crowds. Ben tends to walk as if some force was pulling him upwards with each step. Uplifted.

I am still bracing myself for the stairs up to the Giant Buddha when my phone rings. 'Virginia!' My voice harbours both reproach and remorse; swings towards remorse. 'I've been meaning to get in touch.' I think of her often but don't know what to do with my thoughts.

'Kim…' The line crepitates.

I picture Virginia and her father standing around a hospital bed, machines whirring ominously in the background. 'Yes…? Virginia…?'

'Kim, are you coming or not? We're all waiting for you.' The line gets clearer. A car honks in the background, Spielberg yodels, and the realisation hits me with a blush. It's Saturday. The Hikers are out as usual. 'Sorry. I should have let you know. I'm—busy,' I say, erasing the image of Ben's swinging gait from my mind. 'Helping a friend with work.' I step back to let a cluster of middle-aged women pass and almost walk into the couple behind me.

'…later.' Virginia's voice is already distant as I skirt another group. I shake my limbs, my skin thawing in the sun. All around me, people are taking pictures, trying to fit the Giant Buddha onto their screens.

'He's too big, Daddy.' A boy anxiously studies the display of his camera.

'You can also look through the viewfinder. The little window on top,' the father says to the boy. 'Is that any better?'

'That's worse. It's so small.'

'If the Buddha is too big, just take one part of him.' The father's voice now has a soothing quality. 'Just take whatever portion looks right for you.'

The Buddha is hollow, a giant Russian doll that houses many individuals in its bright stone belly. A columbarium with rows and rows of ancestor tablets, their features sombre on black and white photographs. My steps much too loud on the tiled floor, I move on, leaving their pitiful, drowning faces behind. Compared with the dishevelled gods and dusty shrines tucked away in entrances and on street corners, the Buddha seems aloof, too tidy. Less lived in. Something in me struggles with this, measures this cool, constrained religiosity against Virginia's, so obviously different and yet related. How different death can look. And then the realisation: How we will differ in death, Ben and I, facing dissimilar futures. *Till death do us part.*

'What are you thinking of?'

I turn around. Ben, back already from his appointment. I feel caught.

'That was quick,' I say. 'Nothing.' How can we die such a different death? How dare we share this life of the living? And Virginia, thinking also: *Till death do us part.* But today, in this pale pineapple sunshine at the foot of the Buddha, her pain seems distant. Hardly comparable with my fear, so brand-new, so mine.

He looks at me. 'That was not a "nothing" face you were making,' he says, his voice shining with decided lightness.

That is not a 'nothing' face he is making, either. His features look flatter than moments ago, take in light rather than emanate it.

When we have both reconstructed our smiles and leave for the restaurant, he gestures towards the columbarium. 'My parents wanted to get on a waiting list. It's difficult to get urn space these days. But it turned out to be very expensive.'

I give him a quizzical look.

'Very expensive. I mean, Anita Mui is buried here,' he says, looking around for the entrance. 'The Canto-Pop icon. Did you see her niche, the one with the flowers and letters?'

'A *waiting list.* Isn't that considered bad luck?'

'We're not that superstitious at home,' he says. 'We're Buddhists.'

Holding the door open for me, he says, 'When people were poorer, there used to be the tradition of giving a man a coffin for his sixtieth birthday. A nice, good quality coffin. To make sure things would be done properly when the time came.'

'I see,' I say.

'It's one thing to fear death and try to avoid it. But Chinese are also extremely concerned with death, right? Precisely because it is such an important thing. Time for something to eat.' He steers me towards a table and, walking so close to him, our way across the restaurant is much too short.

*

A contented grunt startles me. Holding the soup bowl to his lips, Ben slurps his *louhfutong* with rapt concentration, eyes closed, a jade charm dangling from his neck. My heart flutters at this animal display of pleasure. Some other part of me cringes, given to a vision of the Angelic Apothecary with her impeccable manners and Great-aunt Frieda's Meissen tureen. I look away, focus on the thin sunbeams floating in through the lotus shaped window grilles. Dust motes rise and fall in a funnel of light.

'That was good.' With another sigh, he lowers his hands.

As if pulled by a rubber band, I turn to my own bowl. 'I have to try it.' I take a spoonful and close my eyes but only taste soup. He is now shovelling rice into his mouth. It makes a sucking noise.

'You're very quiet.' His eyes search mine across the rim of his bowl. Somewhere, a bird calls into the clear, golden light of the afternoon. Women laugh. They must be a group of late visitors, making their way down from the Buddha to the cable car.

'I'm tired. Nothing.' I feel heavy and light in all the wrong places. The cable car. Getting my hopes high. *Till death do us part.* Being a worry wart, as Auntie Hilde would put it.

'Well,' he says, 'if that's it.'

I put my chopsticks down and take another gulp of lukewarm Pu-erh tea from the tiny mugs that could be eggcups. Around us, the groups of elderly worshippers are thinning. I pick up the chilli sauce, lather the remains of my rice until it glistens, crimson and auspicious, in my bowl. The red-hot taste explosion obliterates any subtle complexities of sweet-and-sour, of perhaps-savoury, of lime green. At least one area of my life that is unilateral.

'That was interesting,' I say. 'Thank you for taking me along on such a busy day.'

The sucking stops. He sets down his bowl as if to hear better. 'Reini—'

'Such a perfect day, warm but not too hot.' I take the teapot, refill his cup which is almost filled to the brim.

He lifts it, spilling tea onto the table. He gulps down his drink, stares absentmindedly at two grandmothers who are stacking Styrofoam boxes with leftovers into plastic bags. When he called about today, I feared it already, a meal on plastic stools surrounded by flocks of elderly women worshippers with umbrellas and sun hats.

'Reini.' His voice sounds hoarse. How he has made my name his. 'Next time, you choose a place, okay? Is that it?'

The plastic table cover is soft and sticky under my hands, ready to let go any moment with a snapping sound only to be raised again.

'Alright,' I say. Will it be another date disguised as work or, even worse, work disguised as a date? This is all familiar, too familiar. Somehow, all that was inevitable about Joel has left me marred. Inevitability can be so many things: lack of mate choice; desire unadulterated by reason; or perhaps mad love, grandly messed up. I look into his face, into his eyes that are amber and black in the light of the weakening day. Suddenly, words rush out of my mouth, unbidden. 'But not the cable car—'

He looks up. 'I thought you liked it.'

I am reminded of his hand, my squeeze, and blush. 'No.' My hand flies to my mouth. 'I mean—' Finally, I say, 'I'm afraid of heights. Some mild form of vertigo, I suppose.' I take a napkin, wipe the table with its tea spills and rice kernels, erase all traces of our meal.

And so, I allow myself to fall into the inevitability of things. *Till death do us part.* Will it be Virginia and me, or Ben and me?

Moon Two Day Five
Saturday 4 March

Old and new fuse in an uneasy marriage in Sam Tung Village. Boxy houses line the cement path, streaked with mould under air conditioning vents; an oil drum serves as an outdoor table at the village entrance and there is rubbish strewn throughout. The older buildings, with stone walls and curved roofs, stand abandoned, greenery pushing through in unexpected places, unhinging a door here, unsettling a roof there.

'It's practically deserted.' Involuntarily, I whisper.

'Not quite enough.' Ben lashes out to whisk a mosquito away. A dog sniffs around a boarded up well and disappears around a corner. 'Sorry. And it would be a disaster to lose it to the highway.'

I had imagined one of Hong Kong's oldest settlements to be different. I try it out in my mind, replace the oil drum with a Chinese porcelain stool, the dripping air conditioners with a waterfall and erase the rubbish. Only the backdrop comes close, a mountain of glistening greens, bananas and pomelo trees and all the wilderness that I cannot name. In the soggy March warmth, I feel foolish. We are on another outing. An outing for me and work for Ben, a truth that my mind refuses to take in.

'I thought Green Lotus was about the environment,' I say, kicking a soda can out of the way. 'And now you work on historical sites?'

'For us, this is not about the historical value, it's about the wood above the village. It's an important preserve of rare species. The highway will destroy both, the village and the forest. Wait until we get there, it's beautiful.'

When we stop to apply another layer of mosquito repellent, a sinewy man in a singlet appears in a doorframe. 'Are you from the government?' The old man's eyes are sceptical slits.

'How come you think of government people on a Saturday morning?' Ben asks. 'My friend and I are out for a walk.' *My friend*. The word rings in my ears as I feel it for hidden dimensions.

'They want to destroy our feng shui! They will disturb our ancestors!' The man spits his words out, his neck wiry with strain. Ben pulls out a notebook. The man is speaking so fast now I have trouble following his rural Cantonese. 'And during the war, I fought against the Japanese. The forest protected me.'

'It's hard to believe that he should be that old,' I say when we

106

leave through an arch mottled with fungus. 'That's beautiful.' I run my hand over the carved stone.

Ben nods. 'A Confucian chastity arch, probably. Yeah, that villager must have been a boy back then.'

I duck around the rusty carcass of a car obstructing the path. He pulls me away from the car's oil spill, his hand warm on my sleeve, and I shrink my steps to make the rainbowed puddles last longer.

We climb into the mountain, our steps muted by the leaves on the forest floor, our breath struggling with air that is dense, as if whipped. Ceremonial paper in a faded pink shimmers between the trees and half-broken urns that look like military objects with their olive green glaze. 'Now, you were talking about the biological value. And he was talking about feng shui. So what is this about?'

'Both. Or rather, they are the same in this case.' He runs his hand over his scalp. 'You can figure it out yourself, really. What happens when you leave a piece of forest untouched?'

'It grows wild.'

'And? If you do this for a long time?'

'It grows... even wilder. More and more like a jungle.'

'And if you do this long enough, say over centuries, it becomes a natural preserve of species, right?'

I nod. 'So the old man thinks that disturbing the preserved land will harm its feng shui?'

'This piece of preserved land became what it is *because* it was feng shui land first. Because it embodies good feng shui.' Ben looks at me to see if I'm following. 'Feng shui woods were sacred pieces of land where felling trees was not allowed. They also were places of burial. I guess at one point people noticed that places with feng shui woods had better balanced water resources.' He looks around. 'So that's how we come to have some fantastic pieces of original woodland today.' Without slowing, he gives a half-turn and extends his arms. 'This is a pristine piece of feng shui land. If we had more time...'

'And I thought feng shui was folk religion, not something Buddhists would concern themselves with.' I glance at him. His pace swishes on unperturbed and so I tell him about my run-in with the IKEA delivery men.

His smile is mischievous. 'So, how are you sleeping in your feng shui bed?'

'Non-feng shui bed, you mean. I keep bumping my shin on it. A lot.' I smile ruefully. 'That's more or less the only thing I miss about Sudan. To have a bit more living space.'

'Ah yes, same with Canada. In comparison with my place here, our, er, my student apartment in Victoria was a palatial mansion.' He picks up a leftover soda can. 'I miss the environmental awareness. That oil drum at the village entrance.' Pulling a face, he shakes the can for leftover liquid and places it into the rubbish bag dangling from his knapsack. 'So, how did you end up in Hong Kong? After the Sudan?'

If you end up somewhere, does this mean that there can be no beginnings? Aloud, I say, 'It's a tough place. The first thing I got here, bless this city, were contact lenses.

'They never let people stay for long,' I continue. 'NGOs, I mean. To avoid psychological damage. You know, like the war correspondents. All the journalists have lots of issues. Anyway.' I graze the forest floor for a piece of rubbish until I find a gum wrapper. 'Anyway, that's how I got transferred. Transferred here, I mean.' I walk faster to catch up with him and drop the wrapper into his rubbish bag.

He slows his steps and studies my face, with pupils so trusting that it hurts. I look away, push my fists into my trouser pockets. 'There's also this idea that, if you stay too long, you'll be going native. That's why diplomats are being moved around all the time.' I stretch my arms in the pockets, feel the constraints of the fabric. My pace has quickened. 'Apparently, they felt that in my case there already was… some sort of fraternisation with the natives.' I free my hands and slow down to fall back into step with him.

He raises his eyebrows. 'And that was frowned upon? Being fraternal?' Trust him to know all the shades of the word. There is amusement in his eyes.

'It's not what you think,' I say. Hot and cold, I feel the effect of my words on my skin. 'It was really rather complicated.' We stop. In the sudden stillness, the warm humidity settles like a shadow around me. My eyes beg forgiveness as they search his, tea coloured in the half-shade.

He looks to the side, pulls at a loose thread from his backpack, frowns at the unravelling seam. 'Too bad,' he says and shakes the thread off. Moments later, he is hunched over his camera, squinting at an elephant ear leaf. Maybe it is my eyes, or perhaps the heat, but the fingers adjusting the settings seem to tremble.

'So, tell me more about feng shui and palmistry.' In the forgiving lunchtime shade, things seem easy. I take his hand, rest my fingers on his palm. His skin is warm and dry, unaffected by the moisture that envelops us.

His gaze whispers over my face, skips parts, rests on others. My eyes, and my eyes again. He lifts my hand, strokes my fingers and runs his thumb over my palm, very slowly. As if to clear the surface, read better. There is almost a breeze up here on the mountain. It rained yesterday and the day before, one of the first hard rains of the year, and there is water rushing down the mountain somewhere nearby. I smile to myself. On our makeshift picnic blanket, I edge a bit closer. He examines my hand in more detail, runs his fingers over the lines, and then sits up. He leans forward to inspect it, concentrates. 'Are you eating enough protein? How's your period these days?'

My face erupts scarlet. Heat spills over from my features.

'I, er—' I pull my hand out of his. 'I don't really do Chinese medicine.'

He wipes his hand on his trousers. His features deepen in colour. 'I got carried away. It's none of my business. I'm sorry.'

For the rest of the walk, I keep my hands occupied with water bottles, sunscreen, umbrellas, anything. His hands are also busy, waving away mosquitoes, adjusting settings on his camera. And we talk; about the Hong Kong obsession with distilled water and plastic umbrella rain covers and German *Mülltrennung*, talk about dissecting frogs versus eating them, talk about fundraising and

NGO jargon and our bosses, all to shut out our stuttering hearts.

When we say goodbye, his voice, dark like Chinese liquorice, lifts my eyes, drags the truth to light, lid by lid. 'Reini?' His eyes are limpid. 'Next weekend?'

I look at my feet, hidden in hiking shoes. His gaze travels across my protein-deficient skin, settles on the toilet brush. A smile pulls at my face, defying gravity, slowly inflating my cheeks. He has had lots of business on weekends lately. Always in scenic spots but never with colleagues. And lots of work meetings which always seem to end around dinner time in Yaumatei. Right next to my office.

'Sure,' I say, suddenly not minding it, that this culture sees through secrets and that this man talks about them. I catch his eye, stumble over the smile that forms on his lips, and we burst into laughter, the kind that boils and bubbles and leaves us breathless, both of us. In the end, each of us has his own reasons for falling in love with Sam Tung Village.

Moon Two Day Ten
Thursday 9 March

I am edgy throughout the week, doing countless reruns of the outing with Ben in my mind, combing it against the grain as if searching for something elusive. The weather is grey and has that muggy indecisiveness of the season, a beginning warmth, a starting wetness, all seemingly without commitment. Most people complain about the moisture and battle it with dehumidifiers. But I love the return of the humidity, the way in which it magnifies tastes and smells and the feeling of it on my skin, like a secret breath. It is not a good time for secrets, though; in closets and cabinets, the damp rapidly claims things, dusting them with mould. And so we bring them out into the open, display pillows and blankets on building platforms to air.

To distract myself, I call Virginia. The phone rings for a long time and, all at once, my edginess seems like a childish luxury. When she finally picks up, her hello sounds distant and tired. My stomach tightens. For weeks I've walked around in blood humming euphoria and now this. 'Sorry for having been out of touch,' I say. 'And I'm not quite sure if I can make tomorrow.'

'Yes,' she says. 'Never mind.'

'So many things have been going on at work, I've got two new cases I'm working on, and then I have to attend meetings and we had this international roundtable—'

'Yes.' Her words sound wrung from a dark place deep inside, a pale trickle of half truth.

'And then Jim took me to a new place, and lots of other things have been going on as well.' I pause, wish I could retrieve my babble like a piece of bait on a string. 'How is your mother?'

'She's—' A noise follows, something between a sigh and a hissing breath, all sharp intake. The line falls silent.

'Are you still there?'

Her voice crouches out from somewhere and she sounds even more a stranger than before. 'She's drinking Chinese medicine. To build up her strength. Against... Against the pain.'

'Give her my regards,' I say. I never know what her mother makes of me, whether she finds me an intrusive foreign ghost or a welcome girlfriend for her daughter. And it strikes me that I will never find out. There is also another kind of silence. Virginia has confided in me and I must not talk about it. Ever. That much I have learned about Chinese culture—you avoid the things you fear.

Still, I try. 'Are you at the hospital?' Perhaps that is why she sounds so far away, cut off from mobile phone reception at the clinic.

'No.' The line falls silent again. Plastic whispers, followed by rustling. A nose is blown and then there is only emptiness.

Moon Two Day Twelve
Saturday 11 March

It is easy enough to push the thought of Virginia away, easier even on a late morning like this one, meeting Ben for an outing along the Heritage Trail. When I arrive at the taxi stand in Fanling, he is busy typing into his phone. 'Haikus are the perfect size for text messages.' He flips his phone shut. 'Don't look like that. It's not a sacrilege, you know.'

'Do you read them in Japanese?' This sounds like a question for Jim, who reads his Greek grammar to fall asleep. Although I ask mostly to ignore the trembling of my heart. My eyes cling to the yellow line on the street, follow its unmistakeable message. Sharing poetry over the phone. Just as I was learning to unravel my thoughts and words for him.

He hails a taxi. 'Gosh, no. I write them in Chinese. Something to challenge my brain.' He taps his faded University of Victoria cap. 'I never seem to carry a notebook, so I send them to myself. Sounds autistic, right?' We laugh and my backpack suddenly seems lighter.

When we have boarded the car, I say, 'My ex-boyfriend knew a lot by heart. Lots of Shakespeare. It helped us get through many dusty rides across the desert.'

'Back in the Sudan?'

'Yes. He was a foreign correspondent.' A professional storyteller on and off the page, a working nomad, a wandering ghost like me.

I speak again. 'I read a lot of non-fiction. Books on migration, Chinese culture… I don't have much patience for invented worlds.' I grimace an apology.

'What happened? With the journalist?' How he sometimes resembles a doctor, factual, probing, unconscious of touching sore points.

'What happened? What happened was that another disaster came along and he left.'

'How was it, the Sudan? You never talk about it.'

'I love Hong Kong. But I also loved it when I was there.' Outside, the New Territories rush by with their low-rise houses and exuberant greenery. I close my eyes, smell the sharp, clean smell of the taxi's leather upholstery.

A sharp turn forces me to open my eyes. 'For one, if this was Khartoum, we'd be travelling in a battered thirty-year-old Toyota, nothing like this. So, why do you live in Choi Hung? Do you live with your parents?'

'No. I think I couldn't, not after Canada. I like to get some fresh air on weekends. Choi Hung is a good starting point.' Another bend and I find myself sliding sideways. Ben grips the headrest in front of him.

I hook my fingers into the door card, with some reluctance. I wouldn't mind careening into him. 'I have friends who still live with their parents. Some even after coming back from abroad,' I say. 'But they're women.'

'So, you know about Chinese families.'

I break into a grin. 'The men read the Racing Pages when they go out for dim sum, eight persons around a table. The grannies boss around the rest of the family, especially the daughters-in-law. You have to bow to your parents when you get married and serve them tea.' Another temperamental turn of the car and I allow my shoulders to brush his. 'It all seems to be about eating together and getting the children into the Hong Kong equivalent of Harvard.'

He smiles. 'Lots of families are like that.'

I would love to know how his parents fit into this picture. There exists a more moneyed version to all of this, with ivory chopsticks and upper class British accents, two domestic workers rather than one, and paterfamilias who look like the men in ginseng advertisements.

'Have your parents been to visit?'

'They have toured China and stopped over in Hong Kong. When I was in Khartoum, they went on safari in Kenya and we met up for a few days on the beach.'

'Getting to see the world with you.'

'They probably wished it was other parts of the world, with more Gothic cathedrals and less hepatitis.' I give another half-laugh. That familiar stab, leaving my parents behind. A displaced family we are, wandering the globe. 'And my brother keeps saying that he'll come. He lives in Brussels. European law.'

We get off at Tsung Kyam Church, a cream coloured building on the fringes of a settlement lined with sugarcane fields. The stalks are steaming with humidity after last night's rain.

'Ma Wat Wai,' Ben points the way, his hand trembling slightly against the purple-green backdrop of the sugarcane.

'There are lots of "Wai" around here,' I say as we set out on the cement path, step into the lacquered landscape. To our sides, elephant ears and bamboo glisten.

'Village names ending on "wai" mean a walled village. Or what used to be one.' He shoots me an anxious side look. 'Sometimes, these places can be a bit of a let-down. After all, we're in the land of Spanish villas.'

I smile. A Spanish villa in the New Territories is a flat-roofed, stand-alone building whose main distinction lies in being different from the corrugated tin sheds and mould-blistered houses surrounding it. 'I see, Ma Wat Wai will require a bit of imagination. Why were they walled?'

'There used to be fights. Feuds between the clans that made up the villages, really. And pirates used to be a problem all along the Chinese coast.

'These clans,' he continues. 'came to dominate the entire New Territories, against the locals who were here first. These days you can't walk here without stepping on a Tang or a Lau.'

'Why did they come here?'

'The clans? They were refugees from up north, in the Tang or Song dynasties. Probably fleeing natural disasters or village warfare, or simply needing more land. And getting more pirates and different angry locals in return.'

'That's migration in a nutshell,' I say. 'Trading one sort of problem for another.'

When we arrive at the Tang Chung Ling Ancestral Hall, the

front hall is caged with bamboo scaffolding. A repairman ducks around the corner, trailing black plastic binding around him like a skirt, a Styrofoam lunchbox in his hands. We clamber inside, carefully dodging the bamboo poles and the raised threshold aimed at keeping the evil ghosts at bay. Inside, the main hall is airy, with hundreds of ancestor tablets on display. Rows of foldable mah-jong tables are lined up on the sides.

'For the New Year's dinner,' Ben whispers when he sees my astonished face. 'The clans traditionally have a celebration. There also is a ceremony for all new-born boys. To accept them officially into the clan.'

On the wall hangs a photograph taken on a hillside. A crowd has gathered round an Omega-shaped grave, with a group of Boy Scouts among the worshippers. 'Isn't this kind of religious?' I point at the washed-out image.

'You mean ancestor worship? Or the Scouts?' He squints at it. 'I used to be a Boy Scout. We certainly were a happily syncretistic bunch. For most people sweeping the graves and all that is more about family and community than religion. Like Christmas for many Westerners.'

We step outside, into the open space in front of the hall. 'Welcome to the wilderness!' I turn around to face Ben and open my arms with a flourish. 'I thought... The name 'trail' suggested something different from this.' My arm takes in the tiled plaza, the middle-class vehicles parked at the sides.

'Oh, don't be so bloody literal,' he says. 'This isn't too bad, for an Asian mega-city.'

I stare at him. Belatedly, his hand crosses his mouth, unable to hide an embarrassed smile. I step closer until I can smell him, aniseed and anxiousness married under his shirt. My smile feels endless, willing his eyes to unbrim, his cheeks to unflush. Finally, his eyes relax. 'Off we go,' he says but his voice quivers.

'The ancestral hall was interesting,' I say. I extend a hand, allow it to brush his elbow.

When we have returned to our walking rhythm, I continue, 'Some Chinese parents give their children a lot of pressure. About finding the right kind of job, about marrying, about having children.' Something makes me reckless, maybe his probing into Joel earlier, or maybe his face moments ago. 'Especially about that. It seems as if the "children" didn't get to have a say in this.' A blush flowers on my cheeks. Somehow, I cannot lift my gaze from my feet.

'Aren't people wired for having children? Like all animals?'

The copper frying pans and what they hide, yes. But children? Our footfall is steady like a breath, rising and falling. 'Sometimes, I find it harsh,' I say. 'Berating daughters for not marrying, while the daughters wished they could find their soul mate.'

'It's worse for sons,' he laughs. 'They have to find a great wife *and* a great job.'

I can look at him now, allow my eyes to challenge his in a rare feminist manoeuvre.

'But don't you see?' His eyes don't take up the challenge, remain soft and serious. 'It's also selfish to only have yourself in mind. Disregarding your family.'

'But doesn't this method result in lots of unhappy marriages? Marriages that are compromises of some sort?'

'I thought compromising was the art of staying married.' He offsets his comment with a jesting tone but his cheeks redden. 'Not all parents are like that. My parents pretend that these things don't matter to them. But you should see my mother. Cooing over every baby that she comes across. Then she organises dinner parties to which she invites friends with daughters my age.'

'But don't you feel imposed on? Having other people meddle in your most personal affairs?'

'These "other people" are my parents, Reini. It is their highest duty and honour to see me well settled before they die.'

The columbarium on Lantau with the waiting list that was not to be. 'So you feel bad about disappointing them?'

'Sometimes. But, hey, we're still young.' His eyes averted, he brushes a hand over his scalp. 'Careful.' His head jerks up and he pulls me to the side to let a bicycle pass. I lean into him, extend the moment until the cyclist is almost around the bend.

When we have to let go of each other, he says, 'I did get close to marrying. Back in Vancouver.'

'A Canadian?'

He nods. 'But then she decided to go to Galapagos. To save the Chatham Island tortoise. She loved the nitty-gritty stuff of fieldwork. Sitting for two thousand hours in a drab olive tent to see the turtles mate.'

'And you find a tent hot and stuffy?' Somehow, his voice allows me to tease him. 'The food not up to standard?'

He gives me a playful shove. 'I like policy work, like you. Getting people to change their minds. I'm not good at long-distance relationships.' He steals me a glance. 'I tend to get terribly jealous. And I can't stand the sudden loneliness.' He blushes.

'Jealous of a turtle!'

His blush deepens. 'I know I should have wished her well, with her tracking gear and her camera. But she didn't have to go, so why did she?' He lifts his shoulders to vent his shirt under his backpack. 'So, the job offer from Green Lotus came just at the right time. The perfect opportunity to eat decent Chinese food again.' He rubs his stomach.

'For your parents.'

'Also for myself. Something about my natural habitat, I guess. And they give me pretty free rein at Green Lotus.'

It is hotter than seems possible in these misty surroundings and warmth emanates in waves from my body. It's odd to think back to Joel, in this drenched, fecund landscape so full of everything: water, food, housing. He feels like a distant relative, not somebody I once cradled in my arms. 'The thing is, you're so isolated and your daily routine is so confined, you end up being with somebody who just happens to be there.'

'Exactly.' His voice rises. 'I think that's what I feared. Exactly.'

Gasps rise in my throat and I slow down. 'Not so fast.'

'Are you alright?' He eases me into the pallid non-shade. Moments later, he is fanning my face with his map. A drop of sweat falls from his forehead into my left eye, a trade so intimate it slows my heart, sets it into thin, fluttering motion. I swallow, run my sweaty palms along my trousers, rub my neck. A bird calls out, a forlorn attempt in the middle of the day.

'Mmh.' With closed eyes, I let my lids, cheeks, chin be caressed by the soft swishing air, feel everything in and around me lift.

He shifts hands, causing the breeze to reach me from the other side. His eyes, honey coloured, focus my face, the slender lids crinkled with concern. Another bird calls out, in answer to the first.

He takes my wrist as if to feel my pulse, still fanning. I smile, feed my smile with everything I own, while his smell overwhelms me. The map brushing against my skin, he reaches around me and starts to fan from behind. My face almost hurts from smiling. He anchors me with his arm around my neck, stops fanning, and kisses me.

My lips ring with his kiss, the urge of it. Our lips meet again, and again, while my thumbs tingle with the bristle of his hair. We circle desire, experiment with trust: Here and here and here.

At our feet, the map crumbles under our drunken dance.

Our walk, from then on: smiles, half-swallowed syllables, giggles, mouthed comments, half-eaten remarks. More sunscreen and repellent—'Let me…'—fingers on brows, lips on lips. The foliage lining the street more varnished than ever, golden and green, the high sunlight of the day raising steam, enlarging smells and meanings like a dream.

After a while, we fall silent, collect our feelings, ruffle them back into shape, digest what has happened. A thought, burning secretly somewhere around my spleen, rapidly discarded: *In the middle of nowhere*. To kiss me there and then, he must be either foolhardy or not care either way.

Some days are endless and move in slow motion, flow around bend after bend. We take in more sights along the trail, drag our thoughts to the surface for an ugly stretch along the highway, stop, share water, walk on. Whenever we near a settlement, our hands fall apart and the light between our shoulders grows by inches, as if following a secret choreography.

On our way to the Sin Shut Study Hall, it happens. We bump into Virginia. Like an apparition in the steam-bathed landscape, she grows on the horizon, from an ant-sized suspicion until she fills my field of vision. I drop my gaze. In the lemon sunshine, her fragile, distorted shadow looks small next to mine and is dwarfed by Ben's. Checking out the Heritage Trail she is, just as she announced weeks ago. I take in gulps of overly wet air while thoughts somersault through my love-dazed brain. Blood jubilating. Bones humming.

My smile is broad but crumbling around the edges. I run my hand over my hair and open my mouth, but there is only a croak. Finally, I manage to call, 'Virginia.'

Her gaze darts back and forth between Ben and me, but our bodies are not used to betraying us yet. They still inhabit the world of singlehood.

'Ben is a fundraiser,' I explain. 'He helped me after that disastrous talk at the Ladies League, did I mention that? He's been making some suggestions.'

'*Haih me*?' she says, *Is that so?*

Ben smiles. 'Kim is a good student. She's been very eager to learn.'

'Oh no, not really,' I say.

'I know,' she says. 'I'm her Cantonese teacher.'

Cicadas drill messages into the woolly air, like nails being hammered into cotton. A twig breaks softly under Ben's trainers.

'I tried to call you,' I say. 'We could have done this together, today,' I add, rubbing my nose.

'Yes,' she says and lifts the tips of her feet, clad in trainers almost exactly like Ben's. It is very unlike her to do anything alone. To want to be alone. On a Saturday. In the sunlight, the shine of her hair breaks into a rainbow on black. 'We've both been very busy.'

'We're on our way to the study hall. Sin... Study Hall. Why don't you join us?' My mouth twitches.

'No, thank you,' she says, her eyes carefully neutral. 'I started over at Siu Hang Tsuen. The other way round. You two have a good talk about fundraising.'

We walk back to the train station, taking a detour through the park. We take refuge against a wall, bright like a screen under the moon. Before our bodies touch, the moonlight has already welded us together into one single shadow which trembles against the wall. Tentative at first, then with assurance do our shadow beings merge.

Moon Two Day Twenty-four
Thursday 23 March

Of all people, it is Eva who clarifies things for me. I bump into her on the landing in front of our office toilet, in the grey tiled staircase with its long echoes; thirteen floors up, ten down. She is standing next to the rubbish bin which almost reaches up to her hips. I step into the corridor just as something white is being dropped into it. A paper handkerchief.

'Eva.' My gaze moves over the crisp blouse, the polished pumps, skirting around her red-rimmed lids. She wipes the corner of her eyes with the back of her hand, straightens herself, but makes no effort to go back in. It is stuffy here after the air-conditioned office, and the sweetish smell of rubbish wafts across the landing.

'Anything the matter with Irina?' I ask, although that would not be like her at all.

'No.' She forces a smile, presses the back of her hand against her closed eyes. 'I'll be alright in a moment.'

'Maybe it's PMS,' I say. 'Pre-menstrual syndrome. I tend to get totally weepy.'

Behind her hand, tears start to run again. I am beginning to feel hot and the stench is suffocating.

'I wish…' Her voice is muffled by her fingers. They remain pressed against her lids as if that could keep the tears inside. 'I wish it was PMS. Another month gone.'

'I'm sorry.' Shifting my weight, I reach out, meaning to touch her forearm, but my hand lands on her hip. 'You're still— You're young. For many people it takes a while until… it happens.' From my trouser pocket, I produce a tissue.

She accepts it without looking up. 'Worst of all is my mother-in-law,' she continues. 'Asking me all the time when my belly will swell up, be big and round.' She sniffs. *Daaihtouhpouh*, something in me translates. Big-belly-woman, the Cantonese word for pregnant lady. With surprising force, she blows her nose into my handkerchief and flicks it into the bin with a dismissive turn of her wrist. There is already a collection of wrinkled whites inside.

'Why is it that Chinese are so obsessed with having children? The family line, ancestors, I know. But you're Christian. Your son would never venerate his ancestors.'

'But my in-laws aren't. She always wants to drag me along to the temple for a grandson.' The corner of her mouth trembles, forms a hesitant smile. 'I would hope for a girl.'

I hand her another tissue. She pockets it. 'What happens if the child is a girl? Were a girl? She wouldn't have to participate in the rituals, right? Ancestor worship?'

'There'd be less pressure, yes,' she says. Her voice is losing its shiver.

'But, Eva,' I say, 'this would leave your in-laws… without hope.'

'But that's superstition.'

'What happens to women and girls? They don't participate, but can they be venerated?'

Her gaze falls fully on me. Around her eyes, the skin is freckled from bleaching. Glistening with tears, it looks like a child's. 'That's a curious thing you're asking.' Fingering her silver cross, she continues, 'Women can be venerated as founding mothers of a clan, as wives of important ancestors. Not if they die childless or unmarried, though. Especially if they are unmarried.'

'So, what happens when they're dead?' For the first time in my life, I am tempted to say, *Are they unsaved?* But it sounds grotesque to me.

When she speaks, her voice is soft. 'This is all about family and community, not so much the individual. But… yes. Women without children are not provided for in the afterlife.

'See,' she adds. Her lids flutter, uncertain like butterflies, before her look challenges mine. 'That's why it's so important that we give witness.'

'But can't other people venerate single women? The parents maybe? People used to lose lots of children.'

On her face, another type of smile forms and there is something like compassion in it, or bemusement. 'It would be totally impossible for parents to burn incense for their children. Something against the laws of nature.'

Her upper body turns towards the exit. 'That's why Chinese people have come up with a million ways to avoid that. That vacuum in the afterlife. Adoption, concubines. Communities of unmarried Buddhist women. Ghost marriages.' She pulls a face, wrings the tissue into a tight shape. It must be close to disintegration. She throws it into the bin.

Back at my workspace, I search the sky for the black eared kites but fail to find them. Something in me recoils from her conclusion. Her mission. Eva with her support tights and the cross, and I cannot help thinking of what she has traded one for another, and of what she does not manage to shed, almost like Virginia. The pudgy lawyer with the bad breath who came along to the Museum of Coastal Defence. Frank. (No, I correct myself, Frank was never part of this, he joined Heritage Hikes on his own.) A Mr. Chen who was obviously gay in an unmerry sense of the word. All these attempts, initiated by Virginia's parents, are more than efforts to care for their daughter in this life. They are also attempts to settle her in the afterlife, to create a position for her in which she can be venerated. Keep her from becoming an unhappy ghost.

'Kim.' Irina's blonde head appears over the azure partition of my cubicle.

I give a start. Daydreaming during office hours is not something Irina encourages in her employees. 'I'm trying one of those power breaks.' I fold my hands behind my neck, stretch elaborately, let them fall back.

She leaks a little smile, slightly ironic. 'Lynn is changing the format of Word for the Day. Ed did a wonderful one last week, a Filipino take on the idea of diaspora. It reminded me of yours which we reprinted in the Annual Report.' Her smile changes, becomes warm and uncomplicated. It makes me squirm. She deposits a letter on my desk. For a moment she is a golden vision against the azure partition and I cannot decide whether these colours of Russian icons, of airy saintliness, are wasted on her or not.

'Ronda Pajarillo,' she says. 'The Labour Department has scheduled a new conciliation meeting.'

How much emotion they hide, these documents with their formal letterheads and bureaucratic language. The meeting is scheduled for early May.

She leaves and I file the letter away, right next to the company records. I'm in Irina's good books again. I rub against the phrase, fleetingly touch the green ledger with the blank after my name, and push it back onto the shelf, unopened.

Moon Three Day One
Wednesday 29 March

A postcard from Kazakhstan, from Auntie Hilde. Roaming the world with her Russian language, first for work and now for pleasure. 'The language monster,' my father calls his little sister, the '68 renegade with her string of boyfriends and the suspect politics. Suspect for him, anyway, the Pomeranian refugee child for whom all politics lost their promise early on. I tuck the postcard into my Cantonese textbook.

I wonder what Auntie Hilde would make of Virginia. They are an impossible pair, like snow in the tropics. Mostly, I know what Auntie Hilde would have to say and often ignore it. But she remains silent in my mind even as I sharpen my question, *Her mother, what shall I tell her about her mother?*

Under my textbook, the rattan table mat has furry streaks. I have to talk with Virginia but allow my cowardice to creep up. Poison green and verdigris, it is suffocating, like the mould which erupts so easily at this time of the year, dusts every surface in my flat, blunts knives and takes the shine out of things.

Moon Three Day Twelve
Sunday 9 April

An unseasonal heat wave is steaming the city. In church, the ceiling fans whirr, merely redistributing the soggy air above the black-haired crowd, pushing it into the last corner to the Unreached People Groups. I shift a few inches away from Ronda's warm body. My mind is going fuzzy with the heat. Taking on Eva's jargon I am.

'A reading from the Gospel of Luke,' Jim's voice rings through the sanctuary. I am only half listening, fanning myself with the hymn sheet which sags under my fingers. He looks miraculously cool in his priests' vestments. Fresh-faced, clean-shaven, Sunday-happy.

'The servant answered, "Your brother has come home safe and sound, and your father has ordered us to kill the best calf"—'

The word 'servant' provokes a skip of my heart. Ronda and I will have dim sum afterwards. And Jim loves his Sunday dim sum: 'The suffering of the chosen. Getting up at six on a Sunday morning. I need a decent lunch to get me through the second half of the day.' So, unless there is some counselling crisis among the Filipinas, Jim will come along. Ever the pastor, he will worm out of Ronda where she is staying. And Jim knows Virginia, knows her well enough to see that Ronda is not just staying there but working. Like a slot machine, my mind jingles unlikely options: *Go home right away, claim illness. Tell Ronda to go home right away, claim illness. Tell Jim the truth.*

Throughout the rest of the service, I fidget, distract myself with aperçus: *Christianity is a mobile religion*, not just now as the Filipinas file to the altar for communion, Ronda leading in her Sunday best, me following. 'Amen,' I say, wishing the word had the fullness and conviction it warrants.

'I have called you by your name, you are m-i-n-e…' My throat dry, I join the closing hymn, while my slot machine hasn't come up with a solution yet.

'Sticky rice,' I say but the noise of a thousand happy diners swallows my syllables. At our corner table in the dim sum restaurant, Ronda toys with the ordering sheet and pencil. She is not used to spending money on outside meals, even if this is only the Shamrock Hotel with its greasy chairs and darkened wallpapers. Or she's thinking along the same lines as me, wondering how much to divulge to Jim.

'Sticky chicken rice in lotus leaves,' I repeat, louder, since Ronda is too polite to suggest anything and Jim has already requested, 'Beef balls, rice noodles, and then, what's it called, *louhbahkgou*. Oh, and let's get barbecue pork buns…'

Seeing Ronda take down our orders like a schoolgirl, nodding along, something in me stirs. Jim, unfazed, is washing our bowls and chopsticks with tea from the pot, turning them over in a soup bowl. 'I see you've taken to the local custom of cleaning your dishes with tea,' I say. 'Doing your ablutions.'

'All my parishioners are fervent ablutionists. It creeps in. Nobody has a convincing argument why they do it, but everybody's afraid of not doing it.'

'That's what I would call superstition,' I say.

'The detergents,' Ronda says, still bent over the paper, brow furrowed in concentration. 'People think it helps to clean your dishes from the detergents.'

'But are the detergents really there? You can't see them,' I say.

'Don't we believe in many things we don't see?' Jim has finished with the dishes and is distributing plates and bowls with practised moves.

A waitress stops her trolley. 'Sticky rice, pork buns, rice noodles.' She plonks down the food and ticks our ordering sheet, her hips already on their way to the next table while the rice noodles are still shivering in the soy sauce from the force of her movement.

I divide my pork bun with the chopsticks, watch the steam escape. If I can start a discussion, Jim will have no time to focus on Ronda. 'So often it seems to be only about what you can see. The Bun Festival last year, all that walking on sticks and the buns.' Scrutinising a piece of pork between my chopsticks, I venture, 'Sometimes it's just a lot of hocus-pocus.'

'Careful what you say,' Jim says. 'The word hocus-pocus is derived from Latin, from *Hoc est corpus meus.*'

Ronda nods at the familiar words, chewing.

'This here—' Jim pushes a piece of rice noodle across his plate— 'is folk religion. And medieval Christianity with its "hocus-pocus" also was folk religion. Something more connected to magic than the mind. Yes.' He stares at the noodle, nods at it, finally shoves it into his mouth. 'And are we so different, with our St. Christopher medals pinned to dashboards?'

'I know, what she wants to say.' Ronda puts down her chopsticks and fumbles to tame her zigzagging mane. With a soft pull of her hair, she pushes the ribbon around her ponytail upwards and flicks her hair behind her shoulders. She leans forward to make us hear better. 'They do a lot for religious reasons, but they do it because of fear. There is more fear than joy.'

I nod. 'Yes, that's part of it.'

Jim, his mouth still full, shakes his head. He swallows. 'Now, your faith, for you—' Ronda busies herself with a lotus leaf. I squirm and reach for the chilli sauce. As if to himself, he continues, 'If nothing else, it's probably a set of teachings that you were taught as a child, and a fuzzy warm feeling.'

'Exactly.' Ronda's chopsticks slice the air for emphasis. 'That feeling, Father, that is missing for the Chinese.'

'Chinese religion is… It's more about righting things, be it on a cosmic scale or in the family. Making the sick healthy, the poor rich.' He gulps down some tea, balances the teacup between his fingers, sets it down. 'Which is why you should not compare it with Christianity. Ultimately, they have different concerns.' He tilts his cup. 'Of course it's always up to us to share our version with them.'

Against the background noise I cannot hear whether he says 'version' or 'vision' but keep quiet. I scrape the last bit of sticky rice from my lotus leaf.

'Sorry, jabbering on in my Sunday mode. I have to pastor to my own flock, first of all. But if somebody came to me in distress, of course I would share our Good News with them. Let the Chinese be missionaries to the Chinese, is what I say. They're doing a good job. The Protestant congregations are growing.'

'I know. Being joined by people like Eva.'

'Say, do you really think—' he sits up to see if we are listening— 'do you think God will be bothered by confessional differences? Or even interreligious differences?' He leans back in his chair and looks for the waitress.

Time for dessert, probably. Dessert and some light, pastoral heart-to-heart. To hear how I am doing. And Ronda. 'Maybe God doesn't mind,' I say. 'But what about people? Religion is about liberating people, isn't that what you always say?'

'To make us free from fear,' Ronda says, pouring all of us more tea. 'To promise eternal life.'

'Eternal life is not enough,' I blurt out, a vision of support tights and women in burqas rising in me. Two pairs of eyes look at me, Jim's a curious blue, Ronda's a sceptical black.

'Fundamentalist religions liberate only for the afterlife,' I continue and the rush of recognition makes me spill tea onto the tablecloth. 'But never for the present. And others only liberate for the present, with no afterlife on offer. Like the, like the t'ai chi practitioners in my building.'

'Well put.' Jim sets down his tea. 'You and I are looking for a religion that liberates for both, this life and the next. And that is much harder.' His smile ripples his face.

Ronda shoves the menu in Jim's direction. 'Quick, if we want to have dessert,' she says. 'I promised Miss Virginia to come back in the afternoon.' She gets up and looks around as if searching for the ladies'.

I brace myself for the fall-out from Jim. 'Over there,' he gestures. 'No dessert, then. I'll have a cigar instead.' He grins. 'Or did you want some? That's really a blessing, that Ronda is there to help Virginia through all of this.'

Hysterical laughter wants to rise in me. When the cackling moron inside quietens down, I say, 'Perhaps Ronda's... circumstances could be left to your... pastoral discretion?'

'Reini. Did you really think I didn't talk with her?' He raises his chopsticks, studies the writing on them. 'There is a difference between what is illegal and what is unjust. I won't breathe a word about this.' He puts down the chopsticks, aligns them in two perfectly parallel bars. 'But you should probably stay clear of Irina.'

Somehow it is easier to ask Ronda now, almost as if things had sorted themselves out. 'How are things with Virginia?'

She visibly turns her back-from-the-bathroom briskness down a notch, collects herself. Her fingers play with a charm dangling from the zip of her handbag. Finally, she says, 'Not good. She is... not well. Her mother is— It is really bad.' She focuses me with eyes that always remind me of lychee stones, dark and round. 'She misses you, at the walks. You should call her, or visit her.' As if I had failed to see something, her voice sounds, and she is probably right. And so I still feel chastised after our meal, uncomfortable from more than just the heat plastering my skirt to my skin, while my fingers are already on the phone, longing for Ben.

Moon Three Day Nineteen
Sunday 16 April

Another hot, angry collar around her neck. As usual, I find myself unable to look away from the moxibustion marks on Virginia's skin. In her apron, bent over a recipe, she looks like a battered housewife. *Guard my life and rescue me; do not let me be put to shame, for I take refuge in you.* Like dyspepsia, these echoes rise in me, good food turned sour. Her mother, dying quietly in hospital, trusting in her daughter to guard her, now and forever. Virginia, not rescued but branded, being put to shame because she doesn't take refuge in anything, not even sleep.

She briefly rests her forehead against the heel of her hand before returning to the notes, the sort of Chinese scribble that awes foreigners with its unselfconscious illegibility.

There is another kind of anger as well, anger with myself. Legally, Virginia and Ronda are responsible but whenever I enter the Ngai's flat, I feel uneasy at the sight of Ronda chopping ginger or changing sheets. And so I hide behind my own annoyance, postpone the need to talk with Virginia again and again.

'… And white pepper,' she mutters and looks up from her notebook. '*Louhbahkgou* really is a funny thing to start with.' How long it has taken us to follow up on her promise to teach me how to cook. That dinner at Kosmos, four, no five months ago. She pushes her glasses up with that all-purpose gesture of hers. 'But it's such a Cantonese classic. When you go back, you need to know how to make it.' She wipes her hands, wet from cleaning the counter, on her apron. Next to her, a bowl holds diced ham and dried shrimps which we first soaked and fried moments ago, their aroma still hanging in the air.

I fidget with a knife. 'You're so sure about me going back to Germany.'

'But you always say that you'll be going back.' Her hands stop in mid-motion.

I look at her chopping board, the turnip and the knife neatly lined up. Finally, I say, 'Leaving, you mean,' and in that moment I realise the difference. 'I have a time contract, that is a fact.'

'You... should think about your future.' She lifts the vegetable, assesses it. She says it lightly, hiding her message behind a smile and the housewifely preoccupation with her turnip, dividing it in one assured move. She hands me one half and I take it.

'Mmh,' I say. Ben and I are developing a sort of routine, stealing time around his and my many commitments. Or robbing others of our presence instead. My six foot one Southern Chinese secret which I could reveal today if I wished to. Ben, followed by a talk about religion. *About your mother...*

She starts to peel her half of the turnip. 'Did you know that in your age group there's a real surplus of women in Hong Kong? That's because of all the men who marry women from the mainland. Twenty-five percent.'

And because of the foreigners who marry Chinese women. And it's her age group as well, more or less. 'You know...' I take my half of the root, decapitate it, peel it, carefully cut off all the ugly bits and pieces until it is one smooth piece of truth. Not the original product but not fake either. Something embellished, perhaps even improved on.

'You know—' I infuse my gaze with meaning— 'your time will come.' Through the humidity which is starting to fog up the tiny kitchen, she looks at me, her pupils behind the glasses swimming with steam, or with trust. She takes the turnip and starts to grate it by hand, her tongue sticking out in concentration.

'Anyway,' I say, 'my project at work will be going on for another two years at least.' I shove my half over to her. I wiggle the fried ingredients and set the bowl down again.

She watches the fluffy mound of vegetable sink into the boiling water. 'Five minutes, the recipe says. "Boil the grated turnip for five minutes, then drain over a colander, reserving the liquid".'

Somehow, seeing her bent over her mother's handwriting, that notebook which will remain after her mother is gone, makes it so much harder to speak with her. My silence grows and I wonder whether she feels it bump against her, feels it expand until it fills the kitchen in its entirety. A sweltering form of quiet which causes us to wipe our brows while the water in the pot boils loudly. I open my mouth; close it again. *Did you mean it? What you said a while ago?* Of course she meant it. That look on her face. How do you talk with somebody about the possibility of her mother going to hell?

'Your mother,' I say, 'you know, about your mother—'

'Yes, that's my mother's recipe.' She talks in a brisk, matter-of-fact manner, her eyes scanning the wash basin. She picks up a dishrag and wrings it.

I run my hand over my forehead, wet with steam, and start again. 'I'm sure she will be okay.' I reach over to put the used chopping boards and knives into the sink.

'Don't worry, we can leave everything for Ronda. She can clean up when she comes back.' Her hand still clutching the dishrag, she changes place with me in front of the sink.

'It's her day off.'

'It's her job. She can do it tomorrow. Don't you have many emails in your inbox on Monday mornings?' She lowers the flame under the boiling turnip flakes into a steady blue tongue.

I open the tap, watch the water flow into the basin. 'You know…' I say, 'I'm sure your mother will be alright.'

Virginia is wiping the counter, back and forth her hands go. Under her off-red T-shirt, her shoulder blades follow the movement, opening and closing.

I shut the water off. 'I mean—'

Her shoulders stop. A kind of swallowed noise burps in her but she stifles it at once. She stares at the dishrag in her hands. Her voice, speaking to the gleaming counter, is hoarse. 'No need to fool ourselves.' With a move that is part disgust and part force, she throws the dishrag into the sink, where it drowns without resistance. Suddenly, the marks on her skin are bright crimson, as if illuminated from within. Again, I have to tear myself away from the rosary blooming on her neck, this thing of its own peculiar beauty.

'Let Ronda do it all. You know, I hate it that she is free on Sundays, because I have to cook.'

'Thank you for cooking with me.' My fingers toy with the faucet without opening it.

'I'm thinking of paying her more so that she could work on Sundays. She's really good.' She smiles at me.

'But that's illegal—' I stop. Talking about what is legal with domestic workers and what is not. 'She needs the rest. Why don't you eat out like everybody else?'

'My father really wants a family dinner on Sunday evenings. It's not the same, if it's not at home. Home-cooked.' She plucks a pair of chopsticks from the holder and fishes a shred of turnip out of the boiling water.

We are soaked from the vapour that fills the kitchen to the seams.

'I think the turnip is done.' She drains the vegetables into another bowl and mixes them with rice flour. 'Now, the important part is to get the mixture right.'

I watch, once more rehearsing a thought or two in my mind: *You know…*

Unruffled by the heat, she continues, 'You add rice flour and some of the liquid until the consistency resembles thick congee.' She adds the ham and shrimp, seasons the mixture with salt and pepper and finally transfers it into two steaming pans. 'That's it. Steam it for about an hour.'

Assembling the pot, the water, the pans and the lid is a clattering affair, but finally the turnip cake sits steaming over the flame. I clear my throat. 'I've been meaning to tell you something.'

'Yes?' She looks up.

'I've been thinking, Jim and me, we've been thinking— If you wanted some time off, we'd be glad to run an outing or two for you.'

'But you're helping already.' She places the chopping boards upright on the counter and aligns them, runs her hands around the rims, lifts them and turns to me.

'Anyway,' I say. 'You can think about it.'

Somewhere in the flat, a phone rings. 'Let me get it,' she yells but her father is quicker. She lets her chin sink onto the rim of the chopping boards that still shield her chest and nods. 'Thank you.'

In the living-room, there is a long silence, followed by the sound of house shoes scurrying across the parquet towards the kitchen.

'The hospital.' Her father clasps the doorframe, wheezing. His singlet looks exhausted, greyish cotton that has gone out of shape, and the fly of his shorts is open. 'Mother needs us. She is not well.'

Virginia disappears into the bathroom and so I wait for her while the turnip cake is steaming, browse the stacks of hiking materials on the living-room desk. Between Chinese travel guides and battered maps, a slim volume sits awkwardly, too pink and too new for the familiar piles. *How to Find a Husband*, by somebody called Mei Ling Ng Liu (Mrs). As if marital bliss depended on the right ISBN number. Gingerly, I open it. *Before The First Date: You will have to refresh your eyebrow tattoos if they are faded and make sure that your teeth are well cared for and bleached.*

'Kim, I have to go—'

I drop the book, blush, only to look up into Virginia's face, equally flushed. 'Your time will come,' she says and reaches over, carefully places it back among the guidebooks.

I sneak a look at her eyebrows. They look unchanged. I can virtually feel mine, glaring their unkempt blondeness into the world. 'I could watch the food. It won't be much longer,' I say.

The mass trembles when I turn off the flame and set the pan aside to cool, still very much unlike what it is meant to be, sliced and fried. A fruit salad shows you its origins but with turnip cake, a deeper change of matter occurs. A form of transubstantiation. Already, I can savour our labour of love in my mind, its creamy texture and savoury aromas, turnip and ham, dried shrimp and chilli oil. A very Cantonese mixture that is many things at once yet makes no definite commitment—salty or sweet, mild or spicy.

I pick up the pink volume again, bury my nose in its gluey,

sharp smell. Hot, it feels under my fingertips, and I am tempted to pocket it, to pore over it as if this could make me understand her. As if I hadn't learned how difficult it is to smuggle books back and forth. *Jau si*, the Cantonese call smuggling, to walk privately. To go it alone.

Moon Three Day Twenty-four
Friday 21 April

Laced, with golden trimmings, semi-transparent, frilled and fringed, they hang there in sturdy polyester, whole arrays of bras and underpants, all in red. Bright red, something in between scarlet and cinnabar. A special offers rack on Wanchai Road. Chinese underwear takes some getting used to with its volcanic constructions, stiff like Styrofoam cups. But today I buy a set, a simple cut with V-shaped pants and cross-wise straps on the back. Swinging from my wrist, the bag whispers as I carry it through the early evening, one small noise of promise amid the roar of the rush hour, the beeping of traffic lights, the steps and chatter and phones of seven million people.

At the Fringe Club, I plant a distracted kiss on Ben's cheek and dash past the lobby into the Ladies'. In the sea green toilet stall, I shed my trusty white cottons, look at my body. Untouched by the whitening creams so beloved by the Chinese, its natural tint is not so different from the skin colours around me. Less coconut milk, more very milky coffee. The air conditioning washes over me with its cold breath, lifting every crinkly blonde hair on my body, head to toes. I shiver.

With quick moves, I slide into the new panties, ease myself into the bra. As I climb back into my office clothes, they feel slightly soggy. On my skin, the new pair tugs and pulls, its Chinese red hidden under my blouse. The colour of door blessings and New Year greeting cards, of double happiness coconuts, of taxis and fire engines. The colour of all that is good and new and needs to be protected.

Ben and I.

Slowly, our whispers and sighs rise above the constant hum of air-conditioning and cars, finally shut out everything around us. I reach for him, all of him, his aniseed scent, the silky evasiveness of his hair, and the colour of his skin, like the soft inside of a mangosteen. Even now, it makes me smile, the memory of my first mangosteen, the shock of it with its looks of garlic and its taste of paradise.

My mangosteen. His skin again, here and there and here. A scar, quickly hidden, and a mole, all mine. The world becomes a sea of touch, an ocean of smells, as we unfold our skins under trembling hands, fall into searching curves that thrive on their own fullness, turn in on ourselves, invert our fates, make endings into beginnings, and finally come to a full stop with hunger: *Now*.

Later on, I evoke the aromas of love once more on my tongue, aniseed and salt. On the sheets, a dark patch of sweat frosts the boundaries of our love. Soon, the evidence of this hour will evaporate into the April air.

Moon Three Day Twenty-five
Saturday 22 April

From downstairs, music winds its way up through the air conditioning shaft, tightening and slackening in turns like the breeze at the window. On the platform, a group of elderly women caresses the air, glides through it with soft t'ai chi movements. All ooze, this morning is, inside and outside, a symphony in slow motion. I drink a glass of water.

My apartment is simple, the product of too many moves and too little money. Ben's flat is stark, furnished only with book piles and a mattress. A home sculpted in books: nightstand and fax machine support and dinner table and bed. 'I cheated a bit on that one,' he admitted when my gaze first stumbled over his mattress, floating on a sea of books. 'There are a few bricks hidden somewhere. In strategic places.'

He stirs, smiles before his lids are fully open. The breeze whispers along my legs, plays with the hem of my shirt. His eyes, more awake now, start to softly wrangle with mine.

My eyes savour him, gently at first, getting bolder, going for the hidden places, only to be roped in by his gaze again: *You... in my Polo shirt...*

With care, I lower myself back onto the bookbed. I know the supports are there but it is hard to believe in them, hidden between a battered *Field Guide to the Flora of North America* and Yasunari Kawabata's *Thousand Cranes*. His scent reaches me and my body curls up around him, a smile made form.

There is an enlarged photograph opposite Ben's bed, the only picture in his flat. It is not the fuzzy, calendar-type butterfly poster you might expect in a bedroom, with gentle lighting and buttercups in the background. Rather, it is an almost documentary photograph, showing a creature with huge eyes and absurdly big wings.

'That's a great photograph,' I say. 'I feel like I'm dreaming. Is that me, Reini, waking up in Ben's bed? Or am I only dreaming of being Reini? Like that famous philosophical passage about the butterfly. That Laozi quote.'

'Always so complicated. Zhuangzi, you mean.' He rubs his eyes. His elbow brushes my ribs. 'That's a Tiger Swallowtail.' He studies the poster and smiles. 'I got sunburnt waiting for the right moment.' Up close, the butterfly looks leggy and intricate, revealing its beauty almost reluctantly, with its prisoner's stripes and blond, hairy body.

'Well, that's me, the difficult Cauliflower-Head girl. Always making things complicated.' I sound more peeved than I mean to and tighten my arm around him, mindless of the heat, until I feel his heartbeat.

'Flower, you mean.' Freeing himself from my embrace, he

turns around. With his index, he traces my lobe. He nibbles it, a soft, hot tickle running along the rim of my ear. He affects an expert's voice. 'Not cauliflower. Carrot.' His fingers fall into my hair, gently, and take in its feathery texture, so truly unlike cabbage. 'Have you ever seen carrots in bloom? That's your hair—carrot flowers. Mmh. *My* flower.'

He sits up, raises the hem of his T-shirt, lets it fall down again. 'Gosh, it's hot already.' Settled against the wall, his eyes half closed, he suddenly starts to recite something. '*Sik je jongjau…*' his voice lilts through the yellow morning light.

'You know it by heart.'

His eyes tease me, the pupils slightly misaligned without contact lenses. '*Lengneuih.* This is one of the most famous passages of Chinese philosophy.'

'So-rry.' I smile and dig my nose into his neck, let my carrot flower hair dig into his dark scalp. 'Sorry, Butterfly Lover.'

He laughs. 'The violin concerto. Yet another different thing.'

And so we doze and dream, shut out the world, wrap and unwrap our minds and bodies, wake again. I close my fingers around his jade amulet, so cool and smooth under my fingers, follow the scarlet ribbon around his neck.

'What is it?' I let the ivory creature fall back onto his collarbone.

'You know it.' He lifts the stone with five fingers as if to air the neck under a tight collar. 'A piece of jade.'

'But which animal is it?'

'I'm four years older than you. It's my zodiac animal.'

I pull him over with the pendant until the ribbon cuts into his neck. 'A dragon?'

'Yep, a dragon.' He covers it with his hand and leans over to kiss me. I kiss him back and after a while, the charm knocks softly against my skin, once, twice. I pull away. My eyes closed again, I explore its carving with my fingers, wish to decipher its power like a secret message. *If I don't believe in you, will you still have power over me?*

'Do you believe in it? That the jade will protect you? Like

137

those dead emperors in their jade jackets?'

'They had suits,' he corrects me. 'Almost like armours. My aunt gave it to me.'

'You don't even know yourself whether you believe in it.'

'Let's get something to eat.'

'It's beautiful,' I say. 'A very unusual colour of jade. Like milk and cinnamon.'

We go and fry eggs in his minuscule kitchen, a tangle of arms and skin, kisses and sizzling oil. The smell of hot oil reminds me of my hunger. Against the splutter of the eggs, I ask, 'Did your mother teach you to cook?'

'Do you consider fried eggs cooking?' He inspects the contents of the frying pan. 'No, we had an amah when I was a child. She had a vicious tongue and made the best turnip cake I've ever tasted. That used to be her New Year's treat.' Gently, he lifts one of the eggs, surveys the underside. 'She must have been over ninety when she died. She was already ancient when she came to us and about half my size.' With the spatula, he paints her into the air, a tiny Cantonese woman with a huge bun.

'After she retired, she would still pay her respects to my parents at Chinese New Year, for years.' He turns off the gas. 'I'm sure she would have something to say about my egg frying technique.'

I look at the eggs, flat yellow-white disks, remember their fragile smooth roundness in my hands only moments ago. How things change their shapes and meaning. I kiss the ribbon on his neck. 'Mmh, the kitchen is so small.' I smile.

'I only wear it for my aunt. Careful.' Balancing the pan in one hand, he squeezes past me.

Night and day become entwined, curl up in bliss and forgiveness.

Moon Three Day Twenty-six
Sunday 23 April

My head in Ben's lap, his fingers on my face, we are dozing on my bed, with smells and thoughts and feelings that keep breaking into my conscience and erasing themselves like waves on a beach: our visit to Shek O today, perfunctory really, an excuse almost; the journey to my flat, our steps acquiring more and more urgency until we almost broke into a run—

My phone shrills into the silence. Virginia, who seems to be whispering on top of a bad connection. But I get the gist of it: that I am never at home, that my phone is always turned off, that—

'I can't hear you,' I say. 'You have to speak louder.'

'I can't. I'm… hospital. You have to help me. You work for a medical NGO. Can you come?' Even with my addled brain, I can feel how she is willing me from asking what this is all about.

'What's this about?' I blurt out. My blood sister. When has she ever asked for help? I walk over to the window, stare into my neighbours' flats, breathe in a gulp of noisy, traffic-stricken air. My heart is beating furiously now as if to catch up with the stolen rest. Ominously. Whatever it is, I have to do it because I am a foreign ghost, a *gwailou*, a fox girl.

Her medieval beauty, again. Around Virginia's neck, the moxibustion marks so familiar by now wind along the skin, a dark string of bruises the size and colour of plums. More wakeful nights, more body parts out of order with sorrow and worry. Like love bites, they are. Quickly, I touch my unmarred neck as if to ensure that my secret is safe. Her mother in comparison looks innocuous, still and pale in her hospital bed.

The sight of her mother, her personality fading between the hospital sheets, causes something in me to flare up. 'For heaven's sake, what have you been thinking? She needs medical care. And if you want to bring her home, you need to have her properly dismissed. How are we supposed to move her, IV and all?' And yet I know that to make her mother more of herself again, we need to bring her home.

'I've asked John to come.' Virginia cowers at the sound of my voice, her eyes huge and dark, the shadows underneath a bruised purple. Purple like mangosteens. Another thought to push away.

Brisk steps approach from the corridor.

'Quick.' She shoves me into a chair, jumps into the second one and pulls a visitor's smile into place. The door opens and a nurse comes in, glances at the full drip and Virginia's mother.

'Everything alright?' she asks nobody in particular.

'Everything alright.' Virginia's voice trembles but the nurse is already on her way out.

Her smile falls apart as soon as we are alone. The door opens again and a doctor comes in, white-coated, white-capped, his face half hidden by a mask. 'Ah John!' Her hand flies to her mouth.

The face mask breaks into folds. Above the cellulose fabric, the eyes smile. 'Dr Ngai, please.'

'What on earth is this?' I gape at the two of them. 'John? He's a dentist, for God's sake. You should have brought Ronda.'

'It's her day off.' She is already busy emptying the contents of the nightstand into her mother's handbag.

John steps closer to the bed, takes in Virginia's mother. '*Guma.*' He lowers himself onto the mattress. Careful not to upset the drip, he strokes the back of her hand. Her lids flutter and he closes his palms around her fingers.

'Do you want to go home?' he asks, almost inaudibly, although we are alone with her in the room. On the sheets, his hand still holds hers, his thumb circling softly. 'Even if we can only ease your pain, not give you treatment? Have you thought about it?'

Next to me, I sense Virginia stiffen in the middle of her sorting. There must be a minute change in her mother's face that suffices for John, because suddenly he says, 'Alright then.' Only when he wants to get up do I understand: finger by finger, he has to pry himself loose from her grip.

With quick movements, he pulls out another coat from a plastic bag, drops it onto the bed. 'For you,' he says to Virginia and breaks into a grin. 'Nurse Ngai.'

She picks up the coat and buries her nose in it. When she looks up again, she gives a nervous giggle and pulls a face. 'It does smell like at the dentist's.'

There is a knock at the door, a hammering sound. We freeze, a white-clad doctor in a hospital full of green smocks and two visitors well past visiting hours. 'Let me in!' A woman's voice rings out. The hammering increases. 'I want to come in! I waant…' Her Cantonese becomes difficult for me to understand and turns into wailing. I open the door and look into a tear-stained face framed by grey wisps of thinning hair. Her pupils are milky with age and the top of her pyjamas is unbuttoned, revealing the sagging half moon of a breast.

My whiteness makes her start, brings her into the present. 'Who are you?'

I nod to John and Virginia. 'You go ahead. I'll bring her back.'

The woman's mind is slipping again and she shuffles on my arm to her room without complaint. When I pass the nurse's station on my way back, she nods. 'Thank you.'

At the periphery of my vision, a door opens, followed by rubbery squeaking. 'Nurse,' I say and lift my hand to my temples, 'I have a terrible headache. Would you have something for me?' She assesses me, then trudges to a cabinet in the back and returns with a paracetamol. 'And get some rest,' she says, 'visiting hours are over.'

When I come back into the room, they are all gone, John, Virginia, and her mother. And the bed. Only her belongings are left and, with reluctance, I pack them into the little suitcase I find in the cabinet: ointment against bunions and peppermint mouthwash, her tent-like underwear and a spare nightgown.

I bump into them downstairs as they roll the bed out of the neighbouring lift, a very jumpy nurse in whites that are much too large for her and her more assured looking colleague. Virginia's mother looks tiny in her bed, shrunk with fatigue and oblivious to the fancy dress party staged only for her.

'Emergency exit,' Virginia calls out, her cap falling over her brows.

'The taxi stand,' John barks, the face mask muffling his words.

'An ambulance,' I say and feel ridiculous the moment the words have left my mouth.

The corridor to the exit feels endless, the whining of the hospital bed's wheels much too loud, the creaking of the suitcase on the linoleum too conspicuous. Outside it is pouring, a warm deluge that makes communication almost impossible, rain thundering onto the roof while we wait for a taxi to glide into the curb. Like a young monkey, our charge clings to her daughter's back when we lift her up. Then, Virginia lowers her mother into John's arms and together, they place her into the car like a child.

When we have settled Virginia's mother in her own bed, Virginia disappears into the bathroom. Sounds of rushing water emerge and then quiet. I hunch down on her mother's little suitcase, not yet unpacked in the corner. She is lying motionless, tightly wound around hurt or exhaustion. Just when I want to leave her alone, John returns. He seems oblivious to me, so still in the semi-darkness, and sets down a metal basin on the rosewood nightstand, a reddish dishcloth floating in it. '*Guma*, this will do you good.' With gentle movements, he fishes the cloth out of the bowl, wrings out the surplus water and anoints her forehead. 'Is the temperature okay?'

Quiet moaning emerges in intervals from the bathroom now, interrupted by the opening of the tap.

'Aggh. Ommh.' Virginia's mother focuses on some inner pain but the corners of her mouth shift a few degrees. Upwards. John continues, talking in that birdlike quality that whispered Cantonese can acquire. Ben sounds the same in certain moments and I have to look away from this nephew and his aunt, my eyes burning, my heart raw like meat on market days in the sun. Something poison green rises inside me, like bile. And then the anti-poison: *You shall not covet*.

John finishes with the dishcloth and drapes it over the bowl's rim. As if struck by an idea, he picks it up again and looks furtively around. When he discovers me, he gives a start and averts his gaze at once. He crouches down and lifts the bedspread. Giving off soft puffs, he winds the dishcloth around the left leg of the bed and ties it into a knot. He gets up, wipes his hands on his trousers and pulls the corner of the bedspread back into shape. With a gentle swoosh, it falls over the leg with its improvised protective flag, effortlessly hides its scarlet secret.

Back in the living-room, I wait for Virginia to say goodbye. The bathroom has quietened down. A click is followed by darkness. She comes out, lids fringed pink, her face scrubbed clean of make-up.

'She's asleep now.' Unconsciously, I whisper. 'Where's your father?'

'Kim.' She looks around for her glasses, puts them on with that gesture I know so well. Fingertipped. Behind the glasses, her eyes are earnest. 'Thank you. I don't know how we would have done it. The rain, her things, the nurses...' She touches my hand.

'No problem,' I say and yawn, my limbs suddenly very heavy.

Her fingers around my wrist tighten. 'You must not tell the neighbours,' she says. 'Absolutely not.'

I smile uneasily. 'Why should I? No problem.'

'Not anybody.' Her hands leave my arm but my flesh still throbs from her grip.

I nod.

'My mother beseeched us to bring her home. The doctors wouldn't let her go. And— It's just not done.' Her face shines with determination, a force that pushes through the quickly growing dusk.

I nod again, more slowly. 'But isn't this up to the patient to decide?'

'She's getting afraid of the hospital, of operations.' Her arms wander to her glasses, make a tiny adjustment as if to see me more clearly, but looks to the side. 'It's important to—to go intact into the next world. And people would be afraid if they knew somebody was... somebody so sick was staying at home. The

143

neighbours.'

I remember the temple complex in Taipingshan we visited. And Sago Street in Singapore. A whole street dedicated to the business of death, furnishing last care for the dying and wakes and funeral rites for those passed away. Because the truth is this: so scared are people of death that the sick leave their houses to die, or used to, in the past. To spare the surviving the pollution of death.

'Kim?'

I take her in as if for the first time. Her capacity for harbouring fear I knew but this is something else. The willingness to live with terror, to shelter it in her home. Never before have I smelled valiance, this mix of cold sweat and tired breath and rubbing alcohol.

'You won't tell anybody, right?' Her face, so luminous moments ago, has disappeared in the darkness, leaving only the up and down of her voice. The daytime amah left because of fear, it comes back to me, and I wish I could touch Virginia's face, explore it like Ben did with mine only hours ago.

'I promise,' I say. Not sure what kind of pledge I am making but welcoming the secret between us, equal parts shadow and light.

The metal grille clangs and, in the tense quiet of the flat, all of us jump. With a fluid movement, the entrance door opens and we blink into the sudden light, Virginia extending one arm towards the sofa for support, John standing in the kitchen door, myself firming my grip on the air conditioning remote control.

Virginia's father blinks, takes in our odd threesome in his flat at this time of the day. A bunch of rolled paintings sticks out of his bag.

'Why are you standing here in the dark?' He looks uncertainly at his daughter. His eyes fall on a pair of house shoes in the middle of the floor, beaded and with a slight heel. One of the beads has come loose and a lonely pearl shimmers on the dark wooden floor.

'So you did bring her back.' His words sound harsh, unadorned but his voice is quiet.

144

Virginia's head is bowed, her gaze fixed onto her mother's slippers, lost on our hasty trajectory across the living-room. I try to become invisible and watch him kick off his shoes in silence.

Her father shakes water from his umbrella and shatters it in a single swing, tearing it open until it turns over, distorted, and falls trembling into a corner.

'Shh,' John says, his hand reaching for the door frame once more.

Barefoot, her father tiptoes across the living-room, his upper body inflated with all he must hold back. My eyes go to his feet, *such a shame*, I hear Virginia again in my mind, but his toenails only look yellowed, his feet almost like a woman's in their thinness.

'She's asleep,' John's voice hurries after him.

The toes shift, search for better grip and even in the ashen light of the corridor I sense how his whole body exhales, assembles differently. An emptied out shadow, he stands there, listening to the even breathing of his wife, while the seconds tick by in the darkening flat. His shoulders gel again into their familiar shape, gather brightness and substance as he retreats from the bedroom door and walks towards his eldest daughter.

'I wanted her to stay in hospital. To do everything to get better,' he says. He walks over to the ruined umbrella and picks it up. 'Like the doctors said. Only her best, everything for her best.'

He gives the umbrella a slight shake, handling it like a foreign object. 'Like the doctors, who could never get her to sleep. Thank you.' He hides his face in its wet folds. When he looks up again, his features glisten and start to tremble. Suddenly, he convulses with toneless sobs.

After a while, his voice starts to form a word out of the sobs. Again and again he repeats it and I feel it accumulate meaning and momentum until it brings my heart to a grinding halt: *Haausun*. That most Chinese of praises, the axis around which the world revolves. Filial piety. A dutiful daughter. For a second time today, Virginia makes my heart bloom.

Moon Three Day Twenty-seven
Monday 24 April

Carefully stepping over the ghost sill, I enter Ben's kitchen, feeling around for the switch. A lightness runs over my naked feet, something tickling. I jump. 'Oops!'

When the bluish white lights flare up, the shadow flits into a dark corner under the sink. He must be the father of all cockroaches, shining and broad-backed. The king of Ben's phone-booth sized kitchen. A rustle of newspaper from next room. 'You alright?'

'Just a cockroach,' I yell back. I take off my flip-flop and crouch on the floor. There. The shadow moves again. I wait. He waits. *I know that he exists/Somewhere, in silence.*

'Don't kill it!' Standing in the doorframe, Ben darkens the space under the sink even more.

'I can't see anything.'

'Let me—'

'I can do it. Let me do it.'

'No, don't kill it.'

'Ben.' I get up, feel blood rush into my legs. 'You're the biologist. How many eggs does a cockroach lay?'

'That's not a reason to kill it.'

'In Khartoum—'

He squeezes into the room and extracts the flip-flop from my fingers. With a thud, it lands in the corridor. 'What in Khartoum?'

'Nothing,' I say. The cold of the kitchen tiles bleeds into my back. 'Have you ever had one of those cockroach blooms in your flat? I once helped a friend move out her furniture and clean to get rid of them. We stopped counting after one hundred and thirty-seven.'

'Maybe we'll catch it alive.'

I stare at him. 'Is that what you always do? Catch cockroaches? And then what? Set them free in front of the

146

neighbour's flat?'

He blushes. 'The trick is to avoid them from the start.'

I give him a frown. 'Do you do it for… research purposes? Catch insects alive?' Once more, my eyes pierce the darkness. 'Maybe it's a male,' I say. 'Then you can let him go.'

'And let him spawn dozens of descendants.' He laughs against his will. 'We'd need an entomologist for that. I can't tell a male cockroach apart from a female, not just like that.'

The shadow moves again.

'You better should. Given as you are to breeding them.' I crouch down and lift my remaining flip-flop, only to feel his hand around my wrist. I sigh. *'T is an instant's play/ 'T is a fond ambush.* Clumsily, we get up, hips and elbows brushing against each other, against the sink. He takes a half step back, is stopped by the wall. Raises his lids, searches my eyes with his. Chestnut coloured, they are, very similar to mine in this light.

'Reini.' He lifts the dishwashing sponge, squeezes it to a dry, squeaky echo, puts it down again. 'All life is sacred.' Wiping his hands on his trousers, he turns to go back into the living-room, his broad back filling the door frame almost to the seams.

'Sorry,' I say, following him.

For the rest of the day, we ignore the subject. In my heart, Emily, exploding: *Would not the jest/ Have crawled too far?*

Cockroaches are noiseless, they make their home without you noticing, unlike mice, who sooner or later reveal themselves by sounds or droppings. Later, I lie on Ben's bookbed with its discarded field guides and wait for their silent onslaught. In Sudan, where few lives were sacred, we feared mice. Friendly mammals, they seem now in comparison with the cockroaches, although I know their deadly potential for storage rooms in a hungry country. Next to me in the dark, almost touching, Ben breathes into the quiet. How I have unlearned to see him as a stranger, with his aniseed skin still lodged under my fingernails from our last fond ambush.

Moon Four Day One
Friday 28 April

We almost form a small crowd on the doorstep to the Ngai's flat; three relatives who are leaving under noisy goodbyes just as I arrive. If the family ever meant to keep her mother's illness a secret, the visitors will have revealed it by now. Whenever I ring Virginia these days, there is somebody visiting: John, an aunt, the wife of Second Uncle. I used to think that we're both on our own, Virginia and I, but now I see how different our alonenesses are.

Ronda leads me into the living-room, where Virginia's father is absorbed in a TV show. After the heat outside, the cold tickles my skin. The sight of a window wiper in Ronda's hand reminds me of our shared secret. It is one of the secrets that are secret secrets: I know about her and I know that she knows about me. But we don't know about each other. We both fear heights, Ronda and I.

She follows my gaze and laughs. 'The birds,' she says. 'The windows get dirty, with the cages on the balcony. Miss Virginia will be here in a moment,' she adds, 'she's in the shower.'

Ronda leaves for the kitchen and I feel the togetherness between Virginia's father and me close in on us. But he is smiling, a plate with grapes next to him on his rosewood armchair. 'Ah, you're here to work with Virginia. Take a seat.'

It is difficult for me not to stare at the bedroom door behind which his wife is dying. His eyes trail my gaze. 'She's sleeping,' he says softly. 'She's sleeping most of the time now.' He plucks a grape from the bunch, weighs it in his hands. His clouded eyes focus mine. 'I like to sit with her, watch her sleep.' He opens his mouth for the fruit, chin trembling, and sucks it, the swallowing setting the folds along his neck into gentle shivers.

I slink back into the kitchen to chat with Ronda. 'You look a bit under the weather.'

'I was up last night, with old Ma'am.'

I take a big gulp of ice water. 'They're lucky to have you.'

'If we forget that this is all illegal up to here.' She grins. 'No, I like to work with old people. They don't talk back very much.' She studies her chopping board. 'If they can talk back.' She looks up again. 'And here, I have a room for myself.'

'A broom cabinet, you mean.'

She laughs. 'At my former family, before Mrs Sze, with the twins, we were five people. Five people in a four-hundred square foot flat. And the *pohpo* was staying with us, all the time.' She starts to peel an onion, her vigorous movements suggesting a stern mother-in-law.

'So how is she doing?' I lean against the counter where a cake is setting. 'This looks delicious.'

'Hanging on,' she says, frowning at the onion she is dicing. 'Kind of.'

'You get to see a lot in your—line of work.'

She looks at me. 'It is not easy sometimes, no. To see her mother like this. But Virginia's family, they are good people. Her father, worried all the time, and they stick together. Not like some other families.' Her slicing acquires speed. 'A friend of mine, she used to work for that family with the chicken. The famous one.'

'You mean, the old lady who kept a rooster in her flat? The case that was in all the papers?'

'Yes, that one. Because her husband's soul had gone into the rooster.' She rolls her eyes. 'It was crazy! My friend got tired of the reporters, always hanging around the house.'

'Our religion also must seem crazy to outsiders,' I say. 'All that blood-drinking and body-eating.' I blush.

'But our dead, they don't fill the house with chicken shit. And the feathers, everywhere!'

I laugh. 'If your friend doesn't like cleaning, she should come to Germany. Our most famous cleaner worked in a museum. There was this piece of art, an arrangement with butter by Beuys. Very famous, very expensive. The janitor thought it was rubbish and cleaned it away.'

Ronda laughs so hard a piece of onion shoots out of her hands. It lands on the cream cake where it slowly disappears under the surface. We both stop laughing and stare at the cake's topping, hiding an ugly surprise without effort.

We are still giggling when Virginia appears in the doorframe. 'What's so funny? Sorry for keeping you waiting.' She fiddles with a plastic bag on the counter and lifts out two takeaway cups, her elbow almost brushing the cake.

Following her into the living-room, I mention the rooster's widow and tell her about the Beuys.

'Really? *Ah Ba*, herbal tea from downstairs. For your appetite.' She sets the drink onto a placemat. 'Here, most people would have fired him. Would you like to try the herbal tea?' She stops in mid-movement. 'You know, I think the woman—the one with the rooster—I don't think she is a real widow.'

'Can't do any harm,' I say and pass her my empty water glass. The tea tastes of liquorice and aniseed and two or three more mysterious ingredients. 'You mean, she's making all of this up? As an excuse to keep chickens in her flat?'

'No.' Virginia pulls a tissue out of the box on the table and wipes up the ring of moisture around her tea cup. 'I think the rooster is her ghost husband. This kind of thing used to be fairly common. Ghost weddings, I mean.'

'Ghost weddings?'

'Sometimes, somebody dies young, without a spouse. Maybe engaged to be married. Then, the person can turn into an unhappy ghost, causing trouble. Then you can arrange a wedding with another person who died without a spouse.'

'A wedding between two ghosts?'

'It could also be a wedding between a living person and a dead one,' her father interjects, hardly looking up from the television.

'Yes,' Virginia says. 'I think that is what happened with her. Maybe they were engaged and then he died. A white rooster is used in the wedding ceremony, that's what made me think of it. Although I have never heard of anybody living with it afterwards.'

Her father speaks up again. 'That's because, traditionally, the animal would be killed during the ceremony.' He sips cold tea, smacking his lips.

I take another swig, try to ignore its bitter aftertaste, all subtle notes gone. Chinese medicine, disguised as food, and, as usual, I do not know what to make of it. Or is it food disguised as medicine? My eyes fall on a scarlet card lying next to the tissue box. 'Oh, a double happiness card.'

Virginia flips it open, in a movement that looks as if she wanted to inspect herself in a pocket mirror. 'That's my cousin, Carrie. We overlapped for a year at university.' She drops the invitation back onto the table. 'It's on the 13th,' she whispers. 'The wedding. In two weeks.'

As if in slow motion, her father lifts himself up from the armchair, the heaviness of his movements belying his angular, emaciated body. 'I'm going to sit for a while with your mother.' He is steadying himself against the back of the chair when his gaze falls onto the invitation. 'Carrie getting married.' He sighs. 'My youngest niece.'

He plucks up the card and turns to Virginia. 'And you, attending your "little sister's" wedding. You, an unmarried elder.'

Virginia's stillness speaks of practice, a well-rehearsed way of turning herself inwards, of oiling her surface.

'Don't you feel ashamed?' The card cuts through the air as the words fall between them. 'What will people think of me, sixty-eight years of age and only one granddaughter.' His voice rises. 'In Vancouver.'

'Not so loud.'

'And if she hears us, so what? You make your mother unhappy.'

Her features are stitched up, a carefully closed tightness speaking of a wound underneath. I force myself to look away.

'How can I go and attend yet another wedding?' His face darkens and the paper in his hands brushes against the armchair with an angry swish.

'Shh, you'll wake her up.'

'My daughter, ignoring all I ever taught her.'

Virginia pulls the card out of his grip. When she speaks, her voice quavers. 'Maybe you won't have to attend that wedding after all. Is that what you want?' She rips the card into two, with

151

a dexterity that is almost beautiful.

God, make her mother wake up and call for somebody. Make Ronda come in with a snack. Make a neighbour ring the doorbell. Instead we stand there, frozen in three different stillnesses while the bitterness between us grows. A jingle blares into the room, reminding me of the TV. My whole body feels sticky with sweat. I extend my hand for the drink and let it sink again at the sight of the brownish liquid inside. My fingers ache. I must have clenched them without noticing. On the table, the remains of the invitation shiver in the air conditioning's breeze. Two single happinesses do not always make one double happiness.

'Ma'am, what time for dinner?' Ronda emerges from the bedroom, a thermometer in hand, and for a moment I struggle to reconcile her formality with our laughter in the kitchen. She glances at each of us, tries to make sense of the hot quiet around us. Virginia's father is hunched in his armchair, his breath wheezing, the corners of his eyes glistening. Virginia is bent over him, massaging his shoulders. She looks up, her face sealed, or empty. 'Whenever. Kim and I have work to do.'

Ronda nods. Like a Möbius strip, she embodies two seamless sides, an unflinching willingness to be happy and the humility she needs for it. I give a start. Doesn't Virginia embody two seamless sides as well, though of a different nature? Only much later do I remember the cake and wonder what she did with it; Ronda, this professional keeper of secrets.

Remorse is memory awake. At night, in my cosmically misaligned bed, listening to the air conditioner banging away as it whips the steaming night air, I examine my remorse, *a presence of departed acts / At window and at door.* And the acts that never were but might be. The memory of Virginia, being put to shame, and me doing nothing. For can I want to free her, battle her beliefs with alien medicine, only to shackle her mother? Her mother, who wants to die with the consolation that her daughter will look after her, in death as she does in life, imperfect as a daughter's ministrations may be. Do I want that, let death part them?

There are things which I refuse to believe but still I lie, baking with remorse in my bed. Slowly, too slowly, my thoughts disintegrate with fatigue, collect words on the fringes of my consciousness like flotsam after a storm. *The complement of hell.* Her husband's *cockiness. Bitter tea.* Before I can mould all this into a coherent thought, I fall asleep.

The Beginning of Summer
Friday 5 May

My favourite waiter at the Beijing restaurant killed himself. I only know the bare facts, that his wife died after a long illness so protracted it ate up all the family savings, and that he drowned himself afterwards, but so incredible is his act that it fuels my imagination until I see it clearly in my mind:

One day he cleaned his room, wrote a note in his calligraphy marked by years of jotting down orders for noodles and desserts, and went into the bathroom. He fetched the pail hanging there for water shortages (although the time for water shortages in Hong Kong was long gone) and filled it with water from the shower. He then went back into his room, lit some incense and placed it carefully into the old sand-filled Quaker Oats tin reserved for these purposes. He knelt down in front of his parents' pictures and bowed three times. Then, he went into the bathroom, put his head into the pail and drowned himself.

Moon Four Day Nine
Saturday 6 May

Never again will I hear the waiter's banter while he takes our unchanging orders of vegetable dumplings and *shaobing*. Never again will I listen to him singing Chinese opera, stifled renditions for my ears only, while he is handing out napkins. How this city is able to disguise desperation. I run my hands over the tiles in my bathroom, their tacky, old-fashioned pinkness cold under my hands even in this heat.

In bed, my minty gums suggesting mornings, beginnings, I pull the sheets over my ears only to kick them away at once. 'It's hot.'

'Hmmh.' Ben wets his index and turns a page of his photography magazine.

I lie still for a while, stare at the ceiling with its memories of mould. Heat rises from my body and settles around me. I breathe in. Out. Around my ankles, the sheets form a graceless, suffocating pile. I give them another kick. 'Mind if I turn on the aircon?'

'No, leave it.'

With another sigh, I turn to the wall, roll myself into a ball. Behind me, the magazine flutters to the ground and the light clicks off. The mattress heaves and Ben's fingers tickle my neck, work slowly along my knobbly spine, a gentle warmth running up my back. He whispers, 'What's the matter?'

When my eyes can make out the tangle of clothes behind the door, I say, 'That waiter killed himself. At the Beijing restaurant.'

'*Ah* Lei?'

'Mmh.'

The fingers stop. I unroll myself and turn. It used to be Ben's restaurant. Ben's restaurant and Ben's favourite waiter. In the dim light, my hands frame his face, smother his scalp, the bristles tickling my skin. I feel for his fingers, wrap them in mine. 'He drowned himself. In a pail.' Under my palms, his hands sag, leave

154

me. He sits up and fumbles around in the dark, throwing something to the floor with a thud. In the sudden light, his legs pale against his shorts, he looks smaller than minutes ago, his hand shading his eyes as if to see me better from a distance.

I rise. 'I'll get us a glass of water.'

When I come back, he is still slumped, his face resting on raised knees, his fingers toying with the fraying edge of the sheet.

'What will happen to him?' I ask, the memory of being chosen by *Ah* Lei itching on my skin. Forcing myself to hear an uncomfortable truth. My head leans into Ben's shoulder, nudges him. I rub his thigh.

'Don't you believe that he will go to heaven?' He doesn't look at me as he says this. He frowns at his toenails.

And so we have a suicide lurking in our love-making as if the two were somehow related.

Moon Four Day Ten
Sunday 7 May

More toothpaste, and as usual, it tastes truer to me in the mornings, the confidence it inspires. Downstairs, the t'ai chi women are stirring the soupy air already, carefully cutting through the hot density of the morning. My mouth bulging with the toothbrush, I walk through my flat, tidying up, throwing things into my backpack. Ben's arms stop me, envelop me, and I feel his voice warm on my neck. 'Another hug before you rush off. Or two.'

I snuggle closer, lean into the smell of shaving cream still lingering on his skin, until my nose prickles and I have to dash off into the bathroom to empty my mouth. Over the running water, I hear him ask, 'What's that hike again today?'

Back in the living-room, my hands still dripping, I say, 'From the Peak down to Aberdeen. And there's a family barbecue in the evening to which she invited me. Her cousin is getting married.' I never know why Virginia asks me along to her family affairs, whether it is to let me partake of Cantonese family life or to shield her from her relatives.

Bent over his backpack, fiddling with his camera strap, Ben asks, 'Why do you never take me along? To your friend's outings. The hikes.'

I reach for the blinds, disentangle a knot in the strings. Downstairs, the emptiness on the platform is growing as the women are leaving. 'Would you like that?'

He lowers the camera. 'What's the matter? You've been... odd lately. Rushing off to your friend's that Sunday evening. After... our weekend. You never told me what that was about.'

I promised. So young is he in my life and already splicing the new from the normal. I do not know what scares me more, the way he sees through me or how he can live with it.

'Do you think I don't notice these things? Getting all worked up about the suicide of that waiter. Reini.' His gaze shifts back and forth, falls away. 'You're a medical NGO. Theoretically, at least. Does this have anything to do with drugs? Medication? Are you helping her mother in some way?'

'No,' I say. 'It's... nothing of that sort.' I walk towards the table, drop my sunglasses into my bag. 'I promised Virginia not to tell but it's not what you think.' I close the zip on my bag and look up. 'Big Boy Scout promise.'

For an instant, his shoulders soften. He nudges the small Arab carpet in front of my sofa with his toes, rearranges the tassels. 'Sometimes I feel that I don't know you at all.' His foot traces the oriental pattern.

Apart from my skin under his fingers, venerated molecule by molecule. I lower my head, pick up a lens from his camera. If I were to use it to observe him, what would I see, a truth or a distortion?

He gets up from the sofa and takes a few steps, is stopped by the confines of the room. 'You never told me the whole Sudan story. You avoid it. And now your friend—'

'Virginia,' I say. 'I got transferred here from Khartoum, I told you. Why is that so important?'

'Sent away,' he says, 'you got sent away, is that it?'

I turn to face him. Outside, the morning is bright, casting his face in shadow. I nod.

In my hand, the camera lens is heavy. Carefully, I set the precious weight down. 'I didn't really see myself in Asia and with working migrants.' As if he didn't know the truth, my new love. It feels long ago, my desertion of Sudan and the people I used to know there. Only the punishment still has a sting to it; their absence doesn't hurt anymore.

'So, do you regret it? Cut-throat capitalism and all?'

'Tell me, what do you know about Sudan?'

He feels for the window behind his back, his hands flat against the glass. He glances at me and produces his words carefully. 'It's… a conflict area. With different sides involved, I'm not quite sure who. Parties with different kinds of interests. Oil, ethnic strife, I guess.'

'Yes, different kinds of interests,' I say. 'And you know what? The worst thing was to discover that the NGOs and aid workers also have an interest in it, in the crisis.' Plenty of time to read during the rainy season at the rate of an international salary. Quickly, I continue, 'Of course nobody likes to see the lines of children queuing up for injections.' Thin like evening shadows, they had been, their bodies elongated like plants striving towards the light. 'But the refugee industry feeds the population movements, at least in part. The camps have water. Water and food. And if you think about it, these are the things that the nomads have always migrated for. I said something to that effect which was reported in public.'

'And that integrity was not honoured?'

'Fouling your own nest?'

'That was brave of you,' he says.

His trust hurts more than the truth, this journalistic gift to make the private public. And Fatimah, her hand always on her abdomen. Suddenly, I cannot endure it any longer, his blindness. 'There was something else,' I say. 'Something more complicated. I told you, about the "going native" thing. It was about a local

157

woman. Helping her. It had nothing to do with getting involved with a local. It would be lunacy, to have a Muslim boyfriend under the Sharia. They're all married, anyway.'

I raise my head, force myself to look into his eyes only to quickly avert my gaze. 'I made it possible for a girl to get an abortion.'

Against the light, his face is unreadable, a moon seen from the dark side.

'I recommended her to a Japanese doctor who helped local women. Another aid worker.' Oh Akiko. Working with goodwill and electricity shortages and never enough painkillers. Battling death with death, same with same.

'An abortion?'

'She was our cook's second cousin.'

He stares out of the window, his back turned on me. The silence between us is hardening quickly.

'I would never have thought that... Thought that, of myself,' I say to the back. 'And we are a Christian organisation and don't condone abortion. Nor do the Muslims. So that's why I got sent away.'

The back remains still.

'It's not what you think,' I say. 'She was married. She had been raped by a gang of former soldiers. Like the Niggaz in the south. She could have been stoned for it. For adultery.'

'Is that another tribe?' His voice is very low. 'Another of your sunrise-in-the-desert tribes?'

'No, they're gangs of youth who terrorise people, commit robberies and rape. Against IDPs even, people living in camps where they're supposedly safe.' What a distortion of Islam they had been, the camps, with their fake hospitality, dependent males and alcohol-fuelled, pornography-induced violence against women.

I join him in front of the window, keeping all the distance that the space allows. My forehead sags against the windowpane. 'That was so sickening, to see that you cannot protect people. They have to leave the camps to search for firewood. She could have been blamed for it.'

'So you figured it would be better to have a baby killed rather than her.' Against the glass, his voice sounds flat.

'Her and the baby. If she had been stoned, two would have died instead of one. Does that make it any better for you?' I turn to him, want him to look at me. My throat is very hot and much too tight for all the feelings.

'And how often does this happen?'

'It does happen,' I say, stepping away. 'The whole thing blew rather out of proportion because a foreign journalist caught up on it. And then suddenly, Fatimah wasn't pregnant any more.'

'A foreign journalist?'

Too late, my hand seals my lips. When I swallow, everything hurts, my throat, my ears, my chest.

'So you were sent here because of that story. An *abortion racket.*'

'That's not true! *Ben*, that's not what it was! Ben. I only ever talked with one woman.'

In silence, we let the seconds roll by.

'They needed somebody here anyway,' I say.

Without looking at me, he reaches down to put on his trainers. The grated door falls shut behind him.

'She was very thin,' I call out to him through the door grille as he makes his way to the lift, the metal cold under my fingers. 'Malnourished. Most likely she would have lost the child anyway.'

With a ping, the lift opens. For a moment, Ben hesitates. Finally, he looks me in the face. Thinned, his eyes seem, filled with too much liquid. And very big. He lifts a hand in an undecided greeting. 'Bye.'

Higher and higher I fly, suspended from the laws of earthbound forces, only to fall, seconds later, into a jumping sheet. In a game that seems much too young for those present, we play at fire, Virginia's family and I. A distant cousin who is a fireman in the New Territories has brought the sheet along, a piece of equipment that was mustered out because of the technological progress in fire-fighting but which is still serviceable for a game on the beach. Under my left elbow, the sea blue horizon is greying quickly but when I turn my head I see their laughing faces in a whirl of dark hair against blond sand, anticipating my fall with a smooth catch.

'Enough,' I yell, exhilarated yet ready to exchange my upside-down sky for a solid view of the world. There is some well-meaning laughter, a bit of coaxing, and then it is Virginia's turn. Seeing her on the life net, arms and legs extended like a water bug, it strikes me how rarely I see her let go. Never, really. I burn this image of her into my mind, rising and falling at the hands of her family, hair flying, losing herself in a happy, senseless game.

Later, blood bubbling, we walk back to the barbecue pit where the male half of the clan is busy shrouding fish in foil, spearing crabs onto sticks, embalming meat with barbecue honey.

'I hardly know anybody,' I say to Virginia, trying to detect familiar faces in the cluster surrounding the fire. 'Apart from John, of course.' He had winked at me when he discovered me and I had retorted 'Good evening, Dr. Ngai.'

'That's because of Carrie's family,' she says. Her voice reveals nothing, reminding me all the more forcefully of her father's mood now that Carrie's wedding is approaching. She has stopped mentioning her mother. 'Your place,' she had suggested when we met for our last session and I snatched up a pair of Ben's socks, forgotten behind my bedroom door, just in time.

Hunger is starting to hum in my body, but there is only the empty scent of burning coal and no food yet. It reminds me of the many fires I've witnessed on pavements and roadsides, ashy greetings to the Hungry Ghosts. 'Don't you ever get tired of outings? Aren't you secretly yearning for a cool, quiet evening in front of the TV?'

'Family is different,' she says. 'No index cards, no overweight Americans who're not accustomed to walking or Germans with self-important questions.' She sends me a sideways glance with a smile.

'Are you a vegetarian?' A brush against my arm makes me turn. Spiky hair, short like a boy's, surrounding a very feminine face.

'This is my younger sister, Rebecca,' Virginia introduces her. The individual components of their faces are almost the same but Virginia's frown, etched into her forehead, hems in her features where Rebecca's only look delicate. No wonder Virginia has a hard time defining herself against this sweet-faced girlboy. Rebecca is passing around Vietnamese spring rolls.

Two children loiter nearby, eying us or the food. Virginia extends her arms and catches them, the girl a headful of pink braided antennae, the boy all bones and limbs in a pair of oversized shorts and a Spiderman T-shirt. 'Tina is Rebecca's,' she says. 'Go and speak Cantonese with this foreign auntie. And get rid of your Vancouver accent while you're at it.' She gives the girl a playful shove. The children giggle.

Carrie joins us, beaming. 'Virginia has promised us a wedding city tour.' She extends her hand for a spring roll. 'Hong Kong's secret romantic places.'

'A city honeymoon,' her fiancé adds.

'*Waa*! Sweet as barbecue honey,' John says into the widening circle of relatives.

Back and forth, they banter, flinging their observations with well-practised moves, while my otherness grows, along with my fatigue from hunger, too much rapid-fire Cantonese and too many strange faces.

'Here, take.' Somebody—the wife of Second Uncle?—forces a grilled shrimp into my mouth. I smile, nod, chew, swallow, all at the same time, the shells of the shrimp like plastic in my mouth, its crispy saltiness overlaid with the smoky flavour of the fire. I feel staggeringly out of place. Maybe that is the whole point. Next to my angular, white otherness, Virginia fits perfectly. *Think of her father, his legs thin like clothes hangers. Think of her mother, dying quietly behind shut doors.*

'Eh, Kim, do you know any nice men?' In the sudden quiet, a dozen dark heads turn towards me.

'Somebody extra-special for Virginia?' John asks, a couple of skewers poised in mid-air.

'Yes, it's high time we got to drink her wedding wine,' another cousin chimes in.

161

At the sight of the men with their innocuous faces, their barbecue implements piercing the evening sky like Stone Age weapons, something in me snaps. 'Do you know about her age group, of all the women who cannot marry? You know why? Because—' I drop my gaze, careful not to cross them with my eyes— 'because of all the Hong Kong men who marry women from the mainland. They're financially less demanding, more compliant. Or so I'm told. Besides,' I swallow air, my stomach still churning, 'who says that she wants to get married?'

John looks concerned. 'Virginia does not want to get married?'

Somehow, I cannot stop myself. 'Women today can be anything. Astronauts. Bankers. Women politicians. The Handbag Party. *Saudoihdong*,' I say and the word from me, the foreigner, elicits a weak smile. 'Isn't that what Cantonese parents expect— financial support in old age?'

'Kim,' Virginia implores me.

'Isn't she a role model for your daughters and sisters?' Even so, I get the feeling that I'm arguing all the wrong points. 'Why should you know what is right for her?'

As if paralyzed by the heat, they stand there, smiling the Chinese Embarrassment Smile No. 1, some frowning over my rapid English, others over my garbled Cantonese. And still I cannot stop. 'She could have a boyfriend. She could be a lesbian. Who cares? Why can't you just leave her alone?'

Eyes slither back and forth now, well-lubricated. Between her and me, it seems.

The smoke from the barbecue pit drifts over, makes me cough. My blood sister. Forgive me. A lesbian now, on top of being a spinster. *Moh dauhfuh*, a tofu grinder, as the Cantonese say.

'Virginia likes men,' I say. That talk about copper frying pans, long ago. I exhale slowly, reach out for the stone table behind me, feel it cold against my hot hands. 'That was just an example.' They nod. Emphatically. In unison. Eager. Smiling.

'Quick quick quick! Food is ready!' John appears with a plateful of meat. Relieved laughter. 'What a discussion. An engagement party to discuss the merits of singlehood. We've been neglecting our special guests.' He presses a skewer into Carrie's hands. 'Let's eat!'

'Virginia is such a clever girl, running her business,' somebody—the wife of Second Uncle again—throws in, 'all by herself.' Under her short perm, her face breaks into a well-meaning grin.

'She must be making loads of money. She never tells us how much,' her son teases Virginia.

'Right you are. She should be buying us dinner,' Rebecca calls out.

'Shut up! If you don't shut up, I'll never buy you dinner.' Taking up their playful tone, Virginia pretends to hit them.

Over dinner, only Carrie has the nerve to talk with me. I fill my mouth until I am unable to respond. She shoots me a look. 'It's healthier to have a boyfriend.' Her eyes move critically up and down my body. 'More—natural. All that sticking it out alone is—very foreign.'

Jau si, a voice in me goes off, going it alone. Smuggling foreign ideas into Virginia's life, all on my own. How much good am I doing her? In some moments, I have to dig for what makes me hers or her mine. Maybe it is the fact that she has always taken me for who I am. And maybe what she first loved about me is turning against her: my independence, my being different. I validate her lifestyle but also remind her of where she has failed, of where she is different. I have been her mirror all along, a bright skewedness, right where she has been left, or have I been left where she has been right? How she fades in and out, like an object under a magnifying glass, growing and shrinking while I struggle to get a grasp on her.

Over a dish with cold rice noodles, two cousins whisper. 'Why would she keep her boyfriend from us?' From the fire, smoke rises into the sky until it blends with the dusky evening, two samenesses becoming one.

Moon Four Day Twelve
Tuesday 9 May

'*Mhgoi*!' I call out to attract the attention of the waiters, but they move through the restaurant as if on skates, effortlessly gliding back and forth between tables. 'Sorry,' I say, my voice raised, 'the Macau Restaurant always gets so crowded.'

Ed and Ronda look up from their Tagalog conversation. 'But the food's good.' Ed pulls up his trousers in anticipation. 'Ronda deserves a good lunch today.'

'*Unggoy, unggoy*!' Ronda gives it a try, waving in direction of a woman who is clearing dishes at a nearby table. She looks harried, her uniform too big on her body. The woman nods and calls out to another waiter.

Ed turns to Ronda. There is a smile on his face but it is his lawyerly smile of many meanings. 'Isn't that somewhat beneath you?'

'What?' she says but a blush forms on her cheeks.

'Calling her a monkey.'

She toys with a sugar sachet, a smile curling her lips. 'But she doesn't know that.'

Ed's Tagalog reply is sharp, short.

'But I hear the Filipinas say it all the time,' I say. 'I thought it was the Filipino accent.'

'No, it's Tagalog,' he says. 'Some people seem to find that funny.' He takes a sip from his tea and smacks his lips as if it was a First Flush and not the cheap, lukewarm Puerh you get everywhere for free. Still avoiding Ronda, he says, 'You know, if I had to take the shit some of them have to take, I'd probably do the same.'

I know what he means. Today was the second conciliation meeting for Ronda's case. Her former employers never showed up. Ronda will have to appeal to the Labour Tribunal while Mrs Sze will be free to hire another domestic worker and play golf.

Moon Four Day Nineteen
Tuesday 16 May

At first, I almost overlooked her in the church-like setting of the North Point Funeral Parlour with its pews full of mourners. Virginia's mother is displayed in an open coffin behind a farewell window, a glass front that separates the guests from the back of the room.

As if to remind us of who she really was, a large picture of her is being displayed as well. It is part of an arrangement on the altar to the left of the window and is flanked by a couple of flickering candles, incense and food offerings. Back and forth, my eyes go, between her body and her photograph, as if only one of them could be real. I recognise the chocolate biscuits, a brand that I have eaten many times in Virginia's home and, in the strangeness of my surroundings, I cling to this familiarity longer than necessary.

A wake. Awake. I move my brows up and down, blink my eyes, struggle to feel alert after a day at work, battle the lull of warm stillness. In spite of the air conditioning, my skin sweats and itches under the black cardigan. Is it called a wake because mourners stay awake with the bereaved, or because it serves to accompany the dead across the night into the next realm, as the Chinese believe?

I fidget on the wooden bench, settle my legs into another round of quiet. It is not really a noiseless quiet, just a form of elaborate idleness, with the grown-ups sitting around doing nothing. Disguised by their mourner's headbands and cylindrical hats, it took me a while to locate John and Rebecca among them. So startling was their appearance, so deeply unsettling, that I had to suppress the resemblance right away: *Ku-Kux-Klan, they look like something out of the past, a sick heart, a perversion.* Once in a while, they feed the fire smouldering in a cinnabar burner, commit paper ingots to the flames. At the periphery of the room, the children in their tiny white outfits are growing restless, darting underneath the benches in determined silence like bats.

Moments ago, after entering the room, I was handed a gift, the same kind of funeral giveaway as Jim showed me so long ago. I was instructed to kowtow; nine times to the deceased and three times to the bereaved. A master of ceremonies guides guests along and so I found myself, my knees wobbly, bowing to Virginia's mother while his voice boomed over me. 'First kowtow! Second kowtow!' Afterwards, Virginia walked me through the room, past the display window to the coffin where her mother rests under a glass cover, looking much younger than I ever saw her in life. The small envelope cuts into my flesh. I know its contents without having to look inside: a handkerchief for the tears, a string to keep the soul of the deceased nearby, a coin to thank the visitors for bearing the funeral expenses, and a sweet.

Cymbals and suonas jolt me awake. Opposite us, a group of musicians has started to play, to *wrestle, All day, among the crowded air*. Everything about them is jarring, their bright yellow raincoats and their dissonant tunes, so uneasy to my alien ear, their professional verve and their lack of emotion.

In the noise of the moment, Rebecca's daughter thrusts her head into her mother's side. Her head is bereft of the antenna hairstyle she sported at the barbecue. Tina, her name comes back to me. '*Mamih*, I'm hungry. When can we go home?'

'Shh. Quiet.' Rebecca presses her daughter against her body, gives her a little comforting shake. 'Just be patient, okay?'

Virginia appears next to me and leads me to the burner. 'Here, take,' she says, handing me a piece of gold foil. With swift movements, she folds hers into an ingot and throws it into the fire. 'So that my mother will have money in the afterlife.'

I struggle with mine, mangle it into a brick, a hopeless shape, not unlike the paper boats we used to fold as children. I watch it disintegrate in the flames. 'Where's your father?' I ask, my voice straining against the clamour of the musicians.

'He's not allowed to attend.'

'The doctor didn't allow him to come?'

'No. It is considered bad luck for him to attend the funeral.

His birthday falls into this month.'

My eyes widen. With her hood flattening the meek haircut and the glaring mourning rags brand new and stiff with starch, she looks like an unconvincing rebel.

'It doesn't matter whether you are the husband or not. Sometimes, young people are not allowed to attend. Pregnant women also have to stay away.'

In silence, we fold ingots and throw them into the fire. A group of nuns replaces the musicians and starts to chant tunes. Sanskrit, probably, in its Chinese version, a mind-boggling alliance and utterly incomprehensible to me. With their drab robes, monotonous singing and hairless skulls, they are a sombre presence, where the men were overly loud and bright, and they seem to be more comfortable in their role. There is a sense of roundness about them—the heads, the multiple folds of fabric— that their bodies, shifting angles underneath the cloth, quickly belie.

One of the nuns senses my gaze. Her eyelids flutter, but she does not acknowledge the distraction by the non-chaste non-vegetarian. I return to my gold bars, the scratchy paper under my fingers complying with reluctance. John comes over for a while, smiling shyly at me, and then somebody who must be an aunt, her movements in the heavy body set in a familiar way.

'*Jeje.*' At the sound of the voice, too bright for the surroundings, all of us look up, into Rebecca's face. She pulls Virginia to the side, her whispers rising and falling with force. Her hands are aflutter, gesture towards the altar. Together, they go to inspect the offerings.

When Virginia comes back, she tugs at my sleeve. 'The chocolate biscuits. The biscuits on the altar, you know, the offering. One of them has disappeared. Rebecca thinks… we think… my mother has eaten it. They always were her favourites, you know.' Her eyes, silvered by the neon lighting, shine with barely contained hope.

She sets to work on another pile of ingots. Her arched back, hunched over the paper in concentration, or perhaps because of short-sightedness, ages her without effort, and the sight of her, crouching next to a fire just like the old women burning offerings on roadsides for the Hungry Ghosts, clamps my stomach shut. How easy to see her years from now, dying husbandless, childless, with nobody to venerate her; to become an object of half-hearted devotion from distant relatives and strangers. The truth hits me like a whole mouthful of chilli sauce; blinding and unambiguous it brings tears to my eyes.

'Don't cry. Here, quick.' She is at my side at once, handing me a handkerchief. 'It's unlucky to cry over the coffin.' Obediently, I take it, pretend a coughing fit to hide my tears.

What a pitiful instrument the brain is without the heart to teach it the meaning of things. How we need to see, touch and feel the truth for it to permeate us. On and on, I cough, the walls of my diaphragm banging against each other like in disease. I close my eyes to stop my stomach from churning but I can shut out neither, not the clanging, howling music nor the suffocating smoke. Behind my closed eyes, Virginia's silhouette still burns on my retina.

Finally, when my body has quietened down, I lean over. 'I'm not feeling well. A bit queasy from the smoke.'

She nods. 'Friends never stay for long,' she whispers.

'*Gaje*,' I say, brushing her elbow. Her quivering face, eyelashes darkened with tears, causes me to look away quickly, gulp down saliva, pretend another coughing fit.

'Be sure to eat the sweet when you get home.' Her voice is an insistent hiss against the tears. 'To make the departure of the dead sweeter.'

Moon Four Day Twenty-one
Thursday 18 May

I cannot bring myself to eat the caramel from the pocket, or to use up the dollar coin, and so the ingredients lie undisturbed in their white envelope. Once in a while, I finger it, weigh its promises against its perils—the red ribbon, the sweetness of togetherness here and in the afterlife, of being caught as we fall, against the handkerchief, the loneliness of death as a wandering ghost. Instead of using it, I carry the small package with me as if it were a talisman, crackling whenever I insert a hand into my pocket. Or when Ben does it, like now, his hip brushing against mine as he moves closer on the sofa, fingering for the object that is digging into his skin. I pull away and remove the package, closing my hand around it while I turn to deposit it on the side table, my face glowing in the dusk.

But he is quicker and tugs at my arm, wrestling with more gentleness than force. I open my fist, fully owning my blush. Between us, on my palm, the sachet trembles from our wrangle. My hand, bent like a beggar's, contains it all, apology and appeal and defiance.

'You kept this!'

'The phone numbers,' I say, pointing to the supplier's address on the envelope, 'do you believe in the lucky phone numbers?'

He moves and his jade charm catches light like a sudden moon. 'See, some things just become part of how things are done, even if you don't believe in them.'

I trace the ribbon around his neck, let the pendant dangle against my fingertips. His scent, so familiar by now, has gained substance in the dark.

'Even if you don't believe in them, others do.'

How can I believe in lucky numbers, if this means acceptance of unlucky ones as well? I let the piece of jade fall back onto his collarbone, feel it coolly slip away under my fingers. It never ceases to hurt how faith, this hope-bound, trust-sponsored thing, becomes something else all around me. With incredulity, I envision the unthinkable, a world where not-believing is a blessing. And then I invert my worldview one step further, think of a God who appears and disappears at will, whose biggest mercy to humans is his non-existence. My brain curdles from the effort. Finally, I close my eyes, let Ben cradle me to sleep. Against my hot forehead, the charm feels hard, non-committal.

Moon Four Day Twenty-two
Friday 19 May

Like a wave building from powers deep out in the sea, the heat gathers momentum, grows and gains force until it forms a roaring wall whenever I step outside, hurry from the MTR station to the office, rush over to the shelter, walk, skin moistened from the effort, to the station to meet Ben.

Life goes on and I slip back into my routine. What did I expect, that there would be a delegation of gods knocking on my door, declaring Virginia's mother in hell? That Virginia would break down, lamenting her mother's fate? But tonight I bury my head in my pillow, alone, and shiver in the artificial cold.

There is another kind of recognition, too. Now that her mother cannot die hopeless any more, I could liberate Virginia, share my version of things with her. If I wanted to.

Small Fullness of Grain
Sunday 21 May

After the service, I hang about the vestry, ready to catch Jim before he is swallowed up by the Filipinas. He opens the door in his brisk Sunday manner, surveys the little crowd waiting for him, smiles.

I hesitate, my hand still on the doorframe, before slipping inside. 'I would like to make an offering. Have Mass offered for somebody.'

He gives me his pastoral x-ray look. 'Everything alright back home?'

'Sure. Just in memory of… somebody.'

He starts to search his pockets. Finally, he comes up with a pen and a crumpled paper slip that looks like a 7-Eleven receipt. 'Say again...?'

'My grandmother. And... somebody else. Cheung Sau-fong.' My cheeks flush while I spell her name. I'm glad that it means nothing to him. Cantonese women retain their maiden names in everyday usage.

I turn in the doorframe and bump into Ronda.

She wrinkles her nose. 'A mass for Virginia's mother?'

'Oh.' Jim's gaze wanders back and forth between us. 'I'm sorry to hear she went so fast. When did she die?'

'It was a relief, Father,' Ronda says. 'Not too early, the Lord called her.'

'I didn't realise Virginia's family were Christians.'

'They are not,' she says. 'They are traditional.' Her mobile phone starts to ring. A torrent of Tagalog follows and something that sounds like directions to the church.

'Virginia did seem a bit down during the last hike,' he says to me. 'You haven't been around very much.'

'I went to her mother's wake.'

'So,' he says and his gaze acquires a different kind of quality. 'Is this for her or for you?'

'Do you mean Virginia or her mother? Can't we pray for whomever we want to?'

'Of course we can. It's always good to pray, especially for others.' He smiles down at the discarded vestment, still the liturgical Easter white, spanning the vestry table as if winged.

'Say—' He pats the pockets of his black denim trousers, stops himself and shrugs. 'Do you really think she needs it?'

'Is this a theological quiz?' His brand of pastoral care makes me squirm. I'm sure he does not dare to use it for the Filipinas. Behind me, the Tagalog conversation has abated. The morning sun, piercing the vestry windows with their stained glass panes, throws bits of colour onto Jim's face. I examine the easternmost window, puzzle over the Bible story it illustrates. Jesus, bending down to somebody. A blind person? A woman? A healing story. Golden, green and blue, his cheek shines with an intricate mosaic.

'What is it? You're smiling.'

My smile widens. 'The sun. The light is painting onto your face.'

'Yours too.' He says it matter-of-factly, unsurprised.

I touch my cheek, feel the sun on it, drop my hand again. Look at it as if it could retain some of the colours. 'Do you ever feel that you should be a missionary? I mean, trying to convert people rather than just doing your work as a priest?'

He looks at me, puzzled, a smile slowly forming on his face. 'Is that Eva again?'

'No,' I say. 'Actually, we've been getting on quite well lately.'

For a moment, he remains bent over the table, arms extended. His shoulders relax and he turns towards me. 'You know that we don't believe that only those who "accept Jesus Christ as their Personal Saviour" will go to heaven. After all, what would happen to those who were born in the wrong country?'

'I know, I know that.' I shift my weight onto the other foot. My eyes search his face again. He must have moved, because it looks uniform, the mosaic gone. A priest in his vestry.

'I just wanted to be sure. We *believe* that God's love extends to those who haven't heard of Him.' His whole, wiry body hums with the conviction of his voice. 'That's our doctrine.' He studies the back of his hands resting lightly on the missal as if to put it away.

He straightens until only his fingertips are still touching the volume. 'But I want you to be sure of something else.' His voice is very quiet. He has slipped back into the light. Emerald and yellow, the mosaic reappears on his face. 'If there is a God, He—She—God has to be bigger than any doctrine humans can contrive. God's love is bigger. God's love is not big. It is bigger. Always.'

I nod, feeling numb.

'We,' he says, his voice rising again, 'can only see fragments of Him. Glimpse God. To see God fully, in His full glory—that must be the privilege of those who have gone before us.'

It is a lot to take in and I simply nod again. From my backpack, I dig out some money, deposit it on the vestry table.

'For the Mass. Cheung Sau-fong, remember. And my grandmother.'

Moon Four Day Twenty-nine
Friday 26 May

Hope is a subtle glutton. Rat poison yellow, pus green, alarm pink: a mob of colours, intent on changing fate, the pastry sits in my fridge. Offerings for gods and ancestors, bought at the Buddhist vegetarian restaurant next door. Fruit and flowers that tug at me with their lifelike earnestness, like the paper goods whose fragile egos seem to face an impossible task. In my heart, they fight their battles, helplessness against beauty, despair against comfort. *He feeds upon the fair*, oh how he does. For how can something so alluring, so sophisticated be without effect?

For days now, the pastry has been hovering in my kitchen, revolutionaries in a lull of battle, waiting for the next move: the Buddha's hand, the lotus flower, the chrysanthemum. Imitations of nature, real things and yet nothing like their promise. What would Ben make of them? But I have long crossed beyond the threshold of asking, him or anybody.

Finally, to ward off further corruption, I bite into the pieces. Try them the way Virginia would, hunt their aromas with closed eyes: *And yet, inspected closely…* They taste like nothing much. Sweet above all, cloyingly sweet, a blinding sweetness that numbs all other senses as if to say: it's alright. An absence, Emily would detect, or rather *What abstinence is there!*

Moon Five Day One
Saturday 27 May

Virginia has to keep the hikes going and so we are walking along the Heritage Trail with the Hikers, Spielberg and I. *Again*, something in me complains, although there seems to be a smile hitched to every elephant ear along the way. I do not want to share Ben, my love, even in his absences, a newly learned greed. Instead, I instil my steps on the cement path with rhythm, run my eyes along the railing that lines it, listen to Emily falling away under my feet: *If I can stop one heart from breaking/I shall not live in vain/If I can ease one life the aching…* Virginia seems composed, her feet falling steadily onto the ground, her eyes scanning the group as usual. *Or cool one pain…* I turn Emily down a notch, redirect my attention to Spielberg and his movies.

'… in reality she loves him. It's a great film, you should try to catch it.' If romanticism is the ability to believe in the impossible, Spielberg is the ultimate romantic. Perhaps it comes with believing in invented worlds. Easing life's aches. Cooling pain. And with being single.

Celia and Bertie are walking ahead of us, their bodies very close, their hands not touching. My mind fills in this blank, adds Celia's primness and Bertie's coolness to form this whole. Again, I marvel at how he seems to shrink next to her Asian glamour girl looks, expensive even from behind, slightly out of place between bananas and bamboo, and wonder whether he welcomes it. Whether he believes in impossible things or whether Celia does.

'But people say it's quite a violent movie,' I say to Spielberg. 'Isn't that the one with the tattoo scene everybody talks about?'

'How can you be squeamish about violent movies? After living in Somalia? It's very artistic.'

'Sudan. It wasn't that violent, not really. And it's one thing to see things in reality.' I hesitate. 'A different thing. There's always hope. How can you work in a place like Khartoum and not be

174

hopeful? But to put violence in movies, isn't that a way of... endorsing it?'

'People would argue the opposite, that it's meant to warn us against violence. Which is funny, really. Is that why they put so little love in the movies? To keep us from loving too much?'

We laugh. 'There are ratings for both,' I say. 'Pornography and violence.'

'But love and pornography are not the same.'

'So, make love not war?' I grin, imagine more of Spielberg's brand of love on TVB Pearl, prime time: *Whatcha got cooking?*, a cooking show with Spielberg and Fruit Chan, or perhaps the kung fu movie he mentioned months ago. 'What about kung fu movies, do they count as violent?'

'Kung fu is fantasy.' Spielberg waves it away with a brush of his hand. 'The thing is, we shy away from love more than from violence. Any fully executed act of love will be delegated to private viewing, while it's not difficult to catch whole murders on screen.'

'Entire wars. I know.' My gaze falls on an elephant ear, glistening in brand new green from its gnarled rump. 'Perhaps it's too private.' Turning ourselves inside out. Like a sock, smelly and worn threadbare around the edges. Like a mangosteen, bringing out the vulnerable light flesh hidden underneath the tough maroon surface.

'But, Kim.' Spielberg slows down to face me. 'Movies, artists have always made the private public.' Against the irreverent, bursting greenery around us, his features suddenly seem very earnest.

'The problem is,' he continues, 'love is too complicated. There are so many types of love but only one type of violence.'

Before I can digest Spielberg's words, Virginia leads us into the ancestral hall of the Tang clan. The airiness and the smell of aged wood are familiar but, besides that, my memories of Ben have obliterated the details and I have to take them in again: the beams arching across the hall, the altar with dozens of tablets on it, decorated with paper slips, and a lone flower vase.

When we have all shuffled into the neighbouring hall, she

glances at her index cards. The tangle of notes on them is familiar, her writing and mine mixing, hers tidy like a bookkeeper's, mine too small for my size. We made these cards before her mother died. I drop my gaze.

Her voice rises while she addresses the group. 'This is the tablet of Tang Si-meng. He was a servant who sacrificed himself for his master when they were kidnapped by pirates. He was awarded the honorary title of 'Loyal Servant' after his death. Posthu—posthumously. You can see it here.'

I point to a tablet nearby, a slim wooden board in faded shades of blue, crammed with characters. 'What does it say?'

'That one says "Wife of Lam". They give people's names.'

'But it doesn't give her name,' I say. 'Was Lam particularly famous?'

'No,' she says. 'Women, married women, never use their personal names. In the past, I mean.' Sometimes it hurts, this ambiguity of the Chinese language. Not distinguishing between past and present. Unless you state otherwise.

'It's…' Celia says. 'Like, men do big things. Women are the persons in the house, the family. Sorry.' Her mobile phone has started to ring and she digs into her fake Louis Vuitton bag, comes up with a tangle of USB sticks, earpieces and keychains until she is able to locate it. She pulls a face. 'Work.'

I move a few steps away from Celia. 'But women also do big things. They give birth to the male heirs the families need.'

'Yes,' Virginia says. 'But they do it for their husband's family. The big things that men do, they do them for their own clan, to which they have always belonged. Naming children. Being a businessman.' She looks down at her hands, as if the index card could provide her with the right words. 'Women are… somebody else's. Like "the mother of x" or "the wife of y". So they have… relative names.'

'Relational,' I correct.

Virginia nods. 'So, when women got married they would be addressed by these names. Their position in the family. And their childhood names would stop being used.'

'Even in the family?' I ask. 'How would a husband address

his wife?' *Daling*, he calls me in that Cantonese way of singing vowels. *Flower. Lengneuih*. He has endless names for me, and I am starting to crave them.

'These villages are clan villages.' Zoë wriggles her feet in their flip-flops. There is a fly buzzing around her toes. 'Everybody is family.' With her fatigues and strawberry coloured fringe, she looks as if she had docked a spaceship outside the clan hall. She wriggles again. 'When they were alone, he would probably call her by a nickname. But with other people around, he would call her by a family title. Like "mother of x".'

'His son,' I say.

'Exactly,' Zoë says. 'It would be too intimate to call her by a personal name in front of others. Improper.' The fly is persistent. Now it circles Virginia, who waves it away without even noticing.

'I see,' I say. 'So women basically were nameless.'

'Married women,' Zoë says. 'You could look at it like that, yes.'

When we emerge on the square, shading our eyes against the midday sun, Spielberg is already petting Zoë's husky, tied to the village's letter boxes. Over the course of a few hours, Spielberg's skin has darkened without effort, reminding me of the burnt glow on my own face. I crouch to search for my sunscreen but first sink my hands into the dog's fur. A sensation of depth and warmth that pains me, so clearly unsuited to this climate, and I stroke him again, softly shake his black and white face with the trusting blue eyes as if this might cool him.

'That servant,' I say, giving the dog a final pat, 'who killed himself for his master. It's such a violent tradition. All these Confucian ideals of sacrifice—the chaste widows, the women who are supposed to cut pieces off their flesh to feed to their aging parents…'

'That's just an idea, Kim.' Spielberg's cheeks flush. 'Ideal. Don't you have the same, people who sacrifice themselves? Saints who were killed for their faith?'

'Martyrs,' I say, back on eye level with him. 'But that's— medieval. Or even earlier.' A diffuse image starts to build in me, of distorted bodies, agonised faces. Ochre and brown. 'Maybe you're right,' I say, fiddling with the top on the sunscreen. 'That we've always depicted violence. You know Hieronymus Bosch, the painter? His paintings of hell can give you nightmares.' I squint against the bite of the sunscreen in my eyes.

'The Chinese are the same,' he says. 'Lurid illustrations of purgatory.'

I nod, the black light diorama of Victoria Park still etched into my mind. It took me a long time to figure out that it was a representation of hell. 'Spielberg.' I squeeze the sunscreen back into my bag. 'What you just said. Is it a hell, or is it a purgatory?'

He scratches his head. 'It's not easy.' We quicken our pace to catch up with the group. '*Yihmlouh*, we call it. The realm of the shadows. There are eighteen different kinds of hell, so you can imagine that there is some disagreement about them.'

'Eighteen?' And he was telling me that there are many varieties of love but only one kind of violence. Out of her dark corner, Emily reappears, almost with glee: *There is a fitting a dismay/A fitting a despair.*

Moon Five Day Four
Tuesday 30 May

The many varieties of love. Like a new-found science, we put them to the test, make them our supreme commandment. At first, it seems impossible, to put body to body in this air which is saturated with humidity. Ben, ever the environmentalist, disapproves of air conditioning. It has taken some getting used to, this drenched delirium after my arid love of the Sudan, where the air was all take and no give. Combustible, we always feel in the first moments, until rivers of sweat anoint us. Afterwards, salt frosts my mattress. I have gotten used to the powdery rings that remain long after our skins have separated. I look out for them. Sometimes, I secretly taste the dried patch, like an animal at a salt lick.

'This is new.' His eyes search mine, seek an explanation for the slim gold chain around my neck. A wisp of a chain, really. Thin like a hair. With a cross. Cutting my collarbone in half with its shape. I flatten my hand against it, turn away. Turn to gently bite him on the shoulder, taste the salt on his skin, just underneath the ribbon that holds his jade pendant.

'I thought you hated necklaces.' His voice is muffled, his breath warm against my neck, while I battle unease. *I thought she might ask. Not you.*

Dragon Boat Festival
Wednesday 31 May

It is a liquid evening on Stanley Beach. The heat slows our limbs until they seem to be doing underwater t'ai chi. Even so, each move provokes an outburst of sweat and the mere fact of being alive and breathing seems a humidity-laden affair. This afternoon, we cheered our team of Heritage Hikers on in their dragon boat, racing against sopped Chinese and wet foreigners, boisterous masses rooting from the shore. It needs a certain lunacy, to row a boat in heat like this, to battle the sea, warm and dense like soup, with muscles and drums.

Back on the beach with the sand still seeping warmth into our legs, Virginia and I are waiting for the campfire to gain hold. Somewhere behind us, the men are preparing food; it hisses and sizzles on the barbecue pit. In the thinning transparency of the day, bats dart across the sky. Harbingers of good fortune they are, because their name sounds like it, promises it: *fuk*.

My shin itches. There are mosquitoes around and the smell of repellent sings sharply in the air. I start to draw in the sand, a simplistic bat that could as well be a butterfly. Or maybe even one of the many mosquitoes hovering between us, my blood sister and me. What a John Donne moment. I smile.

'What is it?'

'I was thinking of a poem. By John Donne.' I continue with my drawing, add antennae to my undefined being. 'He wrote a poem about a flea that bit him and his lover, I can't remember the details.'

'A flea?'

How I can sometimes smell her thoughts, the polish of her furniture and the detergents wafting through her flat, where a flea would try to hide in vain. 'He was an English poet. Around the time of Shakespeare. I guess they had problems with hygiene back then.' Scales for my creature. 'His idea was that the flea harboured the souls of himself and his girl, because it fed on them both. Almost like the Holy Trinity.'

I move on knees around my drawing and sit down on the opposite end. In China, you have to revert your fate to make luck happen, turn it around. Another pun: *dou fuk*. 'The idea of the Trinity is a Christian idea. That God has three natures: Father, Son and Holy Spirit.'

Her face glows golden and orange, illuminated by the fire. It is difficult to say how much she understands, so quiet opposite me.

'It's a complicated theological idea,' I say. 'Anyway, Donne thought that the flea hosted three souls and complains when his lover kills the flea.'

'We also have three souls,' she says, gently lifting the end of an ember with her sneaker. When it falls back, sparks sift through the air. 'After death, one soul goes into the grave, one goes into the ancestor's soul tablet, and the third goes into the infernal regions. Some people believe in up to ten souls. But I think it's only three.'

How irrelevant numbers are, how deceitful their promises. Three-in-one shampoo, buy two get one free and save more. Turned upside down, the creature under my hands looks insane. I erase it, flatten the sand again. 'You've known me all this time, and Jim. Would you like to come along one of these days, see what our church is like? We usually go out for dim sum afterwards, it's very relaxed.' I pull up my knees. My trousers, warm and clammy, cling to my skin. Bertie's voice drifts over, telling a tall story. Big talk, the Cantonese call lies, *daaih waah*. The Fox-Bert, I still tend to call him in my thoughts, his stealth from that first meeting etched into my mind.

'Sure. Why not.' She slaps her arm and lifts herself from her Roman dinner pose to sit on her haunches, Chinese-style. '*Aiyo*, the mosquitoes.' Her hand grazes mine as she reaches over for the repellent.

It has become dark, so dark that I cannot say whether the bats have disappeared or I just fail to see them. The night whispers and rustles, the sounds of voices and bursting wood mixing with the strumming of crickets. A smell of coal smoke and fat rises, reminding me of my hunger.

Around the barbecue pit, faces shine with sweat and exhilaration as beer twins with grilled meat for a testosterone-driven aftermath of the races. 'Ladies, help yourselves,' Frank says and we load our paper plates with steaks and salads that are difficult to classify in the dim light.

'… Sometimes you've got to thrust for all it's worth.' That is Bertie's voice and I can virtually smell the beer on his breath.

'Man, we pounded her good, I almost broke my paddle.' Frank raises a bottle of San Miguel to his lips and takes a long gulp.

'Careful what you break.' Bertie grins a sweaty grin, his face surrounded by wet frizzle. 'Got blisters on my bottom last year. Have to be careful. Lots of men have trouble with their— paddles.'

Raucous cheers all around.

'That's cycling.' Frank stifles a belch. 'Harms your balls. Try to think of one famous cyclist with a brood of kids. Nothing wrong with rowing, though.' He takes another swig, lets the bottle dangle in loose circles from his hand. 'Anyway, you gain biceps for anything you might lose elsewhere.' He laughs and makes a half-hearted attempt to hitch up his shorts.

'Back to the fire?' I ask Virginia and she nods. Balancing our plates in front of us, we weave our way back.

A figure separates from the men and joins us, lowering itself onto the sand. She is waiflike, really, with a smell of repellent different from ours clinging to her. Finally, in the golden twilight of the fire, I recognise who she is. Celia Chan, Bertie's girlfriend.

She brings out a bag with *zungzi*, sticky rice steamed in bamboo leaves. The specialty of the day. 'Here, have some, before the men finish them for us.' She presses the cool pyramids with their vegetable feeling into our hands, smiling uncertainly at me. I have missed so many hikes recently that I don't know all of the regulars that well. Or they me. With slow movements, I peel the bamboo leaves from my rice ball.

Rough voices drift over. 'Gimme another piece of meat. Man, I'm hungry.'

'We showed them. Showed 'em good what men with balls can do, the monkeys in their green shirts. Monkeys with their—rice balls.'

Everybody roars with laughter.

'What are they saying?' Virginia frowns and drops a bamboo leaf onto the ground. Celia giggles.

'The way men talk,' I say. 'Joking about how strong and… manly they are.'

'*Haaih-la.*' Bamboo leaves dangle over her wrist as she bites into her rice. Chewing, she continues, 'They can be proud, finishing among the first.' Her eyes wander over the men, their T-shirts with the Heritage Hiker's entwined Hs, white on red, slowly drying on the torsos.

'That's also your making, this group,' I say. It also is the first time in weeks that all angles in her body seem well aligned, or perhaps have disappeared. Her skin looks good with the day's light tan, the way it is meant to be, yet I know I must not compliment her on it. Eighteen different kinds of hell. Ten souls. If only I could give her this: hope for her mother, and herself.

Another lowering next to the fire, heavier, bringing a smell of beer and roast meat with it. Frank. 'Virginia,' he says, his gaze skittering across her clavicle. 'Thank you. Thank you for coming along today.'

Virginia toys with the bamboo leaf between her fingers. 'No

problem,' she says. 'You were great. Everybody was great. I wanted to cheer you on, after you had practised for the whole year.'

'I know things haven't been easy for you,' he says. 'Not easy. Not easy at all. Four weeks, is it?' He runs a hand over his eyes and through his hair. In the dying light of the fire, the white is tinged with orange. Blond, it almost looks. Somewhere on the fringes of the beach, something is moving in the shadows. 'I remember how it was losing my father. Not easy. Not easy at all.'

Suddenly, a woman stands next to us, her body curved with age, a heavy load on her back. 'Coals for barbecue. Very cheap.' Her teeth glimmer in the dark, too bright to be true.

I raise my hand as if in defence. 'No need. We have enough.'

Without a comment, Frank gets up and follows her. He fingers his back pocket, discusses a price and comes back, a sack of coals on his shoulder. 'God knows what she lives on. Her flip-flops, did you see them? Thin like pancakes.' With a thump, he drops the sack onto the sand and sits down again. He lifts a bottle next to the fire and peers into it. 'Not easy. Not easy at all.'

I had all but forgotten about Frank, about his Cantonese, his family ties in the city. I feel heat rise in my cheeks and am glad that nobody can see it in the dark, the shame burning on my skin.

Moon Five Day Nine
Sunday 4 June

Ben's golden body is curled up in the semi-darkness of my flat. Gingerly, I rise to get hold of the remote control for the air conditioning. I turn and bump against the nightstand. Hong Kong flats are an exercise in avoidance. Or perhaps it is the wrong feng shui alignment of my bed again. I rub my hip and reach over for the device, only to set off a pile of books with my knees. *Lives in Limbo—New Paradigms in Migration Studies* (I'm on page four), *Hong Kong for Hikers*, William C. Williams, and Lévi-Strauss's *Tristes Tropiques*.

He opens his eyes, shifts them around until he finds the source of the noise. Almost dinnertime. How we have been turning things inside out lately, making nights into days and days into nights.

'Leave it.' The nap is still audible in his voice, a soft croak, but the environmentalist is already wide awake.

'Ben,' I pout, a last remnant of our catlike hour. 'It's hot.' I used to think that I loved the heat and the velvety quality of the air. These days, it seems more like polyester, drowning my skin in its own sweat. Back in Germany, months ago during my holiday, I missed the unmistakeable presence of Hong Kong air, its *omnipresence*. It can smell used but it never seems used up as it does in Germany. Emptied out. 'More than hot,' I add. 'Suffocating.'

'Come on,' he says, propping himself up on one elbow. 'For millennia, Chinese people have been able to live without air conditioning. Up until around—' he sits, fishes for his underpants— '1976.'

'Well, maybe it's because I'm not Chinese. In case you forget.' As if we could ever forget. Milk white against mangosteen skin. My ancestors against yours. I grab the remote control and press it. 'A few degrees won't hurt.'

With a soft beep, the machine whirrs to life, sending a cold stream of air over our bodies. Blessed, it seems in the first moments. Until.

'Everybody banks on this, this feeling of things not being real,' he scowls. 'When you fly you don't notice how it ruins the climate but it still does.' He grabs his polo shirt, yanks it over his head. 'Cause and effect.' Under the shirt, his voice sounds muffled. 'When you poison somebody's drinking water with pesticides, you don't see it but it still happens.' Another quick pull and his head is free again. 'Not feeling them doesn't mean that they don't exist.' He heaves himself up and walks over to the corner where his shorts lie on my discarded pile of office

184

clothes. 'Do you only believe in things you can see?'

'Of course not,' I say. 'I believe in a lot of things I don't see.'

'We have to take responsibility for our actions.'

'Tell me.'

'It's not enough to tell people about their responsibilities. We also have to live with the consequences of things.' He disentangles his shorts, throws my blouse back onto the dirty pile. 'Not always running away.'

'Are you saying that I avoid responsibility?'

'You—you tell people how to keep maids but you don't even have one yourself. Opting out of the system is not a solution.'

'Ah, really?' I ask. 'Then how come you don't have one? A domestic worker?' I have a suspicion what this is about. Sometimes I catch him staring at my tummy. Wondering. I turn away, suddenly feeling too naked in my T-shirt and underwear. A belly that grows, furtively but steadily, from not acting. Cause and effect. The seen and the unseen.

'Ben,' I say, 'what is this about? Is it the Sudan story again? Yes, acting can have consequences. Not acting can also have consequences. Tell me about taking responsibility. It's not exactly Catholic doctrine, to tell people where they can get an abortion.'

He looks at me, the clothes strewn around. 'I hadn't noticed you were so—bent on Catholic doctrine.'

'Alright, then it's not a matter of doctrine.'

'Oh come on, you don't make any sense.' He sits down on my bed again. Our bed. 'Aren't there exceptions? When the mother's life is in danger?'

'When it's medically endangered, yes.' I look at him, try to taste his mood as if it were a piece of bread. Around me, things are losing their familiar contours. Already, the evening light is distorting them, stretching their shadows into the corners. 'It was so easy,' I say. 'I only gave her a name, nothing more. It was her who made the decision.'

'But did she have a choice, once you gave her the name?' Again, his voice. It sounds so different from his usual self in these moments, shinier in the wrong way, hard and superficial. Of course Ben is right, the feeling of inconsequentiality helped.

A devout Muslim woman, making a decision because she wanted to live. If I had been made to watch the procedure, I would rather have let Fatimah die. But that feels as surreal now as the knowledge of the child's death felt then.

The sun slants in through the shades, cuts our afternoon into sharply delineated slices of light and dark. Indifferent, it seems, to our human plight, without regard for cause and effect.

Moon Five Day Thirteen
Thursday 8 June

Ben. To get hold of him in his absences, I look him up in the dictionary. *An inner room, especially of a two-roomed cottage*. My inner sanctum, my conscience. My Ben Navis of benign benevolence. My benefactor. And so I return to him, day and night. Let myself fall into his very Ben-hood.

Moon Five Day Twenty-one
Friday 16 June

I walk into the Ngai's living-room. And stop. From above the dining table, Virginia's mother is looking at me. Overlooking the whole dining area stands a new rosewood cabinet, much bigger than the previous altar, which had been discreetly tucked into the corner. It is a good portrait, although it has the timeless quality of other Chinese images of the dead; formal, black and white photographs with expressionless faces. Music is playing in the background, barely noticeable, an endless repetition of *Amituofo* calls, the name invoking the Buddha Amitabha. I have always doubted these tapes, with their prayers delegated to a machine, but a lot of believers seem to take a chance. On this gloomy day, the chanting seems even more disembodied than usual, the sound floating in out of nowhere.

A diffuse feeling stirs in me, a sense of familiarity, of déjà vu. Something about Virginia's mother—

'I like this picture.' Ronda leans in the kitchen doorway, a glass of water in hand. 'There were some discussions in the family, about which one to take, but I like this one. Not so serious.'

The bathroom door opens and Virginia shuffles out, half-dressed, a white towel wrapped around her hair. 'Kim!— Sorry, my hike ended late.'

'Virginia—'

She comes to a halt. 'Yes?' Without make-up, her face seems both harder and more vulnerable. The towel reminds me of her headdress at the funeral.

'Last night, I dreamt of your mother.'

'What did she say? What did she say?' She holds up her towel with one hand, eyes narrowed for lack of glasses. It is odd how she seems blurred to me although it is her vision that must be impaired. 'Did she say anything?'

'Er...' *I saw her in my dream*, as the Cantonese say. 'I didn't really see her in my dream.' Her face is an emptiness waiting to be filled. *Pain has an element of blank*, yes, but how often do we overlook the opposite, that blankness also can be a source of pain. I lower my head, rub my forehead with my thumb. 'But it definitely was her. She said... She said that somebody had washed her face. Something... warm and... cold...'

'Ma'am. Miss Kim.' Ronda is now standing in front of the photograph. Her pupils are dilated. She turns to Virginia. 'I cleaned the picture. Yesterday morning, like every Thursday. I wiped it down. I use hot water, then with a dry cloth.' She points to the kitchen, as if to show us the rag drying over the sink.

I gaze at them, feel my lips slowly open. My whole body titillates with warmth.

'What else do you remember?' Virginia grabs my elbow. Slowly, the towel around her head uncoils and slips down. Like manacles, her hands are around my wrists. 'What did she look like?'

'I… I don't know.' I free myself from her grip, let my face fall into my fingers once more. I take a deep breath, summon something. To be able to give her this, *anything*. 'I'm sorry. It wasn't even really a dream. More like a feeling. A voice.'

My eyes still closed, I say, 'She sounded distant. Well, maybe she only seemed distant because I couldn't see her. I think… I would say she seemed well.' I let my hands fall down and take a few steps away from her, from all of them: Ronda, Virginia, her mother. Ronda seems to feel it as well, because she disappears into the kitchen.

There is another new piece of furniture, between the dining corner and the entrance. 'This is beautiful.' I step closer to inspect the cabinet with its butterfly-shaped lock.

Virginia reaches down to pick up her towel, lingering a second or two in the movement, her head still lowered. She comes over and runs her hand over the wood, polished and brown like a chestnut. 'Chinese elm. My father is so pleased with it.'

'Is it very old?'

'Not really. It's more of a family heirloom, from my mother's side in Foshan.'

I let my fingers glide over the satiny finish. 'How did you get it here?'

'Frank arranged for it to be brought over. Don't ask me how he got it through customs.'

For a moment, I am dumbfounded until I remember which Frank she means. The hiker. 'That was nice of him.'

'He works over in Foshan during the week,' she continues, idly moving the lock back and forth. 'The construction sites are all across the border.'

'I never quite know what to make of Frank. He can be so vulgar. Especially when he drinks.' I pull a face. 'That glib line with which he introduces himself. "Laying pipes in Hong Kong's wet places." And then he can be really sweet.'

She looks up, still resting her hand on the smooth surface. 'Do you think so?'

'Sure. Remember that hike when Zoë lost her mobile? He went all the way back with her, calling her phone, hoping that the forest floor would start to ring.'

She laughs. 'I had totally forgotten. I only remember one occasion when we had to divide the group, when that American tourist twisted her ankle.' She gives the shiny wood a final pat. 'I was so nervous during the early hikes. When I think back, they all blend together.'

'You've come a long way. Everybody thinks so.'

She blushes and rearranges the towel over her arm, frowning at a loose seam. 'You know,' she says, 'when my grandmother died, I saw her in a dream. And my sister. She was in London at the time.' She frowns. 'Rebecca had given her a jumper which she quite liked. Cashmere. After Pohpo died, she appeared to her in a dream, saying that she had received a jumper, but that it was the wrong size. And you know what? The day before, I had burnt a paper jumper for her, just like the one she liked so much.'

'Really?'

'Some people… try to get in touch with the dead. To find out.' Her eyes, behind glasses again, swim through the gloom towards me, pin themselves on mine in unspoken question. 'It's called *fu kei*. A spirit medium can do it for you.'

The thing is, if you believe in something, anything at all, where do you draw the line?

And so Virginia's mother starts to oversee the living-room, smiling enigmatically. Ever since my first encounter with her, scrutinizing me across mah-jong tiles, I have felt her inquisitorial gaze on my clumsy foreign ways. And here, standing eye to eye, I am unable to shed them, nor can she abandon hers.

Moon Five Day Thirty
Sunday 25 June

The city is still in that dishevelled state that comes with a heavy typhoon, emptiness and fullness in all the wrong places, twigs and rubbish strewn around sidewalks, umbrella skeletons clustered around dustbins. Yesterday's typhoon cancelled the Heritage Hikes for the weekend and so I asked Virginia to come along today, first to Mass and now for dim sum. She blended in at once in church, squeezed in next to Ronda, one more dark presence amid dozens of heads; long-haired, be-ribboned, ponytailed, some demurely covered. Only her reaction was difficult to gauge as she fumbled with her hymnbook while I did not dare to label my expectations and called them by other names instead: comfort, home, freedom from fear. Somehow, it has become necessary, this mission. Virginia's father, quarrelling daily with his daughter; and her mother, gazing down at us from her rosewood alcove.

Still trailing water, I push the restaurant door open. After the grey and wet outdoors, the Shamrock Hotel seems even greasier than usual. Once more, we ball up our soggy umbrellas.

'A table for four.' Unconsciously, Virginia has taken over and instructs the waitress. We follow her to the back, Jim hurrying, Ronda and I at a more leisurely pace. With practised moves, she starts to fill out the ordering sheet.

'Spring rolls,' Jim throws in, not looking up. His hand is cruising over the table. Searching for his dim sum dishwashing implements. Looking to start off the meal with its proper liturgy. He preached on the Gospel of Matthew today, the story of the workers in the vineyard, the men who are all paid one denar for their work, no matter whether they worked a full day or were hired later. But my thoughts meandered, so familiar is the message of this piece: the love that God bestows on all of us, whether we believe from the beginning or turn to Him later. Instead, I found myself focusing on Jim's voice, its calm assurance, all irony and self-deprecation gone. I like Jim's church voice.

Virginia turns to Ronda. 'Go ask for a soup bowl. So that we can wash the bowls and chopsticks properly. Quick.' Unperturbed, Ronda seems as she gets up, while my face burns. Friends, we are supposed to be here. Sisters and Brothers.

The waitress appears to take our orders.

Jim looks up. 'Is everybody alright with fish congee?'

'No fish,' the waitress replies. 'Because of the typhoon yesterday.'

'Plain, then,' Jim says.

The food arrives and we start to eat, Ronda nibbling her spring roll, Virginia biting into hers with care, Jim chewing his pork bun with bulged cheeks.

'Christianity is funny,' Virginia observes. 'A women's religion. Lots of maids.' I raise my eyebrows mockingly at Jim. She continues, 'They never told us, when I studied Christianity.'

'About the women?' I ask.

'No, that's like Chinese religion,' she says. 'The important rituals are always done by men.' It's Jim's turn to look mockingly at me.

'I never knew that you had studied Christianity.' She knows all about history of course, not just hers but also mine. Sometimes I fear that it is only her knowledge that beguiles me, her familiarity with people whom I have never met but who are still part of me: Charles the Great, Goethe, Hildegard von Bingen. I imagine that knowing them must make her love me more. Understand me.

'We had to take Western art history. No, I meant the Bible reading. So socialist. All earn the same.'

A rash hotness runs over my cheeks. I focus on lifting a spring roll with my chopsticks. 'What does our self-appointed liberation theologian say to that?'

Jim dabs his lips with the napkin, once, twice. 'It's about the Kingdom of God. It's a parable, an allegory.'

'A story behind a story,' Ronda adds, her mouth full.

I put down my spring roll, untouched. 'But does that mean

that we have to believe the first story? The surface story?'

'Well,' Jim says, 'I for my part believe in the surface story. That everybody should earn the same.'

'Ignore him,' I say to Virginia. 'He has socialism already. He lives in a convent.'

'Community,' Jim says.

Ronda has finished her spring roll. 'It is about how God loves all the same.' Like a musical conductor, she moves her chopsticks for emphasis. 'About how, when you turn to God, He will take you in, with love. Like the story of the Prodigal Son.'

'I see,' Virginia says. 'It's like the Filipinas. They all earn the same, no matter how much they work.'

'Yes,' I say. 'The minimum wage. If they're lucky.' I reach for the chilli sauce, daub my plate with the bright red substance and then drown a piece of turnip cake in it.

Virginia observes, 'That's why there's not much point in giving them more time off. We still have to pay them the full wage.'

I swallow, struggle to chew faster, to come up with a reply.

'I don't see, Kim,' Jim says, 'what you should have against socialism. You already dress like a socialist.' Ronda laughs out loud and even Virginia stifles a giggle.

The corners of my mouth bend upwards, but my gaze falls down. Tears well up in my eyes. *Mirth is the mail of anguish*, how could I forget. This was my chance. The workers in the vineyard, God's everlasting love. And here we sit, discussing socialism in a frivolous tone instead.

'I need a mango pudding,' I declare. Jim hates it. He must have been looking forward to a sago dessert.

But when I turn to the waitress, she says, 'No mango pudding either, Miss.'

'I see,' I say. 'The fishermen were unable to go out for mangoes, it that it?'

'We closed early yesterday because of the typhoon, Miss. The pudding has to set.'

The others laugh but my mouth is sour with disappointment. Thin-skinned, that is what I am these days. Too white for this climate. With my chopsticks, I push bits of turnip cake around on my plate. Cause and effect. Ben and our talk about responsibility, about acting and not acting. Virginia, palpating dreams for relief. And me, juggling the seen and the unseen, yearning to be a harbinger of good news.

Moon Six Day Four
Thursday 29 June

Perfect and round, it sits among my messages. A haiku, all mine, from Ben. I gaze at my mobile, ingest the offering with all my might, masticate its words, absorb it until it fills every cell of my being. Once more, and only one more time, I take my phone out, long after I have learned the message by heart. Yearn for its intimacy, its secrecy. If possible, I'd keep it a secret from myself, again and again. To have it reveal itself unto me, over and over. To feel the intimacy spun out of it, of making it, of trading it. My seventeen syllable secret.

Moon Six Day Six
Saturday 1 July
Hong Kong SAR Establishment Day

A time of breaking rules. Virginia stands in her own doorway, presses the bell. Nobody reacts and my heartbeat acquires speed. *Never go to work in pink. You shall not murder. Never eat chocolate before five p.m. Never get into trouble with Immigration.* It always gives me a pang, that last one, whenever I enter the Ngai's flat, the sight of

Ronda—not yet deported—both a relief and a threat. But she does not open and the lengthening silence, growing heavier by the second, causes my palms to itch.

Finally, Virginia digs out her keys and lets us in. We have to step over a broom, cutting the corridor in half, and almost stumble over a bottle with a sulphur liquid. Ronda is perched on the window frame of the dining area, her upper body moving back and forth with the cleaning rag, suspended over emptiness.

'Ronda!' I exclaim.

'Sorry Ma'am.' She smiles in Virginia's direction, the cloth dangling from her hand. 'I was not quick enough.' She wrinkles her nose and smiles again. 'Oh, durian.'

'What, you still haven't finished?' Virginia has entered on bared feet and grabs the remote control of the air conditioning.

'Ma'am, I finish in a minute.' Ronda's breath condenses against the glass pane. She frowns in concentration, her arm wrapped around the window in an uncomfortable-looking way. Passion and prudence. That pronouncement of Irina's, months ago. Which one is Ronda being paid for right now, precariously balanced twenty-two floors above sea level?

'This, this is—' I say. 'You can't have her clean windows like that. Do you want to end up in prison? I can't even look at her.' Instead, my eyes are pulled over to the alcove, as they so often are. Fresh flowers and appetising offerings grace it whenever I visit. Buttering her up. Currying favour with her. Like a child, I always feel, with my stolen glances. The more you try not to think about something, the more it dominates your thoughts. I cannot look her in the eye, not during this confrontation with her daughter.

'Come in,' I say to Ronda. She looks back and forth between us but finally relents. With a practised move, she swings her upper body back into the room.

'Come in. Hurry up now, we want to eat.' Virginia's face folds into harsh lines. She yanks a bunch of spring onions out of the plastic bag and strides out of the room. Singed, the air around her feels.

'And by the way,' I call into the kitchen, 'today is a public

194

holiday. Why is she working?'

'It's Saturday.'

Ronda is gathering her cleaning rags into the bucket. I wished I had never heard the story of the waiter. Afraid of taking up space even in death. Battling same with same, water against the dissolution of his life.

'Any news from your family?' I ask. How I envy Ronda her ability to take life as it comes. Mostly.

She wrings out the rag, carefully drapes it over the edge of the bucket. 'Okay. Thank you.' There is embarrassment in her smile. When we are alone, she avoids addressing me, I have noticed.

From the kitchen, Virginia yells, 'Kim, where did we put the durian?' Plastic bags rustle and the fridge slams with a loud bump. A bang, really.

'It's in my bag,' I shout back. I turn back to Ronda. 'Did your cousin get into that college programme?'

She looks into the pail in her arms. 'Roberto. No. My brother will help him, he knows some people.' With care so as not to upset the dirty water in the bucket, she leaves for the bathroom. A retching and gurgling sound follows. It could be the dirty water being drained into the sink. Who knows.

Over dinner, Virginia's mother continues to peer into our rice bowls, while we avoid any talk of windows or domestic workers, stick to the Hikes and Frank's latest Hawaiian shirt, giggle against our disappointments. Is she benevolent, caressing her daughter with her glances? Or unhappy, merely disguising her discontent with Virginia?

'John has been asking for you,' Virginia interrupts my thoughts, her fork lingering over the fruit platter. The durian, so weapon-like in its natural skin, has been rendered harmless, slimmed down to pale slices of custard flavour. Only the sharp, aromatic smell is the same, the perfume penetrating every corner of the flat.

'Has he?' I assess the remaining pieces of fruit, select the smaller one. How can she still link him with me? Because I haven't told her about Ben yet. Again, my eyes slide over to her mother, this time in apology. Maybe her unhappiness is directed at me. My rules, what good are they now? *You shall not give false testimony against your neighbour. Always start the day with half an hour of running. Never miss a Heritage Hike. You shall not bow down to them or worship them. Never be a missionary. Always let Jim double-check your Word for the Day. Never get involved with the way your friends treat their domestic workers.* It is the painful lesson of the revolutionaries, that breaking rules does not make new ones. Even if breaking them gets easier with practice.

Moon Six Day Eight
Monday 3 July

Dusk, this in-between time, is the holiest of hours. Like all transitions, it inhabits a vulnerability of some kind. And so we seek protection, burn incense and hope for a glimpse of the eternal while heaven and earth readjust themselves like a window being opened, then shuttered for the night. The temple is empty. I take gulps of air, flustered from the heat, and inhale the dry, sharp aroma of sandalwood, while the fruit in my bag weighs down my back.

I kept it a secret from myself throughout the whole day. I kept it a secret when I took the fruit out of the office fridge, thinking of dinner; when I boarded the number six bus in Admiralty, imagining some shopping; when I alighted on Queen's Road East, going for a walk along its many places of worship, the Sikh Temple and the Adventist Hospital, the Hung Shing Temple and the Methodist church.

With shaking hands, I unpack my bag. In the humid, smoke-filled darkness, all sounds seem to be amplified; every rustling of a plastic bag explosive, each footfall on the pavement a thundering threat. My fingers jittery, I build a pyramid of golden oranges, place a single fruit on top of a basis of three, like I have seen it done so many times. Build another one of apples, red as if lacquered, their polished shine jumping up and down in the light of the oil lamp.

I run my palms over my trousers, take deep breaths to calm my heart. Once more, I grope around my backpack, finger an overly warm water bottle and a dishevelled paperback until I hold the bundle of incense, long and hard, in my hand. Feeding the joss into a flame of the oil lamp, I light three sticks. Several times I fold the pieces awkwardly into my hands until I manage to clasp them in the orthodox way. Finally, I offer the incense with three bows. After having placed it on the altar, I start to repeat the ritual with the second batch, sweat running freely down my back.

The sound of a mobile phone shatters the silence, a familiar ring that makes me drop a joss stick. A popular tune, ubiquitous these days, making my heart race, while my white skin glares in the dark. Behind the ghost sill, a slim shadow moves against the blackened wall but, instead of taking the call, the person extinguishes the ringing and hurries away. *Forgive me*, I want to say, not sure who I mean; I, in this temple.

Dusk is short in Hong Kong. I try to recall German summer sunsets, their indecisiveness, their endlessness of *before* and *after*, but these days they are a distant memory only. Without foreplay, night falls on these shores, slicing our days into black and white.

Moon Six Day Fifteen
Monday 10 July

'Kim, I think this must be yours.' Irina appears next to my desk, a lime green leaflet in hand. With some effort, I lift my eyes from Ben's email, try to remember what I am working on.

I fix my eyes onto the seal characters trembling slightly next to her varnished thumbnail. And the lotus logo that I know only too well. My ears radiate heat. I nudge the creole, let the cool metal slip back and forth between my fingers.

She studies me. Something is twitching in her face but she quickly suppresses it. 'Eva had to redo her documents for Ed. Everything came out in poison green.'

'The copy shop was closed because of renovation, so we bought some green paper and did them ourselves.'

'"We"?'

'A friend and I.'

'I asked Eva what it was. Given that *our* material is bilingual.' She pauses as if it was my fault that she doesn't read Chinese. I know it irks her, that in this culture she lacks a capacity as fundamental as reading. She squints at the logo. 'Green Lotus. Eva says they're Buddhist?'

'Environmentalist.'

'Sure.' Irina's eyebrows hover undecidedly in her face.

'*Green Lotus–Upcoming events,*' I say. Even if I cannot read it, I know the leaflet by heart. '*Cleanup Campaign. Setting Free Ceremony. Save the Date: Demonstration—Save Sam Tung—*'

'Okay, okay.' Irina's hand, fanned out in mid-air, stops me. 'Have you ever been to a setting free ceremony?' It is one of her gifts, this ability to be curious about everything. The gift that will probably make her great one day. Besides her ability to shift gears.

I shake my head.

'It's good that you try to understand local culture. Are you still taking your Cantonese classes with your friend?'

'On and off. Right now, it's off,' I say and don't like the sound of it. I hardly notice how often Virginia and I postpone our language exchange, ignore it, drop it. And here is Irina, assuming that I have been doing the leaflet with her. 'I mean, we're still working together. Obviously.' I point at the leaflet, a half-lie. A body lie.

'I'll ask Eva to set up a petty cash box for private photocopies. Alright?'

I nod, my ears still hot. Irina nods back and moves on in that condensed, well-calibrated way she has, so unlike the flailing limbs and awkward elbows of certain other people.

Afterwards, I trudge to the photocopier, like a criminal

returning to the scene of the crime. 'What's a setting free ceremony?' I ask Eva. A bottle of glass cleaner stands on the side table. In the waste paper basket next to her sits a pile of balled-up green paper.

'Sorry about your documents,' I add and glance at the rubbish. Documentation for Ronda, for her Labour Tribunal hearing which has now been scheduled for October. 'If the legislation won't kill us, the paperwork certainly will,' Ed likes to say.

'It's a Buddhist tradition,' she says. Brightly. With assured moves, she feeds sheets into the machine, presses buttons. 'I'm doing triplicates, Ronda will pick up a set later.' She hesitates, re-inserts a sheet. 'My mother used to take me. I loved it. I used to hate the poor creatures being all caged up. When you go to the bird market, you can see birds on sale for setting free.'

I am starting to feel a bit sickly. It could be the hot plastic smell or the sting of the glass cleaner. I raise my voice. 'People buy birds to set them free?'

'Yes, sparrows or other wild birds are captured and then released. It is a good deed to set them free.'

I fish out a screwed up leaflet from the basket and flatten it back into shape. The romantic mind, believing in the impossible. Wasn't that something Spielberg brought up? Or did he mean hope?

Great Heat
Sunday 23 July

Morning smells fill the woods surrounding the Big Buddha. Green smells. Brown smells. Wet smells. And birdcall, even harder to classify, at least for me. Perhaps my companions would know, the budding saviours of the forest, but I doubt it. The Green Lotus crowd is not environmentalist, it is Buddhist. So different are they from the Heritage Hikers that my conscience hardly prickles at letting one go for the other. Older, more Chinese. Less post-colonial.

'… Jason Lau … and Lorena Chan.' Light and shade play on Ben's skin while he sorts out the participants, two dozen fresh-faced volunteers in brand new sports shoes, sunhats and shorts, elderly women with umbrellas, bespectacled men with caps.

A number of Buddhist nuns are with us, from one of the monasteries in the valley below. With their grey habits, they look like a flock of friendly bats, their hairlessness emphasising their smiles. One of them is young, my age perhaps. It is difficult to tell from her face, round like a mooncake. 'I have seen you before.' She smiles.

I have seen you before too, I feel like saying, plying her face under the shaved scalp for something less uniform, more hers, than the look of a Chinese nun in traditional sandals and socks. I have seen you in temples and monasteries, in pilgrim's groups at airports, at interreligious meetings. How can she live with this namelessness? 'The reception! The interreligious New Year's reception, was that it?' I blush, feel Ben's presence next to me enhanced.

She smiles, more to herself now. 'No. At the North Point Funeral Parlour. At a wake and you were the only foreigner.'

'My friend's mother,' I say.

'So, you're quite… immersed in Chinese culture,' she says and her slim brown hand in the wide-sleeved arm encompasses it all in one smooth, restrained gesture: Ben, the Green Lotus volunteers.

'It's not easy, sometimes.' I absorb her lucky mole, follow the sunburnt pigmentation on her cheekbones and want to lose myself in her smile, wide as the universe.

She nods, then pushes me gently towards the group. 'Shh. Ben is giving instructions.'

Laughter reaches us, multiple voices ringing with merriment. Ben, playing to his rapt audience, and I have just missed a joke.

'I knew Plankton would love to go with all the pretty girls.' Ben grins and returns to his list. '*Ah Fuk* and *Wong-je*, you turn left at the Tea Gardens, that gives you a neat circular route. Did I miss anybody?' He scans the group with its backpacks, water bottles and waste bags. In this light, his hair has a brown tinge.

'See you later.' With a pat on my arm, the nun prepares to leave. 'By the way, I'm Fuican.' She nods and starts to descend the hill. Others follow, people in twos and threes, chattering and laughing as they set off.

'Wait a minute,' Ben says when I lift my backpack. 'My parents are joining us.'

'Your parents are coming?' Even the damp, green heat of the forest cannot soften the shrillness of my voice. I glower at him. 'I could at least have worn something decent.' Not my tattered jeans slaughtered into a pair of shorts in a rebellion inspired by Joel. Not my frayed MediMission T-shirt. Above all, not my Green Lotus cap, still stiff and new on my hair.

'To collect rubbish?' Ben's smile is unconcerned, mysterious almost, while anger settles on my skin like a warm cloud. It is not difficult to imagine his parents: The father portly, virile and shining with health, like an Asian life insurance ad, the mother with seamless clothes and ageless skin. A *lady*.

His face softens. 'Reini.'

I try to shield myself against him, to overhear the togetherness he builds around us like a tent, solely with his voice.

'Ben,' a voice calls out.

And another one. '*Josan, josan.*'

Ben turns around faster than I, his breath brushing my ear. 'You'll be fine.' He rests his arm lightly on mine, the soft pressure part apology, part encouraging slap.

A sprightly looking couple has appeared between the trees. They stop, grinning, and give a half bow in our direction. Next to me, I sense Ben frown, tighten. The two resume their walk towards us, taking goose steps. With linked arms, giggling, their legs scissoring as if choreographed, they twist and twirl something like batons in the air. On and on the performance goes, oscillates between something military, cancan and cheerleading. Finally, they come to a halt in front of us, breathless and flushed, holding hands like Hänsel and Gretel.

Ben's face glows crimson. I inch in his direction but he backs off from all of us, from me, from this slice of a man who appears wrapped in his clothes, from the hardly less angular wife who is smiling impishly.

'Ben.' His mother brushes his forearm in greeting. Her son's face shines from her features in a way that makes my heart beat faster. Beautiful genes, assembled in a more peaceful way.

His father hands over a pair of giant pincers with a flourish. 'Rubbish tongs. We thought you might need these.'

I twist my lips, suppress a smile. 'Rubbish tongs are only a nuisance,' Ben declared when we all planned what to bring. 'Only fill up your hands when you need to stick to a bag for the trash, your map, water bottle and other things. Better bring gloves.'

'Perfect,' Ben says, taking the gift. His face has faded back to its normal tan. 'Absolutely perfect. Just what we needed.'

His mother turns to me. 'And you must be Reini.'

'Pleased to meet you,' I say. Absolutely perfect, her pronunciation of my name is, causing the hairs on my skin to tingle.

'I'm Madeleine. A nutcase, obviously.' She laughs and offers me her pair. 'Would you like tongs as well?'

'Ben has enlisted all his troupes, I see.' I extend my hand. Her T-shirt is soothing, of such a faded shade that it is impossible to say whether its original colour was olive, purple or dove-grey. And his father's clothes go back straight to the 1970s.

Cautiously opening the pliers, I say, 'That was a great performance. A mixture between the Changing of the Guards and the Folies Bergère.'

They laugh. Ben's father runs a hand over his hair. 'These things are difficult to carry off with dignity. Especially on public transport.'

Ben heaves his bag up, the tongs slipping from his grasp. 'Ready to rock? Off we go,' he says, picking them up with the slightest of sighs that could also be a wheeze on this hot and still morning.

'Do tell me,' Ben's father says once he has learned that I am a philosopher's daughter. JC, he wants to be called. 'How is Kant viewed these days in Germany?' His eyes are darker than Ben's, of a friendly seriousness. I slow down, shift my rubbish tongs into my left hand to reach an empty soda can high up on the slope.

I cannot remember the Philosopher King ever mentioning Kant. *I think therefore I am.* I drop a piece of bright blue plastic into my bag, stretch for the can. At last I remember a name. 'Sloterdijk!'

'Please, allow me.' JC climbs onto the slope, holding on to a bush. With a metallic clang, the soda can falls into his trash bag.

'Darling, I don't think Reini is joining us this morning to expound on Kant. Now come down, there's enough rubbish to fill your bag without breaking an ankle.' Madeleine turns to me. 'Accidents always happen in the most stupid ways.'

'Absolutely.' I shift the tongs back into my other hand. 'A friend of mine got her hand stuck in the ornamental wiring of her bed, trying to reach for a fallen paper tissue. She had to be rescued by firemen. They had to weld her free. All in her nightie.'

Madeleine laughs.

JC jumps back onto the cement path and wipes his hands on his trousers. 'I once tore a ligament stepping down a sidewalk. Remember, Mad? In Davos. It could at least have been a skiing accident.' Their laugh is short-lived, full of apology.

His arm slips under her elbow. 'And in the long run, what's a torn ligament? There are worse things.' The last words are just for her, said in a voice that could rival his son's for shades of darkness. 'And so,' he continues, opening and closing his empty rubbish tongs in the air, 'and so Maddie worries too much about me.'

It is a slow experience, walking down a hill with a trash bag in hand. Slow and quiet, until Cantonese opera cuts into the silence and, in these surroundings of tea shrubs and camphor trees, it contains even more whine and strangeness than usual. A lone hiker passes us, a stringy elderly man with a transistor radio tied to his belt. With relief, we hear him disappear.

Madeleine has fallen into stride with me. 'So, why Davos?' I ask. 'If you don't ski? Do you enjoy hiking?'

'Oh, that was ages ago,' she says. 'The Swiss holiday. Ben was still a toddler. And we did use to ski, until that holiday.' She looks at her sturdy shoes as if seeing them for the first time.

I study my feet in their trainers. 'I don't ski either,' I say. 'Never did and it doesn't look as if I was going to start with it here.' I give a laugh, but she doesn't pick up on it.

'I lost a child during that holiday in Davos. Cross-country skiing.' Softly, the harsh consonants die away in the still heat under the trees. She speaks without self-pity. Her hand wanders to her belly, rests there for a moment. 'That *was* a skiing accident.'

I search her face, the flawless skin, the perfectly plucked eyebrows, and scan it for guilt. Laughter has weaved creases around her eyes. It is her smile that is apologetic, although right now I could not say who she is apologising to, or what for. Briefly, our eyes touch, amber on Pu-erh tea, until I redirect my gaze away from her, this woman who parts with secrets.

'And then JC tore his ligament. So, the torn ligament was only part of it. The better part.'

Ben reappears at a fast stride, smiling broadly, an empty bin liner billowing in his left hand. 'Got rid of that first bag. Looks like you've been busy as well. Found any treasures?'

'Sorry,' Madeleine says with a glance at me, passing a hand across her temple and straightening her T-shirt in a gesture that could be Irina's. 'What a way to get started off.'

'Yes, getting on well. Ten year old Coke cans and sticky instant noodle packages.' I cast Madeleine a sideways glance and she smiles back.

Ben looks back and forth between us, breaks into a beam.

Backwards, I must learn to read him. A first kiss in the steaming landscape of Fanling, planted in the middle of nowhere: not madness, not recklessness. An invitation to collect trash: not an environmental enterprise, not a Buddhist deed. I must learn to read him backwards, like the character for good fortune that needs to be turned around to make good luck come true.

On the bus back to the ferry, fatigue settles in my limbs as motion sickness and relief mix with the cold from the air conditioning. The driver seems to be intent on breaking some personal record. A sunburn is beginning to cling tightly to my skin and I try to focus on its memory of warmth.

'Look, that's a great one of you and Fuican.' Ben, unperturbed by the bus's potholed trajectory, is reviewing the day on his camera. 'And here's one with you and my parents.'

'Mmh,' I snuggle up to him. 'Admit it, it was bloody hot.' I shiver into my pashmina, wish to ignore the bounding of the horizon that upsets my stomach. After another teeth-clenching turn, I allow myself more heaviness against Ben's shoulder. I point to a fly that is bumping against the window. 'Why do they do that?'

'What?' He looks up from his camera.

'Insects. They always seem to have trouble with their orientation.'

'Not really. Insects are—' for a moment, he steadies himself with one arm, the camera strap dangling from his other hand— 'a great mix of the primitive and the sophisticated.' We are both watching the fly, still struggling against the window. Again and again, it comes up against the glass as if it wanted to break through into the greater reality outside.

'Cockroaches, for example, were around before the dinosaurs. They have an incredible array of instruments for sensual perception. Antennas, cerci, palpi—that's three kinds of feelers and they have two kinds of eyes. Compound eyes and simple eyes.'

I turn off the icy jet of air blasting directly onto my face. 'And the fly? So why are they so disoriented?'

'It depends on what you mean. Flies also have compound eyes.' He eases the camera back into its bag and lowers it into his backpack. I huddle more deeply into my shawl. 'Still cold?' He pulls me closer. For a moment, the smell of rubbish wafts over from his fingers. I shut my eyes and dig my nose into his shoulder.

'Everything,' I say. 'Cold, sunburnt, tired.' I lean over to kiss him. He doesn't like to kiss in public but maybe today I can get away with it.

'Giving me a quiz on insects at this time of the day.' Distractedly, he shuts the air conditioning fuse above him. 'What I do remember is that most insects find it easier to detect a moving object rather than a stationary one.'

I nudge him. 'We should try to catch the fly and release it. The windows don't open.'

When we arrive in Mui Wo, it takes an empty box of Japanese chocolates and some coaxing from Ben to capture the fly and I find myself watching his hands more than the insect, so deft and careful in their task.

We set it free against the gold and blue sky as if seeing off a relative, part relief, part regret. The fly seems to instantly dissolve in the air, and it fills me with envy, its ability to adapt, to take in a new worldview so quickly.

Moon Seven Day Six
Sunday 30 July

I have bought a paper mah-jong set for Virginia's mother. Crisp and golden, the package sits on my table, a mute appeal to do something with it. Burn it, obviously, to dispatch it into the afterlife, but how? I toy with the idea of doing it on the building platform but she is not a hungry ghost. Your ancestor can be my ghost. Was it Jim who said that, ginger sauce dripping from his chin?

Instead, I call my mother the night-owl, still living through Saturday, hear about the effects of Viagra on business and internet pharmacies and the gorgeous summer back home.

I have unlearnt the need for summer and so I say, 'In Brazil, the two sought-after things in pharmacy break-ins are Viagra and adhesive cream for dentures.' I laugh. 'How old must the robbers be?'

'Reinilein,' she says and her voice makes me young again and more pliable, 'it's the young ones who want it. For fear of not being good enough.'

'How come you know? About Brazil?'

Now she laughs. 'Professional duty. And how come you know?'

Medical mothers make for early birds-and-bees lectures and there is nothing I would have to hide. Even so, I tease her. 'Oh, that's my secret.' I meet all kinds, I could have said but find it difficult as usual. I meet more kinds than my parents, which is part of our problem. My problem, really.

Before I get ready for Mass, I hide the mah-jong set in a cabinet. Displacement activities, as Ben the biologist would probably diagnose. Leaving me to wonder who displaces whom or what. And so, I continue to walk around the real issue, because the one person to whom all of this could mean anything is not here.

Festival of the Seven Sisters
Monday 31 July

Remorse is cureless. With its artificial waterfall enclosed by lava stones, the reception of the Fountain of Eternal Youth Spa looks tropical in a pricey way and, as soon as Virginia and I have entered, I wished I was somewhere else—at the dentist's, at Immigration, going over my expense claims with Eva. I almost wished I was at the Beer Festival. This is what I get for my *über*-compensation, for neglecting Virginia for so long. A world all tinsel and lilac and Balinese temple bells in the background.

Worst of all is the voice that haunts me. *For t'is His institution,—/The complement of hell.* Today, I want to free Virginia and free myself as well: of my six-foot-one Ben Navis, of the way an onion can hide under a cream cake, of my sandalwood-scented displacement activities. And still I find myself shirking the mission at hand. It is easy to mistake the intimacy of secrets. My blood sister. *My nyas*. Lately, Joel resurfaces at times, as if to remind me of separations.

'Date of last spa visit?' the beauty therapist barks, white-robed like a doctor.

'This liturgy is alien to me,' I snap back. Last facial? *Sister bless me for I have sinned.* Behind the counter, I vent my soggy shirt which has stuck to my back. Air my socialist garb underneath the toilet brush.

'We'll take the Full Glow Chocolate Package,' Virginia says.

'Please tick.' The beauty therapist shoves a card towards us and the wrongness of it all hits me once more as I am made to confess *dry*, *frizzy* or *discoloured hair*, shall declare my skin *sallow*, *wrinkled* or *blemished*. *Flower*, I coo to myself. Like a mantra, I repeat the names that Ben has given me over the months. Carrot flower hair. Sea anemone feet. Absolute names, not relational; not bigger boned, not taller, not frizzier than the locals.

I was expecting Filipino beauticians, but the girl who massages me is Chinese. Very white, very slim, very nubile. An absolute product of Eternal Youth. *Essential oils are wrung…* Resorting to Emily, I survive an assortment of treatments that remind me of housework, with plenty of kneading and battering of skin.

Finally, Virginia and I are left alone, allowed to soak in two adjacent tubs to absorb the full Chocolate Glow. What would Ben make of me? I let my cheek sink onto the rim and close my eyes, smiling.

'See, you like it after all,' she says.

I open my eyes and regard the surface of the brown bath, then lower my body deeper into the water as if this could hide the blush forming on my cheeks.

'Do you think it's real chocolate?'

'No idea.' I dip a finger into the warm liquid and wave it in theatrical curves before inserting it into my mouth. 'Uggh.'

'You should see your face.'

'It tastes like chocolate that has fallen into the washtub.' Our giggles expand like soap bubbles. The tropical soundtrack runs on without end, like the Amitofo tapes, a mix of bird calls, waterfalls and temple chimes.

I push myself up. 'How's life ? How are things with your father?'

She takes a towel from the side and starts to wipe her face. How I will never be able to see washcloths without thinking of that abduction. That seduction. John, coaxing his aunt into sleep. Throwing the towel away, she says, 'Getting used to things.'

'Do you see John a lot?

'*Ah* John.' She lowers herself back into the water. Somehow, the angle of her shoulders shifts. 'He never comes along to the hikes.' With great deliberation, she rotates her right ankle, spreads out her toes, tilts her foot.

'He was such a big help. With your mother, I mean. Have you... dreamed of your mother lately?'

'No.' She sits up. 'I don't know whether that's a good sign or not. What do you think?'

'I don't know.' I turn around in the slippery tub to better face her and take a deep breath. 'You know, I—I look at it like a Christian. Well, you know that I'm a Christian, you've been to Mass with me. Although maybe that wasn't so—typical, our discussion about socialism and all that.' My heart races. 'Isn't it funny the way we look now, like mud figures? You know, Christians believe that God created the first humans out of a piece of mud. Well, not really—'

'Mud?'

'I mean, we believe that God created us humans in His image.' I pause for breath, my heart hammering like after a run. Bark coloured foam drips from my lids. I wipe my brow, feeling hotter than moments ago.

'You mean, God is a piece of mud?'

I gasp for more air, swallow and break into a cough. 'It—means—that on the inside, God created us like Him.'

'Ah. Then your god is just like our gods. They are also very human inside.'

I take another deep breath, try to reclaim some sort of Eva speech from somewhere. 'You see—you see the way we're all dark right now? We believe that human beings are born with sin attached to them. But then God sent His son—'

'You can wash it all away. Look.' Her washcloth looks like a soiled diaper but under its wipes she reveals flawless, cream coloured skin. With her cocoa-streaked face, she looks very young.

'Like baptism,' I say, louder than intended. 'Exactly. We can be baptised and then God washes our sins away like… chocolate.'

'I like the chocolate. It smells nice.' She closes her eyes and inhales.

'So, for example my grandmother,' I say. The soap bubbles are dying, one by one they implode. Like dishwater, the broth starts to look. 'It makes me happy, to think of her in heaven. The dead go to heaven, that's what we believe.'

'Was she your father's mother or your mother's mother?'

'My mother's.'

'Your *ngoihpoh*, then. *Pohpo* is the other grandmother. On the father's side.' Her shower cap is sliding down, threatening to fall over her eyes. For a moment, she looks like the rebel she was when we freed her mother from hospital. 'And what happens to those who were not Christians in their lives?'

'They still go to heaven,' I say, my voice higher-pitched than I would like it to be. 'They still go to heaven, just like the rest of us.'

She fans out her fingers, studies the back of her hand, watches the dogshit coloured froth drip down. 'But see, our dead are different.'

We rest in a steam bath, wrapped in towels. Virginia sounds sleepy and I also have to drag my thoughts to the surface when she starts to talk. 'Today is the Festival of the Seven Sisters. Remember, what I taught you last year?'

I nod. A festival for unmarried girls, celebrating a pair of lovers. The Cowherd and the Weaving Girl, separated by the Milky Way. On the seventh day of the seventh month, all magpies fly up to the moon to make a bridge for them to meet. I giggle. 'I remember the six unmarried sisters of the Weaving Girl, poor parents.'

She is still whispering. 'Shall we go, later? I used to do that with some former classmates. Make offerings and try to look into the future to see who we'll marry.'

How large he looms in my conscience now, my Cowherd. I turn away and nudge deeper into my towel. 'Sure, we could… do that.'

'Kim?'

'Mmh.'

'Does it make you sad that I'm not a Christian? Is it that?' Her words float through the steam-filled room.

On my skin, the moisture collects in fat drops and falls onto the floor. I press my fists into my eye sockets. Want to disappear like a child, like Virginia under her oversized outfit. If I cannot see you then you cannot see me. Keep still, perhaps blend in. I bite softly into my arm but instead of salt I only taste chocolate soap. Try to calm my breathing, not to let the sobs escape to the surface.

Moon Seven Day Sixteen
Wednesday 9 August

The late afternoon sun pours into the room, spinning gold out of nothing much—my pine dining table, the box in which I collect old newspapers, the catch of my sandal, thrown carelessly off next to the sofa. Virginia and I have finished our language exchange and are slumped on my couch, legs extended, motionless like amphibians in the heat. A poem, grating all upside down in my head. *Furniture.* Furniture and love. Sluggish, with hesitance, the last line assembles in my mind. *His furniture is love.*

'Why don't you turn the air conditioning higher? It's hot.'
Next to me, Virginia shifts, looking around for the remote control. Her eyes scan the surroundings, pass over the Sudanese coffee table in the corner, the Spitzweg poster with the Poor Poet over the sink, my bed with its wrong feng shui in the back; take in all the remaining emptiness. God's residence is next to mine, it comes back to me. 'You don't have any pictures. Not even of your parents.'

'Mmh,' I say. *They are still alive*, but that is beside the point. In the moist density of the afternoon, my thoughts seem to be moving like boulders, rolling slowly. 'If your father is better... Virginia, have you ever thought of moving out?' I return to my ice tea, concentrate on shredding the lemon.

She gets up and walks around. She surveys the bathroom, leans against the doorframe. To my half-turned back, she says, 'I'm not like you, Kim, moving all the time. You will leave again, right?'

I feel for the truth in this sentence, the boulder that came to a halt just in front of me. *Will fail of it above.*

She pushes herself away from the door, takes a few steps in my direction. 'I wish you'd try harder to be a good daughter.'

I set down the ice tea, spilling some of it onto the side table. Like a blow to the foot, the pain travels up inside me. 'But I do. I go home during my holidays. Other expats go backpacking in Vietnam.'

She walks over to the coffee set, straightens a piece or two. When she turns around, her eyes are big and dark. 'You will regret it one day, you know.'

I trace the spilled tea with my finger. 'Maybe we're not that kind of family,' I say. *Who has not found the heaven below.*

She goes into the bathroom, comes back with a piece of toilet paper to mop up my spill. 'That's what everybody thinks.' She balls up the tissue, looks at the soggy mass with disgust. 'Toilet paper. Why don't you get a maid to keep your house in order? And some—*things*?'

'But I have things,' I say, pointing to the pile of books next to my bed, the doorway with its cluster of flip-flops and sandals.

'Library books,' she scoffs. 'And shoes. People need shoes.' She walks off into the bathroom, balancing the disintegrating ball over her left hand. The toilet lid bangs.

Her voice rings out, distorted from the tiles. 'Everybody thinks their families are special.' There is the sound of rushing water and her voice again, raised over the flushing. 'There is only one kind of family. Special ones.' She comes back into the living room, shaking the last drops of water from her hands.

'There's more toilet paper if you need.'

'I wished,' she says, shaking her hands once more, 'you enjoyed being a woman more. You don't really enjoy it, do you?' She blushes and returns to her iced coffee.

I shrug. 'Me? I'm a tomboy, born and bred.'

'All these—dark trousers and white blouses. The stuff you wear for work.' She sets the ice cubes in her drink into clinking motion. 'And the spa.'

The spa. 'Oh,' I say. 'The office uniforms. My own version, anyway.' After a while, I add, 'My parents would hate to be tied down with their grown-up children. "Twenty years is enough," my mother always says.'

We drink in silence.

'I need to go,' she finally says. Her smile looks strained, not quite reaching the corners of her eyes, which shimmer dangerously. She pulls on her sandals, scrutinising her feet. 'I'll ask Ronda for a pedicure when I get home, she took a class at the Y.' She smiles at me. 'She's a good worker.'

My furniture, my home, everything looks bleak now that the sun has disappeared around the neighbouring building. I pick up our glasses and carry them to the sink. The sour aroma of lemon and the bitter scent of coffee linger in the air, two distinct smells that even the humid August heat refuses to mix. I run a finger over my coffee table and wonder how I could ever mistake the dust for gold.

Intercalary Moon Day One
Thursday 24 August

Intercalary month. A thirteenth month slipped in between Moon
Seven and Moon Eight for both ends of the year to fit again, so
that solar and lunar calendars tally and Chinese New Year arrives
at the right time. A moon made to human measure, to make our
view of the world work.

'Kim?'

I pull myself away from the wall calendar. Irina leans on the
partition, composed as usual—colour-coordinated, cool. 'I'd like
to talk with you.'

In Irina's room, it is still July. The speed at which she moves
through the office and life in general sometimes keeps her from
minutiae such as these. Her cough brings me back to the desk.
If she wasn't a fanatical non-smoker, I could swear she was
yearning for a cigarette.

'Kim, you've been with MediMission for, remind me, six
years?'

'Seven,' I say. 'Four years here and three in Khartoum. Well—
almost five here, really.'

'Time flies. Seven, then.'

There is a paperweight on her desk, a mango-shaped crystal
with decorative carving. With some difficulty, I decipher the
upside-down cursive. *25 Years of Life in Abundance. John 10, 10.
With compliments from the Christian Farmers Association.* Her hand
folds around the writing and she weighs the glass orb in her
hand. 'Would you go back?'

'Go back? Go back where?'

'To Khartoum. You didn't want to come here in the first
place, right?'

'No. No, but—' I search her features and break into a smile.
'No, Hong Kong was an arranged marriage,' I say and we both
laugh.

'But a successful one, all in all.' She puts the paperweight down. 'You've worked your way up, you contribute in many ways.' She looks at me from lowered eyes. 'It's changed for you, right?'

I look away, cannot find the right words and simply savour the little warmth inside. Finally, I say, 'It really helps if you immerse yourself in the language.'

'Ah, the language. If only we all had the time.' Her fingers enclose the glass object once more. 'Talking about immersion. Kim, there's no way around this, so I'll just jump in. Sorry if I have to be the nasty mother-in-law in your arranged marriage. The thing is, we've received complaints about you. That you burn incense in temples.'

I stare at the desk where the crystal mango lay minutes ago, the faux grain of the Formica pretending something that is not there.

She lowers the paperweight once more, leaving it shivering unsteadily from the movement. 'Kim. Kim, I know you do all this… with the right kind of attitude. And your interest in local culture is nice.' The paperweight has come to a halt. 'But, you're here to work with the Filipinas and they might feel uncomfortable working with somebody who's—'

'Who's what? They're very conservative.'

'Who's openly sympathetic to local religion,' she says. 'They are. The problem is, to work with them you need their trust.'

'It will do them good to be exposed to other ideas. And— and what about Jim? He works with them. He's even supposed to study Chinese religion.'

'Sure, study it. But…' Irina has folded her hands and looks at me. 'If Jim ever did buy Buddhist offerings, he certainly never placed them in the office fridge.'

The revolutionary pastry which I bought next door and stored for a few hours before taking it home. 'But that's…. food,' I say. 'From their takeaway desk.' How dishonest the truth can feel. And another truth—that we cannot tell them apart here, food from hope. Irina must know this, because she says nothing. 'So?'

'I would strongly recommend that you keep your interest in

local religion to yourself and that you refrain from anything that might be… misconstrued as a—' She looks at her fingers, then raises her head but doesn't look at me. 'A heretical practice in the presence of your clients.'

Dim sum dishwashing. No, that cannot be. Everybody does it, everybody believes in it, like the phone numbers. I nod, my throat suddenly so engorged with feeling that I cannot utter a word.

'Perhaps you can also think of ways to… reinforce your Catholic identity when you are with your clients. Our clients.'

I give her a hard stare. What am I supposed to do, wrap a rosary around my arm, discuss the latest Vatican news and paste a picture of the Pope onto my agenda? The blockage in my throat bursts. 'I'm German. I never was supposed to be that kind of Catholic. Tell me, how do you reinforce your—evangelical identity with your clients? And Lynn Cameron the Methodist? Does she preach on the radio not to gamble in Happy Valley? Remind us not to drink and—'

'Kim.' Irina spins around in her chair. Her legs shift under her skirt. 'We've got freedom of faith here. It's just that—'

'Ah really,' I say, 'do we? I really think we should get the *Osservatore Romano* in here, don't you think so? To reinforce my Catholic identity.' I get up. 'It's good Ed is not a Pentecostal, otherwise he would have to deliver his press briefings speaking in tongues.' Suddenly, I am blinded by tears and my throats hurts as if sore. I feel for the door frame.

'Kim, I'm sorry if—'

I turn around but can hardly see her through my brimming eyes. I swallow. 'I've always loved about MediMission that it's supposed to be ecumenical.'

'We still are. Of course we are.'

'If you're such an authority on ecumenism, you also know what "ecumenical" means,' I say. '"All in the same house" or "all in the inhabited world".'

'I know,' she says, 'I know, I know.'

I cannot suffer her any longer and so I walk out, shoulders bent, while the salt of my tears reaches the corners of my mouth.

My arm brushes her calendar, causing the leaves to rustle.

Irina's voice rings out behind me. 'Just be a bit more careful, that's all.'

Back at my desk, my gaze falls onto the bookshelf. *Wandering Hearts: Filipino Migration and the Global Economy*. *Asian Women in the 21st Century: Between Tradition and Modernity*. Wedged in between, the green ledger, the space after my name still empty. My skin itches as if remembering the chocolate disaster. A dozen old Annual Reports. A stack of DVDs. A farewell card from April Lindsay, off with her family to the next stop in a transnational career. *Cottage cheese is hard to get, but the curries are divine*, she writes, reproducing home-made food under difficult circumstances. Virginia, following decades old recipes bent over her mother's handwriting. And myself, moving and leaving and moving again. A home-maker of yet a different kind.

Once more, my gaze goes to the bookshelf. *Freedom of Movement—a Manifesto*. I taste the shades of the word, try to negate it. The lack of freedom to move. Or the freedom not to move.

Intercalary Moon Day Three
Saturday 26 August

Like a wandering dune, Ben's bookbed meanders through the flat as we dissemble and reassemble it, dusting and spraying books with repellent in the process. Today is cleaning day, after weeks with cockroaches scurrying by while our piles of clothing grew and ungrew on the floor until I felt watched in between.

Ben laughed when I told him so. 'They would see us as a mosaic. Sort of, anyway. Dozens of "eyes" to see Reini in her birthday suit—who wouldn't go for that?'

Still, he agreed to the cleaning plan and so we are bringing up dust bunnies from the corners, blond curls and black wisps of hair tangled into matted, inseparable balls. Once in a while, we close the windows to fumigate a corner or a stack of books. A lone antenna appears, severed from its owner, and I whisk it away, trying not to think of its intricate beauty.

'You're not hiking,' Ben observes. His voice sounds muffled as he lies on his back, a screwdriver in hand, fiddling with one of the bed supports. When he is done, he leans against the wall, his knees almost on eye level, his arms relaxed. 'How's your friend, anyway?'

'She does museums in the summer. It's too hot to hike.'

'What's the matter?'

'Nothing.' I sit down against the opposite wall, my legs almost touching his.

He flips the screwdriver into his other hand. 'You alright?'

'I'm fine.' With the rag, I rub over an invisible blotch on the floor.

He gives an exaggerated sigh. 'You're a fine girl, I know that. But you've been walking around with this screwed up face for weeks. And now this—Mount Everest of books.'

Like a foreign flag, I swing my cloth around my index, first clockwise, then counter-clockwise. Finally, I say, 'Ben, I just need to think this one through by myself.'

He shrugs, gets up and goes to the fridge. Glasses clink, water splashes and he hands me a drink. 'Why do you always have to struggle with things on your own?'

I take a sip. In the poisonous heat of the flat, the water is of an icy purity. 'That's German.'

'Is that supposed to be funny? You always say that. In any case, it's very unhealthy.'

All that worrying, so tempting and so German. As if worrying was a particular type of far-seeing intelligence. I lift the rag and drop it, start to pick lint from it. 'Virginia, she—should move out, or get her father to leave her alone. So—constantly nagging her, for not being married.'

'He sounds bitter.'

I nod, still wringing the cleaning rag. 'He worked like a slave and doesn't have much to show for it.' It only dawns on me as I say it, that without Virginia's previous income as a teacher and her sister's support, he would probably not be living in this middle-class compound.

'Maybe her father is bitter because he doesn't have any sons. Maybe he's ashamed of it. Didn't you say her mother died? That's probably what it is. A phase of transition for the family.'

'By constantly criticising his daughter? That generation with their arranged marriages?' I look to the side but cannot take my words back. Quickly, I add, 'It's wearing her down. Her father.'

'Reini.' His voice is very quiet. 'Semi-arranged, maybe, in that generation. That background.'

We go out for Sichuan noodles. We are hunched over our bowls, slurping the spicy liquid, when he says out of the blue, 'You know, love is always full of contradictions.' His free hand searches mine and his thumb, roughened from our cleaning session, strokes the top of my hand.

I nod. As if I didn't know. I concentrate on my noodles, lift them with my chopsticks, suck them in, the chilli tingling on my tongue.

He somehow manages to eat, use chopsticks and talk all at the same time. 'Maybe he… takes pride in the fact that she is a dutiful daughter. And she as well.'

I look up.

In the dim light of the restaurant, his pupils seem bigger than moments before. 'The way you describe her, that's one of the things she's good at. Being a good daughter.'

Intercalary Moon Day Eleven
Sunday 3 September

Virginia may be a good daughter but I am a bad friend and so I disregard her words and ignore her silences. I must have left my phone in her flat and ring her from my landline. She sounded odd yesterday and sounds odder today. It pains me, how I can read her but rarely bother to do so these days. Leaving her alone even when we are together, going through the motions of our language exchange without ever scratching the surface.

'Wait, I'll ask Ronda.' There is a plonk. Her footfall dies away on the wooden floor. 'Kim. Ronda found it. It had slipped into the sofa—'

'Why is she at home? It's Sunday.' And we quarrel, quarrel to the point of no return, flinging words about that put us both to shame. 'Virginia. You *cannot* pay her instead of giving her time off. If she sues you, you'll be in trouble. It happens all the time.'

'She should take the Chinese as an example. Chinese people work very hard. When my father first came to Hong Kong—'

'Ah yes, foreigners are such ninnies. Thanks for reminding me. He controls you. He manipulates you. You're thirty-eight years old.'

'Hard work won't kill anybody—'

'It's inhuman how you treat her, she needs to be given a day off—' I ball up a leftover Green Lotus leaflet, slam it into the corner. How easy it is to destroy. What did Spielberg say? There ever is only one kind of violence.

When I step outside, I almost walk into an elderly woman assembling offerings on the pavement. The Hungry Ghost Festival. A whole month of celebrations intended to ward off the unhappy dead who come to roam the sphere of the living. The childless, those without remaining descendants, those who were not buried properly, those who died in accidents or killed themselves. There are many ways of being unhappy after all, engendering different kinds of violence.

And if the danger of the ghosts let loose from hell was not enough, this year things feel even more out of sync. The intercalary month extends the time between the Seven Sisters and the Hungry Ghosts. Does this give the ghosts more time among the living? Virginia would know. Siu Yi, these improvised ceremonies are called, the Burning of Clothes, and I imagine myself, incinerating one of my invented office uniforms.

Hungry Ghosts Festival
Wednesday 6 September

After my recording of yet another Word for the Day, dusk has given way to darkness by the time I am on the ferry. With hunger, I bite into a chocolate cookie bought at the ferry entrance. Like a moon, it sits between my fingers, a quickly forming crescent, while the chocolate crumbs in my mouth overpower the aromas around me, gasoline and sea spray and the perfumes and tired breaths of commuters on their way home. There is something else in the air tonight, something that I smell before I see it. Incense is drifting over the sea, uncertain wisps that hover over a lighter nearby.

When we pass the vessel, the women emerge clearly, sharp like paper cuts against the orange lamps of the boat and the silver lighting of the city. Some are scattering rice into the water, others are setting paper boat offerings afloat. A group of monks is with them and, for an instant, their chanting wafts across the sea, bits of sound appearing and disappearing like gusts of wind. They are making offerings to the Hungry Ghosts, to all those who died at sea. The Boat People of Hell.

Fragrant Harbour, Incense Port, *Heung Gong*. There are many explanations for the city's name, the most common one referring to the joss production situated here in ancient times. Tonight, however, there is only one truth as the Hungry Ghosts feed on the incense lit for them, inhale the clouds rising from the water, a whole harbour made fragrant. Fragrant with fear.

White Dew
Friday 8 September

'Auld Lang Syne'. My doorbell rings, upsetting me from my breakfast in various ways at once—because of the ungodly hour, because of the strangeness of Scottish goodbyes on a muggy Southern Chinese morning, because of the overall obsession with invented worlds, again; because of the fact normal people call before they come, nowadays.

Chewing on a piece of toast, my hands sticky with honey, I go to open. Seeing a familiar figure through the grated door, I nod, although for a moment I could not say who is on the inside and who on the outside. In the early morning quiet, the door thunders.

'Ronda!' I smile, refuse to take in the whole message—the church shoes on her feet, the red-blue-and-white plastic bag tugging at her determined brown hand. The kind of bag that holds millions of migrant dreams and wandering belongings. 'Where's Virginia?' I glance over her shoulder but the only sign of life is the joss stick burning quietly in front of my neighbours' door.

'I… left them.' She shifts her weight onto her other foot, then straightens, uncoils her wiry self to full advantage.

Disappointment rises in me and annoyance and I try to put a face on them both and attach them to Ronda. How a pain we foresee hurts less, even if the betrayal is greater; how I could have seen it coming that Virginia might throw her out… and how I would have thought that Ronda's hope would outlive Virginia's. With one single jerk of her chin, she turns from victim to perpetrator.

'I see.' Suddenly, I find it unbearable—the dry, empty texture of the bread in my mouth, my sticky hands that make me helpless, being caught in shorts and a tank top. I struggle to swallow the last bite. 'And may I ask how you found out my address?'

'I—I remembered it, from the time when we brought the nightstand to your flat. Virginia's spare one, remember?' She studiously plays with the zip of her bag. Watching me from the corner of her eye, she pulls the last inch shut.

'That was months ago.' I consciously refrain from waving my hands around which I am itching to wash. But itching less when I think of her walking in once I leave for the bathroom.

I scowl at her. 'And you remembered that it was Block C, Flat G, twelfth floor? Not the seventh or the ninth?' Somehow, I cannot let go of this fact, of her snooping through her employer's mobile phone. As if I didn't know so much more about her and had not always felt entitled to ask for more. *Address? Date of birth? Last employer? Did he sexually harass you?*

She fingers the zip again but there is nothing left to close. She looks up in a way that must come with her job, hot eyes that slide easily back under cool lids.

'And what do you think—' I summon a stern look. Battling same with same. Terrier head with toilet brush. My hands almost hurt from not being able to wash them.

'The shelters, they're all full.'

Once again, I cannot help admiring her command of her body, how it gathers and ungathers itself with meaning. 'The shelters really are for people in much more desperate circumstances than yours.'

'So, you are sending me away?' Trembling slightly, her hair seems to have a life of its own. 'I thought—I thought maybe you need help.' Her eyes dip into my apartment.

'My dust bunnies are none of your business. I can't go hiring every domestic worker in need of a decent employer. The city is full of them.'

'It's inhuman, the way they make me work on Sundays and—'

'And what? They've been going through a difficult time, Ronda.'

Her crimped hair seems to be humming, as if electrified. 'And I think—I thought you meant it. But you're just a, a pretend do-goodie like the rest of them.'

A goody two shoes. My gaze falls to my feet. Barefoot, they

are, the shadow of the water buffalo almost gone. I shift my weight, as if that could change the secrets that have accumulated between my blood sister and me.

'Tell me, tell me one reason why I cannot stay with you.'

'Why do I need to give you a reason?' How I hate myself in this moment, hate her for making me so. Hate my hands, incapacitated by honey and still dying to be washed.

'For a few days, only.' Her eyes challenge me, before they slide away, shuttering themselves until she is fingering her bag again and seems to be speaking to herself, lips frowning in the slightest of pouts. 'And I thought you meant it, treating me like a friend. Talking in the kitchen. How we laughed, at the onion—'

In the opposite entrance, the inner door unlocks with two well-practised bumps. The door grille bangs open and old Ms Chan shuffles out, gluing her gaze onto us. Her eyes savour the moment, the foreign ghost throwing out her helper.

'Come in,' I say to Ronda and I motion us in, a helper and a foreign ghost.

Intercalary Moon Day Nineteen
Monday 11 September

I never hear the word "escape"/Without a quicker blood/A sudden expectation/A flying attitude. Above me, black eared kites are circling the ferry, flying low, on the lookout for something elusive to the human eye, before finally plunging down with force. In a moment, I will come home to find my laundered underwear pressed and folded, my cutlery alphabetically sorted and my cleaning rags disinfected and labelled.

'Ronda,' I say when the door has fallen shut behind me, 'this can't go on, all of this—' My arm sinks to my hip. Your striped bag looming like the Pinatubo in my living-room, my flat which is not mine anymore, our awkward domesticity in the mornings, the non-ringing telephone. 'Give them another chance.'

Ronda looks up, my Sudanese coffee pot balanced in one hand, a dust cloth dangling from the other. She pushes a stray lock behind her ear, looks at the clay vessel in her hands. 'I still have some things, back in the flat,' she says. 'But you have to come with me.'

The sky is soot black by the time we emerge from Tin Hau MTR station, the air weighed down with impending rain. We quicken our pace and our rushing makes it easier to round the convenience store as usual, take the familiar bend into Virginia's estate, hurry past the playground towards the entrance. Heavy drops start to fall, splattering with explosive noise onto awnings and umbrellas. We break into a run.

Upstairs, when Ronda presses the doorbell, nobody opens. She tries to squint through the spy hole. 'That's weird. They should be cooking dinner.' Her shoulders relax. After listening a few more seconds, she lets us in. 'Hello. Hello-o?' Her voice is thinner than necessary, pulled taut.

In the living-room, only the standby buttons glow in the dark and, between the familiarity of it all, the strangeness takes a while to sink in. Then I see it. In front of the picture of Virginia's mother, a couple of candles are burning, their shadows trembling like their own ancestors on the walls. They must have been lit for a special purpose and my brain struggles to understand their message. Their meagre, elongated bodies are falling apart, threatening to set fire to the cabinet underneath.

'That's odd,' I say, 'burning candles without anybody to watch out against fire.'

'Kim.' Ronda hesitates before striding, no, hurrying towards Virginia's room where a pale fringe of light cuts across the threshold. She grabs the door knob and thuds against the unyielding wood. The door doesn't budge.

'It's sealed!' Everything in me plummets. Sealed from inside with duct tape, snaking around the door frame to keep out oxygen.

Together, we throw ourselves against the door until it falls open. It is too much to take in, Virginia on her bed, in her favourite crimson top, a heap of muscle and bones, lifeless like a puppet, the metal wash tub on the parquet filled with embers almost dead, barbecue coals white with heat.

'The window,' I gasp. It is sealed as well. We shove and heave Virginia out of the room, drag and carry her close to the balcony. Old instructions soaring deep inside me (*Erste Hilfe: Bringen Sie das Opfer in stabile Seitenlage*), I position her in the recovery position, feel for her pulse, wait for the oxygen to take hold in her blood. Ronda is already on the phone. Calling an ambulance, phoning Virginia's father. Explaining his daughter's emergency in frayed Cantonese, hectic English. She runs back into Virginia's room; with a grating sound, more tape strips come off. There is a bang of window frame against wall. With gratitude, I feel the rush of fresh air all the way to my place on the living-room floor. The rain has ceased and the air flowing in from the balcony is sweet with purity. On the outside wall the birds, in their habitual muted pose, doze in the cages.

'The ambulance, the damned ambulance.' Suddenly, I cannot suffer their sight any longer, one impatience marrying another, and rush out, my steps too loud on the wooden floor. One by one, I set the cages onto the railing, open the doors, coax their inhabitants to flee. The mynah is the first to go, followed by the hwamei. By the time I am ready to set the finches free, I am shaking so much that I fumble with the minute bamboo doors. I have to rattle their cages until they, too, feel compelled to disappear into the darkness of the city night.

'The ambulance… so slow, so slow,' I whisper into the living-room where Ronda is kneeling next to Virginia, feeling her pulse. At the sound of my voice, Ronda resettles her upper body, pushes a wisp of hair out of her face and doubles her smile for Virginia. I peer down at the ground, wonder whether I can drop the bird cages to make it look like an accident, and shy away from their cannon-like quality. Wiping my hands on my trousers, I summon Ronda. 'Here, take.' I thrust the cages into her arms. 'Bin them, quickly.'

She flinches and, while she hesitates, something hot and quiet gathers in her features, in her face which is so close to my own yet revealing of nothing, her mouth flattened into a line. In the end, she trudges away without a word.

I return to Virginia, take her wrist once more, struggle to make sense of what I feel but lose track. Follow as hope threads its way into my system like the oxygen into hers, and lose track again. Wait and count and wait and count.

'... *now and at the hour of our death.*' Ronda, back from the trash, has started to say Hail Marys. I fall in, bite into the sentences to ungrit my teeth and repeat them and, unable to recover their meaning, cling to individual words. In the alcove, the candles in front of the photograph have burnt down and our gazes interlock in that familiar way, one presence observing the other. Full of grace. If only I could let go of the words churning in my mind. *But I tug childish at my bars/Only to fail again.*

Intercalary Moon Day Twenty-two
Thursday 14 September

This is my letter to the world/That never wrote to me. I wish Virginia had left a note. She was more devious, or perhaps guileless. As a result, all of us feel guilty, each for different reasons. She explains nothing and so nobody gets absolved, her message committed *to hands I cannot see.* During my lonely lunch break, I conjure Emily and the kites—*The simple news that Nature told*—but there is no consolation in them, the kites primitive beasts in constant search for food, Emily producing only garbled pain and nonsense. Surrounded by strangers, clinging to my bitter Yin and Yang, I reject the poem, discard all but one sentence that I carry with me: *Judge tenderly of me!*

After work, I go to see her in hospital, the same one from which we brought her mother home, but the sight of the familiar Buddhist emblem gives no comfort; rather, it unsettles me like a pile of books strewn across the floor, a jumble of titles that evoke all manner of different feelings.

When I enter her room, my stomach is still upset, part motion sickness from the upwards journey in the lift, part something else. Or maybe it is the smell of the detergents, that chemical form of aggression. I scan the beds, search for familiarity between uniform bed linen and dark hair until I find her. The setting sun gives her a terracotta glow.

'Hullo,' I say and extend my present, wrapped in red. My heart allows itself a tiny smugness over this choice.

'You needn't have brought anything.' She fingers the package. Her eyes widen. She pushes it back into my hands, her shoulders shielding it from view. 'Put it out of sight. Into the night stand.'

While I am struggling with the lock of the cabinet, she leans closer. 'Is it a book?' she whispers, her English 'book' standing out starkly in her smooth Cantonese sentence. She smells different, tired and medical.

'Yes,' I answer as if filling in her Cantonese blank, 'that's a *shue.*' With a smooth turn, the drawer locks shut.

'Shh,' she hisses. Her eyes wander to the adjacent beds. 'Don't say it.' But her neighbours seem oblivious to us. One of them is emitting faint snores, the other two are staring into space, dozing.

'What you gave me,' she says, 'was entirely wrong. Wrong for people in hospital,' she continues in English, 'because—that word sounds like the word for "to be defeated", "to lose".'

A blush erupts on my cheeks. It also hurries my stomach along, the boiling feeling which I try to ignore. 'You have to get well soon,' I say. 'Teach me much more.'

'I don't mind.' She tugs at her sheets. She still shields herself, shrouds her body in bed linen pulled up to her shoulders in spite of the heat. The sun has slid behind the mountain and, without its light, her features are ashen, the eyes sunk deep into their sockets. Next to her, so drained on the spotless linen, the night stand is a profusion of colour, crammed with flowers, get well cards, almond cakes and a package of chocolate biscuits. Her family's favourite brand causes my stomach to revolt, again.

'Have you had many visitors yet? These are beautiful.' I point to a very Chinese looking combination, a bunch of red roses, pink lilies and something strange and green in between, all wrapped in lilac foil.

She nods. Her fingers give the blanket free, lower it a few inches. She struggles into a sitting position and extends a waxen arm for the glass on the night stand. Slowly, carefully, she swallows water, one hand clutching the linen again. There must be something wrong with the air conditioning, because every once in a while it starts to make noises, a knocking of metal on metal.

When she turns towards me, her new smell wafts over like a bad memory. 'The almond cakes are from Jim and Spielberg.'

'I'm sorry I didn't come earlier,' I say. 'I wasn't sure…'

Her eyes flutter, travel to her neighbours and back. '*They* are starting to wonder about all the men.' She giggles but her smile looks borrowed, of an awkward fit.

'The Beer Festival,' I say. 'It's coming up. As soon as you've recovered, we'll do that, just you and me.'

She nods and shuts her lids. Her face looks more peaceful with closed eyes.

My stomach flares up again and I find it harder to dismiss. The room has grown dim. I look at my watch. Almost eight. 'I have to go.'

'Thank you for coming.' Her lids are still closed and, against the brightness of the pillow, she looks almost like a woman undergoing a beauty therapy. 'How is Ben?'

'Ben?'

She opens her eyes. In her pallid face, they make a fitful pair of darknesses. 'Why do you never mention him?'

'He's…' I touch my head, straighten my blouse. 'He's fine. He was—shocked to hear about you.' And that makes it worse, to admit that we have been talking about her. That walk along the Heritage Trail when we bumped into her—or she into us. How far away Ben seemed then, and how close Virginia. *I started the wrong way round.* Where did I turn the wrong way? Keeping all the best things to myself. Like a child, I treated her, not thinking her capable of dealing with otherness all the while I was totally incapable of dealing with it myself.

'People talk all the time. Did you really think—' She yanks the sheets up once more. 'You kind of—stand out in a Chinese crowd. One of the nuns mentioned it. You know, from the wake. We had to hire them for the follow-up ceremonies.'

Fuican. Her unintended betrayal hurts me more for her than for me. Can it be a betrayal at all, to speak the truth?

The air conditioning has resumed its unhealthy noise. Something gleams in the corner of her eye and, with excruciating slowness, trickles down her cheek. I shift in my chair, wait for the moment to be able to leave.

'Kim.' The room is almost dark now. 'Are you—have you found… what you are looking for?'

My humpback whale, gentle and vegetarian creature of the sea. Only son and future ancestor. Warrior for cockroaches. Who probes my innermost sensibilities. Turns me inside out. I have to look away and swallow.

There is a soft knock. Frank's face appears in the door frame and, for a moment, it hangs there like a big and pale moon. Behind him, a nurse hurries by in a green smock and the sight of her reminds me of our lab coats all those months ago.

Virginia lifts a hand in greeting, a milky movement on starched white.

He breaks into a smile and comes in. 'Virginia.'

Her smile is simple, almost childlike.

'I—brought you some chocolates.' He seems smaller than usual, perhaps because of his voice, so shrunk and shrivelled in the gloom. Or perhaps it is his shirt which does this, with its muted, dark hues.

'Hi, Frank,' I say. I step forward, push things on the night stand around to create space for his chocolates, will my tears back into their sockets. Take a breath or two. Focus on my surprise at seeing him here.

'You needn't have brought anything. Look, your flowers are still nice.' Virginia half raises herself from the pillow.

'Unless…' he says. 'I don't want to tempt you. Forbidden fruit and all that. We're all eager to have you back soon, aren't we,

Kim?' With a glance at the other beds, Frank lowers himself into the second visitor's chair.

I nod. 'But take your time,' I say. 'We'll keep up your walks. We've got it all figured out, Jim and the others.'

Frank draws his chair closer to the bed and leans forward. Stooped over her bed, there is something new in him, something reminiscent of the old woman on Stanley Beach. The coal vendor humbled by age. 'Get well.' He presses his hand onto her blanket, once, twice, and lets it rest there. Virginia's eyes seem welded to Frank's shirt around the height of his collar, memorising its pattern of dark blue flowers on black. Red spots have appeared on her cheeks. Her gaze heaves itself up, swerves around Frank and falls onto my face. She seems enveloped by fatigue now, heaviness clouding her like another off-key perfume.

'I have to go,' I say, trying to rein in my gaze which darts back and forth between them. I step closer and give her a nod, and another one.

In the darkness of the surroundings, it is barely noticeable but her gaze flits to the night stand and back to me. 'Never mind,' she says. 'How could I believe in—linguistics?'

Frank shoots me a look but Virginia only smiles.

'Take care,' I say into the room and with relief hear the door fall shut behind me.

Intercalary Moon Day Twenty-four
Saturday 16 September

There is a constant stream of Virginia's relatives at my door, loaded with presents. Toddler-sized teddy bears in bonbon colours and with satin bows, choice Chinese medicine for each bodily organ conceivable, homemade soups like the broths given to women in childbed, flowers in bulky heart-shaped plastic and foil contraptions, fruit baskets.

Her father approaches me, in long trousers and a freshly ironed shirt, and hands me a gift. I know better than to open it in his presence. 'What would we have done without you? You saved her.' He swallows, his voice shakier than I remember it.

Tension gathers inside me, congeals like soup. Indeed, without me things would have been so much easier. 'Don't speak of it,' I say, producing a smile. I shift my weight. 'I'm… sorry that your birds died from the coals.'

His smile, so warm and soft moments ago, tightens. For an instant, he looks to the side, a private grief tearing at his features.

'Don't speak of it,' I say again. 'And there was Ronda.' Ronda, who has quietly moved back in with the family. I avert my eyes from his thin frame. Will he get a new pair of birds, now that the park has swallowed his old ones?

Intercalary Moon Day Twenty-six
Monday 18 September

It is a time of disease. I fall ill with a summer cold. Virginia instructs Ronda to bring me herbal tea and Chinese medicine, leaving me to wonder whether to take it, whether to believe in it.

I drag myself to work. It is only a cold, after all.

'The air conditioning,' Eva nods. 'Take some hot Coca-Cola with ginger.'

'Saturday Night Fever,' Ed says. 'Get some sleep.' He looks up from the paper clip which he is twisting into a new shape. He likes to clean his fingernails with them. 'Come on, admit it.' But when I tell him about Virginia, he whistles under his breath. 'So sorry to hear that.'

'You need to take things more lightly,' Irina says, a concerned look on her face. 'And you're running a fever. Go home.'

The fever blurs my perception until it frays at the edges. Ben, tucking me into bed like a child, feeding me rice porridge, watching over my heated sleep while the air conditioner drums its insistent rhythm, keeping the ghosts at bay. Because this is how it is: The gods have won. Everywhere they glare at me, at the IKEA entrance and from rosewood cabinets, underneath banyan trees and in doorways. The gods have won, and I have done nothing.

And there is a part of me which is glad to shed this responsibility, to revert to my state of lonely faith, to feel responsible for nobody's salvation but my own. Because isn't this what she has taught me to fear, to entrust your salvation to others?

Moon Eight Day Three
Sunday 24 September

Fragrant Harbour, Incense Port, Pearl of the South China Sea. Like an incantation, I repeat the words in my mind. They have become meaningless, a medium to calm myself only. Below us, between the avocado green of the hills and the silver grey of the sea, the city lies in the distance, shimmering like a Fata Morgana.

We are walking along the Dragon's Back, Ben and I. He has decided that I need some exercise. My cold has passed but my whole body still creaks with a dry ache. My throat rasps, my stomach clamps in emptiness and, if I wasn't so dried up, there would be tears behind my lids. Even my heart feels sore, thumping its dogged rhythm as we climb the hill in silence.

Blinded with sweat, my voice pumping with exertion, I say, 'This really is Virginia's kind of thing.' I stop to wipe my brow. Fumbling to put the soggy handkerchief back into my trousers, I add, 'I wish I could have done something for her.'

Ben says nothing.

'I mean, I should have,' I say.

'That's… normal, that you spent less time with her after you met me. Okay, she felt left alone, yes. But all of you overlooked it. Probably because she wanted you to.'

Virginia, keeping still, trying to blend in.

Sometimes I hate his glib manner, his easy way of getting over problems. 'I should have done more. I know I should.'

'Reini.' He comes to a halt. 'If somebody is… determined in that way, or maybe suffering from disease, nobody can make that kind of a difference.' His eyes beseech me, the pupils growing until there is hardly any brown left.

We resume our walk.

'I know I could have,' I finally say and I tell him about the secrets that have grown between her and me: Ben, and how I knew all along what was behind the copper frying pans. Her mother's abduction and Ronda, although these two secrets feel different. (A fleeting thought for later: that secrets and counter-secrets are two different currencies.) And I tell him about Virginia's fear of hell, although I leave out the chocolate spa and my socialist religion.

'Maybe… maybe I should talk with her about religion,' I conclude. 'To help her overcome that fear.'

'To offer her what? An Eva-type of religion? Long skirts and virginity and no Coca-Cola?'

'That's the Mormons,' I say, blushing nonetheless.

'Alright, then with Coca-Cola. But a heaven-and-hell-type of story again, with a narrow worldview?'

'Ben.' It hurts, this surprise, how he can knock me over with the force of his words, the impurity of his assumptions.

'She was lonely and overwhelmed,' he says. 'The death of a parent sometimes does this. Unbalances people in a fundamental way.' His stride lengthens and I have to struggle to keep up with him.

'But don't we have to—talk with people?'

He stops and turns to face me. He pulls out his water bottle, gulps down some water. With the back of his hand, he wipes his forehead. 'Reini.' His expression changes. 'I swore to myself I wouldn't have this kind of discussion with you.'

I take a step back, look to the side, my heart beating furiously. That must be the steep ascent.

'You must not feel responsible for everything and everybody.' He steps closer. His voice softens. 'Don't make this kind of face. Virginia is a grown-up person. Feelings are a subjective thing.' Like a breeze, his fingers are on my cheeks, gently shift my sunhat a few inches. 'What she believes in, what you believe in—what can you do about it?' His eyes draw me in with their darkness.

I know what I don't believe in. Or so I thought. I don't believe in invented worlds. The Diorama Hell in Victoria Park. I turn away and stay mute. Today, I'm skipping church.

His voice again, persistent like a fly against a window. 'About the rest, it's not up to you to decide. That's also a form of hubris, don't you think so?' He approaches me again, lets his arms dangle into emptiness when I withdraw once more. '*Lengneuih*. Feeling responsible for everything is also a kind of... of making yourself superhuman. Taking on more than humans can take.'

We continue along the narrow path, single file. Fragrant Harbour, Incense Port, Pearl of the South China Sea... My hat lowered over my face, I march to the silent rhythm of the invocation drumming in my skull until I almost step on a butterfly. And another one.

'What's that?' In the bright light, there is something deeply unsettling about them, their yellow and black wings scattered like petals on the forest floor.

'It's their life cycle. They go through different stages, changing from one form into the next. You know that.' He is talking over his shoulder. 'Being a butterfly is just the final part of what being a butterfly is about.' He slows down and inspects one of the dead creatures. 'Looks like a Jezebel to me.'

'But this is the final stage. Being a butterfly, I mean.' I pick up a wing, hold it against the light. 'It looks scary. A battlefield of dead butterflies.' I blow the wing from my palm.

'It looks like the end to us but, from the species' point of view, life goes on.' He sets himself into motion again. 'They lay eggs before they die. That's probably why they come here, there must be some plant the caterpillars need after hatching.'

Every few steps, my eyes return to the ground, only to stumble across another butterfly wreck. Dead as they are, I catch myself avoiding them. Finally, we crest another hill and the city springs up again in the distance, bruised white against the sea, grey like a blunt mirror, its clamour stunted into a faraway hum. An off-white noise.

'How can you live with this?' I don't look at him while I ask, aim my eyes at the city instead; the hectically straining high-rises, the haze fading their edges like a tacky picture.

'You mean—me, the biologist, in a mega city?'

'No, I mean, the total... denial of the natural world. Reclaiming land as if it had always been there for us to use. All that plastic. And a lot of ignorance. One woman in the hiker's group thinks that high tide has to do with high noon. I've never lived in a place in which people... almost cultivate their ignorance of nature.'

'I thought you loved it.' His eyes are fastened to the dead leaves and the dismembered butterflies at our feet.

'I do.' Don't I feel its ache pull every day at my heart? The cicadas with their shrill mating calls, loud like jackhammers, the brilliant blood-red writing of a double happiness coconut, its tender sprout like a wing, trying to lift an impossible weight.

After a while, he says, 'Hong Kong is— There's a lot of upward mobility, not just among the immigrants. Oops, careful.' He stops so abruptly I almost bump into him. A net spans the width of the path, watched over by a spider the size of my palm. 'A woodland spider. People who have just left the rice paddies and fishing boats behind don't want to be reminded of their rural origins.' He lifts his camera. I duck under the net and wait for him.

When he has finished, he says, 'But there are people who love nature. Your friend—Virginia brings you to all these places and knows all about Chinese history.'

'I think she does it because she knows foreigners like it. Local girls would never go hiking, it's always, "Ugh, the suntan."'

'A moment ago you were saying that this is really her thing. Now you're saying she is a clever businesswoman. Come on,

236

continue.' His sneaker kicks a stone, sends up a bird in flight. 'Now that you're coming clean with your feelings for the locals.'

I follow his example and set off another piece of gravel, some internal heat firing the movement. 'Well, if you really want to know, I hate it how Western women are treated differently from Western men. Hong Kong people adore Western men. Western women are just an oddity with their yellow hair and un-Chinese directness. That's sick. Colonial. Proto-colonial.' I glance at him. 'And Chinese people have disgusting ear cleaning habits and are incredibly prudish. And, and—' For a moment, I cannot think of anything more to say. Then it comes back. The servitude of grown-up children and the indecisiveness of Cantonese food, sweet and savoury all rolled into one; the obsession with being white, again.

'So, we are disgusting and prudish?'

I raise my eyes to the curves and planes of his golden skin, each fold made mine, feel the familiar pull inside my body. 'Not all of you,' I concede. Still, the rage which I nurtured moments ago cannot be stifled so easily. 'But—what kind of place is this? With pineapple buns without pineapple? With fake frogs barking in the parks and snow installations for Christmas?'

'You mean—too perfect? Always going for the picture perfect?'

'No, not perfect at all. Like Kowloon Tong. An ice-rink in the tropics.'

'Striving for the impossible? Always bettering oneself?' He looks at me, his eyes half shut against the sun. We walk around another bend. The canopy opens and the city reappears, slender skyscrapers stretching like fingers into the clouds.

'It's… It's something about the senses,' I say. 'About duping the senses.' All these mirrored façades hiding their insides, promising one thing and delivering another. It is a shimmering reality, a city of changing meanings and invented worlds. Offered up to me to take it or leave it. To see it one way or another like a hologram.

We stop at a T-forked crossroads and sit down on a pair of rocks. My gaze travels into the distance, into the white horizon with its thousand amalgamated noises, hiding its colours like a rainbowed spectrum spun into white nothing.

'Where are we going?' With a sweeping movement, my hand slices the heat in two. For a moment, I cannot say whether it is mine and his heat, or ours and theirs.

'Where we are going?'

My heart flips, flutters like a bird, but something in me shies away from the tone of his voice. 'Just—which direction we'll take. In a moment.'

He wipes moisture from his upper lip, points down the hill. 'That one. To the right.'

Around us, the city pulses on, invisible from this vantage point. For the briefest of moments, I am tempted to tell him about the *white noise*, to share my discovery with him, but pull the idea back like a dog on a leash. Something is brimming behind my eyes, while my stomach is churning self-righteously. I almost wished we'd bump into Virginia, or even Irina. I kick a stick away, then a lump of gravel, and finally a piece of desiccated orange peel.

'Ye…es?' The remains of a smile slink away from his face when he takes me in, my crumpled, dejected posture. 'Come on, Reini, spill it out.'

I disregard my eyes and settle for my stomach instead, let its hot self-sufficiency fire me on. 'You're always so, so—'

'So what?'

'So detached. Cucumber cool.'

'Would you rather have me jump at every provocative remark that you make? Just because I'm not the nervy type doesn't mean that I don't care, Reini. You know that.'

'Aloof. That's what you are. Sitting like the Giant Buddha on the mountain to see what people around you are up to.' My hand flies to my mouth. 'Sorry.'

'So, I'm a stone sculpture on a mountain? Watching the world go by? Not caring?'

'You do care, I know that. All the cleanup campaigns and the feeding of the poor. But…' I need something more personal, a more individual rage. Somebody like Irina, her face burning with the creed of justice and sisterhood, lashing out regardless of any collateral damage. Somebody more black and white.

He jumps up and starts to pace around, his head lowered, his eyes trained on the ground. Finally, without looking up, he says, 'I cannot reconcile you with a whole culture.'

His words send my stomach into free fall. I can hardly look into his face, its shades of darkness. 'But I love Chinese culture.'

'You won't stop brushing up against certain things, nor can I make you stop. I sometimes feel like your apology.' He is still not looking at me, scrutinising his right foot where a piece of gravel has lodged in the sole of his sneaker. With a dull thump, he kicks it against a rock. It doesn't budge. He kicks again, with more force.

My sinking acquires speed. It reminds me of our cable car journey, so long ago now. 'My... apology?'

'Your... apologetic... native.' Again, he sends his right foot flying against the stone. 'Towards yourself. Or Chinese culture.' This time, the force of his movement raises a cloud of dust.

I remain silent. After a while, I say, 'You can get it out with a chopstick when you get home.'

He turns towards me. I recoil as if from a glaring fire. The shine of his face frightens me. If Joan of Arc had been a Chinese man, this is what she would have looked like. 'But don't you see? There is no need to apologise. Not to anyone.'

On our descent from the Dragon's Back, there are fewer and fewer dead butterflies until they vanish altogether. Instead, I discover a lone specimen dithering over a bush. It is big as my palm, dark brown, almost black, with a row of bright dots on each wing. 'These are very common, they seem to be everywhere. Why are they not dying?'

'They have a different life cycle,' he says. 'Look at their size. It takes a while to grow to that size. That's a Mormon. A Lesser Mormon, I guess.'

'So, are there Greater Mormons as well?' I let irony seep into my question, deflate it with a half-laugh.

Ben ignores my voice. 'Yes, there are, actually. Greater

Mormons, Common Mormons, Lesser Mormons.' He stops to lift his camera, squints at the settings on the display.

'Is this how you see us? A bunch of religious nutcases?'

Slowly, Ben's arms sink back, the camera still in his hands. His eyes rest on my face. 'But it's you who brings these things up. You seem to feel bad because you're not one of them. But you aren't and that's good. Fine with me, anyway. Come on, you—you hardly ever wear skirts. You have your… office uniforms.' He averts his gaze, lets his camera dangle from its strap until its weight cuts into his neck. The Mormon has disappeared.

'Thank you very much.' There is a new glare in my face. 'It's good to know how you see me after all. A religious nutcase on an impossible mission. You're probably glad for all that suffering in her life and her mother's as well. So many Buddhist chances.' My voice whines with strain and the fear of tears. I yank my sunhat deeper into my face, so deep that it almost reaches the bridge of my nose.

For the rest of our walk, I can barely see beyond my knees, so reduced is my field of vision, but at least I don't have to take in any more of this: not the butterfly graveyard, not the city with its faux shine, appearing and disappearing like a cruel vision, not Ben's El Greco eyes. Above all, he does not get to see my face, it's liquid glaze on this suffocating day.

Back home in my bed, I cry until salty trickles run into my ear. I cry for my injustice and for the pain of loving all this like mad, the black eared kites soaring in front of my office window, the noise of the dim sum restaurants humming under the city's surface, the chattering of the carefully made-up girls, the lanky animation of the young men. The turquoise of the sea along the shore, the heat sapping against my skin, drenching each pore in sweat, like love.

It is the aching love for something that you know you will lose one day.

Moon Eight Day Six
Wednesday 27 September

Remorse is cureless,—the disease/Not even God can heal. Like an old friend, this part of Kowloon always takes me in, with its scents of sandalwood and exhaust fumes, coconut tarts and durian, and so I wander around in search for solace, my stomach growling. But today, the magic is not there, the friendship gone, and the oddity of everything jarring, plywood furniture next to Kwun Yam statues, office supplies next to incense. And the paper gifts for the dead.

I walk on, quickly.

Virginia is still recovering. In her absence, I measure the emptiness she leaves behind, palpate it for its size and substance like a foreign body. With hesitance, I label it: Loyalty. Intellectual challenge. Sisterhood. More paper goods, card games and a race course, dim sum and soft drinks and, suddenly, I see her with more clarity. New York cheesecake and hiking shoes, a set of city maps and a compass. And a paper servant, would I have burnt a paper servant for her?

I continue and almost walk into a stack of mooncakes, the boxes piled waist-high in a shop entrance. Life goes on. Already, mooncakes are seeping into our lives like a new currency, the gift cartons containing the lacquered spheres filling every inch of sales space. Mung bean and egg yolk, Maxim's Ice Cream and Hello Kitty, lotus seed and red bean paste. Soon, it will be Mid-Autumn Festival, a night for family reunions and moonlit picnics. What will Virginia's family do about it, the picnic and the remorse?

Moon Eight Day Nine
Saturday 30 September

After getting off the bus, the Hikers assemble next to a row of whitewashed houses. A cul-de-sac or a plaza, it is hard to say what the open space before us is, with that indecisiveness that many New Territories villages share, an accumulation of rusty sheds, abandoned houses and tiled two floor buildings. With a whine, the minibus turns around and disappears.

Jim is running the Hiker's outing today and so I come along, even though it is the Heritage Trail. *Again.* It has become heavy, the silence Virginia has left behind. Heavier even, the silence between Ben and me. I listen to it every day.

Trailing his map, Jim approaches a villager who is cataloguing our group with narrowed eyes, our easy togetherness, our black-and-whiteness: Celia and Bertie, Spielberg and Frank, Zoë and her husky and all the others. After stepping carefully over a dog dozing next to the man's wiry calves, Jim asks, 'Is this the way to San Wai?'

'Can't read maps,' the old man grunts but his eyes have widened at the sound of a foreigner speaking Cantonese. He heaves himself up from his stool, leans against the doorframe. 'See that white house over there?' His calloused hand points out a large, colonial-looking structure. 'The old missionary building,' he continues, his head now moving with more vigour.

When he has finished with his explanations, Jim asks, 'What about that old house?'

'Ah.' The old man nods, rubs his chin. '*Yip Ga*, we used to call it. The Yip Family. A home for abandoned girls, it was, after the government banned *muijai*. The lady missionary took them in, sent them to school. My sisters used to play with the Yip Family girls. Such a good person, she was.'

'Did you grow up around here?' Frank steps forward as if to show how different old age can look, parrot coloured or drab, with teeth like an advertisement or a mouth full of stubs, until I remember that there must be two decades between them.

'Oh, that was when I was in primary school,' the old man says. 'In the 1930s.'

The group spreads out, some members gathering around the old man, others lingering to take in the surroundings. Jim and I go into a nearby temple. It's more of a shrine really, small and unkempt-looking. Lukewarm, the devotion that went into it looks to me, the incense dead, the offerings untidy. 'Do you think that's on purpose?' I ask. 'The oranges like that, all scattered? Empty peanut shells?'

'Looks like a monkey if you ask me,' he says. 'The famous, infamous New Territories macaques.' He starts to wipe down the altar with a handkerchief, collects the peanut shells in his left palm. Holding his hand aloft, he looks around for a place to deposit the rubbish. His eyes reach the ceremonial furnace, hesitate.

'I've got a trash bag,' I say. As if this could conjure Ben. In the quiet of the shrine, the rustling of the plastic bag seems noisy.

Jim peers at the group outside and frowns. 'Still talking with that old man.'

'What's *muijai*?' I ask. 'What the old man was talking about.'

He looks at me, his brows rising over the steel rim that frames his eyes. 'Don't tell me you've never heard of *muijai*.' He takes off his glasses, wipes them with his shirt. 'They used to be young servant girls. A system of bondage with a timeline, you could probably call it.' Behind the clean lenses, the blue of his eyes seems lighter, more transparent.

We step outside. The group is now standing in front of a decrepit building with a tree growing out of it, snapping pictures.

'This way,' Jim gestures, then turns back to me. 'Poor families would sell their girls to richer people when they were about ten years old. The girl would work as a servant for them until she was old enough to be married. Working off the money they had paid for her, as it were.' He gives a half-turn to assess the progress of the group. 'The family taking her in was obliged to marry her off, by which time the servitude would end. So her family, her

243

real family, would be saved the expenses of feeding her.'

'And providing her with a dowry and all that—*Mui-jai*,' I try out the new syllables in my mouth. Not so new, really. *Muimui*, the little girl, the younger sister. 'So you're part of the family,' Ronda and the other Filipinas joke when they trade stories of exploitation. Having been told, 'We treat you just like family'. Having had to share beds with children. My steps come to a halt. 'Jim. It's the same *mui*, right? Like *banmui*. The Filipino servants.'

Jim stops. He takes out his water bottle, closes his eyes and takes a long gulp. 'Ah.' He wipes his mouth, looks at me and nods.

'So.' Warmth seeps through the concrete into my feet. I struggle to attach a single feeling to this piece of information. 'So,' I say again. 'There's a history of—of exploitation here. A kind of cultural concept attached to it, you could say.' Even now, I cannot seem to get rid of Sudan, of Joel's voice, years ago, telling me, 'Some of the Arab tribes have been doing this for centuries. Selling humans as if they were cattle. And the Nubians. Which is why we better don't meddle with it.'

The water bottle suspended in mid-air, Jim smiles, an expression that is part apology, part pity. His eyes take me in, dripping with sweat in this alien climate. 'You could put it that way, yes.' Struggling to wrestle the water bottle back into the bag, his voice comes in fits and starts. 'You—really hadn't heard of this—before?'

'No,' I say. 'I probably should have.' Irina's masterpiece would have enlightened me, no doubt. Or any of the other books Jim has been trying to foist on me.

In San Wai, a parking space has replaced the moat around the village but the walls sheltering it are still intact. Slowly, the group winds its way through the maze of houses until we reach the ancestral temple at the end of the compound. Even without Virginia, it feels good to be hiking again, listening to the inconsequential chatter of people on an outing, throwing in a careless remark or two. Being young and unbonded. Not ready to die.

244

'Zoë grew up in a walled village, did you know that?'

'The door gods look just like her. Fierce, colourful.'

'Back, back, back to the entrance. I need a ciggy.'

I hesitate on the temple's doorstep. 'Jim, look at these door gods.' I study the pair in its two-dimensional, graceful eeriness, the flowing robes, the swords raised high over heads. A riot of colours. 'Beautiful or scary, what are they really? No wonder people have all these ideas of dangerous gods.'

'They are the good ones, Reini. They guard people against evil spirits.'

I lean against the door, the lacquer of the paintwork smooth under my fingers. 'All that violence. How can you beat evil with violence?' Battling same with same, like Chinese medicine. 'It seems so alien. Hell and punishment and all that.' I open my camera again, compare the photo with the originals on the door. 'Quite different from our idea of a loving God, isn't it?'

'Don't we have a similar God? Jealous if we worship other gods? Strong and protective of his people? A God who stops the sea and does all kinds of miracles to save them.'

'That's in the Old Testament.' Another one of Jim's theological quizzes. I squirm, my damp trousers clinging to my thighs, and focus on the Hikers in the distance. Tiny like insects they seem from where we stand. 'So, how come in the New Testament we suddenly have this gentle father figure with his all-encompassing love?'

'There's both, Reini, don't be fooled. The parables warn as well as instruct. There's always the danger of rejection besides the redemption.' He pats his trouser pockets, takes in the approaching group and changes gear, takes out his notes instead. He flips a piece of paper over and looks at it with furrowed brow. 'Maybe—'

He starts to fold the sheet. 'Maybe God has changed.' He frowns at the paper in his hands, unfolds it partly, tries again. 'If we're all given the capacity to become somebody different, then God above all must be able to change. Don't you think the God shown in the New Testament is a God of change?'

'A God of change?'

He is bent over his origami now, uses the altar as support. Wings emerge. A plane?

'Think of it. God changing into a human being, to bring about reconciliation—change. The miracles, feeding a crowd with two fish, making the blind seeing, making the witnesses faithful, again—change. Everybody changes in these stories, I think even Jesus does.' He squints at the paper object and nods. 'Yes, I think he does. And he tells stories of change, about the Prodigal Son and others.' Jim beams at his product.

'And changing water into wine, don't forget.'

He laughs. 'Yes, what a fine trick to have up your sleeve.' He gives his creation a final tug. With a soft, papery sigh it unfolds into a bird. He takes a step back, looks at it. 'How do you like my dove?'

'I thought it was a plane.'

'No, it's a dove. Noah's dove. The one that returned after the flood. God's offering of peace. Because, you see... Wait a minute—' he looks around. 'It is God who changes during the flood. Becomes more compassionate, while poor Noah is stuck with all the animals on the ship.' Gently, he pulls a dead joss stick out of the incense burner and inserts it into the dove's beak. 'There you go. Complete with the olive branch.'

'You'll have trouble recreating the rainbow, though,' I laugh.

He clicks his tongue. 'Reini. Insatiable as ever.'

Mid-Autumn Festival
Friday 6 October

Whenever I go into the Ngai's flat, the smell of fire seems to be lingering. I never know whether I imagine it or whether it is real. After all, carbon monoxide is odourless and nothing in the flat was damaged. But I cannot shake it off. And then there is Virginia's mother, observing us incessantly, her eyes dark with reproach.

We need a new beginning, Virginia and I, and start by tidying up her materials. Our materials, really, textbooks and hiking guides, files and leaflets. We are surrounded by piles of old papers when she suddenly asks, 'Do you believe in dreams?' Her eyes remain fastened onto the photocopy on her knees but her voice is eager. She is sitting cross-legged, a ring binder on her lap.

I finger an exercise sheet filled with my early Cantonese attempts. 'They always seem to mean something,' I say. 'Even the most stupid ones. Especially the stupid ones. But if you ask me, we often understand them the wrong way.' They shine with importance but dazzle us with details. The paper in my hand is full of mistakes. I throw it onto the trash pile.

She pauses, her eyes resting on me. 'I don't even know if it was a dream or… something else.' When her gaze leaves me, the folder on her legs wobbles softly. She rolls in her lower lip. 'When I was… lying there. In my room.'

I nod while trust spreads its fragile wings.

'I saw my mother.'

I nod again, stare at my knuckles clenched around a stack of leaflets. Suddenly, I am aware of my breathing, each measure of air hard won against my tightening throat.

'She talked with me and seemed really well.'

I put down the leaflets and shift on my haunches. I swallow, painfully. 'That's… good.'

'I was walking. I mean, not just along the street. More like… hiking. Going somewhere.' She looks at the folder across her knees, her face thinned to a pale inverted U from where I sit. 'I asked her if she needed anything. She said she was well provided for but could do with something to drink. You see, afterwards— afterwards we discovered that all of us had forgotten to refill the tea cups.'

Her mother's niche looks tidy as usual, a well-kept arrangement of fruit, teacups, flowers. My ankles are starting to hurt.

'She—she said more, with a really strong voice. "But I agonise over my dear daughter," she said, "Daughter, don't be distressed about me. I thank you for your provisions. Now do take care of yourself.'" She leans back, becomes herself again.

My feet are tingling. I shift and resettle on my knees. When I swallow, the strain reaches up to my ears and my eyes feel hot. I reach for another sheet. 'It's good to hear that she... that she is well.'

'I wanted to ask more, what exactly did she mean with looking after myself, and how she's doing. But she had disappeared already.'

I flatten the paper under my hands, lay it on the floor to even out the folds. A map of Hong Kong Cemetery, still good. 'It... it doesn't sound like a dream.' With a final move, I smooth down the map and place it onto the usable pile.

Virginia's face gives an almost invisible twitch. Her gaze slides sideways, in my direction, but her shoulders remain curved over the folder. Absentmindedly, she snaps the ring mechanism open, shuts it again. 'No,' she says, 'it wasn't a dream.'

When I prepare to leave, she presses a bulky plastic bag into my hands. 'Mooncakes. For you. And one box for Frank.' Her face reddens. 'I meant to pass this on to him earlier. You will see him at the hike tomorrow, won't you?'

'Yes,' I say. 'That's Spielberg's hike. The Avenue of Fame.' A visit to the waterfront, really, but these days, we do anything to keep the hikes going.

'Frank has been so kind. Always bringing me snacks, looking after me. He even,' her blush deepens, 'updated the website for me. You were sick, remember? I gave him the password.'

Before I can search her face, she shoves me towards the door. 'Ronda and I have to start cooking for tonight.'

I give her a smile. 'Happy Moon Festival.' In my hand, the bag cuts into my flesh. Most foreigners hate mooncakes with their intrepid combinations of rock sugar and pork, sweet bean paste and salted duck egg. Like nouveaux riches, they cannot hide their poor origins, crammed with fat, sugar and protein. They are heavy and to a foreign palate taste garbled. But it might be like Frank to love them.

Monkey God Festival
Saturday 7 October

I have a new paper obsession, two slips of green and yellow material which I constantly finger. They are dotted with auburn spots. Blood. There are the things that we strive for and there are those that are gifts, things that even our hopes don't cover for lack of imagination. How the two sides of this day come together as one: noise and quiet, ecstasy and contemplation. And so I arrive at harbouring a new secret, my golden green revelation that rightens everything, finally.

With its primary coloured swings and bouncy rubber flooring, the playground of the Sau Mau Ping housing estate seems like an unlikely backdrop for a religious festival. But when I arrive, the open space is already a multicoloured riot, a turbulence of noise and people. A swarm of elderly women worshippers flocks around a shrine while a group of musicians, clad in silk, drowns everything in clashing, whining, drumming sound.

After a while, the proceedings fall into a familiar rhythm. I have witnessed gods' birthday parties before, have followed the god as he was being escorted in a little shrine to the festival matshed, have watched him being placed with a premium view of the opera to be performed in his honour, have absorbed the roast pig offerings and the incense coils, the crowds and the parasols.

Everything changes when the Monkey God separates himself from the worshippers. He changes. He is in his forties perhaps, with the wiry, compact build of the Southern Chinese and absolutely inside his truth, very far away and totally here. He jumps and cavorts, twitches and grins, hammers his hands on his chest and scratches himself. Like a giant child, he seems in conjunction with the toboggan and the seesaw and looks as if he might use them any moment, make them part of his ecstasy. I step to the side to avoid my neighbour's piercing umbrella. My eyes devour him, cannot let go of this ape in front of me.

After a while, he comes to a halt, his wide buttery trousers soaked around the waist, and settles down at a desk. People jostle and a line forms in front of him. I crane my neck to see. When I move, my feet tingle, unable to shake off their terrestrial make-up. The umbrella to my right shifts and an elbow pokes into my side.

'You come,' the woman hisses. 'I too go.' With steps that seem far too decisive for her stature, she leaves for the queue. My eyes follow her through the crowd with its sunhats and mobile phones. The noise and her weasel-like quality make it difficult, as if listening to the TV and the radio at the same time. Then I understand what the Monkey God is doing. He is holding practice, listening to believers describing ailments, advising on remedies. It is a confrontation that I, the non-believer, have always shirked.

When I stand in front of him, I am seized by fear that my white face will snap him out of it, will make him come untrue, but nothing of the sort happens. His face is everything at once, Man and Monkey God, shiny with sweat and tanned as a hide. A translator interprets his Monkey language, moulds it into classical Chinese. I stare at them both and nod, although I do not understand a word.

'Strong heart. No fear,' the aide finally pronounces and I do not know whether this is the diagnosis or the cure. He scribbles something onto a piece of paper and hands it to me. I rush off, my legs nimble again.

As the day wears on, the harsh light of noon mellowing into a strong afternoon sun, all of us take a break at one point, step out, have a drink, make a phone call. He, however, inhabits the Monkey God and the Monkey God him, not for seconds but for entire minutes, moments, hours. At one point, he slashes his tongue with a sword, dripping with blood. There is walking on knives, bathing in boiling oil and more stepping on knives, until my mind refuses to take in any more of this.

Monkey. The word rings with multiple meanings, like everything around me. The heavenly creature of the zodiac,

Virginia's sign. The mischievous jester. The Buddha Victorious with Strife. The Great Sage Equal to Heaven. I stop the name-dropping. A fire has been lit, has gathered into a white force while we were busy admiring the invulnerability of the Monkey God. And so he proves his power one more time, crosses a bed of red-hot charcoal only to appear unscathed on the other side.

My neighbour has fashioned her umbrella into a walking stick and rushes back to the front. When she returns, her hand seeks mine, a bony thinness meeting my fingers, smuggling something into my grasp. Two paper slips, yellow and green, spotted with blood.

'Powerful,' she says. 'No sick, no bad.'

'*Doje*,' I thank her, struggling with the magnitude of the day, its endless October skies, the way it floods me with otherness and with a feeling of being strangely at home, finally: to see otherness venerated, to see it make unique sense. How did he learn that, to ease himself into this, to give himself up and be more than he could ever be alone, and feel whole?

After the multitudes in Sau Mau Ping, I need to be alone. Not just in a space devoid of other people but still with myself. And so, instead of taking the MTR all the way home, I walk the stretch from the Star Ferry pier to Hong Kong Park and look for a bench in the wilting shade. The late afternoon light is starting to blur the boundaries of things. Already, the shade under the trees is becoming meaningless, the day's heat almost gone.

A woman is about to leave when I sit down. Her English is careful, cultivated. 'There is an amphibian there. I first thought it was a branch.' She nods towards a nearby lantana. With meticulous movements, she folds the bookmark into her hardcopy and, before I can glean the title, she is on her way, heels clicking softly on the pavement. 'Have a nice evening.'

An amphibian, moving between worlds. I scan my surroundings, the cassia tree, the elephant ear leaves, the Buddha's hand. Nothing. Ambition seizes me and I try in a more systematic way. Plants. Creek. Walls. Pelleted ground. Nothing.

I give up and relax against the bench, settle into the quiet as the silence around me grows, takes on substance like the humid air of the park.

A flock of white birds flaps through the sky, the sun dyeing them the palest of apricots. The cockatoos in Central lack the grace of the black eared kites, yet I love them, though in a more detached way, less mine. Refugees of war, they are, descendants of one single pair that a colonial officer set free to spare them Japanese occupation. I love the surprise of their whiteness blooming against office towers, the chutzpah with which they make this place home, oblivious to their luck.

And then, to my side, I discover it, at the corner of my vision. It does not blend into the surroundings, it is the surroundings, a green golden stillness on a lichen-covered stone. Moments ago, for the woman, it was the bark of a tree, the lengthened arm of a branch it sat on. Breathless, I wait for it to move, to reveal itself, as if action alone could prove it.

The lizard blinks. I wink back, into its eyes with their surround sight. Into the Eye of God. What did Jim say at the walk, about a God who loves to change? Suddenly, my lungs are close to bursting from holding my breath. I sift oxygen into my mouth, urgently, quietly, somehow. Trying to outdo an amphibian in stillness, trying to do more than humanly possible, as always. Even here on the hill the air has a salty tang to it, a reminder of the harbour below. The Changeable Lizard. Another blink and then the heavenly creature disappears behind a curtain of leaves, like an actor preparing his next incarnation. Who knows what it will be next, sand coloured and mottled with grey perhaps, fusing with the ground, motionless and graceful.

I would like to tell Ben about it, although I know that this is the one truth that will be difficult to name. Suddenly, I ache to be near him, to share everything with him again, meaningful or not, the lizard and new books, the Monkey God and my cantankerous toaster. I close my eyes, gulp down big mouthfuls of sea-scented air as if this could bring him back to me, the soft salt of sweat under my tongue, his five-spice skin.

On my way out, I pass a shrine, a small offering to the Earth

God. It must be the gardener's, tucked away near the park entrance, a small island of sun-bleached vermilion in a sea of emerald and moss green. Every day, dozens of bridal pairs pass him without noticing, their minds on photographs set against silver high rises and tropical foliage. What a city this is, allowing God to appear in so many shapes, from ferocious door gods to sweet faced maidens. To take on so many different lives and meanings. Lizard and monkey, Kwun Yam and Mary. Being all things to all people, a stone to me or a branch to you. Keeping still and blending in. I feel for the paper slips in my pocket, let their green and golden hope rub off onto my fingers. *No disease. No evil.* Paradise is, for all of us, a place where we can be all we want to be and more, and feel whole.

Moon Eight Day Twenty-two
Friday 13 October

Superiority to fate/is difficult to learn. Against the dark wood panelling of the District Court, the presiding officer's face blooms like a sickly yellow moon. Liver trouble, too much anger, Ben would probably detect in one of his Chinese medicine moods, a tendency to not take things lightly. Even so, it will be difficult for Ronda to prove her case. How do you show that something never happened? That there never was a warning, a verbal announcement of her impending dismissal? I twist my legs around each other to keep them from wriggling, and chew on Emily Dickinson to calm myself.

'Where are you staying now? Is that address in Tin Hau still correct?' With an air of superiority, the officer peers over his glasses, his voice flaccid like his features. A man who does not need to shout. Or who is weary.

'Yes sir, that is correct. In Tin Hau, I am staying at a friend's place. She is my friend's friend.' She glances in my direction.

At my blood sister's, I think, and quickly rein in my thoughts as if the officer could read them. *A pittance at a time.* My fears—one for Ronda, one for myself—dampen my fingers against the smooth wood of the bench. In their court suit, my legs twitch helplessly, the material of the trousers adding to the slipperiness of it all.

The officer has followed her glance, sees a white face at the end of it and nods. He proceeds to check the personal details of Mrs. Sze, Ronda's former employer. It takes a while because in spite of her Oxbridge English, Mrs Sze has insisted on her right for translation. Finally, the officer turns again to Ronda. 'Will you please outline your complaint in your own words.'

At first, her sentences spit and sputter. The surroundings temper her, flatten her hair and make her skin dull like dishwater. I give her the slightest of nods and a smile, and her words acquire more fluidity.

'… fired me without warning. And the salary for the last month, and the compensation for having to leave, I never got it,' she finishes.

'Thank you.' The officer taps his pen against the desk. 'You, the claimant, must realise that in the meantime, the defendant—your former employer—has produced a letter of resignation from your side. This alters the case completely.'

'A letter? But I have never—'

'Will you please speak only when asked. A letter of resignation with your signature.' He scans the papers in front of him in a cursory manner, then regards Ronda again. 'Am I to understand that you were not aware that the defendant had produced new evidence?'

'No sir. Yes sir.—I mean, I did not know about the letter. I did not write anything.'

'But we have it here.' He gestures towards the bailiff, who proceeds to bring over the document.

A neatly typed letter of resignation, with Ronda's signature sitting slightly askew at the bottom. A bit of glitter clings to her signature and a Pokémon sticker sits between the words. Between her two signatures really, because there is a pair of them, one next to the other.

Ronda's cheeks and forehead turn such a transparent grey that I can see her temple throb.

'Is that your handwriting?'

'Yes sir but I see it for the first time, I do not have a—'

'Will you please respond to my question. So, this is your handwriting?'

'Yes sir, but—'

'Quiet!' On the benches, restless whispering has started in at least three different languages at once. The presiding officer glares at the bailiff to keep the order.

'Sir.' Ronda's rolling R rings out and makes the word into a command more than a plea. She is standing very straight. 'Please excuse me, speaking without being asked. I was playing with Ivy.' For the first time, her eyes brush Mrs Sze. 'The girl. We practised signatures. We pretended to be rich ladies, how to sign cheques. We liked to play that we were rich. Ivy always wanted to open a hospital.'

The officer looks at her in her jeans and flamingo coloured T-shirt. He shifts his gaze to Mrs Sze, who fidgets in her long-sleeved dark suit but looks him in the eye. He sighs. Seconds tick by while he stares down at his desk. Finally, he lifts the stack of documents in front of him, shuffles and pushes the papers into alignment. For a moment, he shrivels behind his shield. He sighs again. 'The hearing is adjourned for fifteen minutes.'

When the meeting resumes, the presiding officer exudes a businesslike manner. 'I am asking the defendant: Would you be willing to settle the case by paying half the amount demanded by the claimant? This would not be construed as an admission of guilt but would help us all to close the case.'

When the translator has finished, Mrs Sze folds her hands on top of each other. Slowly, she raises her eyes to the officer, a smile slinking around her mouth. 'Why should I?'

The officer's pallor is cold now, more chalk than jaundice. 'A settlement of this kind is the speediest way to resolve cases like this one. Cases that waste time—yours, mine, Ms, er, Pajarillo's. And taxpayer's money.'

Looking down at her flawless hands, where a discreet diamond glints on one finger, Ms Sze follows the translation.

The officer continues, 'Let me repeat that this would carry no implication of guilt on either side. So, would you be willing to agree to this kind of compromise?'

Ms Sze inclines her head. A slight smile has built on her face. 'Yes, Sir.'

'I am asking the claimant: Can you accept this solution, or do you want to drag this case on for another six months or a year and try to prove that you did not write the—Pokémon letter?'

Ronda searches my features but, even if I was allowed to advise her, I would not know what to say. She lowers her head. Seen in this pose, leaning on her bench, she seems almost as if in church. When she finally looks up, she does not face the officer. Instead, she steadies her shoulders, lifts her chin and slightly turns to Ms Sze. Her lids are hammering but, when she speaks, her voice hardly shakes. 'Yes Ma'am. Yes Ma'am, I will accept your—incredibly generous offer.'

Outside, relief sweeps through me, relief that the charade with her is over, while professional disappointment tugs at me, but only a little. Not even Irina will blame me for this, the way these things go. Nor will Ed, for whom cases like Ronda's are on the periphery of his lawyer's vision.

I summon Emily again, cling to her words as if they could change things. *Until, to her surprise/The soul with strict economy/Subsists till Paradise.* None of this is a surprise, neither the result nor the cool way in which Ronda handles it, but for some reason I resent her aloofness. Pulling her into the MTR entrance to avoid the traffic noise, I say, 'You shouldn't have let them get away with this.'

'To wait another year? Trying to prove something impossible?' She shakes her head. 'No, life goes on. But I do not want to stay here, I think.'

'Join me for lunch. Even if we can't celebrate.'

She hesitates, shakes her head once more and smiles, embarrassed. 'I want to call my family.' For an instant her countenance cracks, setting her corkscrew hair in shivering motion. She looks away, leaving me to admire her quaking profile, until she is ready to meet my eyes again. 'Thank you.'

Seeing her disappear through the turnstiles of the MTR, she looks clumsy, fragile even in an unknown way as the tentacles of the machine spill her forth, render her unable to turn back. Something in me relishes her vulnerability, the same part of me that craves her paradise, so much sturdier than mine.

She waves. 'See you, at Virginia's.' A soul of economy, subsisting.

Moon Eight Day Twenty-four
Sunday 15 October

At home, something has to be done about the Green Lotus leaflets. They appear everywhere; misprints serving as cupboard lining, as notepaper next to my telephone, balled up in shoes put away to dry months ago, during the typhoon season. I finger the newest one, printed only days before Virginia toppled our lives. *Save Sam Tung Village—Demonstration—October 15*. I put it on the growing stack of castaways.

I've never been good at saying sorry. I like to think that it comes with being tall. And now Ben, who is certainly taller than me. The realisation weighs me down. He is stubborn. With a sigh, I pull the leaflets out of my running shoes. Another thing that I have neglected, while the whole point of living in Causeway Bay and working in Yaumatei was to go running in Victoria Park. I step into my trainers, allow them to close around my feet. After a summer of sandals, they feel heavier than they should. It is odd how habits persist in your heart long after they have left your life. Or you have left them.

Victoria Park is full of people, buzzing with New Territories villagers and environmental activists, brimming with the usual

Sunday crowds of Indonesians on their day off. I wriggle past market stalls with cheap hijabs and long skirts. The Green Lotus volunteers are easy to spot, a cheerful group behind a long table overflowing with publicity materials. Fuican is there, together with another nun. And Ben. I swallow.

'Reini!' His eyebrows shoot up. A smile hurries across his face, quickly hides behind the ears. He looks down again, busies himself with some leaflets.

'Just out for a run,' I say and pull at the Lycra enclosing my thighs.

'Sure. Always good to do sports. Good for your health.' His gaze falls onto my legs, their tanned, toned length, and scurries away, into the asphalt next to my running shoes.

'Reini, long time no see.' Fuican's smile is placid as ever, unsurprised. 'Come here, I've got something for you. Something I've been meaning to give to you.' She rummages in a removals box and comes up with a package, her face reddened from bending down. 'For you. For you and Ben, really. Don't be polite, open it.'

It is a beautiful edition of the Lotus Sutra, bilingual. I place it on the table. 'Thank you,' I say and feel Ben's eyes on Fuican and me. Louder, I say, 'I just, I just dropped by to see if you need help. Like I used to do. I figured you could do with some help today.'

'That's good of you.' She smiles, pats the table once or twice, and moves to let me in next to her.

'Sorry—' I squeeze past Ben, carefully avoiding him, and take my place between him and Fuican.

'Sure. Er, good of you to come,' he says. His voice sounds odd.

'Oh, I'm just… doing my bit,' I say, looking askance. He is unshaved. His trousers seem to be sagging. A little bit.

'Could you pass me that stack of reports, please?'

When I lean over to get them, my elbow brushes his. Like an electric jolt, our touch flits through me, seems to immobilise my heart. I search his face and flinch, because in that very moment he is doing the same with mine. Back and forth, our hands move on the table, arranging and rearranging brochures, fanning them out and making them into stacks, all the while we sieve the air for hope.

When the demonstration gets under way, Ben thrusts something into my hands. A bamboo rod attached to a length of white cotton, and the recognition that it is a discarded piece of bed linen shoots through me. It looks familiar.

'Would you— Mind taking this? Care for carrying this together?' He hoists the banner into the air and shuffles it into shape. Automatically, my arms follow. Seen from behind, the characters look even more intractable than usual. Feng shui First, the English caption reads.

After a while, we fall into a stride. It is impossible to carry a banner without some sort of harmony between you and your fellow bearer. Our harmony is distance, a safe distance. To keep the sheet afloat, we take great care to keep that distance, all along the park and underneath the overpass crowning Yee Wo Street.

'Ben—' I have to raise my voice against the people and the megaphones. He looks at me as if testing a temperature. Another spasm of the sheet and we continue.

We turn into a side street. Suddenly, the banner releases its tension on my fingers, sags and withers. He looks around, pulls me into a doorway, trailing the sheet behind him like a veil. 'Reini—'

The linen settles around our legs, wraps our feet.

'Reini, I...'

My arms go around him, fasten him, are fastened in return. The doorway reeks of dog urine. I shut my eyes, follow the soft texture of his T-shirt under my fingers, wish to garner courage from it. I nudge closer. 'We should have talked,' I whisper. 'Earlier. I'm sorry.'

He eases himself against the wall. Behind his back, paper shudders noisily as a management notice disintegrates under our impact. His palms on my shoulder blades are warm, warm and of an infinite, exquisite slowness. Outside, people continue to march past, a blur of sound and motion. I fold myself into him, dig into his aniseed scent. Under my fingers, the hair on his neck bristles and his cheek against my face feels damp. My heart quietens, gradually, like after a hard run, until our heartbeats fuse.

The door opens and I sense a woman coming out, a brisk step full of perfume and purpose. The rush stops. Ben's hands on my back shield me from her gaze, from the impropriety, the incredulity. I lean even more into him, let myself fall.

Above the door, a lucky mirror takes us in, collapses Ben and me into an octagon, holds us still while the masses roar by.

How easy it is all at once, to adopt a fly's point of view, travelling in the first row of the upper deck and overflowing with love. Ben and I are taking the bus to Stanley, to have an outdoor dinner and linger on the beach afterwards. To celebrate, although none of us says so. Perched high on my travelling throne, I ride through Wanchai, pass neon signs reaching far into the street and catch glimpses of first-floor karate studios next to hair dressers. Floating and flying, I am invulnerable behind my shield of glass, disembodied and omniscient, know the smells and sounds outside without touching them, sweet-warm and soapy, biting and briny, throbbing and beeping.

Never again will I fear it, the suspension of flying. How easy it is from this vantage point, to take in the mosaic of views along Queen's Road East and fuse them into one, the Hung Shing Temple and the English Speaking Methodist Church, the Pak Tai Temple hidden up Stone Nullah Lane and the Adventist Hospital. Finally, the meringue shape of the Sikh Temple appears, and my hunger garlands it with visions of curry and rice.

'Ben,' I ask, aching for a piece of him that I can touch in public and finally settling for his wrist, 'what if you release an animal that doesn't resettle well?' At this time of the day, few people get off in Stanley and long queues of tourists are waiting at the bus stop to return downtown. 'Remember the fly that was so difficult to catch, in Mui Wo?'

'Careful.' He holds me back as a taxi rushes by and the warmth of his fingers on my elbow distracts me for a moment.

'It was just a fly, come on.'

'Just a fly?' I give him a playful tug. 'And who's the biologist here, doesn't even a fly have a natural habitat?'

He looks right and left, then pulls me along, his fingers busy with mine. 'How bad is your hunger? Can we hop over to Stanley Market before dinner?'

'The tourist trap? You, the anti-materialist?'

He drops my hand. 'Even anti-materialists need clothes. They have my size,' he adds, bringing his T-shirt a few more inches down. 'Flies are universal. *Musca domestica* has been shown to live everywhere.'

'That was a fly, okay. But what about other animals? Don't you have these ceremonies, setting animals free?' Under the awning of Stanley Market, our voices sound different. We weave our way towards one of the clothes shops at the back, barely avoid ringing electronic toys whizzing around our feet, rush past snatches of Italian and German.

Delirious, I feel after all that has happened today, my pulse dancing with hunger and anticipation, and still cannot let go. 'It's birds that you set free, right? How does it work from a biological point of view?'

'I don't think people transport them a long way. It's sparrows, mostly.' Ben checks the size tag of a shirt and throws it back onto the heap. 'So, same as the fly. A fairly common type of bird.'

'I'm just—' the smell of textile chemicals cuts into my nose and I sneeze— 'afraid that the idea might be better in theory than in practice.'

'Our little Kant today?' But his voice is soft as he says this.

'Ben.' I start looking through the shirts, disentangle two dark blue pieces. 'What about this?' I shove them in his direction. 'We have this romantic idea of setting birds free. But maybe they'd be better off being left alone in the first place.'

'This is all symbolic.' He picks up the shirts, fingers the material, drops them. 'Too shiny,' he mutters and digs into the pile again, brings up another piece of dark fabric. On an on, he pulls until he holds a pair of trousers in his hands. 'Oh— We don't release highly specialised species. Or endangered species.

This is not about coral reef fish or the Siberian Crane or anything. It's about gaining karma.'

'It's beautiful, absolutely.' I drag another shirt out of the pile. He looks up, pulls a face. 'Too 1970s.'

'The custom, I mean.' I look at the discarded shirt with its print pattern of flamingos, parrots and cockatoos. 'Or too Hawaii. This could be Frank's.' I giggle. 'Virginia has changed a lot.'

'You always seem to forget that I've met her only once.'

'Why is it that we say "something is beginning to change" if change sometimes also is an ending?'

'You mean— What you were saying about Frank?' He examines a dark green Polo shirt. When he has laid it aside, he continues, 'Nothing ever stops changing. People change, things change.'

'He's alright, I guess. Here, more green ones.'

'He does sound a bit… coarse the way you describe him.'

'When he drinks too much. Maybe it comes with his job. He's an engineer. Public sewage systems, that kind of thing. "Laying pipes in Hong Kong's wet places." Uggh… Here, another one just like your favourite. But he's generous.'

'Give it some time. Maybe he'll lighten her up. If he wears Hawaiian shirts.'

Some need to love and others need to be loved. Who said that, ages ago at the Lover's Rock? My gaze falls back onto the shirt with its tropical birds, yellow-crested cockatoos like the ones in Central. I have even seen flamingos in the wild, sweet pink in a fatigues coloured world, on a trip to Kenya when I was fleeing Sudan for a holiday. 'How do we make sure that we do things for others and not for ourselves?'

'And where is this coming from now?'

'All this business of setting free.' I stroke the shirt with its satiny surface, uncrimple the birds. 'I just don't know why I do certain things. Or did. Maybe I always do things for myself. Maybe even the girl in Khartoum. Maybe it's a way of feeling in charge. My way of gaining karma.' My palm rushes to my mouth.

His hands stop their mechanical task in mid-air. Slowly, they sink to his sides. 'Why would you have done it for yourself? You didn't gain anything from it, far from it.'

'Can this be the measure? Whether we suffer in the course of doing something for others?'

'Kim-chi. You *are* in full form today. Come on. They're closing in a moment, you are hungry, I am hungry. There's been lots of stupid martyrdom in history, and senseless forms of self-flagellation.'

As if on cue, my stomach growls.

He adds another shirt to his pile of dark greens and muted blues and then walks over to the cashier. 'I think the fact that she asked is an important thing. The Sudanese girl requested your help. And then you made it possible for her to make a decision— No plastic bag, please.'

With some effort, he squeezes the polo shirts into his backpack stuffed with Green Lotus materials and closes it. 'Time to eat. Your choice today, huh?' With his hand on the small of my back, he steers us out of the market, his fingers broadcasting their own unmistakeable message. How we make choices every minute of our lives, for ourselves and for others.

In total silence they appear, dart through the sky like inconsequential thoughts, zip and unzip the dusk. 'Bats.' I move closer to Ben, guide his gaze with my hand. 'Over there. Near the trees.' How that smell of mosquito repellent will always remind me of our walk in Lung Yeuk Tau, the taste of kisses mixed with so much else. We watch them on their silent mission through the night, full of purpose where humans only see erratic behaviour.

I drowsily snuggle into his arms, his belly soft against my spine, and let the warmth of the fire wash over me. The night is still mild and Germany, battling the first night frosts in October, seems very far away. 'Ben.' I turn around to face him. 'I got it.'

'What?'

'You know, why bats are linked with luck.'

'It's— The words sound the same. *Fu.*' He pokes the fire with a barbecue skewer, chasing up sparks, sending tiny particles of ash into the air.

'I know. But there is another way of looking at it. Mosquitoes transmit diseases. Malaria, Dengue fever. And what do bats feed on? Mosquitoes!'

'Some bats do. Yes. Some bats also act as pollinators. You might have a point there.' He rubs his chin. 'Bats as part of a healthy living environment. Part of the local feng shui.'

Like velvet, the evening wraps around us, bleeding peace into the gentle air. It makes it easy to talk, the way our words evaporate into the dim light as if they had no owner. And so I tell him more about Virginia, lift the secret which has been eating me all along: *me, missionary*.

'You made it possible for her to have a choice,' he says. 'And choose she did.'

'She never really seemed much interested.' I say. 'In having a choice, I mean.' I breathe in deeply, taste the remnants of the sea in the air. 'Is there really a choice, with religion?'

'You mean, are we free to choose at all? With our families, our cultures at our backs?'

'No.' I gaze into the fire, its heat beating against my skin. 'There's something else besides the choice. Something needs to happen, right? Like a chemical catalyst. A kind of... grace.'

In the dark, I sense his grave look more than I see it. 'If that is so, you have even less to blame yourself for.'

'But choices...' We quarrelled about choices, after all, a long time ago. Something else is weaving itself into this conversation, I can feel it coming along sideways. 'Choices can also be harmful. Not good. The things you choose between.' I swallow. 'We've been brought up to believe that having choices is the hallmark of development, of civilisation.' A sort of human dignity, where in reality some people only manage to exchange one type of death for another.

'*Lengneuih*. Sometimes there is no real choice. Sometimes we have to decide between two impossible things. You know that. Better than I do.'

Still it is there, that heat on my face.

His voice is almost black and crumbles at the edges. 'Choices are not only important because of the possibilities but of the process. They make us grow. The other side of deciding is responsibility.'

Virginia, choosing to be a devoted and dutiful daughter. Perhaps one day a loving wife. Choosing responsibility for others over herself. I, choosing to be a non-missionary. Fatimah, who really had no choice but to survive.

'That colleague of yours, Eva?' he interrupts my thoughts. 'She has all decisions already made for her. How can she learn responsibility if her god doesn't even trust her to decide on her beverages?'

'Why do you always think she's a Mormon? I think she's a Pentecostal or something. She drinks everything. Well, apart from alcohol.'

'See?'

'But Muslims also don't drink. I always used to think that was a good thing.' How it always sidles up to us, Fatimah's child. 'And you're the one who hates the Friday night packs in Lan Kwai Fong. So…' I say.

'So,' he says.

'You never mentioned these things when we… talked about choices before.'

He turns around to face me, his eyes gleaming. 'I'm only human, Reini. Some choices are outside of my worldview. Refusing them is to grow as well. That's what you call temptation.'

He sees my face, moves closer. 'You're still thinking of that Sudanese baby, right?' He gathers me into his arms, settles my head against the worn mellowness of his T-shirt. 'I think you did… I guess—I trust your judgement of the situation.'

Like forgiveness, night settles around us, reluctant at first. We watch the darkness grow, eat up the fringes of our vision, the beach, the sea. We watch the fire consume itself. One by one, he collects my fingers in his fists and starts to stroke them. His breath brushes my hair. 'Flower. *Daling*. Why do you always have to deal with things on your own?'

My pulse quickens, rushing to my defence. It will take a while to unlearn that habit. To unlearn my secrets. Whenever did he say that—not to take on more than humanly possible? Because that, too, can be a temptation.

I lean back into him, let his aniseed scent overpower the smell of the fire. 'Maybe I could learn.' The fire casts an orange glow onto our hands. One by one, I raise his fingertips to my lips, kiss them. I fold my hands into his, allow him to smother my fists in a new mudra. 'Not to do everything on my own.'

'It's high time,' he says, his voice dark like the night around us. Ben. My bat.

Moon Eight Day Twenty-five
Monday 16 October

'The congee is divine.' Eyes closed, I savour another mouthful. My colleagues nod in between slurping and smacking their lips. We are squeezed around a table at our corner restaurant and Ed's elbow threatens to upset my bowl. Eva is beaming at Irina, spoon adrift, her other hand protecting her stomach. She has spent a lot of meals with one hand under the table lately. Ever since my bout of disease, I have been craving rice gruel. I used to find it too plain, couldn't quite see the point of a gluey porridge if I could have decisive, red-hot kimchi instead. Now I yearn for its gentleness along my throat, its soothing all-lovingness. Congee is the perfect comfort food, the first solid thing Chinese babies eat, the kind of dish mothers cook for their sick children.

'I think Kim has something interesting to share about her weekend,' Irina's voice pushes through the background noise and our conversation. Suddenly, it is very quiet. She shoves a newspaper across.

Howling and cheering erupts around the table and it takes me a while to get hold of the paper.

It is a great picture. Ben and I, marching against a blazing blue sky, in our midst a banner, *Feng shui First*. I'm wearing a borrowed Green Lotus T-shirt, the exact replica of his, mine loose where his stretches over his belly. Today, the whole city will see us, greeting customers from newspaper stands and K-Mart entrances, glaring from the front page of the *South China Morning Post*. Seven million Hong Kong people including thousands of devout Filipino Catholics. And I can only wonder what they will make of me, protesting with the locals, shadowed by a bunch of Daoist monks.

Irina's silver fingernail taps against the newsprint.

I swallow, press my cool palm against my forehead.

'They only do it for the government compensation,' I hear Ed say. 'The feng shui villagers. Don't be fooled, Kim.'

It would be so easy and so acceptable. *This was an environmental thing. My boyfriend is a Buddhist. Sometimes, on weekends, I volunteer just to be with him.* But I don't open my mouth. Too easy and only part of the truth. The wrong part of the truth.

When we are seated in her room, Irina starts to toy with her paperweight right away. On the wall, the calendar lags several days behind again. 'Christianity is a good thing. Buddhism is a good thing. The Muslim faith is a good thing. Chinese religion...' She hesitates. 'Anyway, religion as such is a good thing but you can't do them all at the same time.'

'How odd. I would see it just the other way round.' I refrain from looking in direction of Eva's cubicle. With difficulty, I recapture the taste of congee in my mouth, its mothering quality. 'I'm not quite sure this is something one can discuss.'

'Really.' Irina deposits the paperweight back on the table. With a swivel of the chair, she turns away from me, lets her gaze roam the upper half of Yaumatei as if the unlit neon lights and grey façades could give her an answer. 'Kim, I appreciate your work. Your creativity, the many ways in which you contribute.'

That must be the Christmas parties—the only staff member who can sing 'Stille Nacht' in the original version. Against the padding of the office chair, my body feels weighed down and too warm. My fingers itch for the cool assurance of her paperweight. I fold them in my lap but they break free immediately and go into wringing, wrenching motions.

'You do realise that you're making things more difficult for yourself.'

'Irina—'

She moves around as if the tone of my voice had surprised her. Her eyes dip across my face.

'When were you ever one to go for what is easy?'

She grins and I know that I've got her. I get up, an impish grin building on my face. 'I love Buddhist food.'

She wags her pen at me. 'You better be careful.'

On my way out, I stop in front of the calendar. 'I can't stand this any longer,' I say and yank down the surplus leaves. 'Just bringing you up to date.'

In the work space to my right, Eva's support tights shine in familiar brightness under her desk. There is something jarring about them in this heat, like the women missionaries who fought against foot binding but were so repressed in other ways.

'And Kim—' Irina's voice rings through the office once more— 'you know it's your turn with Word for the Day, right?'

'Roger,' I shout back and to be able to raise my voice at her is a relief. 'The recording is on Wednesday.'

And then I have an idea.

Moon Eight Day Twenty-seven
Wednesday 18 October

As if to deny all that Hong Kong is about, the recording studio in Kowloon Tong is a cool, dry, airless place where 'wall to wall carpeting' takes on a new meaning. I lean against the grey partition, the polyester pile scratchy under my fingers, and watch Ronda record her last few beats. Since she has to leave Hong Kong, she will probably have something to say to the city, I figured, and asked her to do one Word for the Day. 'We're doing two recordings,' I said to Lynn Cameron before she left us alone with the Chinese technician. 'I've gotten an extra slot for you. Ronda Pajarillo here has agreed to do one as well.'

Lynn looked startled at Ronda's cheap T-shirt, black leggings and plastic flip-flops, the unofficial domestic workers' uniform. Then she broke into a broad smile that folded her chin into her neck. 'Of course,' she said, her hand wandering to her cheek. 'Of course, of course. The more the merrier.'

The truth is, this is only the first half of the surprise that I have in store for Lynn. As promised, I will do my Word for the Day, but I will not do it alone. Fuican is joining me. Because this is what I have learned from her book—there are things that we share. I look at my watch. She is running late. Against my back, the polyester is starting to feel hot.

Like a make-believe mantra, I repeat my motivation to myself: to talk about what we have in common, to take a stance. Not to play a practical joke on Irina or Lynn. Not to go it alone, *jau si*. Not to smuggle things or people, although this is what I will be doing, really, smuggling Fuican and her message into the recording studio.

'Stop,' the technician calls out to Ronda. 'We're still seventeen seconds over. Try cutting out some words. Take a break and then we'll do it again.'

Ronda has brought a friend from the shelter along for moral support, a petite Indonesian with a bashful smile. Her lilac headdress looks vaguely familiar. I steal another glance at my watch. I remember where I have seen this scarf before, several of them. 'Were you at the New Year's Reception?'

'At the hotel, the interreligious meeting?' She nods. It turns out she used to volunteer for a Muslim charity helping Indonesian domestic workers. Just as I am checking the time again, Fuican slips into the room. 'Sorry, missed the ferry,' she whispers. 'We're not supposed to go out alone.' When the technician sees her shaved head and grey habit, his eyes open wide but he says nothing. My heart beats faster at the sight of her, her clothes blending into the studio's carpeting as if to underline her innocuousness, while she holds so much power over me in this moment. A power I submit to out of choice but even so, my skin gets clammy with fear.

'Back to work,' the technician says and Ronda finishes her shortened recording in one smooth go. It occurs to me Fuican is another secret Ronda and I share, one that she isn't even aware of.

Then it is Fuican's turn and I resume my position at the wall, joined by Ronda and her friend. As if she had done this many times, Fuican starts to read. 'This story from the Lotus Sutra goes back to a tale that is well known in the oriental world.'

My back is beginning to itch against the carpet. Over the studio door, the red recording light has flicked on. I relax somewhat, shift my weight noiselessly against the partition. Fuican retells the story of a young man who asks his father for his share of the inheritance, turns his back on the family and leaves home to explore the world.

'Years later he comes back, destitute, and begs for a job as a pig keeper in his father's house. The father sees his change of heart and forgives him, calling a feast and showering the boy with lavish gifts.' At the sound of the familiar words my stomach softens. I must have heard it dozens of times, a typical Lenten story of reform and redemption, even if it feels unseasonal and strange in this functional room full of static electricity.

Calm and with hardly inflected English, Fuican continues her narration. 'For the devout Buddhist believer, this story embodies the promise of Buddhahood, it is about salvation that comes at an unexpected time and in an unexpected way.'

I reach out for the cool metal filing cabinet at my side. With a gently whizzing sound, a jolt of static electricity runs through me and I flinch. Next to me, Ronda is listening with big eyes. Her friend is nodding, fingering her scarf absentmindedly.

'The father, whose wealth symbolises the riches of enlightenment, takes an active role in winning his son back,' Fuican continues and concludes with remarks about the blindness that keeps us from seeking enlightenment. 'This story has also found its way into the Bible, where it is known as the

Prodigal Son.'

I get up. The moment of truth, Spielberg would say in his inimitable manner and I miss him, how he would crack the situation like one of his jokes. The technician must sense something, because he says, 'You've done this before, Kim. No need to get nervous.'

I clear my throat. 'We are used to reading this story as a parable about the Kingdom of God,' I start. 'As a story about the son who mends his ways and returns to the father, God-father, late, but not too late, because the father still takes him in. It is a story that illustrates God's never-ending love for those who turn to him, no matter when.'

I look up and take in my audience on the carpet; Ronda with her legs pulled up, her friend kneeling and Fuican in a position that I can only guess at, her limbs hidden underneath her robes. Their faces are turned towards me, of a trust that glazes their eyes, or perhaps it is the late afternoon sun that does it. *My friends*, and my eyes brim at the realisation, shine back to them. I nod, once, twice, swallow, give silent assent to something none of us has voiced, and continue.

'It is not only the son who has a change of heart,' I say, 'but also the father. The Heavenly Father, who at the beginning of the story sends off the departing son for good. We have a God of change. God's love is all-encompassing and eternal. All-pervasive, and because of that, God will reach out to different people, will reach different people, in different ways.'

I look at them again, lined up against the partition, and half expect them to stick prayer slips into the carpet wall, bow towards Mecca, everything at once. 'Not only does God exhibit different sides; no, God also inhabits different forms across places and times. God changes, constantly, to be all things to all people. Don't you think God gets bored with being only a limited vision to a limited people?'

I sense a smile in my audience, but when I look up, it is gone already. Ronda is frowning, her hair quivering against the pearl coloured backdrop, one strand standing out in a scraggly line like medical machinery detecting life. Her friend seems indrawn, two fingers pushed under the sash of her scarf, wriggling. Fuican is smiling, but she is always smiling and I have trouble reading this particular version. My heart is beating hectically against its ribcage now, robbing me of air.

Somehow, I come to a conclusion with my Word and, in spite of the studio's air conditioning, find myself sticky with sweat when I am done. Fuican and I have to repeat some of it and, by the time we finish, the sun is already disappearing behind the Kowloon Tong mountains. Lynn returns as we are packing up and looks with puzzlement at our group with its various garments.

'The more the merrier,' I say and grin. 'Some friends who wanted to see the studio,' and push them out of the door before she can suspect anything.

Behind his desk, the technician is sliding his controls back and forth, inscrutable. I am sorry for Lynn, for the breach of trust she will perceive in this. It is one thing to find a truth and overflow with it and another thing to do so at the expense of others. But this is the only way I can think of to do this. Against all odds, one part of me hopes that this episode will be without consequences. I fear it, the revelation, but there also is that other part of me which craves it.

Moon Eight Day Thirty
Saturday 21 October

'What about Chinese medicine? And can you practice both at once, Chinese and Western medicine?' The tourist turns towards me, her eyes very light and blue in her tanned face, and I feel like an impostor, taking my friends through King George V Memorial Park and the side alleys around the former Chinese Lunatic Asylum as if I had anything to say about them. We are standing in the garden of the Medical History Museum, surrounded by carefully labelled plants. But it seems one of the few things that I can do for Virginia, to take the Hikers along the Medical History Trail in Taipingshan, so easy with its guidebook and signs.

If I don't believe in you... I feel the familiar question surge in me but disregard it. 'What I know is this: it helps to have faith. Everywhere, always. That is an agreed-upon fact. Tested double-blind.'

The woman nods and her eyes are suddenly surrounded by wrinkles. 'Yes, the placebo effect.'

Something about it sounds wrong but I don't contradict her. Before she can raise any more questions, I change tack. 'Here's the surprise I promised,' I say and the laughter in the group subsides at once. How childlike they are, fastening their believing looks onto me for a treat. 'See that house on the corner? That's the public bath going back to the plague of the 1890s. It's open to the public. Have fun.'

The group ambles over to the bathhouse and I follow them, my washbag rattling in my backpack. But when I open it, I find that I have only packed body lotion. 'I forgot my shampoo,' I call out from my shower stall. 'Anybody has some for me?'

'Here.' Celia appears in the middle corridor, tanned against the gleaming tiles. More bottles appear from the stalls. *Anti-Dandruff. Smooth'n Shiny. Man's Miracle.*

'Whoa,' I say, 'where did that come from?'

Zoë grins while Celia twists her hair into a coil.

'I'll have some of each. I can do with all of this. Make it three-in-one.'

With awe, they watch as I start to create a mixture in my palm, stir it with my index.

'Careful what *you* wish for.' Zoë pulls her bottle away. 'This one's for black hair only.'

'Let's see.' I grab the bottle from her and press it until a transparent liquid fills my palm. 'Looks safe enough.'

'Or try it in a hidden place. Like they always recommend for shoe cream,' Zoë says.

'Behind my ears?'

'In an invisible place.' Celia giggles and puts her hand in front of her mouth. Her gaze rests with fascination between my legs.

'Don't get too envious. Yep, cauliflower from head to toe.' I move, feel her gaze reattach itself to my scalp while I try not to look at the eggplant smoothness of her abdomen. 'Careful what you wish for!' I lift my palm. 'Maybe my special three-in-one mix will do it for you.' She flees, yelping, and all at once we are in the middle of a water fight, soapy and hot, slipping across the floor, playing catch.

'Anti-dandruff. Yuk.' Celia frowns, then waves the hot pink bottle threateningly.

'Here, here!' Zoë raises her arms and Celia flings her anti-dandruff shampoo over to her like a practised baseball player. Zoë catches it, runs after me, scooting dangerously across the floor, legs scissoring.

'The black one, the black one! Dip her, dip her!' I yell, jumping up and down, until Zoë sees and catches it from me. Celia, in her fashionable maroon tint, takes flight.

Back and forth we run, shrieking and slithering, until Spielberg's voice calls out from the doorway. 'Ladies, no problemo, take a few more hours. We'll just go ahead and have dinner without you.'

When we emerge, giggling and flushed, the men eye us with suspicion, their crew cuts almost dry. 'Welcome back.' Jim, halfway through a cigar, exhales blue rings into the evening air thickening already with night noises, dinner being chopped nearby, the sound of a TV. 'The frolicking Fräuleins.'

Only later, on our way to the MTR, do I remember. Today was the day of the radio broadcast. But the evening air against my skin feels cool and, with the smell of shampoo still clinging to my hair, it is easy to believe that my life is clean and unchanged.

Frost Descends
Monday 23 October

'Mor-ning.' My mouth full with a cross bun from the bakery downstairs, I enter the office, trying for some panache. I stride past Eva, already clattering away on her keyboard. Toothpaste freshness and morning devotions rise off her like warmth from a freshly ironed blouse.

'Now look who we've got here.' Ed, his arms full of files, plonks them down next to the photocopier. There's something wrong with him, with the way his gaze hovers around me without meeting my eyes. Not with him. With me. The realisation hits me like a kick to the shin. He turns and starts to move Immigration papers around. It takes rather long. I watch his bent back, his hands shuffling documents whose writing is still glaring at him from the glass surface, the intentional muteness of it all, the stiffness of his movements.

'Ed.' My voice, hungry again, wills him to be my ally.

His hands stop moving. There is the slightest twitch in direction of Irina's room. When he starts talking, I have to strain to understand him. 'In the taxi Saturday morning, on our way to the Anglicans. You know, that IMMINENT thing. The Interdenominational Migrants Network.' His voice is directed at the glass surface. 'The taxi driver had the radio on.' The whispering emphasises his Filipino accent. *Taaksi*. It sounds almost Swiss. On any other day, it would make me smile.

I gather my lips into my body as if I could turn myself outside in with this move, roll myself up like a stocking. Ed's breath brushes against my ear. 'What on earth were you thinking? Irina is livid.'

I close my eyes against his wounded look, the moisture in his eyes.

His voice comes back without a trace of his usual happy-go-lucky accent. 'Kim…'

In this moment, Irina's door bangs open and we jump apart.

Ed blushes a deep auburn. My face radiates heat and I feel the heaviness of my backpack on my shoulders.

'Kim.' Irina coughs, pulls at her skirt. 'I want to have a word with you. My Word for the Day.' Another tug at the fabric covering her slim hips, an invisible internal straightening that seems to inject her with a steel rod that quickly hardens, and she disappears into her room. Around her, the air is upset, like asphalt shivering in the heat. How easily heat and cold look the same.

In my cubicle, I don't bother with turning on the computer and only drop off my bag on the desk. There is a Green Lotus mug which I have used for weeks without raising suspicion. It looks familiar in a new way, like a relative who you haven't seen for a while. *How did she grow to be like that?*

Her room is already hot, the October light beating in from outside, the air conditioning fighting a futile battle. When I come in, she is sitting very still, watching her paperweight trundle like an insecure compass. She stops it in mid-move, sits up and motions me to take a seat. Her face, so clear-cut normally, is rigid and the light draws harsh lines onto her skin.

Into the silence, I say, 'We should have thought ages ago about giving slots to others.'

She does not respond.

'It's... post-colonial, to have only Westerners for Word for the Day. And Lynn Cameron is always desperate for new voices.'

'I'm not talking about Ronda, you know that.' Her gaze sharpens. 'You act without consulting me. You've abused your position of trust. You've been given certain tasks and you do something else instead. Something else entirely.'

'For me, it was about religion. Not about—you.'

'And Lynn Cameron, for heaven's sake. This is not only about me.'

Next door, the office machinery gives off its usual mechanical sighs, whines and beeps. My first, self-righteous flush has passed, leaving my limbs shaky.

'Kim. I think we both need to make a decision.'

For the first time, our gazes lock and they seem incapable of letting go. The silence between us expands until it threatens to burst. Finally, I tear myself away.

'I don't know what to make of this any more,' she says.

I nod. It is a feeling I know. But it seems distant now, like a disease long overcome. *25 Years of Life in Abundance*… I have learned it by heart, feel the words form in me before I can think them, like a well-chewed prayer.

'Kim, I ask you to take some time off,' she says. 'We can call it a holiday, for the time being. You didn't go on holiday at all this year.'

She sighs and her hand reaches for the glass orb. I never found out how she came by that paperweight, in this city with hardly any farmers or fishermen left. *Fishers of Men*. It rings odd, this exhortation from the Gospel of Matthew, now more than ever, in this city with more gods than fishermen. Gods in abundance.

'But, Kim.' Gently, she sets down the paperweight.

I fidget and my trousers, damp, clinging to my skin, are loosened by the movement.

Her voice is very low. 'I can't promise anything at this point, you know that, right?'

She will want to speak with Jim. In his capacity as Father James. And with our headquarters. About my developing *history*. My golden green secret, simmering deep inside, now laid open. In this moment, my face glows.

I squirm in my seat. 'Is that all?'

'Isn't that enough?' She allows herself a smile. With that lubricated movement I know so well, (which I will probably not see again, I chastise myself), she glides from her chair. Two quick strides and she hugs me, quickly, in an embrace that is neither here nor there. Blonde against blonde, I realise incoherently, as if I had missed something all along.

I have been fired. Immediately, I banish the word with its many connotations, make it less ashen. Suspended. From work. And then, tumbling: My work visa. Ben.

*

277

Before I leave, I take out the company records one more time. I shield myself with the heavy green ledger for a moment before opening it on the desk. One final thing to do, whether I will return or not. *Reinhild Kranich*, blank. My finger rubs over the correction fluid. It has hardened into a rubbery mass. I can already hear it in my mind, months from now, in a blurred phone connection, 'Somebody seems to have messed with our company records. Kim, was that you?' I smile to myself. One day, I will have to make a confession but at least now I know what to fill in behind my name. Slowly, I start to write.

I cannot bring myself to tidy up my work space like somebody who departs for good and so I pack only a few things, my Cantonese grammar, my thesaurus, my mug still discoloured with tea stains.

'I'm leaving,' I call into the office to whoever wants to hear it. At her work station, Eva hunches more deeply into her files, hesitation written all over her tense shoulders, one hand protecting her abdomen again. Finally, she looks up.

'Kim.' She rises from her seat, pulls at her bright shirtsleeves, smiles nervously. 'Irina says that you'll be... away for a while.' Her eyes linger somewhere around my ears.

'Yes,' I say. 'It's called a holiday, officially. Time to think.'

'I listened to your radio speech. Sorry. I mean, the one that was supposed to be yours. The podcast.' She blushes.

It annoys me, how even this seems to fill her with a bad conscience, as if she had broken a rule. 'Trying to stay abreast of office politics,' I hear myself say. 'I see.' I lean closer across the counter. 'Eva, that's the normal thing to do. Finding out about the office scandal of the day.'

'If you look at it that way.' She smooths down the dog-eared, stapled corner of a document. When she raises her head, she looks me straight into the eye. 'My mother-in-law will be glad to hear that Buddhists and Christians have things they share.'

I allow my gaze to rest on her stomach, raise my eyebrows.

She gives me a hardly perceptible nod while her hand glides back onto its resting place.

I nod back once, twice, with emphasis, and beam at her.

'Thank you,' she says. 'Bye, Kim.'

The office door falls shut behind me with its usual soft click. If I come back, I want to be Reini, I suddenly know. Tell people that I have outgrown Kim. And shed my office uniforms. Perhaps I will even let my hair grow.

Moon Nine Day Six
Friday 27 October

The late afternoon light filtering through the museum's picture windows illuminates the painting as if from within and I am glad that we have come to the special exhibit, Virginia and I. Being a work renegade has its advantages. Botticelli's *Pietà*. An image which I have seen countless of times, on calendars, in books, on a prayer card stuck into Ronda's hymnal, and yet it seems new today. We take it in, each of us clouded in her own silence, while around us groups of visitors gather and disperse again.

There's something wrong with the painting, with its attitude. A reversal of roles, an upside down sort of feeling. I toy with explanations. The ever living one, toppled by death. An ascension hiding between broken bones, earthbound. A grown man, lying in the arms of his mother. For some reason, I think of my mother, how she reclaimed Alex's room, threw him out when he refused to leave 'Hotel Mama'. 'I had to, Reini,' she declared. 'Otherwise, he'd still be expecting his breakfast in bed. Boys take so long to grow up nowadays.'

Virginia's face is golden and dark, almost like the Botticelli. In a half-shivering motion, she comes out of her reverie and leans over. 'It's so different, seeing it in real life.'

I wriggle deeper into my shawl and follow her into the museum's cafeteria, still struggling with the painting's obscenity. A mother, holding her still son in her arms. A dead child. There is almost a limp in Virginia's walk these days, lumbering and lurching around some kind of inner pain.

'You know, this is such a Catholic classic. Not just as an image but as a *feeling*. The *Pietà*, I mean,' I say, bent over the tiny reproduction on the exhibition ticket. 'And I'm sure it inspires the Filipinas when they decide to go away. It's become an excuse for taking all kinds of crap.' I close my mouth, abruptly, but too late.

She peers at the ticket, flattens it carefully and moves it with her fingertips like a ruler. 'But it can be wonderful, this kind of… unconditional giving. Ronda was wonderful with my mother, you know.'

'Any news from her?'

'She texted me after her arrival. Her husband has already lined up a job for her in Dubai.' Her fingers let go of the ticket. 'She was really devoted. A true *sin keih leung mouh*.'

'The loving wife and doting mother,' I respond, feeling as if in class with her. How long ago that seems. I pick up the ticket, almost the same size as Ronda's prayer card.

'I think you've got the same ideal.'

'What?' I push the ticket away. 'And don't you normally put it the other way round, children sacrificing themselves for their parents?' I try it on the *Pietà*. A son, sacrificing himself. That is what happened, after all and, in a flash, I understand my unease. Mary, giving her son, becoming a cultural icon for suffering motherhood, while the story was the other way round. A Chinese story. A son, giving himself for the rest of the family.

She ignores the ticket, trembling from the force of my movement. For a moment, we drink in silence. 'Oh!' She claps her hands in sudden recognition. 'I heard you on the radio. Ronda turned it on, saying that you would be on the radio.'

I nod wearily. A grown-up ache is tied to that radio show, part soreness, part pride.

'It's a very Confucian story,' she says. 'I like it.'

'The Prodigal Son?' Abruptly, I set down my drink.

She stifles a giggle. 'But where does your radio voice come from? So different!'

Of course she is right. The emphasis on harmony, on keeping

the family and its fortune together, the web of duties and loyalties. The belief in the goodness of people and their ability to change. Another story with a dominant father figure. I brush her elbow with the ticket stub, a whispering touch of paper on skin. 'Your mother, when you dreamed of her the other day—'

'It wasn't a dream.'

'Sorry. I mean, when you saw her.'

She looks away, to the side, fingers her T-shirt around the hip as if to tuck in a loose seam. It is a new gesture. There is a certain kind of quiet around her now. At first it felt odd, this reticence, but I think it is good, a way of being more with herself.

I run my fingertips along the edge of the ticket. 'I'm so glad about that.' The paper cuts into my skin. I drop it.

She looks me fully into the face. 'When you did that radio broadcast… You're religious but not like Ronda.'

I pick up the ticket again, careful to skim the edges. 'I'm sorry about the spa. I hope it wasn't… too awkward for you.'

She sets down her coffee. 'The spa?' Her eyes rest seriously on mine. 'You mean—the way you treated the beauty therapist?'

I frown, have a vague memory of a person, thin and white. 'The beauty therapist?'

'Never mind. I think you were just nervous. I liked it, us doing something together. We should do more of that.'

I can already see it, the Beer Festival first and then the chocolate spa. Or the other way round. Queasy, the thought makes me. 'I'm starving,' I say. 'I'll get us something to eat.' She nods and I go to buy muffins and sandwiches at the counter.

When I set the tray down, she is being still with herself again, absentmindedly stirring her iced coffee. Gathered in. I start on a muffin, push hers over, but she ignores it.

With visible effort, she comes back to the present—the cafeteria, the pastel walls, our small square table. She straightens herself. '*Ah* Kim.' Her fingertips stroke the glass, a tentative movement that leaves transparent traces on the surface. 'For you, how is it? How do you know that Ben is right for you?' She picks up the muffin, with a movement of shoulders and arms that is a bit too quick for the question.

The enormity of it whacks me. *He makes me hear colours, see sounds. He feeds me.* Finally, I say, 'It just feels right. Natural.'

She has started to break off bits from her muffin, crumbles it into pieces without eating.

'Frank is a good person,' I say.

She looks up and quickly looks away.

My drink is still half full. I sip with my eyes closed, search for the familiar bittersweet taste, and set the glass down again. The moisture has condensed on the glass, rained a ring onto the table. I trace the damp with my fingers. 'At the beginning, I didn't know what to make of him. Just—in general. Anyway. You have to… find out what you feel.' I draw a heart into the liquid on the table. It feels childish, reminds me of the hearts that we used to draw onto every surface when we were teenagers, onto exercise books, rulers, misted windows.

She drops her crumbled muffin, picks up a napkin and mops up the damp patch.

'What you want,' I add.

Her smile, cornering her mouth, is difficult to read, sad and hopeful at once. She is half turned away now, the soggy tissue still in her hands. 'I used to be afraid of so many things. Still am.' Her voice is so low now that I have to guess half of the words.

She lets the napkin sink onto the table. 'I don't feel old enough for him. At least… that's what I used to think. But he's… nice.'

The moment is so dense my lungs threaten to explode. I exhale, feel my heart under my ribcage pick up its pace again. 'He really… likes you, you know.'

Suddenly, her eyes dominate everything, two dark orbs beseeching me.

After a while, she says, 'He seems like a… trustworthy person. He's very reliable.'

'He is,' I say, pushing away the thought of his beery exhalations, the loud pipe laying jokes, and her interest in quiet things, the intricacies of historic tablets and ancient pottery. Some love and some need to be loved. Maybe there are more ways to read him, his light skin with its unapologetic sunburn, his exotic shirts in a place bent on fashion, his sturdy selfhood in this city of changing meanings. 'I mean, he is. He's... authentic. And he already knows all about Cantonese families, remember?'

She smiles, her head lowered again, and tucks a strand of hair behind her ear. Ever since the hospital, her hair has looked a bit unkempt, more Punk than librarian. She looks around the table, pushes the plate with the rejected pastry away and takes a sandwich. Finally, she starts to eat, sinking her teeth into the bread.

Her shoulders soften as if somebody had rearranged them from inside, like a freshly plumped pillow. 'I'm looking forward to going back to the hikes,' she says, her mouth full. 'I owe all of you endless thanks. I know you're doing your best.'

'And probably failing on many accounts,' I say. 'This is really so much harder than it looks. What did you find the most difficult thing when you started with the walks?'

She looks up, her cheeks bulging with food. 'I think... to have the right kind of attitude towards my clients, to be service-minded.' She chews, swallows. 'To like everybody and like everybody the same.'

'That sounds big.' I laugh. 'The Goddess of the Hong Kong Heritage Hikers. Scary, even. That sounds like family, loving everybody the same.'

She tilts the sandwich in her hands back and forth. 'You know, when I travelled to Scotland, the landlady had that kind of attitude. When she came to meet me at the door, she greeted me like her long-lost daughter.'

Virginia's sandwich smells good, a smell of warm bread mixed with seafood. I reach for the second one. 'But love has to... see you,' I say. 'How could the landlady who didn't know you mean you?' I bite into the sandwich. Dried fish and something else, a very Chinese combination. I wipe my chin, powdered with fish flakes. 'Family is forever. Loving who you won't leave.'

'But your parents—' She stops herself.

Leave my parents out of this, I want to say, although I cannot quite say why, as I take the liberty of discussing hers all the time. 'Does your father know about Frank?'

'Do you really think my father doesn't support me?' She folds the napkin under her hands into a roll, moves it as if she was rolling sushi. 'He gave me the money to start the Hikers. He helped me with people he knew in museums, to get me slots for guided tours.' She releases the sushi roll and we watch it unfold, become napkin again. 'Of course our families see us.'

'But what about the... candidates? All that pressure to marry?'

She tosses her napkin away. 'It doesn't matter how you meet somebody if it works out in the end.' A smile steals into her face. 'Would your parents ever have chosen Ben for you?' Suddenly, her face throbs with suppressed mirth. I start to giggle at the recognition and our faces feed on each other, brimming, bursting, until we finally explode into a salvo of gulping, hiccupping laughter.

'The... part-time vegetarian.' She looks at me sideways, half stifling her joke with her napkin.

'A man who loves cockroaches.'

Her cheeks bulge behind her hands.

'A man who sleeps on books,' I add and even this piece of information wings past with newly-won confidence. I can sense it, soon she will lift the copper frying pans.

'Of course he loves cockroaches,' she says, still flushed. Another smile creeps into her face. 'You have a cockroach tummy.'

'What?' I pretend to hit her over the head.

'Crazy girl, that's an expression. A compliment if you have a super-flat tummy, like a cockroach.'

My hand slides under my T-shirt, onto the smooth surface that seems to be made to cradle Ben's head. 'Yeah, I can already feel the scales,' I declare, mock seriousness distorting my voice. 'And the antennae.' Reluctantly, my hand leaves its warm cocoon, brushes over my bristles. 'Already breaking through, can't you see them?'

We don't want to let this day end, its giggles, its boy

284

confessions, and hesitate to step outside, our bodies still humming with laughter. At this time of the afternoon, the harbour promenade is busy with tourists and peddlers, photographers and locals, but we ignore them all. Slowly, savouring it, we make our way to the ferry, absorb everything in big, quiet gulps; the harbour, brimming with boat traffic, the smell of the sea, our skins so close together.

The day with its azure late summer skies is aging gracefully around the edges. Behind the ferry pier, the horizon is quickly changing, a blaze of candyfloss turning marshmallow pink. Above us, the palms lining the promenade wave their fronds like banners, hail our delirious mirth, all anguish vanished. *Much madness is divinest sense/To a discerning eye.*

Remembrance of Kwun Yam
Thursday 9 November

Paradise is… I pull my eyes away from Ben, let my gaze drop onto the water greyed by rainclouds. They are crossing the horizon fast, and under the waves rising from our ferry, the warm sea seems to be shivering.

Fragrant Harbour, Incense Port, Pearl of the South China Sea. I inhabit them, these words, have ingested them and made their meaning mine until they ring from my skin like a mantra. Below my feet, the ferry rumbles towards Kowloon. Automatically, I feel in my trousers for melon seeds but only find a dented piece of caramel. Something else disintegrates under my probing fingers. The envelope from the wake, given to me so many months ago by Virginia, now falling apart from the heat and humidity. The sweet soothes my hungry stomach. I dig in my pockets again, wipe my sticky fingers with a handkerchief.

Above us, black eared kites ribbon their way through the sky, growing out of the light grey only to fade back into it, an endless cycle of apparitions and disappearances. Around this time of the year, they will start to cruise again in front of my office window, diving deep between the Yaumatei buildings. Irina called while we were away. 'Interfaith cooperation, that is the next big thing,' she declared while I was squinting into the brilliant sunshine, standing up straight. She was working on a project proposal and would I consider being part of it? The Filipinas would have to do without me, since I would be working with representatives of other faiths, or perhaps South East Asian refugees… I held the phone away from my ear, tried to soften the impact of her voice that still holds so much power over me.

Deep inside, the memory of the green ledger stirs but breeds only mild discomfort. One day, I will have to explain my tampering with the company records. I look forward to it, to crediting that space behind my name with its new meaning. A meaning which it always owned, now reinforced with yellowed correction fluid: *Reinhild. From Germanic 'ragina' (will of the gods, fate) and Old High German 'hiltja' (battle, warrioress)*. The Angelic Apothecary and the Philosopher King were right after all.

The sound of a phone cuts through the dense afternoon. Virginia. 'Zoë wants to organise a welcome back party. What do you think?'

'I'll call you later,' I say, clinging to the kites, the clouds, Ben. In an instant, it comes back, the evening at Zoë's, almost a year ago, the party that made us into blood sisters, Virginia and me, surrounded by pink garden gnomes and that odd assortment of virgins, the Lourdes grotto on the ground floor and Kwun Yam on the roof. On that night, I first mistook it for tacky art connoisseurship; later learned that it was a Confucian act of piety. *Some love and some need to be loved.* Spielberg said that, about humans, but I try it out on the gods. An angled truth, to be further examined, perhaps dismissed after all. But this I do know: rather than love a stranger, Virginia will need to love her own gods, grow to love rather than fear them.

Ben looks up from his camera. 'I got a great one of a kite. Here.' I step over and we peer at the display. He sighs. 'Wants to make you take off, doesn't it?'

I nod into his neck.

'Airports employ falconers,' he continues. 'Gosh, I always think that must be the coolest job on earth.'

'It does sound great,' I say. 'What do they need falconers for? Rich Saudis on stop-over?'

'Yes,' he says with a roll of his eyes, his voice an extra notch deeper. 'To entertain them while they're away from their harem— No, they do it to keep off birds that would disturb air traffic.'

'The falcons,' I say, my mind straining for their image after the kites, the falcons so different in their sleek, meaningful beauty, bred with a purpose. On my tongue, the taste of Virginia's sweet still lingers. 'What do you think, are they free?'

'Free?'

'I mean, how do you define free? Is freedom the wish to stay even if you could leave? Or is it the simple fact that you do stay?'

'Reini, making things complicated as usual.' He pretends to shake his head in dismay.

'Going away,' I say. 'Going away certainly would be a sign of being free.' Sea and horizon have divided into two different shades of grey now the rainclouds are starting to clear up.

'Are you trying to tell me something?' His voice belies his words.

I smile. He smiles back.

For a while, our gaze lingers over nothing in particular and we take in the tang of the air, both sweet and briny after the rain. He moves closer and puts his arm around my waist, almost. Side by side, we watch Kowloon approach, leave the rounded windows of the library behind us. Like portholes, they look, and remind me of MediMission and the comparison with Noah's Ark. I close my eyes, allow the salty air to rush over my tongue.

Ben's arm suddenly leaves my waist. 'Look.'

A rainbow envelops the harbour behind us, a perfect arch that bridges the shores, water and light fused into a myriad different hues. So imperceptible is the series of changes within the arch that it forms an inevitable whole. And another one, its silent echo, grows out of the thunder-dark sky. The shower has softened the air, become part of it. A late rain, very late, I think while I try to comprehend its grace: a rainbow, embracing this heavenly city.